Let the Right One In

Let the Right One In

John Ajvide Lindqvist

THOMAS DUNNE BOOKS
ST. MARTIN'S GRIFFIN
NEW YORK

This is a work of fiction. All of the characters, organizations, and events portrayed in this novel are either products of the author's imagination or are used fictitiously.

THOMAS DUNNE BOOKS.
An imprint of St. Martin's Press.

www.thomasdunnebooks.com
www.stmartins.com

The Library of Congress has catalogued the hardcover edition of this book as follows:

Lindqvist, John Ajvide.
   [Låt den rätte komma in.]
   Let me in / John Ajvide Lindqvist ; translated by Ebba Segerberg.—1st U.S. ed.
      p. cm.
   ISBN-13: 978-0-312-35528-9
   ISBN-10: 0-312-35528-9
   I. Segerberg, Ebba. II. Title.
PT9877.22.I54L48 2007
839.73'8—dc22

2007023510

ISBN-13: 978-0-312-35529-6 (pbk.)
ISBN-10: 0-312-35529-7 (pbk.)

First published in Sweden under the title Låt den rätte komma in by Ordfront

First published in the United States under the title Let Me In

20 19 18 17 16 15

To Mia, my Mia

The Location

Blackeberg.

It makes you think of coconut-frosted cookies, maybe drugs. "A respectable life." You think subway station, suburb. Probably nothing else comes to mind. People must live there, just like they do in other places. That was why it was built, after all, so that people would have a place to live.

It was not a place that developed organically, of course. Here everything was carefully planned from the outset. And people moved into what had been built for them. Earth-colored concrete buildings scattered about in the green fields.

When this story begins, Blackeberg the suburb had been in existence for thirty years. One could imagine that it had fostered a pioneer spirit. The Mayflower; an unknown land. Yes. One can imagine all those empty buildings waiting for their occupants.

And here they come!

Marching over the Traneberg Bridge with sunshine and the future in their eyes. The year is 1952. Mothers are carrying their little ones in their arms or pushing them in baby carriages, holding them by the hand. Fathers are not carrying picks and shovels but kitchen appliances and functional furniture. They are probably singing something. "The Internationale," perhaps. Or "We Come Unto Jerusalem," depending on their predilection.

It is big. It is new. It is *modern.*

But that wasn't the way it was.

They came on the subway. Or in cars, moving vans. One by one. Filtered into the finished apartments with their things. Sorted their possessions into the measured cubbies and shelves, placed the furniture in formation on the cork floor. Bought new things to fill the gaps.

When they were done, they lifted their eyes and gazed out onto this land that had been given unto them. Walked out of their doors and found that all land had already been claimed. Might as well adjust oneself to how things were.

There was a town center. There were spacious playgrounds allotted to children. Large green spaces around the corner. There were many pedestrian-only walking paths.

A good place; that's what people said to each other over the kitchen table a month or so after they had moved in.

"It's a good place we've come to."

Only one thing was missing. A past. At school, the children didn't get to do any special projects about Blackeberg's history because there wasn't one. That is to say, there was something about an old mill. A tobacco king. Some strange old buildings down by the water. But that was a long time ago and without any connection to the present.

Where the three-storied apartment buildings now stood there had been only forest before.

You were beyond the grasp of the mysteries of the past; there wasn't even a church. Nine thousand inhabitants and no church.

That tells you something about the modernity of the place, its rationality. It tells you something of how free they were from the ghosts of history and of terror.

It explains in part how unprepared they were.

No one saw them move in.

In December, when the police finally managed to track down the driver of the moving truck, he didn't have much to tell. In his records he had only noted *18 October. Norrköping-Blackeberg (Stockholm).* He recalled that it was a father and daughter, a pretty girl.

"Oh, and another thing. They had almost no furniture. A couch, an armchair, maybe a bed. An easy job, really. And that . . . yeah, they wanted it done at night. I said it would be more expensive, you know, with the overtime surcharge and that. But it was no problem. It just had to be done at night. That seemed real important. Has anything happened?"

The driver was informed of the events, of whom he had had in his truck. His eyes widened, he looked down again at the letters on the page.

"I'll be damned. . . ."

He grimaced as if he had developed a revulsion for his own hand-writing.

18 October. Norrköping-Blackeberg (Stockholm).

He was the one who had moved them in. The man and his daughter.

He wasn't going to tell anyone about it, not for as long as he lived.

Part One

Lucky is he
who has such a friend

Love trouble
will burst your bubble
boys!

—Siw Malmkvist, "Love Trouble"
trans. Laurie Thompson

I never wanted to kill. I am not naturally evil
Such things I do
just to make myself more attractive to you
Have I failed?

—Morrissey, "The Last of The Famous
International Playboys"

Wednesday

And what do you think this might be?"

Gunnar Holmberg, police commissioner from Vällingby, held up a little plastic bag of white powder.

Maybe heroin, but no one dared say anything. Didn't want to be suspected of knowing anything about stuff like that. Especially if you had a brother or a friend of your brother who did it. Shoot horse. Even the girls didn't say anything. The policeman shook the bag.

"Baking powder, do you think? Flour?"

A mumble of answers in the negative. They didn't want him to think class 6B was a bunch of idiots. Even though it was impossible to determine what was really in the bag, this lesson was about drugs, so you could draw certain conclusions. The policeman turned to the teacher.

"What do you teach them in Home Economics these days?"

The teacher smiled and shrugged her shoulders. The class laughed; the cop was OK. Some of the guys had even been allowed to touch his gun before class. It wasn't loaded, but still.

Oskar's chest felt like it was about to burst. He knew the answer to the question. It hurt him not to say anything when he knew. He wanted the policeman to look at him. Look at him and tell him he was right. He knew it was a dumb thing to do, but he still put his hand up.

"Yes?"

"It's heroin, isn't it?"

"In fact it is." The policeman looked kindly at him. "How did you know?"

Heads turned in his direction, curious as to what he was going to say.

"Naw . . . I mean, I've read a lot and stuff."

The policeman nodded.

"Now there's a good thing. Reading." He shook the little bag. "You won't have much time for it if you get into this, though. How much do you think this little bag is worth?"

Oskar didn't feel the need to say anything else. He had been looked at and spoken to. Had even been able to tell the cop he read a lot. That was more than he had hoped for.

He let himself sink into a daydream. How the policeman came up to him after class and was interested in him, sat down next to him. Then he would tell him everything. And the policeman would understand. He would stroke his hair and tell him he was alright; would hold him and say . . .

"Fucking snitch."

Jonny Forsberg drove a hard finger into his side. Jonny's brother ran with the drug crowd and Jonny knew a lot of words that the other guys in the class quickly picked up. Jonny probably knew exactly how much that bag was worth but he didn't snitch. Didn't talk to the cop.

It was recess and Oskar lingered by the coat rack, indecisive. Jonny wanted to hurt him—what was the best way to avoid it? By staying here in the hallway or going outside? Jonny and the other class members stormed out the doors into the schoolyard.

That's right; the policeman had his car parked in the schoolyard and anyone who was interested could come take a look. Jonny wouldn't dare beat him up when the policeman was there.

Oskar walked down to the double front doors and looked out the glass window. Just as he thought, everyone in the class had gathered around the patrol car. Oskar would also have wanted to be there but there was no point. Someone would knee him, another pull his underpants up in a wedgie, policeman or no policeman.

But at least he was off the hook this recess. He went out into the schoolyard and snuck around the back of the building, to the bathrooms.

Once he was in the bathroom he listened, cleared his throat. The sound echoed through the stalls. He reached his hand into his underpants and quickly pulled out the Pissball, a piece of foam about the size of a clementine that he had cut out of an old mattress and put a hole in for his penis. He smelled it.

Yup, he had pissed in his pants again. He rinsed it under the tap, squeezing out as much water as possible.

Incontinence. That was what it was called. He had read about it in a pamphlet that he had sneaked from the drugstore. Mostly something old women suffered from.

And me.

There were prescription medicines you could get, it said in the pamphlet, but he did not intend to use his allowance so he could humiliate himself at the prescription counter. And he would definitely not tell his mother; she would feel so sorry for him it would make him sick.

He had the Pissball and it worked for now.

Footsteps outside, voices. Pissball in hand, he fled into the nearest stall and locked the door at the same time as the outer door opened. He soundlessly climbed up onto the toilet seat, curling into a ball so his feet wouldn't show if anyone looked under the door. Tried not to breathe.

"Pig-gy?"

Jonny, of course.

"Hey Piggy, are you here?"

Micke was with him. The worst two of the lot. No, Tomas was worse but he was almost never in on stuff that involved physical blows and scratches. Too smart for that. Was probably sucking up to the policeman right now. If the Pissball were discovered, Tomas was the one who would really be able to use it to hurt and humiliate him for a long time. Jonny and Micke, on the other hand, would just beat him up and that was fine with him. So in a way he was actually lucky. . . .

"Piggy? We know you're in here."

They checked his stall. Shook the door. Banged on it. Oskar wrapped his arms tightly around his legs and clenched his teeth so he wouldn't scream.

Go away! Leave me alone! Why can't you leave me alone?

Now Jonny was talking in a mild voice.

"Little Pig, if you don't come out now we have to get you after school. Is that what you want?"

It was quiet for a while. Oskar exhaled carefully.

They attacked the door with kicks and blows. The whole bathroom thundered and the lock on the stall door started to bend inward. He should open it, go out to them before they got too mad, but he just couldn't.

"Pi-ggy?"

He had put his hand up in class, a declaration of existence, a claim that he knew something. And that was forbidden to him. They could give a number of reasons for why they had to torment him; he was too fat, too ugly, too disgusting. But the real problem was simply that he existed, and every reminder of his existence was a crime.

They were probably just going to "baptize" him. Shove his head into the toilet bowl and flush. Regardless of what they invented, it was always such a relief when it was over. So why couldn't he just pull back the lock, that was in any case going to tear off at the hinges at any moment, and let them have their fun?

He stared at the bolt that was forced out of the lock with a crack, at the door that flung open and banged into the wall, at Micke Siskov's triumphantly smiling face, and then he knew.

That wasn't the way the game was played.

He couldn't have pulled back the lock, they couldn't simply have climbed over the sides of the stall in all of three seconds, because those weren't the rules of the game.

Theirs was the intoxication of the hunter, his the terror of the prey. Once they had actually captured him the fun was over and the punishment more of a duty that had to be carried out. If he gave up too early there was a chance they would put more of their energy into the punishment instead of the hunt. That would be worse.

Jonny Forsberg stuck his head in.

"You'll have to open the lid if you're going to shit, you know. Go on, squeal like a pig."

And Oskar squealed like a pig. That was a part of it. If he squealed they would sometimes leave it at that. He put extra effort into it this time, afraid they would otherwise force his hand out of his pants in the process of punishing him and uncover his disgusting secret.

He wrinkled up his nose like a pig's and squealed; grunted and squealed. Jonny and Micke laughed.

"Fucking pig, go on, squeal some more."

Oskar carried on. Shut his eyes tight and kept going. Balled his hands up into fists so hard that his nails went into his palms, and kept going. Grunted and squealed until he felt a funny taste in his mouth. Then he stopped and opened his eyes.

They were gone.

He stayed put, curled up on the toilet seat, and stared down at the floor. There was a red spot on the tile below. While he was watching, another drop fell from his nose. He tore off a piece of toilet paper and held it against his nostril.

This sometimes happened when he was scared. His nose started to bleed, just like that. It had helped him a few times when they were thinking about hitting him, and decided against it since he was already bleeding.

Oskar Eriksson sat there curled up with a wad of paper in one hand and his Pissball in the other. Got nosebleeds, wet his pants, talked too much. Leaked from every orifice. Soon he would probably start to shit his pants as well. Piggy.

He got up and left the bathroom. Didn't wipe up the drop of blood. Let someone see it, let them wonder. Let them think someone had been killed here, because someone *had* been killed here. And for the hundreth time.

✝

Håkan Bengtsson, a forty-five-year-old man with an incipient beer belly, a receding hairline, and an address unknown to the authorities, was sitting on the subway, staring out of the window at what was to be his new home.

It was a little ugly, actually. Norrköping would have been nicer. But having said that, these western suburbs didn't look anything like the Stockholm ghetto-suburbs he had seen on TV: Kista and Rinkeby and Hallonbergen. This was different.

"NEXT STATION: RÅCKSTA."

It was a little softer and rounder than those places. Although, here was a real skyscraper.

He arched his neck in order to see the top floors of the Waterworks' administrative building. He couldn't recall there being any buildings this tall in Norrköping. But of course he had never been to the downtown area.

He was supposed to get off at the next station, wasn't he? He looked at the subway map over the doors. Yes, the next stop.

"PLEASE STAND BACK FROM THE DOORS. THE DOORS ARE CLOSING."

Was anyone looking at him?

No, there were only a few people in this car, all of them absorbed in their evening newspapers. Tomorrow there would be something about him in there.

His gaze stopped at an ad for women's underwear. A woman was posing seductively in black lace panties and a bra. It was crazy. Naked skin wherever you looked. Why was it tolerated? What effect did it have on people's heads, on love?

His hands were shaking and he rested them on his knees. He was terribly nervous.

"Is there really no other way?"

"Do you think I would expose you to this if there was another way?"

"No, but . . ."

"There is no other way."

No other way. He just had to do it. And not mess up. He had studied the map in the phone book and chosen a forested area that looked appropriate, then packed his bag and left.

He had cut away the Adidas logo with the knife that was lying in the bag between his feet. That was one of the things that had gone wrong in Norrköping. Someone had remembered the brand name on the bag, and then the police had found it in the garbage container where he had tossed it, not far from their apartment.

Today he would bring the bag home with him. Maybe cut it into small pieces and flush it down the toilet. Is that what you did?

How is this supposed to work anyway?

"THIS IS THE FINAL STATION. ALL PASSENGERS MUST DISEM-
BARK."

The subway car disgorged its contents and Håkan followed the stream of people, the bag in his hand. It felt heavy, although the only thing in it that weighed anything was the gas canister. He had to exercise a great deal of self-restraint in order to walk normally, rather than as a man on the way to his own execution. He couldn't afford to give people any reason to notice him.

But his legs were leaden; they wanted to weld themselves onto the platform. What would happen if he simply stayed here? If he stood absolutely still, without moving a muscle, and simply didn't leave. Waited for nightfall, for someone to notice him, call for . . . someone to come and get him. To take him somewhere.

He continued to walk at a normal pace. Right leg, left leg. He couldn't falter now. Terrible things would happen if he failed. The worst imaginable.

Once he was past the checkpoint he looked around. His sense of direction wasn't very good. Which way was the forested area? Naturally he couldn't ask anyone. He had to take a chance. Keep going, get this over with. Right leg, left leg.

There has to be another way.

But he couldn't think of any other way. There were certain conditions, certain *criteria*. This was the only way to satisfy them.

He had done it twice before, and had messed up both times. Hadn't bungled it quite as much that time in Växjö but enough that they had been forced to move. Today he would do a good job, receive praise.

Perhaps a caress.

Two times. He was already lost. What difference did a third time make? None whatsoever. Society's judgement would probably be the same. Lifetime imprisonment.

And morally? How many lashes of the tail, King Minos?

The park path he was on turned a corner further up, where the forest started. It had to be the forest he had seen on the map. The gas container and the knife rattled in the bag. He tried to carry the bag without jostling the contents.

A child turned onto the path in front of him. A girl, maybe eight years old, walking home from school with her school bag bouncing against her hip.

No, never!

That was the limit. Not a child so young. Better him, then, until he fell dead to the ground. The girl was singing something. He increased his pace in order to get closer to her, to hear.

> "Little ray of sunshine peeking in
> Through the window of my cottage . . ."

Did kids *still* sing that one? Maybe the girl's teacher was older. How nice that the song was still around. He would have wanted to get even closer in order to hear better, so close in fact that he would be able to smell the scent of her hair.

He slowed down. Don't create a scene. The girl turned off from the park path, taking a small trail that led into the forest. Probably lived in a house on the other side. To think her parents let her walk here all alone. And so young.

He stopped, let the girl increase the distance between them, disappear into the forest.

Keep going, little one. Don't stop to play in the forest.

He waited for maybe a minute, listened to a chaffinch singing in a nearby tree. Then he went in after her.

†

Oskar was on his way home from school, his head heavy. He always felt worse when he managed to avoid punishment in *that* way, by playing the pig, or something else. Worse than if he had been punished. He knew this, but couldn't handle the thought of the physical punishment when it approached. He would rather sink to any level. No pride.

Robin Hood and Spider-Man had pride. If Sir John or Doctor Octopus cornered them they simply spit danger in the face, come what may.

But what did Spider-Man know, anyway? He always managed to get away, even if it was impossible. He was a comic book action figure and had to survive for the next issue. He had his spider powers, Oskar had his pig squeal. Whatever it took to survive.

Oskar needed to comfort himself. He had had a shitty day and now he needed some compensation. Despite the risk of running into Jonny and Micke he walked up toward downtown Blackeberg, to Sabis, the local grocery store. He shuffled up along the zigzaging ramp instead of taking the stairs, using the time to gather himself. He needed to be calm for this, not sweaty.

He had been caught shoplifting once at a Konsum, another grocery chain, about a year ago now. The guard had wanted to call his mother but she had been at work and Oskar didn't know her number, no, really he didn't. For a week Oskar had agonized every time the phone rang, but then a letter arrived, addressed to his mother.

Idiotic. It was even labeled "Police Authorities, District of Stockholm" and of course Oskar had ripped it open, read about his crime, faked his mother's signature, and returned the letter in order to confirm that she had read it. He was a coward, maybe, but he wasn't stupid.

What was cowardly, anyway? Was this, what he was about to do, cowardly? He stuffed his down coat full of Dajm, Japp, Coco, and Bounty chocolate bars. Finally he slipped a bag of chewy Swedish Cars between his stomach and pants, went to the checkout, and paid for a lollipop.

On the way home he walked with his head high and a bounce to his step. He wasn't just Piggy, whom everyone could kick around; he was the Master Thief who took on dangers and survived. He could outwit them all.

Once he walked through the front gate to the courtyard of his apartment complex he was safe. None of his enemies lived in this complex, an irregular circle of buildings positioned inside the larger circle formed by his street, Ibsengatan. A double ring of protection. Here he was safe. In this courtyard nothing shitty had ever happened to him. Basically.

He had grown up here and it was here he had had friends before he started school. It was only in fifth grade that he started being picked on seriously. At the end of that year he had become a full-fledged target and even friends outside his class had sensed it. They called more and more seldom to ask him to play.

It was during that time he started with his scrapbook. He was on his way home to enjoy that scrapbook right now.

Wheeee!

He heard a whirring sound and something bumped into his feet. A dark red radio-controlled car was backing away from him. It turned and drove up the hill toward the front doors of his building at high speed. Behind the prickly bushes to the right of the front door was Tommy, a long antenna sticking out from his stomach. He was laughing softly.

"Surprised you, didn't I?"

"Goes pretty fast, that thing."

"Yeah, I know. Do you want to buy it?"

". . . how much?"

"Three hundred."

"Naw, I don't have that much."

Tommy beckoned Oskar closer, turned the car on the slope and drove it down at breakneck speed, stopping it with a huge skid in front of his feet, picked it up, patted it, and said in a low voice:

"Costs nine hundred in the store."

"Yes."

Tommy looked at the car, then scrutinized Oskar from top to bottom.

"Let's say two hundred. It's brand new."

"Yes, it's great, but . . ."

"But what?"

"Nothing."

Tommy nodded, put the car down again, and steered it in between the bushes so the large bumpy wheels shook, let it come around the large drying rack and drive out on the path, going further down the slope.

"Can I try?"

Tommy looked at Oskar as if to evaluate his worthiness, then handed over the remote, pointing at his upper lip.

"You been hit? You've got blood. There."

Oskar wiped his lip. A few brown crusts came off on his index finger.

"No, I just . . ."

Don't tell. There was no point. Tommy was three years older, a tough guy. He would only say something about fighting back and Oskar would say "sure" and the end result would be that he lost even more respect in Tommy's eyes.

Oskar played with the car for a while, then watched Tommy steer it. He wished he had the money so they could have made a deal. Have that between them. He pushed his hands into his pockets and felt the candy.

"Do you want a Dajm?"

"No, I don't like those."

"A Japp?"

Tommy looked up from the remote. Smiled.

"You have both kinds?"

"Yeah."

"Swiped 'em?"

". . . yeah."

"OK."

Tommy put his hand out and Oskar gave him a Japp that Tommy slipped into the back pocket of his jeans.

"Thanks. See you."

"Bye."

Once Oskar made it into the apartment he laid out all the candy on his bed. He was going to start with the Dajm, then work his way through the double bits and end with the Bounty, his favorite. Then the fruit-flavored gummy cars that kind of rinsed out his mouth.

He sorted the candy in a long line next to the bed in the order it would be eaten. In the refrigerator he found an opened bottle of Coca-Cola that his mom had put a piece of aluminum foil over. Perfect. He liked Coke even more when it was a little flat, especially with candy.

He removed the foil and put the bottle next to the candy, flopped belly down on his bed, and studied the contents of his bookcase. An almost complete collection of the series *Goosebumps*, here and there augmented by a *Goosebumps* anthology.

The bulk of his collection was made up of the two bags of books he had bought for two hundred *kronor* through an ad in the paper. He had taken the subway out to Midsommarkransen and followed the directions until he found the apartment. The man who opened the door was fat, pale, and spoke in a low, hoarse voice. Luckily he had not invited Oskar to come in, just carried out the two bags, taken the two hundred, nodded, said "Enjoy," and closed the door.

That was when Oskar had become nervous. He had spent months searching for older publications in the series in the used comics stores along Götgatan in South Stockholm. On the phone the man had said he had precisely those older volumes. It had all been too easy.

As soon as Oskar was out of sight he put the bags down and went through them. But he had not been cheated. There were forty-five in all, from issue number two to forty-six.

You could no longer get these books anywhere. And all for a paltry two hundred!

No wonder he had been afraid of that man. What he had done was no less than rob him of a treasure.

Even so, they were nothing compared to his scrapbook.

He pulled it out from its hiding place under a stack of comics. The scrapbook itself was simply a large sketchbook he had swiped from the discount department store Åhléns in Vällingby; simply walked out with it under his arm—who said he was a coward?—but the contents . . .

He unwrapped the Dajm bar, took a large bite, savoring the familiar crunch between his teeth, and opened the cover. The first clipping was from *The Home Journal*: a story about a murderess in the US in the forties. She had managed to poison fourteen old people with arsenic before she was caught, tried, and sentenced to death by electric chair. Understandably, she had requested to be executed by lethal injection instead, but the state she was in used the chair and the chair it was.

That was one of Oskar's dreams: to see someone executed in the electric chair. He had read that the blood started to boil, the body contorted itself in impossible angles. He also imagined that the person's hair caught on fire but he had no official source for this belief.

Still, pretty amazing.

He turned the page. The next entry was from the newspaper *Aftonbladet* and concerned a Swedish murderer who had mutilated his victims' bodies. Lame passport photo. Looked like any old person. But he had murdered two male prostitutes in his home sauna, butchered them with an electric chain saw, and buried them out back behind the sauna. Oskar ate the last piece of Dajm and studied the man's face closely. Could have been anybody.

Could be me in twenty years.

†

Håkan had found a good place to stand watch, a place with a clear view of the path in both directions. Further in among the trees he had found a protected hollow with a tree in the middle and there he had left the bag of equipment. He had slipped the little halothane gas canister into a holster under his coat.

Now all he had to do was wait.

Once I also wanted to grow up
To know as much as Father and Mother . . .

He hadn't heard anyone sing that song since he was in school. Was it Alice Tegnér? Think of all the wonderful songs that had disappeared, that no one sang anymore. Think of all the wonderful things that had disappeared, for that matter.

No respect for beauty—that was characteristic of today's society. The work of the great masters were at most employed as ironic references, or in advertising. Michelangelo's "The Creation of Adam," where you see a pair of jeans in place of the spark.

The whole point of the picture, at least as he saw it, was that these two monumental bodies each came to an end in two index fingers that *almost, but not quite* touched. There was a space between them a millimeter or so wide. And in this space: life. The sculptural enormity and richness of detail of this picture was simply a frame, a backdrop, to emphasize the crucial void in its center. The point of emptiness that contained everything.

And in its place someone had superimposed a pair of jeans.

Someone was coming up the path. He crouched down with the sound of his heart beating in his ears. No. An older man with a dog. Two wrongs from the outset. First a dog he would have to silence, then poor quality.

A lot of screams for so little wool, said the man who sheared the pig.

He looked at his watch. In less than two hours it would be dark. If no one suitable came along in the next hour he would have to settle for whatever was available. Had to be back home before it got dark.

The man said something. Had he seen him? No, he was talking to the dog.

"Does that feel better, sweetpea? You really had to go, didn't you. When we get home daddy will give you some liverwurst. A nice thick slice of liverwurst for daddy's good little girl."

The halothane container pressed against Håkan's chest as he leaned his head into his hands and sighed. Poor bastard. All these pathetic lonely people in a world without beauty.

He shivered. The wind had grown cold over the course of the afternoon, and he wondered if he should take out the rain jacket he had stowed away in his bag as protection against the wind. No. It would restrict his movement and make him clumsy where he needed to be quick. And it could heighten peoples' suspicions.

Two young women in their twenties walked by. No, he couldn't handle two. He caught fragments of their conversation.

". . . she's going to *keep* it now . . ."

". . . is a total ape. He has to realize that he . . ."

". . . her fault because . . . not taking the pill . . ."

"But he, like, has to . . ."

". . . you imagine? . . . him as a dad . . ."

A girlfriend who was pregnant. A young man who wasn't going to take responsibility. That's how it was. Happened all the time. No one thought of anything but themselves. *My* happiness, *my* future was the only thing you heard. Real love is to offer your life at the feet of another, and that's what people today are incapable of.

The cold was eating its way into his limbs; he was going to be clumsy now, raincoat or no raincoat. He put his hand inside his coat and pushed the trigger on the canister. A hissing noise. It was working. He let go of the trigger.

He jumped in place and slapped his arms to get warm. Please let someone come. Someone who was alone. He looked at his watch. Half an hour to go. Let someone come. For life's sake, for love.

> But a child at heart I want to be
> For children belong to the Kingdom of God.

By the time Oskar had read through the whole scrapbook and finished all the candy it was starting to get dark. As usual after eating so much junk, he felt dazed and slightly guilty.

Mom would be home in two hours. They would eat dinner, then he would do his English and math homework. After that he would read a book or watch TV with her. But there wasn't anything good on TV tonight. They would have cocoa and sweet cinnamon rolls and chat. Then he would go to bed, but have trouble falling asleep since he would be worried about tomorrow.

If only he had someone he could call. He could of course call Johan, in the hope that he wasn't doing anything else.

Johan was in his class and they had a good time when they hung out, but if Johan had a choice, he never chose Oskar. Johan was the one who called when he had nothing better to do, not Oskar.

The apartment was quiet. Nothing happened. The concrete walls sealed themselves around him. He sat on his bed with his hands on his knees, his stomach heavy with sweets.

As if something was about to happen. Now.

He held his breath, listening. A sticky fear crept over him. Something was approaching. A colorless gas seeping out of the walls, threatening to take form, to swallow him up. He sat stiffly, holding his breath, and listened. Waited.

The moment passed. Oskar breathed again.

He went out into the kitchen, drank a glass of water, and grabbed the biggest kitchen knife from the magnetic strip. Tested the blade against his thumbnail, just like his dad had taught him. Dull. He pulled the knife through the sharpener a couple of times, then tried it again. It cut a microscopic slice out of his nail.

Good.

He folded a newspaper around the knife as a stand-in holster, taped it up, and pushed the packet down between his pants and left hip. Only the handle stuck up. He tried to walk. The blade was in the way of his left leg and so he angled it down along his groin. Uncomfortable, but it worked.

He put his jacket on in the hall. Then he remembered all the candy wrappers that lay strewn around his room. He gathered them all up and stuffed them into his pocket, in case mom came home before he did. He could hide the wrappers under a rock in the forest.

Checked one more time to make sure he hadn't left any evidence behind.

The game had already begun. He was a dreaded mass murderer. He had already slain fourteen people with his sharp knife without leaving a single clue behind. No hair, no candy wrapper. The police feared him.

Now he was going out into the forest to select his next victim.

Strangely enough he already knew the name of his victim, and what he looked like. Jonny Forsberg with his long hair and large, mean eyes. He would make him plead and beg for his life, squeal like a pig, but in vain. The knife would have the last word and the earth would drink his blood.

Oskar had read those words in a book and liked them.

The Earth Shall Drink His Blood.

While he locked the front door to the apartment and walked out of the building with his hand resting on the knife handle he repeated these words like a mantra.

"The earth shall drink his blood. The earth shall drink his blood."

The entrance he had used on his way into the yard lay at the right end of his building, but he walked to the left, past two other buildings, and out through the entrance where the cars could drive in. Left the inner fortification. Crossed Ibsengatan and continued down the hill. Left the outer fortification. Continued on toward the forest.

The earth shall drink his blood.

For the second time this day Oskar felt almost happy.

†

There were only ten minutes left of Håkan's self-imposed time limit when a lone boy came walking down the path. Thirteen or fourteen, as far as he could judge. Perfect. He had been planning to sneak down to the other end of the path and then come walking toward his intended victim.

But now his legs had really gotten stuck. The boy was walking nonchalantly along the path and Håkan was going to have to hurry. Every second that went by reduced the chance of success. Even so his legs simply refused to budge. He stood paralyzed and stared at the chosen one, the perfect one, who was moving forward, who was about to pull up next to where he was standing, right in front of him. Soon it would be too late.

Have to. Have to. Have to.

If he didn't do it, he would have to kill himself. Couldn't go home empty-handed. That's how it was. It was him or the boy. Go ahead and choose.

He finally got going, too late. Now he made his approach by stumbling through the forest, straight at the boy, instead of simply meeting him calmly on the path. Idiot. Clumsy oaf. Now the boy would be on his guard, suspicious.

"Hello there!" he called out to the boy. "Excuse me!"

The boy stopped. He didn't run away, he could be grateful for that. He had to say something, ask something. He walked up to the boy who was standing on the path, alert, uncertain.

"Excuse me . . . Could you tell me what the time is?"

The boy's gaze went to Håkan's watch.

"Yes, well, mine has stopped, you see."

The boy's body was tense as he checked his watch. He couldn't do anything about that. Håkan put his hand inside his coat and rested his index finger on the trigger while he waited for the boy's answer.

†

Oskar walked down the hill past the printing company, then turned onto the path into the forest. The weight in his belly was gone, replaced with an intoxicating sense of anticipation. On his way to the forest the fantasy had gripped him and now it felt like reality.

He saw the world through the eyes of a murderer, or so much of a murderer's eyes as his thirteen-year-old's imagination could muster. A beautiful world. A world he controlled, a world that trembled in the face of his actions.

He walked along the forest path looking for Jonny Forsberg.

The earth shall drink his blood.

It was starting to get dark and the trees closed around him like a silent crowd, following his smallest movements with trepidation, fearful that one of them was the intended target. But the killer moved through them, past them; he had already caught sight of his prey.

Jonny Forsberg was standing at the top of a hill some fifty meters from the trail, hands on his hips, a grin pasted on his face. Thought it was going to be business as usual. That he would force Oskar to the ground, hold his nose, and force pine needles and moss into his mouth, or some such thing.

But this time he was mistaken. It wasn't Oskar who was walking toward him, it was the Murderer, and the Murderer's hand closed hard
around the handle of the knife, preparing himself.

The Murderer walked with slow dignified steps over to Jonny Forsberg, looked him in the eyes, and said "Hi Jonny."

"Hello Piggy. Are you allowed out this late?"

The Murderer pulled out his knife. And lunged.

†

Uh, it's . . . a quarter past five."

"OK, thanks."

The boy didn't leave. Just stood there staring at Håkan, who took the
opportunity to step closer. The boy stood still, following him with his gaze.
This was going to hell. Of course the boy sensed something was wrong.
First a man came storming out of the woods to ask him what the time was
and now he had struck a Napoleon pose with his hand inside his coat.

"What do you have there?"

The boy gestured at Håkan's heart region. Håkan's head was empty;
he didn't know what he was going to do. He took out the gas container
and showed it to the boy.

"What the hell is that?"

"Halothane gas."

"What are you carrying it around for?"

"Because . . ." He felt the foam covered mouthpiece and tried to think
of something to say. He couldn't lie. That was his curse. "Because . . . it's
part of my job."

"What kind of job?"

The boy had relaxed somewhat. He was holding a sport bag similar to
the one Håkan had stowed in the hollow up in the woods. Håkan gestured to the bag with the hand that was holding the gas canister.

"Are you on your way to work out or something?"

When the boy glanced down at his bag he had his chance.

Both arms shot out, the free hand grabbing the boy by the back of
the head, the other pressing the mouthpiece of the canister against his
mouth. Håkan released the trigger. It let out a hissing sound like a large

snake and the boy tried to pull his head away but it was locked between Håkan's hands in a desperate vice.

The boy threw himself back and Håkan followed. The hissing of the snake drowned out all other sounds as they fell onto the wood shavings on the trail. Håkan's hands were still clenched around the boy's head and he held the mouthpiece in place as they rolled around on the ground.

After a couple of deep breaths the boy started to relax in his grip. Håkan still made sure the mouthpiece was in place, then looked around. *No witnesses.*

The hissing sound of the canister filled his head like a bad migraine. He locked the trigger in place and teased his free hand out from underneath the boy, loosened the rubber band and then drew it back over the boy's head. The mouthpiece was secured.

He got up with aching arms and regarded his prey.

The boy lay there with his arms thrown out from his body, the mouthpiece over nose and mouth, and the halothane canister on his chest. Håkan looked around once more, retrieved the boy's bag, and placed it on his stomach. Then he picked him up and carried him to the hollow.

The boy was heavier than he had expected: a lot of muscle. Unconscious weight.

He was panting from the exertion of carrying the boy over the soggy ground while the hissing of the gas cut through his head like a chain saw. He deliberately panted more loudly so as not to hear the sound.

With numb arms and sweat pouring down his back he finally reached his destination. There, he laid the boy down in the deepest part of the hollow and then stretched out beside him. It grew quiet. The boy's chest rose and fell. He would wake up in approximately eight minutes, at most. But he wouldn't.

Håkan lay beside the boy, studied his face, caressed it with a finger. Then he pulled himself closer to the boy, took the floppy body in his arms, and pressed it to him. He kissed the boy tenderly on the cheek, whispered "forgive me," and got up.

Tears threatened to well up into his eyes as he looked at the defenseless body on the ground. He could still refrain.

Parallel worlds. A comforting thought.

There was a parallel world where he didn't do what he was about to do. A world where he walked away, leaving the boy to wake up and wonder what had happened.

But not in this world. In this world he now walked over to his bag and opened it. He was in a hurry. He quickly pulled on his raincoat and got out his tools. A knife, a rope, a large funnel, and a five liter plastic jug.

He put everything on the ground next to the boy, looking at the young body one last time. Then he picked up the rope and got to work.

✝

He thrust and thrust and thrust. After the first blow Jonny had realized this wasn't going to be like those other times. With blood gushing from a deep cut on his cheek, he tried to escape, but the Murderer was faster. With a couple of quick moves he sliced away the tendons at the back of the knees and Jonny fell down, lay writhing in the moss, begging for mercy.

But the Murderer wasn't going to relent. Jonny was screaming . . . like a pig . . . when the Murderer threw himself over him and let the earth drink his blood.

One stab for what you did to me in the bathroom today. One for when you tricked me into playing knuckle poker. And I'm cutting your lips out for everything nasty you've ever said to me.

Jonny was bleeding from every orifice and could no longer say or do anything mean. He was long since dead. Oskar finished by puncturing his glassy eyeballs, *whack whack*, then got up and regarded his work.

Large pieces of the rotting, fallen trees that had represented Jonny's body had been hacked away and the tree trunk was full of perforations. A number of wood chips were scattered under the healthy tree that had been Jonny when he was still standing.

His right hand, the knife hand, was bleeding. There was a small cut right next to his wrist; the blade must have slipped while he was stabbing. Not the ideal knife for this purpose. He licked his hand, cleaning the wound with his tongue. It was Jonny's blood he was tasting.

He wiped the last of the blood on the newspaper holster, put the knife back, and started walking home.

The forest that, starting a few years back, had felt threatening, the haunt of enemies, now felt like a home and a refuge. The trees drew back respectfully as he passed. He didn't feel an ounce of fear though it was starting to get really dark. No anxiety for the next day, whatever it would bring. He would sleep well tonight.

When he was back in the yard, he sat down on the edge of the sandbox for a while to calm himself before he went back home. Tomorrow he would get himself a better knife, a knife with a parry guard, or whatever it was called . . . so he didn't cut himself. Because this was something he was going to do again.

It was a good game.

Thursday

His mom reached over the kitchen table and squeezed Oskar's hand. There were tears in her eyes.

"You are absolutely *not* allowed to go into the woods by yourself, do you hear me?"

A boy about Oskar's age had been murdered in Vällingby yesterday. It had appeared in the afternoon papers and his mother was completely beside herself when she came home.

"It could have been . . . I don't even want to think about it."

"But it was Vällingby."

"And you mean to say that someone who is capable of doing this to a child wouldn't be able to go two subway stations? Or walk? Walk all the way here to Blackeberg and do the same thing again? Do you spend a lot of time in the woods?"

"No."

"You are not allowed to go past the yard now, as long as this . . . Until they've caught him."

"You mean I can't go to school?"

"Of course you can go to school. But after school you come straight here and you don't leave this complex until I get home."

"Big deal."

The pain in his mother's eyes mixed with anger.

"Do you *want* to be murdered? Do you? You want to go into the woods and be killed and I have to sit here and worry while you're lying out there in the forest and . . . you're being butchered by some bestial . . ."

The tears welled up in her eyes. Oskar put his hand on hers.

"I *won't* go into the woods, Mom. I promise."

His mother stroked his cheek.

"Little sweetheart, you're all I have. Nothing is allowed to happen to you. I would die too."

"Mmmm. How exactly did he do it?"

"What do you mean?"

"You know. The murder."

"How should I know? The boy was killed by some kind of maniac with a knife. He's dead. His parents' lives have been ruined."

"Aren't the details in the paper?"

"I can't bear to read it."

Oskar took the copy of *Expressen* and flipped through the pages. The crime filled four pages.

"You shouldn't read things like that."

"I'm only checking something. Can I take it?"

"Don't read about it, I'm serious. All that violent stuff you read isn't good for you."

"I'm just seeing what's on TV tonight."

Oskar got up intending to take the paper to his room. His mother hugged him clumsily and pressed her wet cheek against him.

"Sweetheart, can't you understand that I'm worried about you? What if something were to happen to you—"

"I know, Mom, I know. I'm careful."

Oskar hugged her a little back and then carefully extracted himself, went to his room wiping his mother's tears from his cheek.

This was amazing.

From what he could understand the boy had been killed while he was out playing in the woods. Unfortunately the victim had not been Jonny Forsberg, only some unknown boy from Vällingby.

The atmosphere in Vällingby that afternoon had been funereal. He had seen the headlines before he came home and perhaps he was only imagining things but it seemed to him that people in the main square had been talking more, walking more slowly than normal.

In the hardware store he had swiped an incredibly alluring hunting knife that cost three hundred. He had made up an excuse in advance in case he was caught.

"Excuse me, Sir, but I am just so afraid of the killer."

He would probably also have been able to squeeze out a few tears, if it came to that. They would have let him go, no doubt about it. But he had not been caught, and now the knife was tucked into the hiding place next to his scrapbook.

He needed to think.

Could it be that his game had in some way caused the murder to happen? He didn't think so, but he couldn't completely rule out the idea. The books he read were full of things like this. A person's thoughts in one place causing an action somewhere else.

Telekenesis. Voodoo.

But exactly where, when, and above all *how* had the murder been committed? If it had involved a large number of stab wounds on a prone body he had to seriously consider the possibility that his hands possessed a terrifying power. A power he would have to learn to control.

Or is it . . . the TREE . . . that is the link.

The rotten log that he had cut. Maybe there was something special about it, something that meant that whatever you did to the tree . . . spread further.

Details.

Oskar read all of the articles on the murder. A photograph of the policeman who had been to their school and talked about drugs appeared on one page. He was not able to comment further at this stage. Technical experts from the National Laboratory of Forensic Science had been called in to secure evidence from the crime scene. One had to wait and see. There was a picture of the murdered boy, taken from the school yearbook. Oskar had never seen him before. He looked like a Jonny or Micke. Maybe there was now an Oskar in the Vällingby school who had been set free.

The boy had been on his way to handball practice at the Vällingby gym and never come home. The practice had started at five-thirty. The boy had probably left home at around five o'clock. So at some point in between—Oskar's head started to spin. The time matched up exactly. And the boy had been murdered in the forest.

Is it true? Am I the one? . . .

A sixteen-year-old girl had found the body around eight o'clock in the evening and contacted the police. She was described as being treated for "extreme shock." Nothing about the state of the body, but if this girl was in a state of *extreme* shock it indicated the body had been mutilated in some way. Usually they only wrote "shocked."

What was the girl doing in the woods after dark? Probably nothing interesting. Been picking pine cones or something. But why wasn't there anything about how the boy had been murdered? The only thing they offered was a photograph of the crime scene. Police tape demarcated an ordinary wooded area, a hollow with a large tree in the middle. Tomorrow or the next day there would be a photo in this place, lots of candles and signs about "WHY?" and "WE MISS YOU." Oskar knew how it went; he had several similar cases in his scrapbook.

The whole thing was probably a coincidence. But what if.

Oskar listened at the door. His mom was doing the dishes. He lay down on the bed and dug out the knife. The handle was shaped to fit the hand and the whole thing weighed about three times as much as the kitchen knife he had used yesterday.

He got up and stood in the middle of the room with the knife in his hand. It was beautiful, transmitted power to the hand holding it.

The sound of clinking dishes came from the kitchen. He thrust a few times into the air. The Murderer. When he had learned to control the power Jonny, Micke, and Tomas would never bother him again. He was about to lunge again, but stopped himself. Someone could see him from outside. It was dark now and the light was on in his room. He looked out but only saw his own reflection in the glass.

The Murderer.

He put the knife back in its hiding place. This was only a game. These kinds of things didn't happen in reality. But he needed to know the details. Needed to know them *now*.

†

Tommy was sitting in an armchair with a motorcycle magazine, nodding his head and humming. From time to time he held the magazine aloft so Lasse and Robban, who were sitting in the couch, could see a particularly interesting picture, with a caption about cylinder volume and maximum speed. The naked light bulb in the ceiling was reflected in the shiny pages, throwing pale cat's eyes over the cement and timber walls.

He had them sitting on pins and needles.

Tommy's mother was dating Staffan, who worked in the Vällingby police department. Tommy didn't like Staffan very much, quite the opposite, in fact. A know-it-all, oily-voiced kind of guy. And religious. But from his mom Tommy got to hear this and that. Things Staffan wasn't really allowed to tell his mom and things that his mom wasn't really allowed to tell Tommy, but . . .

That was how, for example, he had heard about the state of the police investigation into the radio store break-in at Islandstorget. The break-in that he, Robban, and Lasse had been responsible for.

No trace of the perpetrators. Those were his mom's exact words: "No trace of the perpetrators." Staffan's words. Didn't even have a description of the getaway car.

Tommy and Robban were sixteen years old and in the first year of high school. Lasse was nineteen, something wrong with his head, and he worked at LM Eriksson in Ulvsunda, sorting metal parts. But he had a driver's license. And a white Saab–74. They had used a marker to alter the plates before the break-in. Not that it mattered, since no one had seen the car.

They had stored their bounty in the unused shelter room across from the basement storage area that was their meeting place. They had removed the chain with metal cutters, supplied it with a new lock. Didn't really know what to do with all the stuff since the job itself had been the goal. Lasse had sold a cassette tape to a friend at work for two hundred but that was it.

It was best to lay low with the goods for a while. And not let Lasse handle any selling since he was . . . a little slow, as his mom put it. But now two weeks had gone by since the caper and the police had something else to occupy them.

Tommy kept turning the pages of the magazine and smiling to himself. Yup, yup. A whole lot of something else to occupy them. Robban was drumming his fingers against his thigh.

"Come on, let's hear it."

Tommy held up the magazine again.

"Kawasaki. Three hundred cubic. Fuel injection and—"

"Get a grip, man. Tell us."

"What . . . the murder?"

"Yes!"

Tommy bit his lip, pretended to think it over.

"How did it happen?"

Lasse leaned his tall body forward, folding in the middle like a jackknife.

"Uh. Let's hear it."

Tommy put the magazine away and met his gaze.

"Sure you want to hear it? It's pretty scary."

"Phft. So what."

Lasse looked all tough, but Tommy saw a flash of concern in his eyes. You only had to make an ugly face, talk in a funny voice, and not agree to cut it out to make Lasse really scared. One time Tommy and Robban had used Tommy's mom's makeup to make themselves look like zombies, unscrewed the light bulb, and waited for Lasse. It had ended with Lasse shitting himself and giving Robban a black eye under his dark blue eye shadow. After that they had been more careful about scaring Lasse.

Now Lasse was sitting up in his seat and crossing his arms, as if to show he was ready to hear anything.

"OK, then. So . . . this wasn't your usual murder, you understand. They found the guy . . . strung up in a tree."

"What do you mean? Was he hanged?" Robban asked.

"Yeah, hanging. But not by his neck. By his feet. So he was hanging upside down in the tree. By his feet."

"What the fuck—you don't die from that."

Tommy looked long at Robban as if he had made an interesting point, then he continued.

"No, you're right. You don't. But his neck had been cut open. And that'll kill you. The whole neck, sliced open. Like a . . . melon." He pulled a finger across his neck to show the path of the knife.

Lasse's hand went up to his neck as if to protect it. He shook his head slowly. "But why was he hanging like that?"

"Well, what do you think?"

"I don't know."

Tommy pinched his bottom lip and made a thoughtful face.

"Now I'll tell you the strange part. First you slice someone's neck open so they die. You'd expect to see a lot of blood, right?" Lasse and Robban both nodded. Tommy paused for a while in the midst of their expectation before he dropped the bomb.

"But the ground underneath . . . where the guy was hanging. There was almost no blood at all. Just a few drops. And he must have gushed out several liters, hanging up like that."

The basement room was quiet. Lasse and Robban stared straight ahead with a vacant look until Robban sat up and said, "I know. He was murdered somewhere else and then brought there."

"Mmmm. But in that case why did the killer bother to hang him up? If you've killed someone you normally want to get rid of the body."

"He could be . . . sick in the head."

"Yeah, maybe. But I think it's something else. Have you ever seen a butcher's shop? What they do with pigs? Before they butcher them they drain all the blood. And do you know how they do that? The hang them upside down. From a hook. And cut their throats."

"So you mean . . . what, the guy . . . that he was planning to *butcher* him?"

"Aaaah?" Lasse looked uncertainly from Tommy to Robban to Tommy again to see if they were pulling his leg. He found no indication of this, and said,

"They do that? With pigs?"

"Yeah, what did you think?"

"That it was some kind of machine."

"And that would be better, in your opinion?"

"No, but . . . Are they alive then? When they're hanging up like that?"

"Yeah, they're alive. And kicking around, screaming."

Tommy made a noise like a stuck pig, and Lasse sank back into the couch staring at his knees. Robban got up, walked a few steps back and forth, and sat down again.

"But it doesn't make sense. If the murderer was going to butcher him there would be blood everywhere."

"You're the one who said he was going to butcher him. I don't think so."

"Oh. And what do you think, then?"

"I think he was after the blood. That's why he killed the guy, in order to get the blood. I think he took it with him."

Robban nodded slowly, picked away at the scab of a large pimple in the corner of his mouth. "Yeah, but why? To drink it, or why?"

"Maybe. For example."

Tommy and Robban sank into their respective inner reenactments of the killing and what had happened thereafter. After a while Lasse raised his head and looked at them. He had tears in his eyes.

"Do they die fast, the pigs?"

Tommy met his gaze with equal seriousness.

"No, they don't."

†

I'm going out for a while."

"No."

"Just out into the courtyard."

"And nowhere else, do you hear?"

"Sure, sure."

"Do you want me to call for you when . . ."

"No, I'll be back in time. I have a watch. *Don't* call for me."

Oskar put on his jacket, his hat. He paused as he was putting his boot on. Went quietly back to his room and took out the knife, tucked it inside his jacket. Laced up the boots. He heard his mom's voice again from the living room.

"It's cold out there."

"I've got my hat."

"On your head?"

"No, on my feet."

"This is no joking matter, Oskar, you know how it is. . . ."

"See you in a while."

". . . your ears."

He walked out, looked down at his watch. A quarter past seven. Forty-five minutes until the program started. Tommy and the others were probably down in their basement headquarters but he didn't dare go down there. Tommy was alright, but the others . . . They could get strange ideas, especially if they had been sniffing.

So he went down to the playground in the middle of the yard. Two big trees, sometimes used as a soccer goal, a play structure with a slide, a sandbox, and a swing set consisting of three tire-swings suspended from chains. He sat down in one of the tire-swings and rocked gently to and fro.

He liked this place at night. Hundreds of lighted windows all around him on four sides, himself sitting in the dark. Safe and alone at the same time. He pulled the knife out of the holster. The blade was so shiny he could see windows reflected in it. The moon.

A bloody moon . . .

Oskar got up, snuck over to one of the trees, talked to it.

"What are you looking at, you fucking idiot? Do you want to die?"

The tree didn't answer and Oskar carefully drove the knife into it. Didn't want to damage the fine smooth edge.

"That's what happens if you so much as look at me."

He turned the knife so a small wedge of wood popped out of the trunk. A piece of flesh. He whispered, "Go on, squeal like a pig."

He stopped, thought he heard a sound. He looked around, holding the knife by his hip. Lifted the blade to his eyes, checked it. The point was as smooth as before. He used the blade as a mirror, and turned it so it reflected the jungle gym. Someone was standing there, someone who had not been there a moment before. A blurry contour against the clean steel. He lowered the knife and looked directly at the jungle gym. Yes. But it wasn't the Vällingby killer. It was a child.

There was enough light for him to determine that it was a girl he had never seen before. Oskar took a step toward the jungle gym. The girl didn't move, just stood there looking at him.

He took another step and suddenly he grew scared. Of what? Of himself. He was on his way toward the girl with his hand tightly closed around the knife, on his way to stab her with it. No, that wasn't true. But that was how he had felt, for a moment. Wasn't she scared?

He stopped, pushed the knife back in its holder, and put it back inside his jacket.

"Hi."

The girl didn't answer. Oskar was so close now that he could see she had dark hair, a small face, big eyes. Eyes wide open, calmly looking at him. Her white hands were resting on the railing.

"I said hi."

"I heard you."

"Why didn't you answer?"

The girl shrugged. Her voice was not as high as he would have expected. Sounded like someone his own age.

There was something strange about her. Shoulder-length black hair. Round face, small nose. Like one of those paper dolls in *Hemmets Journal*. Very . . . pretty. But there was something else. She had no hat, and no jacket. Only a thin pink sweater even though it was cold.

The girl nodded her head in the direction of the tree that Oskar had cut.

"What are you doing?"

Oskar blushed, but she probably couldn't tell in the dark.

"Practicing."

"For what?"

"For if the murderer comes along."

"What murderer?"

"The one in Vällingby. The one who killed that guy."

The girl sighed, looked up at the moon. Then she leaned forward again.

"Are you scared?"

"No, but a murderer, that's like . . . it's good if you can—defend yourself. Do you live here?"

"Yes."

"Where?"

"Over there," the girl gestured to the front door next to Oskar's. "Next door to you."

"How do you know where I live?"

"I've seen you in the window before."

Oskar's cheeks grew hot. While he was trying to think of something to say the girl jumped down from the top of the jungle gym and landed in front of him. A drop of over two meters.

She must do gymnastics or something like that.

She was almost as tall as he was, but much thinner. The pink sweater fit tight across her chest, which was still completely flat, without a hint of breasts. Her eyes were black, enormous in her pale little face. She held one hand up in the air in front of him as if she were warding something off that was coming toward her. Her fingers were long and slender as twigs.

"I can't be friends with you. Just so you know."

Oskar folded his hands over his chest. He could feel the contours of the knife through his jacket.

"What?"

One corner of the girl's mouth pulled up in a half-smile.

"Do you need a reason? I'm just telling you how it is. So you know."

"Yeah, yeah."

The girl turned and walked away from Oskar, toward her front door. After a couple of steps Oskar said, "What makes you think I'd *want* to be friends with you? You must be pretty stupid."

The girl stopped. Stood still for a moment. Then she turned and walked back to Oskar, stopped in front of him. Interlaced her fingers and let her arms drop.

"What did you say?"

Oskar wrapped his arms more tightly around himself, pressed one hand against his knife, and stared down into the ground.

"You must be stupid . . . to say something like that."

"Oh, I am, am I?"

"Yes."

"I'm sorry. But that's just how it is."

They stood still, about half a meter between them. Oskar continued staring into the ground. A strange smell was emanating from the girl.

About one year ago his dog Bobby had gotten an infection in one paw and in the end they had been forced to have him put down. The last day Oskar had stayed home from school, lain next to the sick dog for several hours, and said good-bye. Bobby had smelled like the girl did. Oskar screwed up his nose.

"Is that strange smell coming from you?"

"I guess so."

Oskar looked up at her. He regretted having said that. She looked so . . . fragile in her pink top. He unfolded his arms and made a gesture in her direction.

"Aren't you cold?"

"No."

"Why not?"

The girl frowned, wrinkling up her face, and for a moment she looked much much older than she was. Like an old woman about to cry.

"I guess I've forgotten how to."

The girl quickly turned around and walked back to her door. Oskar remained where he was, looking at her. When she reached the heavy front door he fully expected that she would need to use both hands to pull it open. But instead she grasped the door handle with one hand and pulled it open so hard it banged into the wall stop, bounced, and then closed behind her.

He pushed his hands into his pockets and felt sad. Thought about Bobby and how he had looked in the makeshift coffin Dad had made for him. Thought about the cross he had made in wood shop that had snapped in two as they hammered it into the frozen ground.

He ought to make a new one.

Friday

Håkan was sitting on a subway train again, on his way downtown. Ten thousand kronor bills in his pocket, secured by a rubber band; he was going to do something good with them. He was going to save a life.

Ten thousand was a lot of money, and when you thought about the fact that those Save The Children campaigns claimed that "One thousand kronor can feed one family for a whole year" you would think that ten thousand could save a life even in Sweden.

But whose life? And where?

You couldn't just walk up and give the money to the first drug addict you bumped into and hope that . . . no. And it had to be a young person, anyway. He knew it was silly, but ideally it would be a weeping child like in one of those pictures. A child who took the money with tears in his eyes and then . . . and then what?

He got off at Odenplan and, without knowing why, walked in the direction of the public library. In the days that he had lived in Karlstad, when he was a Swedish teacher at the high school level and still had a place to live, it was generally known that the Stockholm public library was a . . . good place.

Not until he saw the cupola, familiar to him through pictures in books and magazines, did he know why he had come here. Because it was a good place. Someone in the group, probably Gert, had told him how you went about buying sex there.

He had never done that. Buy sex.

Once Gert, Torgny, and Ove had found a boy whose mother had been brought back from Vietnam by someone Gert knew. The boy was maybe twelve years old and knew what was expected of him, was well-paid for his trouble. And yet Håkan couldn't bring himself to do it. He had sipped his Bacardi and Coke, enjoyed the boy's naked body as he writhed and turned in the room where they had gathered.

But that was the limit.

The others had, one by one, been sucked off by the boy, but when it was Håkan's turn a hard knot formed inside him. The whole situation was too disgusting. The room smelled of arousal, alcohol, and mustiness. A drop of Ove's cum glistened on the boy's cheek. Håkan pushed the boy's head aside when he lowered it to Håkan's groin.

The others had taunted him, called him names, finally threatened him. He was a witness; he needed to be a partner in crime. They taunted him about his scruples, but that wasn't the problem. It was simply too ugly, the whole thing. The single room of Åke's commuter apartment, the four mismatched armchairs arranged for the event, the dance music from the stereo.

He paid for his part of the affair and never saw the others again. He had his magazines and photos, his films. That had to be enough. Probably he also had his scruples, that only showed themselves this once in the form of a distaste for the situation.

Why then am I on my way to the City Library?

He was probably going to take out a book. The fire three years ago had consumed his life, and his book collection. Yes. He could borrow *The Queen's Diadem* by Almquist, before he performed his good deed.

It was quiet inside the City Library this morning. Older men and students, mostly. He quickly found the book he was looking for, read the first few lines,

Tintomara! Two things are white
Innocence—Arsenic

and put it back on the shelf. A bad feeling. It reminded him of his earlier life.

He had loved this book, used it in his class. Reading the first few words made him long for his reading chair. And the reading chair was supposed to be in a house that was his, a house filled with books, and he should have a job again and he should and he would. But he had found love, and that dictated his life nowadays. No reading chair.

He rubbed his hands together as if to erase the book they had been holding, and walked into an adjacent reading room.

There was a long table with people reading. Words, words, words. At the very back of the room there was a young man in a leather coat. He had tipped the chair back and was flipping uninterestedly through a book of photographs. Håkan moved in his direction, pretended to be interested in a shelf of geology books, glancing now and then at the youth. Finally the boy lifted his gaze and met Håkan's, raised his eyebrows in a question:

Want to?

No, he didn't want to. The youth was around fifteen years old, with a flat, Eastern European face, pimples and narrow, deeply set eyes. Håkan shrugged and walked out of the room.

Outside the main entrance the youth caught up with him, gestured with his thumb and asked "got a light?" Håkan shook his head. "Don't smoke," he said in English.

"OK."

The boy pulled out a lighter, lit his cigarette, and stared at him through the smoke. "What you like?"

"No, I . . ."

"Young, you like young?"

He pulled away from the youth, away from the main entrance where anyone could come walking by. He needed to think. He hadn't expected it to be this straightforward. It had only been a kind of game, to check if what Gert had said was true.

The youth followed him, came up right next to him by the stone wall. "How young? Eight or nine? Is difficult, but—"

"*No!*"

Did he really look like such a fucking pervert? Stupid thought. Neither Ove nor Torgny had looked particularly . . . remarkable. Normal guys with normal jobs. Only Gert, who lived on the proceeds of a huge inheritance from his father and could indulge himself in whatever he wanted. After multiple international trips he had acquired a truly appalling appearance. A flaccid mouth, glazed eyes.

The boy stopped talking when Håkan raised his voice, still studying him through narrowed eyes. Took a puff on his cigarette, then dropped it on the ground and crushed it under his foot, stretched out his arms.

"What?"

"No, I just . . ."

The boy took half a step closer.

"*What*?"

"I . . . maybe . . . twelve."

"Twelve? You like twelve?"

"I . . . yes."

"Boy."

"Yes."

"OK. You wait. Number Two."

"Excuse me?"

"Number two. Toilet."

"Oh. Yes."

"Ten minutes."

The boy zipped his leather jacket and disappeared down the steps.

Twelve years old. Booth number two. Ten minutes.

This was really, really dumb. If a policeman came by. They must know about these transactions after all these years. That would be the end. They would connect him to the job he had done yesterday and that would be the end. He couldn't do this.

Go over to the bathroom and take a look, that's all.

The bathroom was empty. A urinal and three booths. Number two had to be the one in the middle. He put a one crown coin in the lock, turned it, and walked in. Closed the door behind him and sat down on the toilet seat.

The walls of the booth were covered with scribbles. Not at all what you would expect from the City Library clientele. Here and there a literary quotation:

Harry me, Marry me, Bury me, Bite me

but mostly obscene drawings and jokes:
Killing for peace is like fucking for virginity.
Here I sit
I am elated
Came to shit
Ejaculated
as well as an impressive selection of telephone numbers that one could call for a variety of interests. A few of them had the sign and were probably authentic. Not just someone trying to have a joke at someone else's expense.

So, now he had checked it out. He should leave. Never knew what the young man in the leather jacket would think of. He stood up, urinated into the toilet, sat down again. Why had he urinated? He didn't really need to go. He knew why he had done it.

Just in case.

The outer door opened. He held his breath. Something in him hoped it was a policeman. A large male policeman who would kick open the door to the booth and beat him up with the baton before he arrested him.

Low voices, soft steps, a light knock on the door.

"Yes?"

Another knock. He swallowed a glob of saliva and unlocked the door.

A boy about eleven or twelve stood there. Blond hair, heart-shaped face. Thin lips and large, blue eyes devoid of expression. A red puffy jacket that was a little too big for him. Right behind him was the older boy in the leather coat. He held up five fingers.

"Five hundred."

The way he said "hundred" sounded like "chundred."

Håkan nodded and the older boy carefully guided the younger one into the booth and shut the door. Wasn't five hundred a bit much? Not that it mattered but . . .

He looked at the boy he had bought. Hired. Was he on drugs? Probably. The look in his eyes was far away, unfocused. The boy stood pressed up against the door half a meter away. He was so short that Håkan didn't need to tilt his head to look into his eyes.

"Hello."

The boy didn't answer, just shook his head, pointed to his groin, and made a gesture with his finger: *unzip your pants.* He obeyed. The boy sighed, made a new gesture: *take out your penis.*

His cheeks grew hot as he obeyed the boy. That was how it was. He was following the boy's orders. He had no will of his own. He wasn't the one doing this. His small penis was not in the least erect, hardly made it down to the toilet lid. A slight tickle when the head touched the cold surface.

He narrowed his eyes, tried to imagine the boy's gestures so they more closely resembled his beloved. It didn't work so well. His beloved was beautiful. This boy, who now bent down and pushed his head toward his groin, was not.

His mouth.

There was something wrong with the boy's mouth. He put his hand to the boy's forehead before he reached his goal.

"Your mouth?"

The boy shook his head and pushed on his hand so he could continue his work. But now Håkan couldn't. He had heard about this kind of thing.

He put his thumb against the boy's upper lip and pulled up. The boy had no teeth. Someone had knocked or pulled them out in order to make him more fit for his work. The boy stood up, a frothy, whispering sound as he crossed his arms across his chest in the puffy jacket. Håkan tucked his penis back into his pants, zipped them, and stared onto the floor.

Not like this. Never like this.

Something came into his line of vision. An outstretched hand. Five fingers. Five hundred.

He took the pack of bills out of his pocket and handed it to the boy. The boy took off the rubber band, ran his pointed finger across the ten pieces of paper, replaced the rubber band and held the packet aloft.

"Why?"

"Because . . . your mouth. Maybe you can . . . get new teeth."

The boy smiled a little. Not a wide grin, but the corners of his mouth pulled up. Perhaps he was only smiling at Håkan's folly. The boy thought for a moment, then took a thousand kronor note from the packet and put it in his outer pocket. Put the rest in an inner pocket. Håkan nodded.

The boy unlocked the door, hesitated. Then he turned to Håkan, stroked his cheek.

"Sank you."

Håkan put his hand over the boy's, held it against his cheek, and closed his eyes. If only someone could.

"Forgive me."

"Yes."

The boy pulled his hand back. Its warmth was still on Håkan's cheek when the outer door banged shut after the boy. He stayed in the booth, staring at something someone had written on the wall.

Whoever you are. I love you.

And right underneath it someone had written,

Do you want some cock?

The warmth had long since left his cheek when he made his way back to the subway and bought an evening paper for his last few kronor. Four pages were devoted to the murder. Among others was a picture of the hollow where he had done it. It was full of lighted candles, flowers. He studied the picture and didn't feel much.

If you only knew. Please forgive me, but if you only knew.

†

On his way home from school Oskar stopped under the two windows of her apartment. The closest one was only three meters from his own room. The blinds were drawn and the windows formed light gray rectangles against the dark gray concrete walls. Looked suspicious. Probably they were a . . . strange kind of family.

Drug addicts.

Oskar looked around, then walked in the front door and looked at the list of names. Five surnames neatly spelled out in plastic letters. One line was empty. The name that had stood there before, HELLBERG, had been there so long you could read it from the dark contours left against a sun-bleached background. But no new letters, not even a note.

He jogged up the two sets of stairs to her door. Same thing there. Nothing. The name plate attached to the mail slot was blank, the way it looked when an apartment was unoccupied.

Maybe she had been lying. Maybe she didn't live here at all. But she had walked in this entrance. Sure. But she could have done that anyway. If she—

The front door downstairs opened.

He turned away from her door and quickly walked down the stairs. Let it not be her. She would think that he was somehow . . . But it wasn't her.

Halfway down the stairs Oskar met a man he had never seen before. A short, stocky man who was half bald and smiled in an unnaturally wide way.

The man saw Oskar, lifted his head and nodded, his mouth still pulled up in that clownlike smile.

Oskar paused in the front entrance, listening. Heard keys pulled out and a door open. Her door. That man was probably her dad. Granted, Oskar had never seen a real life drug addict, but that man looked sick.

No wonder she was strange.

Oskar went down to the playground, sat on the edge of the sandbox, and kept an eye on her window to see if the blinds had been pulled up. Even the bathroom window looked like it had been covered on the inside. The frosted glass was much darker than in other peoples' apartments.

He took his Rubik's Cube out from his pocket. It creaked and squeaked as he turned it. A copy. The original was much more supple, but cost five times as much and could only be found in the well-guarded toy store in Vällingby.

Two sides had been completed, all one color, and on a third side only one little bit was out of place. But he couldn't get it there without destroying the two completed sides. He had saved an article from *Expressen* that described the various kinds of turns—that was how he had managed to solve two sides, but after that it was much harder.

He looked at the Cube, tried to think out the solution instead of just turning. He couldn't. His brain couldn't manage it. He pressed the Cube against his forehead, as if to delve into its interior. No answer. He placed the Cube on a corner of the sandbox half a meter away. Stared at it.

Glide, glide, glide.

Telekenesis, that was the name for it. In the USA they had run experiments. There were people who could do stuff like that. ESP. Extra Sensory Perception. Oskar would have given anything to be able to do something like that.

And maybe . . . maybe he could.

Today at school hadn't been so bad. Tomas Ahlstedt had tried to pull his chair out in the cafeteria, but he had seen it in time. That was all. He

JOHN AJVIDE LINDQVIST ⸺ 48

was going to go out into the forest with his knife, to that tree. Make a more serious attempt. Not get all carried away like yesterday.

Cut into the tree calmly and methodically, hack it apart and concentrate on Tomas Ahlstedt's face in his mind the whole time. But . . . there was the whole thing with the murderer. The real murderer who was out there somewhere.

No, he had to wait with this until the murderer was caught. On the other hand, if there was a normal murderer then the experiment was useless. Oskar looked at the Cube, imagined a line connecting his eyes to the Cube.

Glide, glide, glide.

Nothing happened. Oskar stuffed the Cube into his pocket, got up, brushed some sand from his pants, and looked at her window. The blinds were still drawn.

He went inside to work on his scrapbook, to cut out and paste the articles about the Vällingby murder. There would probably be a lot of them, in time. Especially if it happened again. He was hoping a little that that would be the case. Hopefully in Blackeberg.

So the police would come to his school, the teachers would be serious, concerned, that kind of atmosphere. He liked it.

†

Never again. No matter what you say."

"Håkan . . ."

"No. It's just—no."

"I'll die."

"Then die."

"Do you mean that?"

"No. I don't. But you could do it yourself."

"I'm still too weak."

"You're not weak."

"Too weak for—that."

"Well, then I don't know. But I won't do it again. It's so—horrible, so . . ."

"I know."

"You don't know. It's different for you, it is . . ."

"What do you know about how it is for me?"

"Nothing, but at least you're . . ."

"Do you think I like it?"

"I don't know. Do you?"

"No."

"No, of course not. Well, anyway . . . I'm not doing it again. Maybe you've others who have helped you who have been . . . better at this than me."

". . ."

"Have you?"

"Yes."

"I see."

"Håkan?"

"I love you."

"Yes."

"Do you love me, even one little bit?"

"Would you do it again if I said I loved you?"

"No."

"I should love you anyway, you mean."

"You only love me to the extent I help you stay alive."

"Yes. Isn't that what love is?"

"If only I thought you would love me even if I didn't do it . . ."

"Yes?"

". . . maybe I would do it again."

"I love you."

"I don't believe you."

"Håkan. I can manage for a few more days but then . . ."

"Make sure you start to love me, then."

†

Friday night at the Chinese restaurant. It's a quarter to eight and the whole gang is there. Everyone except Karlsson who's at home watching the TV quiz show *Nutcrackers* and just as well. No great loss there. He's the sort who'll probably roll in when everything's over and tell you how many questions he knew the answers to.

In the corner table for six nearest the door there's Lacke, Morgan, Larry, and Jocke. Jocke and Lacke are talking about what kinds of fish can live in both fresh and salt water. Larry is reading the evening paper and Morgan is swinging his leg in time to some song other than the Chinese Muzak softly piped in through the hidden loudspeakers.

On the table in front of them are some more or less full glasses of beer. Their faces are hanging on the wall above the bar.

The restaurant owner was forced to flee China in conjunction with the cultural revolution, on account of his satirical caricatures of people in power. Now he has instead transferred his talents to his regulars. On the wall there are twelve tenderly drawn felt-pen sketches of them.

All the guys. And Virginia. The pictures of the guys are close-ups, where the irregularities of their physiognomies have been exaggerated.

Larry's lined, almost hollowed-out face, and a pair of enormous ears that stick straight out from his head, make him look like a friendly but starving elephant.

In Jocke's picture it is his large eyebrows that meet in the middle that have been emphasized and transformed into a rose bush and a bird, perhaps a nightingale.

Because of his style, Morgan has been given features from the young Elvis. Big sideburns and a "Hunka hunka burnin looooove, baby" expression. The head is perched on a small body holding a guitar, in Elvis-pose. Morgan is more pleased with this picture than he wants to admit.

Lacke looks mostly worried. Here the eyes have been enlarged and given an intensified expression of suffering. He has a cigarette in his mouth and its smoke has gathered into a rain cloud above his head.

Virginia is the only one who appears in full body. In an evening gown, shining like a star in her sparkling sequins, posed with outstretched arms, surrounded by a flock of pigs gazing at her in bewilderment. At Virginia's request the restaurant owner has made a duplicate of this picture that Virginia has taken home.

Then there are a few others. Some who aren't part of the gang. Some who have stopped coming. A few who have died.

Charlie fell down the stairs in his building on his way home from the restaurant one night. Cracked his head on the mottled concrete. The Gherkin got cirrhosis of the liver and died of an internal hemorrhage.

One evening a few weeks before he died he had pulled his shirt up and showed them a red spider's web of blood vessels branching out from his navel. "Damn expensive tattoo," he said, and he died soon thereafter. They had honored his memory by putting his picture on the table and making toasts to it all evening.

There is no picture of Karlsson.

This Friday night is going to be the last one they will ever have all together. Tomorrow one of them will be gone forever. One more picture will be nothing more than a memory. And nothing will ever be the same.

†

Larry lowered the newspaper, put his reading glasses on the table and sipped some beer from his glass. "I'll be damned. What's going on inside the head of a person like that?"

He showed them the paper with the headline CHILDREN IN SHOCK above a picture of the Vällingby school and a small inset of a middle-aged man. Morgan glanced at the paper, pointed.

"Is that the guy?"

"No, it's the principal."

"Looks like a murderer to me. Just the type."

Jocke stretched a hand out for the paper.

"Let me see."

Larry gave him the paper and Jocke held it at arm's length, studied the snapshot.

"Looks like a conservative politician to me, guys."

Morgan nodded.

"That's what I'm talking about."

Jocke held up the newspaper to Lacke so he could see the photograph. "What do you think?"

Lacke looked at it reluctantly.

"Ah, I don't know. I get creeped out by that kind of thing."

Larry breathed on his glasses and polished them against his shirt.

"They'll get him. You don't get away with something like that."

Morgan tapped his fingers on the table, stretched his hand out for the paper.

"How did Arsenal do?"

Larry and Morgan switched to talking about the currently pathetic state of English soccer. Jocke and Lacke sat quietly, nursing their beers, lighting cigarettes. Then Jocke started in on the whole cod thing, how the cod was going to die out in the Baltic. The evening wore on.

Karlsson didn't turn up, but just before ten another man came in, someone none of them had ever seen before. The conversation was more intense at this hour and no one noticed him until the man was sitting alone at a table at the far end of the room.

Jocke leaned toward Larry.

"Who's that?"

Larry looked over discreetly, shook his head.

"Don't know."

The new guy got a big whisky and quickly emptied it, ordered another. Morgan blew air out through his lips with a low whistle.

"This guy means business."

The man did not appear to notice that he was being observed. He simply sat motionless at the table, studying his hands, looking like all the trouble in the world had been stuffed into a backpack and strapped onto him. He quickly downed his second whisky and ordered a third.

The waiter leaned down and said something to him. The man dug around in his pocket and showed him a few bills. The waiter made a gesture as if to say that wasn't what he meant, when of course that was exactly what he had meant, and then he walked off to fill the man's order.

It wasn't surprising to them that the man's credit had been in question. His clothes were wrinkled and stained as if he had slept in them, in some uncomfortable place. The ring of hair around his bald spot was straggly and hung halfway to his ears. The face was dominated by a large pink nose and a jutting chin. Between them were a pair of small, plump lips that moved from time to time as if he were talking to himself. His expression didn't change at all when the whisky was placed in front of him.

The gang returned to the subject they had been discussing: if Ulf Adelsohn would be worse than Gösta Bohman had been. Only Lacke looked over at the lone man from time to time. After a while, when the man was on his fourth drink, he said, "Shouldn't we . . . ask him if he wants to join us?"

Morgan glanced at the man, who had sunk together even more. "No, why? What's the use? His wife has left him, the cat is dead and life is hell. I know it all already."

"Maybe he'll offer to buy us a round."

"That's a different story. Then he's allowed to have cancer as well." Morgan shrugged. "It's OK by me."

Lacke looked at Larry and Jocke. They made small gestures of assent and Lacke got up and walked over to the man's table.

"Hello."

The man looked up at Lacke, bleary-eyed. The glass in front of him was almost empty. Lacke rested his hands on the chair on the other side of the table and leaned down toward the man.

"We were just wondering if maybe . . . you wanted to join us?"

The man shook his head slowly and made a befuddled, dismissive gesture, brushing the suggestion away.

"No, thank you, but why don't you sit down?"

Lacke pulled the chair out and sat down. The man drained the last of his drink and waved the waiter over.

"You want something? It's on me."

"In that case. Same as you, then."

Lacke didn't want to say the word "whisky" since it sounded presumptuous to ask someone to buy you something expensive like that, but the man only nodded, and when the waiter came closer he made a V-sign with his fingers and pointed to Lacke. Lacke leaned back in the chair. How long had it been since he had last ordered whisky in a bar? Three years? At least.

The man showed no signs of wanting to start a conversation, so Lacke cleared his throat and said, "Some cold weather we're having."

"Yes."

"Could snow soon."

"Mmm."

Then the whisky arrived and made further conversation unnecessary for the moment. Even Lacke got a double, and he felt the eyes of the gang burning in his back. After a few sips he raised the glass.

"Cheers. And thanks."

"Cheers."

"You live around here?"

The man stared out into space, as if this was something he had never thought about before. Lacke couldn't determine if the nodding of his head indicated an answer to the question or if it was part of an inner dialogue.

Lacke took another sip and decided that if the man didn't answer the next question then he wanted to be left alone, not talk to anyone. If that was the case, Lacke would take his drink and return to the others. He had done his duty. He hoped the man wouldn't answer.

"So, then. What do you do to make the time go by?"

"I . . ."

The man furrowed his brow and the corners of his mouth were lifted spasmodically into a grin, then relaxed again.

". . . I help out a little."

"I see. With what kind of thing?"

A spark of alertness flashed under the man's transparent cornea. The man looked straight at Lacke, who felt a shiver at the base of his spine, as if a black ant had bitten him just above the tailbone.

Then he rubbed his hand over his eyes and pulled a few hundred kronor bills out of his pocket, laid them on the table and stood up.

"Excuse me, I have to . . ."

"OK. Thanks for the drink."

Lacke raised his glass to his host but he was already on his way over to the coat rack. He got his coat down with clumsy hands and walked out. Lacke stayed put with his back to the gang, looking at the heap of bills in front of him. Five one hundred kronor bills. A tumbler of whisky cost sixty kronor and this outing had consisted of a total of five, maybe six.

Lacke looked surreptitiously to the side. The waiter was busy settling the bill of an older couple, the only dining customers. While Lacke stood up he crumpled one of the notes into a ball, slipped it into his pocket and walked back to his regular table.

Halfway there he turned back, emptied the remaining whisky from the man's glass into his own, and took it with him.

A successful evening all around.

†

But *Nutcrackers* is on tonight!"

"Yeah, but I'll be back for it."

"It starts in . . . half an hour."

"I know."

"Where are you going?"

"Out."

"Well, you don't have to watch *Nutcrackers*, of course. I can watch it by myself. If you really have to go out."

"But . . . I'll be back for it."

"I see. I guess I'll wait on heating up the crepes."

"No, you can . . . I'll be back later."

Oskar was torn. *Nutcrackers* was one of the highlights of their TV week. Mom had made crepes with shrimp filling to eat in front of the TV. He knew he was disappointing her by going out instead of sitting here . . . and sharing the anticipation with her.

But he had been standing by the window since it got dark and just now he had seen the girl come out of the building next door and walk down toward the playground. He had immediately pulled back from the window. He didn't want her to think that he . . .

Therefore he had waited five minutes before putting on his clothes and heading out. He didn't put on a hat.

†

He couldn't see her on the playground. She was probably sitting high up on the jungle gym somewhere, like yesterday. The blinds in her window were still drawn but there was light coming from the apartment. Except for the bathroom window, a dark square.

Oskar sat down on the sandbox ledge and waited. Like he was waiting for an animal to come out of its hole. He was simply planning to sit here for a while. And if the girl didn't come out he would go back in again, play it cool.

He got out his Rubik's Cube, started to twist it in order to have something to do. He had gotten tired of having that one corner piece to worry about and so he mixed up the cube completely so he could start over.

The creak from the Cube was amplified in the cold air; it sounded like a small machine. In the corner of his eye Oskar saw the girl get up from her perch in the monkey bars. He kept working, creating a new one-colored side. The girl stood still. He felt a flicker of worry in his stomach but took no notice of her.

"You here again?"

Oskar lifted his head, pretending to be surprised, let a few seconds pass and then:

"*You* again."

The girl said nothing and Oskar twisted the Cube again. His fingers were stiff. It was hard to tell the colors apart in the dark and so he only worked with the white side that was easiest to differentiate.

"Why are you sitting here?"

"Why are you up there?"

"I came here to be by myself."

"Me too."

"So why don't you go home?"

"You go home. I've lived here longer than you."

Take that. The white side was done now and it was harder to keep going. The other colors were one big dark gray blur. He kept moving pieces, at random.

The next time he looked up the girl was standing on the railing and getting ready to jump. Oskar felt a quiver in his tummy when she hit the ground; if he had tried the same jump he would have hurt himself. But the girl landed as softly as a cat, walked over to him. He turned back to the Cube. She stopped right in front of him.

"What's that?"

Oskar looked up at the girl, at the Cube, then back at the girl.

"This?"

"Yes."

"You don't know?"

"No."

"It's a Rubik's Cube."

"What did you say?"

This time Oskar overenunciated the words.

"Ru–bik's Cube."

"And what's that?"

Oskar shrugged.

"A toy."

"A puzzle?"

"Yes."

Oskar held the Cube out to her.

"Want to try it?"

She took the Cube from his hand, turned it, examined it from all sides. Oskar laughed. She looked like a monkey examining a piece of fruit.

"You really haven't seen one before?"

"No. What do you do?"

"Like this . . ."

Oskar got the Cube back and the girl sat down next to him. He showed her how you turned it and that the point was to get the sides to be one color. She took the Cube and started to turn it.

"Can you see the colors?"

"Naturally."

He snuck glances at her while she was working on the Cube. She was wearing the same pink top as yesterday and he couldn't understand why she wasn't freezing. He was starting to get cold from sitting still, even though he was wearing his jacket.

Naturally.

She talked funny too, like a grown-up. Maybe she was *older* than him, even though she was so puny. Her thin white throat jutted out of her turtleneck top, merged with a sharp jaw bone. Like a mannequin.

But now the wind blew in Oskar's direction and he swallowed, breathed through his mouth. The mannequin stank.

Doesn't she ever take a bath?

The smell was worse than old sweat; it was closer to the smell that came when you removed the bandage from an infected wound. And her hair . . .

When he dared to take a closer look at her—she was completely absorbed by the Cube—he noticed that her hair was caked together and fell around her face in matted tufts and clumps. As if she had put glue or . . . mud in it.

While he was studying her, he happened to breathe in through his nose and had to suppress the urge to vomit. He got up, walked over to the swings, and sat down. Couldn't be close to her. The girl didn't seem to care.

After a while he got up and walked over to where she was sitting, still preoccupied with the Cube.

"Hey there, I have to go home now."

"Mmm . . ."

"The Cube . . ."

The girl paused. Hesitated for a moment, then held the Cube out to him without saying anything. Oskar took it, looked at her and then handed it back.

"You can keep it until tomorrow."

She didn't take it.

"No."

"Why not?"

"I may not be here tomorrow."

"Until the day after tomorrow, then. But you can't have it for longer than that."

She thought about it. Took the Cube.

"Thanks. I'll probably be here tomorrow."

"Here?"

"Yes."

"OK. Bye."

"Bye."

As Oskar turned and left he heard softs creaks from the Cube. She was going to stay out here in her thin top. Her mother and father must be . . . different, letting her go out dressed like that. You could end up with a bladder infection.

✝

Where have you been?"

"Out."

"You're drunk."

"Yes."

"We agreed you wouldn't do this anymore."

"You agreed. What's that?"

"A puzzle. You know it isn't good for you—"

"Where did you get it?"

"Borrowed it. Håkan, you have to—"

"Borrowed—from who?"

—

"Håkan. Don't be like this."

"Make me happy, then."

"What do you want me to do?"

"Let me touch you."

"Alright, but on one condition."

"No. No, no. Not that."

"Tomorrow. You have to."

"No. Not one more time. What do you mean, 'borrowed'? You never borrow anything. What is it anyway?"

"A puzzle."

"Don't you have enough puzzles? You care more about your puzzles than you do about me. Puzzles. Cuddles. Puzzles. Who gave it to you? *Who gave it to you?*, I said!"

"Håkan, stop it."

—

"What do you need me for anyway?"

"I love you."

"No, you don't."

"Yes. In a way."

"There is no such thing. You either love someone or you don't."

"Really?"

"Yes."

"In that case I have to think about it."

Saturday

The suburban mystique is the absence of riddles.
—Johan Eriksson

Three thick bundles of advertising catalogs lay outside Oskar's apartment door on Saturday morning. Mom helped him fold them. Three different pages in every package, four hundred and eighty packages total. For each package he made about fourteen *öre*. In the worst case he only got one page to deliver, yielding seven öre. In the best case scenario (or the worst in a way, since it involved so much folding prep) he received up to five pages a package yielding twenty-five öre.

He was helped by the fact that the large apartment buildings were included in his district. He could dispatch up to one hundred and fifty packages there per hour. The whole round took about four hours, including a trip home in between to fill up on packets. If it was a day when there were five papers per packet he needed to go home twice.

The packets had to be delivered by Tuesday at the latest but he usually did it all on Saturday. Got it over and done with.

Oskar sat on the kitchen floor, his mom at the kitchen table. It wasn't fun work but he liked the chaos he made in the kitchen. The large mess that bit by bit transformed into order, into two, three, four overstuffed paper bags full of neatly folded packets.

His mom put one more pile of packets' into one of the bags, then shook her head.

"Well, I really don't like it."

"What?"

"You can't . . . I mean, if someone were to open the door or something . . . I don't want you to . . ."

"No, why would I?"

"There are so many crazy people in the world."

"Yeah."

They had this conversation, in some form or another, almost every Saturday. This Friday evening his mom had said she didn't think he should make any deliveries this Saturday, on account of the murderer. But Oskar had promised to scream to high heaven if anyone so much as said "hi" to him, and then his mom had given in.

No one had ever tried to invite him in or anything like that. Once an old guy had come out and yelled at him for filling his mailbox "with this garbage" but since then he had just avoided putting anything in the man's mailbox.

The man would have to live without knowing he could get a haircut with highlights for that special event for only two hundred kronor at the hair salon this week.

By eleven-thirty all the pages were folded and he set off on his rounds. There was no point in stuffing the bags into the garbage can or something; they always called and checked up on him, made random tests. They had made that perfectly clear when he called up and signed up for the job six months ago. Maybe it was a bluff, but he didn't dare take the chance. And anyway, he didn't have anything against this kind of work. Not for the first two hours, at least.

He would pretend, for example, that he was an agent on a secret mission, out to spread propaganda against the enemy occupying the country. He sneaked through the hallways, on guard against enemy soldiers who could very well be dressed up as old ladies with dogs.

Or else he pretended that each building was a hungry animal, a dragon with six mouths whose only source of nourishment was the virgin flesh—made to look like advertisements—that he fed it with. The packet screamed in his hands when he pressed it into the jaws of the beast.

The final two hours—like today, just after the second round—he was overcome by a kind of numbness. The legs kept walking and the arms kept moving mechanically.

Put the bag down, place six packets under his arm, open the downstairs door, arrive at the first apartment, open the mail slot with his left arm, put a packet in with his right hand. Second door, and so on. . . .

When he finally came to his own complex, to the girl's door, he stopped outside and listened. He heard a radio on, low. That was all. He put the packet in the mail slot and waited. No one came to get it.

In the usual way, he ended with his own door, put a packet in the mail slot, unlocked the door, picked up the packet, and threw it in the garbage.

Done for the day. Sixty-seven kronor richer.

Mamma had gone to Vällingby to do the shopping. Oskar had the apartment to himself. Didn't know what to do with it.

He opened the cabinets under the kitchen sink, peeked in. Kitchen utensils and whisks and an oven thermometer. In another drawer he found pens and paper, recipe cards from a cooking series that his mom had started subscribing to, and then stopped since the recipes called for such expensive ingredients.

He continued on into the living room, opened the cabinets there.

His mom's crochet—or was it knitting?—things. A folder with bills and receipts. Photo albums that he had looked at a thousand times. Old magazines with unsolved crossword puzzles. A pair of reading glasses in their case. A sewing kit. A little wooden box with his and his mom's passports, their government-issued identification tags (he had asked to be allowed to wear his but his mom had said only if there was a war) a photograph and a ring.

He went through the cabinets and drawers as if he were looking for something without knowing exactly what it was. A secret. Something that would change things. To suddenly find a piece of rotting meat in the back of a cabinet. Or an inflated balloon. Anything. Something unfamiliar.

He took out the photograph and looked at it.

It was from his christening. His mom was holding him in her arms, looking into the camera. She was thin back then. Oskar was dressed in a white gown with long blue ribbons. Next to his mom was his dad, looking uncomfortable in his suit. Looked like he didn't know what to do with his hands and had therefore let them fall stiffly by his side, almost like he was standing at attention. Was looking straight at the baby. The sun was shining on the three of them.

Oskar brought the image closer to his eyes, studied his dad's expression. He looked proud. Proud and very . . . unpracticed. A man who was happy to be a father but who didn't know how to act. What you did. You could have thought it was the first time he had seen the baby, even though the christening was a full six months after Oskar's birth.

His mom, however, held Oskar in a confident, relaxed way. Her look into the camera was not so much proud as . . . suspicious. Don't come any closer, her look said. I'll bite you in the nose.

His dad was leaning forward slightly, as if he wanted to get closer without really daring to. It was not a picture of a family. It was a picture of a boy and his mother. And next to them there was a man, presumably the father, judging by his facial expression. But Oskar loved his dad, and so did his mom. In a way. In spite of everything. How everything had turned out.

Oskar took out the ring and read the inscription: *Erik 22/4 1967.*

They had divorced when Oskar was two. Neither of them had found another partner. "It just didn't work out that way." They had both used the same expression.

He replaced the ring, closed the wooden box, and put it back on the shelf. Wondered if his mom ever looked at the ring, why she kept it. It was made of solid gold. Probably ten grams worth. Worth about four hundred.

Oskar put his jacket on again, walked out into the yard. It was starting to get dark even though it was only four o'clock. Too late to go out into the forest.

Tommy walked by outside the building, stopped when he saw Oskar.

"Hi."

"Hi."

"Anything going on?"

"I don't know . . . Delivering flyers, and stuff."

"Any money in that kind of thing?"

"Some. Seventy, eighty kronor. Each time."

Tommy nodded.

"You want to buy a Walkman?"

"Don't know. What kind?"

"Sony Walkman. Fifty."

"New?"

"Yup. In the box. With ear phones. An even fifty."

"I have no money on me. Right now."

"I thought you said you made seventy or eighty doing that stuff."

"Yeah, but I'm paid by the month. One more week."

"OK. You can have it now and then I'll get the money from you later."

"Yeah . . ."

"OK. Go and wait over there and I'll get it."

Tommy gestured to the playground and Oskar walked over and sat down on a bench. Got up and walked over to the jungle gym. No girl. He quickly walked back to the bench and sat down, as if he had done something forbidden.

After a while Tommy came back and handed over the box.

"Fifty in a week—OK?"

"Mm."

"What are you listening to?"

"KISS."

"What do you have by them?"

"*Alive*."

"You don't have *Destroyer*? You can borrow it from me if you like. Tape it."

"Great."

Oskar had the double album *Alive* by KISS, had bought it a few months ago but never listened to it. Mostly looked at the pictures from their concerts. Their made-up faces were cool. Like live horror figures. And "Beth," the one where Peter Criss sang, he actually liked, but all the other songs were too . . . there was no melody or anything. Maybe *Destroyer* was better.

Tommy got up to leave. Oskar squeezed the box.

"Tommy?"

"Yeah?"

"That guy. Who was killed. Do you know . . . *how* he was murdered?"

"Yeah. He was strung up from a tree and had his throat slit."

"He wasn't . . . stabbed? Like the guy had stabbed him. In the chest, I mean."

"No, only his throat—*phhhhhssst.*"

"OK."

"Anything else?"

"No."

"See you."

"Yeah."

Oskar stayed put on the bench, thinking. The sky was dark purple, the first star— or was it Venus?—was already clearly visible. He got up and went in to hide the Walkman before his mom got back.

Tonight he would see the girl, get his Cube back. The blinds were still drawn. Did she really live there? What did they do in there all day? Did she have any friends?

Probably not.

✝

Tonight—"

"What have you been doing?"

"I took a shower."

"You don't normally."

"Håkan, tonight you have to . . ."

"No, I told you."

—

"Please?"

"This isn't about . . . I'll do anything except that. Say the word. I'll do it. Take some of mine, for God's sake. Here. Here's a knife. No? OK, then I'll have to—"

"Stop it!"

"Why? I'd rather do this. Why did you take a shower? You smell like . . . soap."

"What do you want me to do?"

"I can't!"

"No."

"What are you going to do?"

"Do it myself."

"And you need to shower for that?"

"Håkan . . ."

"I would help you if it was anything else. Anything else, I . . ."

"Yeah, OK. Fine."

"I'm sorry."

"Yeah."

"Be careful. I—was careful."

†

Kuala Lumpur, Phnom Penh, Mekong, Rangoon, Chungking . . .

Oskar looked at the photocopied map he had just filled out, weekend homework. The names told him nothing, were simply collections of letters. It gave him a certain feeling of satisfaction to sit and look them up in the geography book, to see that there actually were cities and rivers in just that place where they were marked on the photocopy.

Yes, he was going to memorize them and then his mom could test him. He would point to the dots and say the foreign names. Chungking, Phnom Penh. His mom would be impressed. And sure, it was kind of fun with all these strange names for places that were far away, but . . .

Why?

In fourth grade they had been given photocopies of Swedish geography. He had memorized everything back then too. He was good at that. But now?

He tried to recall the name of even one Swedish river.

Äskan, Väskan, Piskan . . .

Something along those lines. Ätran, maybe. Yes. But where was it? No idea. And it would be the same thing with Chungking and Rangoon in a few years.

It's meaningless.

These places didn't even *exist*. And even if they did . . . he would never see them in person. Chungking? What would he do in Chungking? It was just a big white area and a little dot.

He looked at the straight lines that his scrawled letters were balancing on. It was school. That's all. This was school. They told you to do a lot of things and you did them. The whole thing had been invented so the teachers would be able to hand out photocopies. It didn't mean anything. He could just as well be writing *Tjippiflax, Bubbelibäng* and *Spitt* on these lines. It would be equally meaningful.

The only difference actually would be that his teacher would say it was *wrong*. That it wasn't the correct name. Then she would point to the map and say "Look, here it says Chungking, not Tjippiflax." Pretty weak argument, since someone had made up the names in the geography book. Nothing spoke for it being true. And maybe the Earth really was flat, but this was being kept secret for some reason.

Ships falling over the edge. Dragons.

Oskar got up from the table. The photocopy was done, filled with letters that his teacher would accept. That was all.

It was past seven, maybe the girl had gone outside? He moved his face to the window and cupped his hands around it so he could see better in the dark. Wasn't there something moving down by the playground?

He went out into the hall. His mom was knitting or maybe crocheting out in the living room.

"Going out for a while."

"You're going out again? I thought I was supposed to test you."

"We can do that in a while."

"Wasn't it Asia this time?"

"What?"

"The worksheet you had. Isn't it Asia?"

"Yes, I think so. Chungking."

"Where is that? China?"

"I don't know."

"You don't *know*? But—"

"I'll be back."

"Alright. Be careful. Are you wearing your hat?"

"Sure."

JOHN AJVIDE LINDQVIST   68

Oskar put the hat in his coat pocket and went out. Halfway to the playground his eyes had grown accustomed enough to the dark that he spotted the girl in her usual place on the jungle gym. He walked up and stood below her, his hands in his pockets.

She looked different today. Still the pink top—did she not have any other?—but her hair didn't look so matted. It lay smooth, black, slick against her head.

"Hey there."

"Hi."

"Hi."

He was never in his life going to say "hey there" to someone ever again. It sounded incredibly stupid. The girl stood up.

"Come up here."

"OK."

Oskar climbed up onto the structure until he was next to her, discreetly drawing air into his nose. She didn't stink anymore.

"Do I smell better today?"

Oskar blushed. The girl smiled and held something out to him. His Cube.

"Thanks for lending it to me."

Oskar took the Cube and looked at it. Looked again. Held it up to the light as best he could, turned it and examined it from all sides. It had been solved. All of the sides were a solid color.

"Did you take it apart?"

"What do you mean?"

"Like . . . did you take it apart . . . and then put the pieces back in the right place?"

"Can you do that?"

Oskar tested the pieces to see if they were loosened from having been taken apart. He had done that once, marveled at how few twists it took to lose one's movements and forget how to make the sides all one color again. The pieces had of course not been loose when he took it apart, but did she actually solve this thing?

"You must have taken it apart."

"No."

"But you've never even seen one of these before."

"No, it was fun. Thanks."

Oskar held the Cube up to his eyes, as if it could tell him what had happened. In some way he was sure she wasn't lying.

"How long did it take you?"

"Several hours. If I did it again it would probably go faster."

"Amazing."

"It's not so hard."

She turned toward him. Her pupils were so large that they almost filled the whole iris, the lights from the building reflected in the black surface and it looked like she had a distant city in her head.

The turtleneck sweater, pulled high onto her neck, further accentuated her soft features and she looked like . . . a cartoon character. Her skin, its quality—he could only compare it to a wooden butter knife that had been polished with the finest sandpaper until the wood was like silk.

Oskar cleared his throat.

"How old are you?"

"What do you think?"

"Fourteen, fifteen."

"Do I look it?"

"Yes. Or—no, but . . ."

"I'm twelve."

"Twelve!"

For crying out loud. She was probably younger than he was, since he was going to turn thirteen in a month.

"What month were you born?"

"I don't know."

"You don't know? But . . . when do you celebrate your birthday and that?"

"I don't celebrate it."

"But your mom and dad must know."

"No. My mom is dead."

"Oh. I see. How did she die?"

"I don't know."

"And doesn't your dad know?"

"No."

"So . . . you mean . . . you don't get any presents or stuff?"

She stepped closer to him. Her breath wafted onto his face and the city of light in her eyes was extinguished when she stepped into his shadow. Her pupils were two marble-sized holes in her head.

She's so sad. So very, very sad.

"No, I never get any presents. Ever."

Oskar nodded stiffly. The world around him had ceased to exist. Only those two holes, a breath away. Their breaths mingled and rose, dissipated.

"Do you want to give me a present?"

"Yes."

His voice was not even a whisper. Only an exhalation. The girl's face was close. His gaze was drawn to her butter-knife cheek.

That was why he didn't see her eyes change, how they narrowed, took on another expression. He didn't see how her upper lip drew back and revealed a pair of small, dirty white fangs. He only saw her cheek and while her mouth was nearing his throat he drew up his hand and stroked her face.

The girl froze for a moment, then pulled back. Her eyes resumed their former shape; the city of light was back.

"What did you do that for?"

"I'm sorry . . . I—"

"What did you do?"

"I . . ."

Oskar looked at his hand, still holding the Cube, and relaxed his grip on it. He had been squeezing it so hard the corners had left deep imprints in his hand. He stretched it out toward her.

"Do you want it? You can have it."

She slowly shook her head.

"No. It's yours."

"What's . . . your name."

"Eli."

"My name is Oskar. What did you say your name was? Eli?"

"Yes."

The girl seemed suddenly restless. Her gaze flitted around as if she were looking for something, something she couldn't find.

"I'm . . . going now."

Oskar nodded. The girl looked him straight in the eyes for a few seconds, then turned to go. She reached the top of the slide and hesitated. Then she sat down and slid to the bottom, started off toward her front door. Oskar squeezed the Cube.

"See you tomorrow?"

The girl stopped and said "Yes" in a low voice without turning, then kept going. Oskar watched her. She didn't go home, though; she walked through the archway that led to the street. Disappeared.

Oskar looked at the Cube again. Unbelievable.

He twisted a section one rotation, broke up the unity. Then he turned it back. Wanted to keep it like this. At least for a while.

✝

Jocke Bengtsson was chuckling to himself on his way home from the movies. Damned funny film, *The Charter Trip*. Especially that part with the two guys running around the whole movie looking for Peppe's Bodega. When the one pushed his hungover friend in a wheelchair through Customs: "invalido." Damn, that was funny.

Maybe he should go off on a trip like that with one of the guys. But which one.

Karlsson was so boring he made the clocks stop; you'd get sick of him in two days. Morgan could get ugly when he had too much to drink and he was sure to do that when it was cheap. Larry was OK but way too sickly. In the end you'd have to push him around in a wheelchair. "Invalido."

No, Lacke was the only one who would do.

They could have a lot of fun down there for a week. But Lacke was poor as a church mouse, and could never afford it. He could sit and drink beers and smoke every night and that was totally cool by Jocke, but he'd never have the dough for a trip to the Canary Islands.

He may as well face the facts—none of the regulars at the Chinese restaurant were good travel companion material.

Could he go by himself?

Stig-Helmer had done it. Even though he was a total loser. Then he met Ole, and everything. Got together with a chick and all that. Nothing wrong with that. It was eight years since Maria had left him and taken the dog, and since then he had not known anyone in the biblical sense, not one single time.

Would anyone want him? Maybe. At least he didn't look as bad as Larry. Of course the booze was staking its claim in his face and body, even though he had managed to keep it under control to a certain extent. Today for example he hadn't had a single drop yet, even though it was almost nine o'clock. But now he was going to have a couple of gin and tonics before going down to the Chinese restaurant.

He'd have to think more about that trip. It would probably go the way of so much else these past few years: nothing. But you could always dream.

He walked along the park path between Holbergsgatan and Blackeberg school. It was pretty dark, the streetlights stood about thirty meters apart and the Chinese restaurant glowed like a lighthouse up on the hill to the left.

Should he throw caution to the wind tonight and go directly up to the restaurant and . . . no. Too expensive. Then the others would think he had won the lottery or something and call him a cheapskate for not buying them a round. Better to go home and get started first.

He passed the commercial laundering center, the chimney with its single red eye, the muted rumble from inside.

One night when he was on his way home—drunk to the gills—he had experienced a kind of hallucination and seen the chimney detach itself and start gliding down the hill toward him, growling and hissing.

He had curled up on the path with his hands over his head, waiting for the attack. When he finally put his arms back down the chimney stood where it always was, magnificent and unmoving.

The streetlight nearest the Björnsongatan underpass was broken and the path under the street a dark hole. If he had been drunk right now he would probably have walked up the stairs next to the underpass and gone up to Björnsongatan, even though that was slightly longer. He could get such strange visions in the dark when he had had something to drink. Always slept with the light on for that reason. But right now he was stone sober.

He had a hankering to take the stairs anyway. The drunken visions had started to seep into his perception of the world even when he was sober. He stood still on the path and summed up the situation for himself:

"I'm starting to get soft in the head."

Let me make this clear to you, Jocke. If you don't get ahold of yourself and make it just that little bit further through the underpass, you won't make it to the Canary Islands either.

Why not?

Because you always jump ship at the first sign of a hurdle. The law of least resistance, in every situation. What makes you think you could manage to call a travel agent, get a new passport, buy things for your trip, and above all, take that step out into the unknown if you don't even have the guts to walk this short stretch?

You have a point. But so what? If I walk through the underpass, that means I'll make it to the Canary Islands, that it'll happen?

It makes me think you'll call and book the ticket tomorrow. Tenerife, Jocke, Tenerife.

He started to walk again, summoning images of sunny beaches and drinks with little umbrellas. Damn it, he was going. Wouldn't go down to the restaurant tonight, no. He would stay home and check the ads in the paper. Eight years. Fucking time to pull himself together.

He had just started to think about palm trees, whether or not there were palm trees in the Canary Islands, if he had seen any in the movie, when he heard the sound. A voice. He stopped in the middle of the underpass, listening. A moaning voice was coming from the side.

"Help me . . ."

His eyes were starting to get used to the dim light, but he could still only discern the contours of the leaves that had blown in and collected in heaps. It sounded like a child.

"Hello? Is anyone there?"

"Help me . . ."

He looked around. No one in sight. He heard a rustling in the dark, could see movement in the leaves.

"Please, help me."

He felt a strong desire to walk away. But that was impossible. A child had been hurt, had maybe been attacked by someone. . . .

The murderer!

The Vällingby murderer had come to Blackeberg, but this time the victim had survived. . . .

Oh, for heaven's sake.

He didn't want any part of this. He who was on his way to Tenerife and all. But what could he do? He took a few steps in the direction of the voice. The leaves crunched under his feet and now he could see the body. It was curled into a fetal position in the leaves.

Damn, damn.

"What happened?"

"Help me...."

Jocke's eyes were now fully accustomed to the dark and he could see the child stretch out a pale arm. The body was naked, probably raped. No. When he got close he saw that the child was not naked, was simply wearing a pink top. How old? Ten or twelve. Maybe he had been knocked down by his "friends." Or her. If it was a girl that was less likely.

He crouched down next to the girl and took her hand.

"What happened to you?"

"Help me. Lift me up."

"Are you hurt?"

"Yes."

"What happened?"

"Lift me up...."

"Is it your back?"

He had been drafted into the medical corps during his compulsory military training and knew you shouldn't lift people with neck or back injuries unless you secured their heads first.

"It's not your back, is it?"

"No. Lift me."

What the fuck was he supposed to do? If he took the child home to his apartment the police would think . . .

He would have to take him or her to the restaurant and call an ambulance from there. Yes. That was a plan. The child had a small, thin body—must be a girl—and even though he wasn't in the greatest shape he thought he could manage to carry her there.

"OK. I'll carry you to a place where we can call, alright?"

"Yes . . . thank you."

That "thank you" stung his heart. How could he have hesitated? What kind of bastard was he? Well, he had managed to keep his head and now he was going to help the girl. He coaxed his left arm under her knees and put the other arm under her neck.

"OK. Up we go."

"Mmm."

She weighed almost nothing. It was incredibly easy to lift her up. Twenty-five kilos, at most. Maybe she was malnourished. Problems at home, or anorexia. Maybe a stepfather or something who abused her. Fucking pathetic.

The girl put her arms around his neck and leaned her cheek against his shoulder. He was going to manage this.

"How does that feel?"

"Good."

He smiled. A feeling of warmth rushed through him. He was a good person, in spite of everything. He could imagine the others' faces when he came in, the girl in his arms. At first they would wonder what the fuck he was up to and then they would be more and more impressed. "Well done, Jocke," etc.

He turned to start walking up to the restaurant, consumed by his fantasies of a new life, the new start he was in the process of making, when he felt the pain in his throat. What the fuck? It felt like a bee-sting and his left hand wanted to go up and wave it away, examine it. But he couldn't drop the child.

Stupidly he tried to bend his head to see what it was, even though he naturally couldn't see his own throat from that angle. He couldn't bend his head anyway because the girl's jaw lay pressed against his chin. Her grip around his neck grew tighter and the pain stronger. Now he understood.

"What the hell are you doing?"

He felt the girl's jaws working up and down against his chin as the pain at his throat grew more intense. A warm trickle of fluid ran down his chest.

"Stop it!"

He let go of the girl. It wasn't a conscious thought, simply a reflex: must get this off my throat.

But the girl didn't fall. Instead she established an iron grip around his neck—good god how strong her little body was—and wrapped her legs around his hips.

She clung to him like four hands wrapped tightly around a doll, while her jaws continued to work.

Jocke grabbed her head and tried to pull it away from him but it was like trying to tear a fresh branch from a birch tree with your bare hands. Her head was, like, glued to him. Her grip on him was so strong that it pressed the breath from his lungs and didn't allow him to draw in fresh air.

He staggered backward, desperate for air.

The girl's jaws had stopped working on him; now he only heard a quiet lapping. She had not loosened her grip for a moment, quite the opposite. Her grip on him was even tighter now that she was sucking. A muted crunch and his chest radiated with pain. Several ribs had been broken.

He had no more air for screaming. He pummeled the girl's head with a few feeble blows as he staggered around in the dry leaves. The world was spinning. The distant street lamps danced like fireflies in front of his eyes.

He lost his balance and fell backward. The last sound he heard was the leaves crunching as they were crushed by his head. A microsecond later he hit the stone pavement and the world disappeared.

†

Oskar lay wide awake in his bed, staring at the wallpaper.

He and his mom had watched *The Muppets* but he had not followed the story at all. Miss Piggy had been angry about something and Kermit had been looking for Gonzo. One of the sour old men had fallen from the theater balcony—but the reason why he had done so had escaped Oskar. His thoughts had been elsewhere.

Then he and his mom had had hot cocoa and cinnamon buns. Oskar knew they had chatted but couldn't remember about what. Something about painting the kitchen sofa blue, maybe.

He stared at the wallpaper.

The whole wall that his bed was pushed up against was decorated with a photograph wallpaper depicting a forest meadow. Wide tree trunks and green leaves. He would sometimes lie in bed and dream up figures in the leaves nearest his head. There were two figures he always saw as soon as he looked. The others he had to try harder to summon forth.

Now the wall had developed another significance. On the other side, on the other side of the forest, there was . . . Eli. Oskar lay there with his hand pressed against the green surface and tried to imagine what the other side looked like. Was the room on the other side her bedroom? Was she also lying in her bed right now? He transformed the wall into Eli's cheek, stroked the green leaves, her soft skin.

Voices on the other side.

He stopped stroking the wallpaper, and listened. One high and one low voice. Eli and her father. It sounded like they were arguing. He pushed his ear against the wall to hear better. Damn it. If only he had had a glass. He didn't dare get up and get one because maybe they would stop talking before he got back.

What are they saying?

Eli's dad was the one who sounded angry. You could hardly hear Eli's voice at all. Oskar had to concentrate to catch the words. He only heard the occasional swear words and ". . . unbelievably *cruel.*" Then there was a thud as if something had been knocked over. Had he hit her? Had he seen them when Oskar stroked Eli's cheek . . . could that be it?

Now Eli was talking. Oskar could not hear a word of what she was saying, only the soft tones of her voice as it rose and sank. Would she be talking that way if he had hit her? He *couldn't* hit her. Oskar would kill him if he hit her.

He wished he could vibrate himself through the wall, like Lightning, the superhero. Disappear through the wall, in through the forest and out the other side, see what was happening, if Eli needed help, comforting, anything.

Now it was quiet on the other side. Only the sound of his heart drumming out its sucking whirling beats in his ear.

He got up out of bed, went over to his desk, and poured out a number of erasers from a plastic cup. Took the cup back with him into bed and held the open end against the wall, the closed end against his ear.

The only thing he could hear was a distant clanking, hardly from the room next door. What were they doing? He held his breath. Suddenly there was a loud bang.

A gun shot!

He had taken out a gun and—no, it was the front door, slammed so hard the walls were ringing.

He jumped out of bed and walked over to the window. After a few seconds a man emerged. Eli's dad. He was carrying a bag in his hand and walked with quick, angry strides toward the exit, and disappeared from sight.

What should I do? Follow him? Why?

He went back to bed. It was only his imagination working overtime. Eli and her dad had argued, like Oskar and his mom sometimes. It even happened that his mom stepped out like that afterward if it had been really bad.

But not in the middle of the night.

His mom sometimes threatened to move out when she thought Oskar was being bad. Oskar knew she would never do it, and she knew he knew. Maybe Eli's dad had simply taken this game of threats a step further. Took off in the middle of the night with a bag and everything.

Oskar lay in his bed with his palms and forehead pressed against the wall.

Eli, Eli. Are you there? Has he hurt you? Are you sad? Eli . . .

There was a knock on Oskar's door and he flinched. For a terrible moment he thought it was Eli's dad coming in to take him on as well.

But it was his mom. She tiptoed into his room.

"Oskar? Are you asleep?"

"Mmm."

"I just have to say . . . about these new people . . . what neighbors. Did you hear them?"

"No."

"You must have heard them. He was screaming and banged that door like he was crazy. Good god. Sometimes I'm so relieved I don't have a man in my house. Poor woman. Have you seen her?"

"No."

"I haven't either. Well, I haven't seen him either for that matter. Blinds drawn all day. Probably alcoholics."

"Mom."

"Yes?"

"I want to sleep now."

"Yes, sorry, honey. I just got so . . . Good night. Sweet dreams."

"Mm."

His mom walked out and closed the door carefully behind her. Alcoholic? Yes, that seemed probable.

Oskar's dad drank too much from time to time. That was why he and mom weren't together anymore. Dad could have tantrums like that when he got too drunk. He never hit anyone but could scream so he got hoarse, bang doors, and break things.

Something in Oskar was cheered by this thought. Ugly, but still. If Eli's dad was an alcoholic then they had something in common, something they shared.

Oskar leaned his forehead and hands against the wall again.

Eli, Eli. I know how it is for you. I'm going to help you. I'm going to save you.

Eli . . .

†

The eyes were wide open, staring blindly toward the arched ceiling of the underpass. Håkan brushed a few dry leaves away, revealing the thin pink sweater Eli usually wore, now discarded on the man's chest. Håkan picked it up, at first intending to hold it up to his nose to smell it, but he stopped when he felt that the sweater was sticky.

He dropped it back onto the man's chest, then pulled out his hip flask and took three big swallows. The vodka shot down his throat in fiery flames, licking his stomach. The leaves crunched under his rear end as he sat down on the cold stones and looked at the dead man.

There was something wrong with his head.

He dug around in his bag, found his flashlight. Checked that no one was coming along the path, then turned on the flashlight and directed it toward the man. His face was a pale yellow-white in the beam of light, the mouth hung half-open as if he was about to say something.

Håkan swallowed. The thought that this man had been allowed closer to his beloved than he ever had revolted him. His hand fumbled for his flask, wanted to burn away his anguish, but he stopped himself.

The neck.

There was a wide red mark running around the man's neck like a necklace. Håkan leaned over him and saw the wound Eli had opened in order to get at the blood.

Lips against his skin.

—but that didn't explain the neck . . . lace . . .

Håkan turned the flashlight off, drew a deep breath, and involuntarily leaned back in the tight space so that the cement walls scraped against the bald spot in the back of his head. He clenched his teeth together in response to the stinging pain.

The skin on the man's neck had split because . . . because the head had been rotated 360 degrees. One full rotation. The spine had snapped.

Håkan closed his eyes, breathed slowly in and out to calm himself and to stop the impulse to get up and run far, far away from . . . all this. The cement wall pressed against his head, the stones underneath him. To the left and right, a path where people who would call the police could come walking along. And in front of him . . .

It is only a dead body.

Yes. But . . . the head.

He didn't like knowing that the head was loose. It could fall back, perhaps come off if he lifted the body. He curled up and rested his forehead on his knees. His beloved had done this. With bare hands.

He felt a tickle of nausea in the back of his throat when he imagined the sound it had made. The creaking when the head was twisted around. He didn't want to touch this body again. He would sit here. Like Belacqua at the foot of the Mountain of Purgatory, waiting for dawn, waiting for . . .

A few people came walking from the direction of the subway. Håkan lay down in the leaves, close to the dead man, pressed his forehead against the ice cold stone.

Why? Why do this . . . with the head?

The risk of infection. You could not allow it to reach the nervous system. The body had to be turned off. That was all he had been told. He had not understood it then, but he did now.

The steps grew quicker, the voices more distant. They were taking the stairs. Håkan sat up again, glancing at the contours of the dead, gaping face. Did that mean this body would have sat up and brushed the leaves off itself if it hadn't been . . . turned off?

A shrill giggle escaped him, fluttering like birdsong in the underpass. He slapped his hand over his mouth so hard it hurt. The image. Of the corpse rising out of the leaves and sleepily brushing dead leaves from its jacket.

What was he going to do with the body?

Maybe eighty kilos of muscles, fat, bone that had to be disposed of. Ground up. Hacked up. Buried. Burned.

The crematorium.

Of course. Carry the body over there, break in, and do a little burning on the sly. Or just leave it outside the gate like a foundling and hope that their enthusiasm for burning was so great they would pop it in without bothering to call the police.

No. There was only one alternative. On his right the path continued on through the forest, toward the hospital, and down to the water.

He stuffed the bloody sweater under the man's coat, hung his bag over his shoulder and pushed his hands under the back and knees of the corpse. Got to his feet, staggered a little, regained his balance. Just as he had expected, the head fell back at an unnatural angle and the jaws shut with an audible click.

How far was it to the water? A few hundred meters maybe. And if someone came by? Nothing to do about that. Then it would be all over. And in a way it would be a relief.

†

But no one came by and once he was safely down by the shore he crept— his skin steaming with sweat—out along the trunk of a weeping willow that grew almost horizontally over the water. With some rope, he had secured two large stones from the shore around the feet of the corpse.

With a slightly longer rope wound in a noose around the chest of the corpse he dragged it out as far as he could, then untied it.

He stayed there on the tree trunk for a while, his feet dangling slightly above the water, staring down into the black mirror, now less and less frequently disturbed by bubbles.

He had done it.

Despite the cold, drops of sweat ran down his forehead and stung his eyes. His whole body ached from the strain but he had done it. The corpse lay right under his feet, hidden from the world. Did not exist. The bubbles had stopped rising to the surface and there was nothing . . . nothing to show that there was a dead body down there.

A few stars twinkled in the water.

Part Two

The Humiliation

. . . and they steered their course toward parts where Martin had never been, far past Tyska Botten and Blackeberg—and there ran the border for the known world.

—Hjalmar Söderberg, *Martin Bircks Ungdom*

But he, whose heart a skogsrå* steals
it never will recover
His soul will long for moonlight dreams
and no mere mortal lover . . .

—Viktor Rydberg, "Skogsrået"

*TRANSLATOR'S NOTE: a beautiful but sinister forest spirit.

On Sunday the papers published a more detailed account of the Vällingby murder. The headline read:

"Victim of Ritual Murder?"

Pictures of the boy, the hollow in the forest. The tree.

The Vällingby murderer was at this point no longer the topic on everyone's lips. The flowers brought to the hollow had wilted, the candles burned down. The candy cane striped police tape had been removed, all evidence to be found there had long since been secured.

The Sunday paper article revived people's interest. The epithet "ritual murder" suggested it was going to happen a second time, didn't it? A ritual is something that is repeated.

Everyone who had ever taken that path, or been anywhere near it, had something to tell. How creepy that part of the forest was. Or how beautiful and calm it was around there, and how you could never have guessed.

Everyone who had known the boy, no matter how superficially, said what a fine young man he was and what an evil person the murderer must be. People liked to use the murder as an example of a crime where the death penalty would be justified, even if you were against that sort of thing in principle.

Only one thing was missing. A photograph of the killer. People stared at the insignificant hollow, at the boy's smiling face. In the absence of a likeness of the perpetrator this had all simply . . . happened.

It was not satisfying, satisfactory.

Monday the twenty-sixth of October police announced through radio and morning papers that they had made the largest drug seizure ever recorded in Sweden. They had arrested five Lebanese men.

Lebanese.

Now that was something you could get your head around. Five kilos of heroin. And five men. One kilo per Lebanese.

The Lebanese men had also—on top of everything else—taken advantage of the extensive Swedish social welfare system during the time they were smuggling heroin. There were no photos of the Lebanese men, but none were needed. You knew what they looked like. Arabs. Say no more.

There were speculations that the ritual murderer was also a foreigner. It seemed plausible enough; weren't blood rituals common in those Arab countries? Muslims. Sent their kids off with plastic crosses or whatever it was they wore around their necks. Small children working as mine removers. You heard about that. Brutal people. Iran, Iraq. The Lebanese.

But on Monday the police released a composite sketch of the suspect, and it was published in the evening papers. A young girl had seen him. The police had taken their time, taken every precaution in constructing the image.

A normal Swede. With a ghost-like appearance, a vacant gaze. Everyone was in agreement about that: yes, this is what a murderer looked like. No problems imagining this mask-like face creeping up on you in the hollow and . . .

Every man in the western suburbs who resembled the phantom picture was subjected to long, scrutinizing looks. These men went home and looked at themselves in the mirror, saw no resemblance whatsoever. In the evening, in bed, they wondered if they should change something about their appearance in the morning or would that seem suspicious?

It would turn out they didn't need to bother. People would soon have something else to think about. Sweden would become a changed nation. A *violated* nation. That was the word that was continually used: violated.

While those resembling the police sketch lie in their beds weighing the benefits of a new hairstyle, a Soviet submarine has just run aground outside of Karlskrona. Its engine roars and echoes across the archipelago as it tries to free itself. No one goes out to investigate.

It will be discovered by accident on Wednesday morning.

𝔚𝔢𝔡𝔫𝔢𝔰𝔡𝔞𝔶

28 OCTOBER

The school was buzzing with rumors. Some teacher had listened to the radio during recess, had subsequently told his class about it, and by lunchtime everyone knew.

The Russians were here.

The biggest topic of conversation among the children over the past week had been the Vällingby murderer. Many had seen him, so they said, some even claimed to have been attacked by him.

The children had seen the murderer in every sketchy-looking character who walked past the school. When an older man in ratty clothing had taken a short cut across the school grounds the children had run for cover—screaming—to the nearest building. Some of the tougher guys had armed themselves with hockey sticks and prepared themselves to knock him down. Luckily someone had finally identified the man as one of the local alcoholics from the main square. They let him go.

But now the Russians were here. They didn't know much about the Russians. There once was a German, a Russian, and a Bellman—or so the joke went. The Russians were best in the world at hockey. They were called the Soviet Union. They and the Americans were the ones who flew in outer space. The Americans had made a neutron bomb to protect themselves against the Russians.

Oskar talked it over with Johan during the lunch break.

"Do you think the Russians have it too—the Bomb?"

Johan shrugged. "Sure. Maybe they've even got one on that submarine."

"I thought you had to have an airplane to drop it?"

"Nah. They put them in rockets that can be fired from wherever."

Oskar looked up at the sky. "And a submarine can have those?"

"That's what I said. They can put them anywhere."

"The people die but the houses are left standing."

"Exactly."

"Wonder what happens to the animals."

Johan pondered this for a moment.

"They must die too. At least the big ones."

They sat down on a corner of the sandbox, where none of the smaller kids were playing. Johan picked up a large rock and threw it so the sand whirled up around it. "Pow! Everyone dead!"

Oskar picked up a smaller rock.

"No! One person survived. Pshiuuuu! Missile in the back!"

They threw rocks and gravel, exterminating all the cities of the world, until they heard a voice behind them.

"What the hell are you doing?"

They turned around. Jonny and Micke. Jonny was the one who had spoken. Johan tossed the rock he had in his hand.

"Uh—we were just . . ."

"I wasn't talking to you. Piggy? What were you doing?"

"Throwing rocks."

"Why were you doing that?"

Johan drew back a few steps, was busy retying his shoes.

"Just—no reason."

Jonny looked at the sandbox and then thrust his arm out so suddenly that Oskar flinched.

"The little kids are supposed to play here. Don't you get it? You're wrecking the sandbox."

Micke shook his head sadly. "They could trip and hurt themselves on the rocks."

"You're going to have to clean this up, Piggy."

Johan was still busy with his shoes.

"Did you hear me? *You're going to have to clean this up.*"

Oskar stood still, unable to decide what to do. Of course Jonny didn't care about the sandbox. It was just the usual. It would take at least ten minutes to clear away all of the rocks that they had thrown and Johan wouldn't help. The bell was going to go off at any moment.

No.

The word came to him like divine inspiration. Like when someone says the word "god" for the first time and really means . . . God.

An image of himself picking up rocks after the others had gone back to class, only because Jonny had told him to do so, had flickered past inside his head. But something else had too. In the sandbox there was a jungle gym like the one in Oskar's courtyard.

Oskar shook his head.

"What's this?"

"No."

"What do you mean 'no'? You seem to be a little slow today. I'm telling you to pick this up and *that means you do it.*"

"NO."

The bell rang. Jonny stood there looking at Oskar.

"You know what this means, don't you? Micke."

"Yes."

"We'll have to get him after school."

Micke nodded.

"See you, Piggy."

Jonny and Micke went in. Johan got up, finished with his shoes.

"That was pretty dumb."

"I know."

"What the hell did you do that for?"

"Because . . ." Oskar looked at the jungle gym. "Because I did, that's all."

"Idiot."

"Yes."

†

Oskar lingered at his desk after school was over. Took out two blank pieces of paper, got the encyclopedia from the back of the room, started turning the pages.

Mammoth . . . Medici . . . Mongol . . . Morpheus . . . Morse

Yes. Here it was. The dots and dashes of the Morse alphabet took up a fourth of a page. He started to copy down the code in large, legible letters on the first piece of paper.

A= .-

B= - . . .

C= -.-.

and so on. When he was done he wrote it out again on the second sheet of paper. Wasn't satisfied. Threw the piece of paper away and started over, making the symbols and letters even neater.

Of course it was only important that one of the pages came out well: the one for Eli. But he liked the work and it gave him a reason to stay there.

Eli and he had been meeting every evening for a week now. Yesterday Oskar had tried knocking on the wall before he went out and Eli had answered. Then they went out at the same time. That was when Oskar had the idea of developing this communication through some kind of system, and since the Morse alphabet already existed . . .

He scrutinized the finished pages. Nice. Eli would like it. Just like him she liked puzzles, systems. He folded the pages, put them in his school bag, rested his arms on the bench. There was a sinking feeling in his stomach. The clock on the classroom wall showed twenty past three. He took out the book he had in his desk, *Firestarter*, and read it until four.

They couldn't have waited for him for two hours, could they?

If he had just picked up the rocks like Jonny had said, he would have been home by now. Been OK. Picking up rocks was certainly not the worst he had been asked to do, and done. He regretted it.

And if I do it now?

Maybe the punishment tomorrow would be milder if he told them he stayed after school and . . .

Yes, that's what he would do.

He gathered up his things and went out to the sandbox. It would only take him ten minutes to fix this. When he told them about it tomorrow Jonny would laugh, pat him on the head and say "good little Piggy" or something like that. But that was better, all things considered.

He glanced at the play structure, put his bag down next to the sandbox, and started to pick up the rocks. The big ones first. London, Paris. While he was picking them up he imagined that he was now *saving* the world. Cleaning up after those terrible neutron bombs. When the stones were lifted the survivors crawled out from their ruined houses like ants out of an anthill. But weren't the bombs supposed to *not* hurt the houses? Oh well, there were probably some atom bombs too.

When he walked to the edge of the sandbox in order to dump out a load of rocks, they were just standing there. He hadn't heard them coming, had been too busy with his game. Jonny, Micke. And Tomas. They held three long thin hazel branches. Whips. Jonny used his whip to point at a rock.

"There's one."

Oskar dropped the rocks he was holding and picked up the rock Jonny was pointing at. Jonny nodded. "Good. We waited for you, Piggy. We waited a long time."

"And then Tomas came along and said you were here," Micke said.

Tomas' eyes remained without expression. In elementary school Oskar and Tomas had been friends, played a lot in his yard, but after the summer between fourth and fifth grade Tomas had changed. He had started to talk differently, more grown up. Oskar knew that the teachers thought Tomas was one of the most intelligent boys in the class. You could tell from the way they talked to him. He had a computer. Wanted to be a doctor.

Oskar wanted to throw the rock he was holding straight into Tomas' face. Into the mouth that now opened and talked.

"Aren't you going to run? Get going now. Run."

There was a whistling sound as Jonny whipped the branch through the air. Oskar squeezed the rock harder.

Why don't I run.

He could already feel the stinging pain on his legs when the whip hit its mark. If he could only make it out to the park road where there would maybe be grown-ups around, they wouldn't dare to beat him up.

Why don't I run.

Because he didn't have a chance. They would have him on the ground before he had taken five steps.

"Let me go."

Jonny turned his head, pretended like he hadn't heard.

"What did you say, Piggy?"

"Let me go."

Jonny turned toward Micke.

"He thinks we should let him go."

Micke shook his head.

"But we've made such nice-looking . . ." He waved his whip in the air. "What do you think, Tomas?"

Tomas looked at Oskar as if he were a rat, still alive, writhing in his trap.

"I think Piggy needs a whipping."

There were three of them. They had whips. It was a maximally unfair situation. He could throw the rock in Tomas' face. Or hit him with it if he came close. There would be a talk with the principal and so on. But they would understand. There had been three of them, armed.

I was . . . desperate.

He wasn't desperate at all. In fact he felt a streak of calm through the fear, now that he had made up his mind. They could whip him as long as it gave him the opportunity to smash the rock in Tomas' disgusting face.

Jonny and Micke stepped up. Jonny whipped Oskar across one thigh so he doubled over in pain. Micke went up behind him and locked his arms by his side.

No.

Now he couldn't throw it. Jonny whipped his legs, spun around once like Robin Hood in that movie, hit again.

Oskar's legs burned from the lashes. He writhed in Micke's hold but couldn't get free. Tears welled up in his eyes. He screamed. Jonny gave Oskar one last hard lash that grazed Micke's legs so that he yelled "watch it, will you" but without releasing his hold.

A tear ran down Oskar's cheek. It wasn't fair. He had picked up all the rocks, he had bent over backwards, so why did they have to hurt him?

The rock that he had been holding onto so hard fell out of his hand and he started to cry for real.

Jonny said with a pitying voice, "Piggy's crying."

Jonny seemed satisfied. His work was done. He gestured to Micke to let him go. Oskar's whole body was shaking, wracked with sobs, and from the pain in his legs. His eyes were filled with tears when he lifted his face to them and heard Tomas' voice.

"What about me?"

Micke grabbed Oskar's arms again and through the fog of tears over his eyes he saw Tomas walk closer. He snivelled,

"Please don't."

Tomas raised his whip and struck. One single blow. Oskar's face exploded and he jerked to the side so violently that Micke either lost or let go of his grip and said,

"What the hell, Tomas. That was . . ."

Jonny sounded angry.

"Now *you* can talk to his mom."

Oskar didn't hear what Tomas answered, if he said anything.

Their voices disappeared into the distance; they left him with his face in the sand. His left cheek burned. The sand was cold, soothed the heat in his legs. He wanted to put his cheek in the sand as well, but realized it wasn't a good idea.

He lay there so long he started to get cold. Then he sat up and carefully felt his cheek. Blood came off onto his fingers.

He walked over to the outside toilets and looked in the mirror. The cheek was swollen and covered in half-congealed blood. Tomas must have struck him as hard as he could. Oskar washed his cheek and looked in the mirror again. The wound had stopped bleeding and it wasn't deep. But it ran right across almost his entire cheek.

Mom. What do I tell her?

The truth. He needed comforting. In an hour mom would be home and then he would tell her what they had done to him and she would be completely distraught and hug him and hug him and he would sink into her arms, into her tears, and they would cry together.

Then she would call Tomas' mom.

Then she would call Tomas' mom and they would argue and then Mom would cry about how mean Tomas' mom was and then . . .

Woodshop.

He had had an accident in woodshop. No, then maybe she would call the teacher.

Oskar studied his wound in the mirror. How did you get something like this? He had fallen off the play structure. It didn't really work but Mom would *want* to believe it. She would still feel sorry for him and comfort him, but without all that other stuff. The play structure.

His pants felt cold. Oskar unbuttoned them and checked. His underpants were soaked. He took out the Pissball and rinsed it out. He was about to put it back but stopped and looked in the mirror.

Oskar. That's . . . Oskar.

He took the rinsed Pissball and put it on his nose. Like a clown nose. The yellow ball and the red wound on his cheek. Oskar. He opened his eyes wide and tried to look crazy. Yes. Creepy. He talked to the clown in the mirror.

"It's over now, it's enough. Understand? This is it."

The clown didn't answer.

"I'm not standing for this. Not even one more time, understand?"

Oskar's voice echoed in the empty bathroom.

"What should I do? What should I do, do you think?"

He twisted his face into a grimace until it hurt, distorted his voice by making it as raspy and low as he could. The clown spoke.

". . . kill them . . . kill them . . . kill them."

Oskar shivered. This was a little creepy for real. It really sounded like someone else's voice, and the face in the mirror wasn't his own. He took the Pissball from his nose, put it back in his pants.

The tree.

Not because he really believed in this and all . . . but he would go stab the tree. Maybe, just maybe. If he really concentrated, then . . .

Maybe.

Oskar picked up his bag and hurried home, filling his head with lovely images.

Tomas is sitting at his computer when he feels the first stab. Doesn't understand where it is coming from. Staggers out into the kitchen with the blood gushing from his stomach. "Mom, Mom, someone is stabbing me."

Tomas' mom would just stand there. Tomas' mom who always took his side no matter what he had done. She would just stand there. Terror stricken. While the stabs continued to puncture Tomas' body.

He falls to the kitchen floor in a pool of blood, "Mom . . . Mom . . ."
while the invisible knife cuts open his stomach so his intestines spill out onto
the linoleum.

Not that it really worked that way.

But still.

✝

The apartment reeked of cat piss.

Giselle lay on his lap, purring. Bibi and Beatrice were wrestling on the floor. Manfred sat in the window like usual, his nose pushed up against the windowpane, and Gustaf was trying to get Manfred's attention by buffeting his side with his head.

Måns and Tufs and Cleopatra were relaxing in the armchair, Tufs pawing at a few loose threads. Karl-Oskar tried to jump up onto the windowsill but missed and fell backwards onto the floor. He was blind in one eye.

Lurvis was out in the hall keeping an eye on the mail slot, ready to jump if any advertising was pushed in. Vendela was resting on the hat shelf keeping an eye on Lurvis. Her deformed right front paw hung down between the wooden slats and flinched from time to time.

A couple more cats were out in the kitchen, eating or lazing around on tables and chairs. Five were sleeping on the bed in the bedroom. A few more had their favorite hideaways in closets or cupboards they had learned how to get into on their own.

After Gösta had stopped letting them out—relenting to pressure from his neighbors—no more fresh genetic material had come in. Most of the kittens born were either dead or so deformed they died a few days after birth. About half of the twenty-eight cats that lived in Gösta's apartment had some kind of congenital defect. They were blind or deaf or were missing teeth or had motor damage.

He loved them all.

Gösta scratched Giselle behind the ear.

"Yes . . . my little darling . . . what are we going to do? You don't know? No, neither do I. But we have to do *something*, don't we? You can't get away with something like this. It was *Jocke*. I knew him. And now he's dead. But no one else knows. Because they didn't see what I saw. Did you see it too?"

Gösta lowered his head, whispered,

"It was a *child*. I saw it coming down the path. It waited for Jocke. In the underpass. He went in . . . and never came out. Then in the morning he was gone. But he's dead. I *know* he is.

"What's that?

"No, I can't go to the police. They're going to ask questions. There will be a lot of people and then they will ask . . . why I didn't say anything. Shine one of those lights in my face.

"It was three days ago. Or four. I don't know. What day is it today? They're going to ask. I can't do it.

"But we have to do something.

"I just don't know what."

Giselle looked up at him. Started to lick his hand.

†

When Oskar came home from the forest, the knife was smeared with splinters of rotten wood. He washed it under the kitchen tap, drying it off with a dishcloth that he then rinsed clean and held against his cheek.

His mom would soon be home. He had to go out again, needed a little more time—tears were still clumped in his throat, his legs ached. He took the key from the kitchen cupboard, wrote a note: *Back soon, Oskar*. Then he put the knife back and walked down to the basement. Unlocked the heavy door, slipped in.

The underground smell. He liked it. A reassuring blend of wood, old things, and locked-in-ness. A little light filtered in through a window at ground level and in the dim light the basement promised secrets, hidden treasure.

To his left there was an oblong section divided into four storage compartments. The walls and doors were made of wood, the doors secured with various-sized locks. One of the doors had a reinforced lock; a person who had been robbed.

On the wooden wall at the very end of the area someone had written KISS with a marker. The "S"s were formed like elongated, backward "Z"s.

But the most interesting area was to be found at the end opposite all this. The room for recycling and oversized trash. Oskar had once found a still-intact globe that now stood in his room, as well as several issues of the series *The Hulk*, and some other stuff.

But today there was almost nothing. It must have been emptied recently. A few newspapers, some folders with the labels "English" and "Swedish." But Oskar had enough folders. He had scavenged a whole bunch from the container outside the printing shop a few year ago.

He walked through the basement room and out to the next stairwell in the building, Tommy's stairwell. Continued on to that basement door, unlocked it, and walked in. This basement had a different smell: a trace of paint, or thinning solution. This basement also contained the safety shelter for the whole complex. He had only been in once, three years ago, when some of the older guys had had a boxing club there. He had been allowed to go with Tommy and watch, one afternoon. The guys had gone after each other with boxing gloves on their hands and Oskar had been a little scared. The groaning and sweating, the tense, concentrated bodies, the sound of the blows muffled by the thick concrete walls. Then someone had gotten hurt, or something like that, and the wheels that you turned in order to pull away the fastening mechanism on the door had been blocked with chains and lock. The end of the boxing.

Oskar turned on the light and walked over to the shelter room. If the Russians were coming it would have to be unlocked.

If they hadn't lost the key.

Oskar stood in front of the massive iron door and a thought appeared. That someone . . . someone was locked in here. That that's what the chains and lock were for. To restrain a monster.

He listened. There were distant sounds from the street, from people's movements in the apartments above. He really liked the basement. It was like being in another world, while knowing that the other world was still there outside, above you, if you needed it. But down here it was quiet, and no one came and said anything, did anything to you. Nothing you had to do.

Across from the safety room was the clubhouse. Forbidden territory.

Of course, they didn't have a lock, but that didn't mean just anyone was allowed in. He took a deep breath and opened the door.

There wasn't much in this storage unit. Just a badly sagging couch, and an equally sagging armchair. A rug on the floor. A chest of drawers with peeling paint. A clandestine lighting arrangement had been rigged up consisting of a cord feeding from the light in the corridor connected to a single naked bulb suspended from the ceiling. It was turned off.

He had been down here a few times before and knew that all he had to do to turn it on was twist the bulb. But he didn't dare. Enough light filtered in through the gaps between the planks to see. His heart beat faster. If they found him here they would . . .

What? I don't know. That's what's so horrible. Not beat me up, but . . .

He kneeled on the rug and lifted a sofa cushion. A few tubes of glue and a roll of plastic bags, a container of lighter fluid. In the other corner of the sofa, under the seat cushion, there were porno magazines. A few well-thumbed issues of *Lektyr* and *Fib Aktuellt.*

He took one of the *Lektyr* and shifted closer to the door where there was more light. Still kneeling he laid the magazine out on the floor in front of him, flipped the pages. His mouth was dry. The woman in the picture lay in a deck chair wearing only a pair of high-heeled shoes. She was pushing her breasts together and pouting. Her legs were spread and in the middle of the bushy hair between her thighs there was a strip of pink flesh with a groove down the middle.

How do you get in there?

He knew the words from talk he had heard, graffiti he had read. Cunt. Hole. Labia. But it wasn't a hole. Only that groove. They had had sex education at school and he knew there was supposed to be a . . . tunnel leading in from the vulva. But in what direction? Straight up or in or . . . you couldn't tell.

He kept turning the pages. The readers' own stories. At the swimming pool. A stall in the girls' changing rooms. Her nipples stiffened under her bathing suit. My dick was thumping like a hammer in my swimming trunks. She gripped the clothes pegs, turned her little ass toward me, and moaned, "Take me, take me now."

Did this kind of thing go on all the time, behind closed doors, in places where you couldn't see?

He had started a new story, about a family reunion that took an unexpected turn, when he heard the basement door being opened. He shut the magazine, put it back under the sofa cushion and didn't know what to do with himself. His throat contracted; he didn't dare to breathe. Footsteps in the corridor.

Please God let it not be them. Let it not be them.

He squeezed his knee caps with his hands, clenched his teeth so hard he hurt his jaw. The door opened. Tommy was standing there, blinking.

"What the hell?"

Oskar wanted to say something, but his jaws were locked shut. He simply stayed where he was, kneeling on the rug of light that rolled out from the door, breathing through his nose.

"What the hell are you doing here? And what have you been up to?"

Almost without moving his jaws Oskar managed to press out a ". . . nothing."

Tommy took a step into the storage area, towering over him.

"With your cheek, I mean? How did you get that?"

"I . . . it's nothing."

Tommy shook his head, screwed the light bulb so it turned on, and closed the door. Oskar got to his feet, standing in the middle of the room with his hands by his side, unsure of what he should do. He took a step toward the door. Tommy sank down in the armchair and pointed to the couch.

"Sit down."

Oskar sat down on the middle cushion, the one that didn't have anything stashed underneath it. Tommy sat quietly for a few moments, looking at him. Then he said: "Alright, let's hear it."

"What?"

"What happened to your cheek."

". . . I . . . I just . . ."

"Someone beat you up. Right?"

". . . yeah . . ."

"How come?"

"I don't know."

"What? They beat you up with no reason?"

"Yes."

Tommy nodded, picked at a few loose threads that hung from the armchair. Took out a wad of chewing tobacco and tucked it into his lip, held out the jar to Oskar.

"Want some?"

Oskar shook his head. Tommy put it back, adjusted the wad of tobacco with his tongue, and then leaned back in the armchair, with his hands folded on his stomach.

"I see. And what were you doing down here?"

"Um, I was just going to . . ."

"Check out some of the babes, right? Because you aren't into sniffing yet, are you? Come over here."

Oskar got up, walked over to Tommy.

"Come closer. Breathe on me."

Oskar did as he was told and Tommy nodded, pointed at the couch, and told Oskar to sit down again.

"You stay away from that shit, you understand?"

"I haven't . . ."

"No, you haven't. But you stay the hell away, you understand? It's no good. Tobacco is good. You can try that." He paused. "OK, are you planning to sit there gawking at me all night?" He gestured to the cushion next to Oskar. "Want to read more?"

Oskar shook his head.

"OK, then get lost. The others are coming soon and they won't be too pleased to see you here. Go home, go on now."

Oskar got up.

"And Oskar . . ." Tommy looked at him, shook his head, sighed. "No, forget it. Go on home. And one more thing. Don't come down here anymore."

Oskar nodded, opened the door. He stopped in the doorway.

"Sorry."

"It's OK. Just don't come here anymore. Oh—you got the money yet?"

"Tomorrow."

"Great. I made a tape for you with *Destroyer* and *Unmasked*. Come by and pick it up later."

Oskar nodded. He felt a lump growing in his throat. If he stayed here he would start to cry. So he whispered "thanks" and left.

†

Tommy stayed in his armchair, sucked on the wad of tobacco, and stared at the dust bunnies that had collected under the couch.

Hopeless.

They would keep beating on Oskar until he finished ninth grade. He was the type. Tommy would have liked to do something but once it got started there was nothing you could do. No stopping it.

He dug a lighter out of his pocket, put it in his mouth, and let out the gas. When it started to feel cold inside his mouth he took the lighter away, lit it, and breathed out.

A burst of fire in front of his face. But he felt no happier. He was restless, got up, and walked around. The dust whirled up around his feet.

What the hell can you do?

He paced around the small space, thinking it was a prison cell. You can't get away. Have to make the best of it, bla bla. Blackeberg. He was going to get away from here, he was going to be . . . a sailor or something. Anything.

Swab the deck, go to Cuba, heave ho.

A broom that was almost never used was leaning up against the wall. He took it and started to sweep. Dust flew up his nose. When he had been sweeping for a while he realized he had no dustpan. He swept the dust pile under the couch.

Better to have a little shit in the corners than a clean hell.

He flipped through the pages of a porno, put it back. Wound his scarf around his neck and pulled it tight until his head felt like it was about to explode, released it. Got up and took a few steps on the rug. Sank to his knees, prayed to God.

†

Robban and Lasse came around half past five. When they walked in Tommy was relaxing in the armchair and looked like he didn't have a care in the world. Lasse was sucking on his lips, seemed nervous. Robban grinned and thumped Lasse on the back.

"Lasse needs another tape."

Tommy raised his eyebrows.

"Why?"

"Tell him, Lasse."

Lasse snorted, didn't dare look Tommy in the eyes.

"Uh . . . there's a guy at work . . ."

"Who wants to buy?"

"Mmm."

Tommy shrugged, got up from his chair, and picked the key to the safety room out of the stuffing. Robban looked disappointed. He must have been expecting some kind of amusing scene but Tommy didn't care. Lasse could shout out *"Stolen goods for sale"* from the rooftops at his job for all he cared. It didn't matter.

Tommy pushed Robban aside and walked out into the corridor, turned the key in the lock, pulled the heavy chain out of the wheels and threw it over to Robban. The chain fell through his hands, rattling to the floor.

"What's your problem? Are you high or what?"

Tommy shook his head, turned the wheel mechanism, and pushed the door open. The fluorescent lighting inside was broken, but there was enough light from the corridor to see the boxes piled up along one wall. Tommy picked up a carton of cassette tapes and gave it to Lasse.

"Have fun."

Lasse looked uncertainly at Robban, as if to get help interpreting Tommy's behavior. Robban made a face that could have meant anything, then turned to Tommy, who was locking up.

"Heard anything more from Staffan?"

"Nope." Tommy clicked the lock together, sighed. "I'm going over there for dinner tomorrow. We'll see."

"Dinner?"

"Yes—why?"

"No, nothing. Just thought cops ran on . . . gas or something."

Lasse laughed out loud, glad the tension was broken.

"Gas . . ."

†

He had lied to his mother. And been believed. Now he was stretched out on his bed, feeling sick to his stomach.

Oskar. That guy in the mirror. Who is he? A lot of things happened to him. Bad things. Good things. Strange things. But who is he? Jonny looks at him and sees Piggy whom he wants to beat up. Mom looks at him and sees her Little Darling whom she doesn't want anything bad to happen to.

Eli looks at me and sees . . . what?

Oskar turned to the wall, to Eli. The two faces peeked out from between the trees in the wallpaper. His cheek was still swollen and tender, a crust had started to form on top of the wound. What would he tell Eli, if Eli came out tonight?

It was all connected. What he would tell her depended on what he was to her. Eli was new to him and therefore he had the opportunity to be someone else, say something different from what he said to other people.

What do you do anyway? To make people like you?

The clock on his desk read a quarter past seven. He looked into the leaves, tried to find new shapes, had found a little gnome with a pointy hat and an upside-down troll when he heard a knock on the wall.

Tap-tap-tap.

A careful sound. He tapped back.

Tap-tap-tap.

Waited. After a few seconds a new tap.

Tap-taptaptap-tap.

He filled in the two missing ones: *tap-tap.*

Waited. No further tapping.

He took down the paper with the Morse code, pulled on his jacket, said good-bye to his mom, and walked down to the playground. He had only taken a few steps when the door to Eli's building opened and she came out. She was wearing tennis shoes, blue jeans, and a black sweatshirt with *Star Wars* written across it in silver letters.

At first he thought it was his own shirt; he had one just like it that he had been wearing a couple of days ago. It was in the laundry basket now. Had she gone out and bought one just like it to match his?

"Hey there."

Oskar opened his mouth to say the "Hi" he had had prepared, closed his mouth. Opened it again to say "Hey there" and said "Hi" anyway.

Eli frowned.

"What happened to your cheek?"

"Phhh . . . I . . . fell."

Oskar kept going toward the playground. Eli followed. He walked past the jungle gym, sat down in a swing. Eli sat in the swing next to it. They swung back and forth in silence for a while.

"Someone did that to you, didn't they?"

Oskar kept swinging.

"Yes."

"Who?"

"Some . . . friends."

"*Friends?*"

"Some kids in my class."

Oskar got the swing moving fast, picked up the rhythm.

"Where do you go to school anyway?

"Oskar."

"Yes?"

"Slow down a little."

He slowed himself down with his feet, looked at the ground in front of him.

"Yes, what is it?"

"You know what?"

She reached her hand out and grabbed his and he stopped completely, looked at her. Eli's face was almost completely blacked out against the lighted windows behind her. Of course it was just his imagination but he thought her eyes were *glowing*. At any rate, they were the only thing he could see clearly in her face.

With her other hand she touched his wound and that strange thing happened. Someone else, someone much older, harder, became visible under her skin. A cold shiver ran down Oskar's back, as if he had bitten into a Popsicle.

"Oskar. Don't let them do it. Do you hear me? Don't let them."

". . . no."

"You have to strike back. You've never done that, have you?"

"No."

"So start now. Hit them back. Hard."

"There's three of them."

"Then you have to hit harder. Use a weapon."

"Yes."

"Stones, sticks. Hit them more than you really dare. Then they'll stop."

"And if they keep hitting back?"

"You have a knife."

Oskar swallowed. At this moment, with Eli's hand in his, with her face in front of him, everything seemed simple. But if they started doing worse things if he put up resistance, if they . . .

"Yes, but what if they . . ."

"Then I'll help you."

"You? But you are . . ."

"I can do it, Oskar. *That* . . . is something I can do."

Eli squeezed his hand. He squeezed back, nodded. But Eli's grip hardened, so hard it hurt a little.

How strong she is.

Eli loosened her grip and Oskar took out the page of code he had written down for her at school, smoothed out the folds, and gave it to her. She wrinkled her forehead.

"What's this?"

"Let's go over to the light."

"No, I can see fine. But what is it?"

"The Morse code."

"Oh, right. I see. *Awesome.*"

Oskar giggled. She said it in such a—what was it called?—artificial way. The word somehow didn't fit in her mouth.

"I thought . . . we could like . . . talk through the wall to each other."

Eli nodded. Looked like she was thinking of something to say. Then she said:

"That will be amusing."

"You mean fun?"

"Yes. *Fun.* Fun."

"You're a little strange, you know that?"

"Am I?"

"Yes, but it's OK."

"You'll have to show me what to do, in that case. Not to be strange."

"Sure. Want to see something?"

Eli nodded.

Oskar showed her his special trick. He sat on the swing like before, kicked off. With each pump of his legs, with every arc a notch higher, something grew in his chest: freedom.

The illuminated apartment windows went past like multicolored, glowing strands and he swung higher and higher. He didn't always manage to do this trick, but now he was going to do it, because he was as light as a feather and could almost fly.

When the swing got so high that the chains loosened and started to jerk on the back swing he tensed his whole body. The swing went back one more time and then at the top of the next forward swing he let go of the chains, and pushed his legs forward, as high as they would go. The legs went around half a turn and he landed on his feet, bending over as far as he could so the swing wouldn't hit him in the head, and when it had gone past he stood up and stretched out his arms. Perfect.

Eli applauded, shouted: "Bravo!"

Oskar caught the swing, put it back in its normal position, and sat down. Yet again, he was grateful for the dark that hid a triumphant smile he couldn't suppress, even though it pulled at his wound. Eli stopped clapping, but his smile was still there.

Things were going to be different from now on. Of course you couldn't kill people by hacking up trees. He knew that.

Thursday

29 OCTOBER

Håkan sat on the floor in the narrow corridor and listened to the splashing from the bathroom. His knees were pulled up so his heels touched his buttocks; his chin rested on his knees. Jealousy was a fat, chalk-white snake in his chest. It writhed slowly, as pure as innocence and childishly plain.

Replaceable. He was . . . replaceable.

Last night he had been lying in his bed with the window cracked. Listened to Eli saying good-bye to that Oskar. Their high voices, laughter. A . . . lightness he could never achieve. His was the leaden seriousness, the demands, the desire.

He had thought his beloved was like him. He had looked into Eli's eyes and seen an ancient person's knowledge and indifference. At first it had frightened him: Samuel Beckett's eyes in Audrey Hepburn's face. Then it had reassurred him.

It was the best of all possible worlds. The young, lithe body that gave beauty to his life, while at the same time responsibility was lifted from him. He was not the one in charge. And he did not have to feel guilt for his desire; his beloved was older than he. No longer a child. At least he had thought so.

But since all this with Oskar had started something had changed. A . . . regression. Eli had started to behave more and more like the child her appearance gave her out to be; had started to move her body in a loose-limbed and careless way, use childish expressions, words. Wanted to *play*. Hide the Key. A few nights ago they had played Hide the Key. Eli had become angry when Håkan had not showed the necessary enthusiasm for the game, then tried to tickle him to get him to laugh. He had relished Eli's touch.

It was attractive, naturally. This joy, this . . . *life*. But also frightening, since it was something so foreign to him. He was both hornier and more scared than he had ever been since meeting her.

Last night his beloved had gone into Håkan's bedroom and locked the door and proceeded to lie there for half an hour tapping on the wall. When Håkan once again was allowed in he saw a piece of paper taped to the wall above his bed. The Morse code.

Later, when he was lying there and trying to fall asleep, he had been tempted to tap his own message to Oskar, something about what Eli *was*. Instead he had copied the code onto a scrap of paper so he could decode what they said to each other in the future.

Håkan bent his head, rested his forehead on his knees. The splashing from the bathroom had stopped. He couldn't go on like this. He was about to explode. From desire, from jealousy.

The bathroom lock turned and the door opened. Eli was standing in front of him. Completely naked. Pure.

"Oh—you're sitting out here."

"Yes. You're beautiful."

"Thank you."

"Will you turn around for me?"

"Why?"

"Because . . . I want you to."

"No; why don't you get up and move?"

"Maybe I'll say something . . . if you do this for me."

Eli looked quizzically at Håkan. Then turned 180 degrees.

Saliva spurted into his mouth, he swallowed. Looked. A physical sensation of how his eyes devoured what was in front of them. The most beautiful thing there was in the world. An arm's length away. An endless distance.

"Are you . . . hungry?"

Eli turned around again.

"Yes."

"I'll do it for you. But I want something in return."

"What is it?"

"One night. All I want is one night."

"OK."

"I can have that?"

"Yes."

"Lie next to you? Touch you?"

"Yes."

"Can I . . ."

"No. Nothing more. But that. Yes."

"Then I'll do it. Tonight."

Eli crouched down next to him. Håkan's palms burned. Wanted to ca-ress. Couldn't. But tonight. Eli looked up and said,

"Thanks. But what if someone . . . that picture in the paper . . . there are people who know you live here."

"I've thought of that."

"If someone comes here during the day when . . . I'm resting."

"I've thought of that, I said."

"How?"

Håkan took Eli's hand, got up and went out into the kitchen, opened the pantry, and took out an old jam jar with a twist-on glass lid. The jar was half-filled with a clear liquid. He explained what he had planned to do. Eli objected vehemently.

"You can't."

"I can. Do you understand now how much . . . I care about you?"

†

When Håkan was ready to leave he put the jam jar into the bag with the rest of his equipment. During that time Eli had gotten dressed. She was waiting in the hall when Håkan came out. Eli leaned over and lightly planted a kiss on his cheek. Håkan blinked and looked at Eli's face for a long time.

I'm lost.

Then he went to work.

✝

Morgan was slurping his way through Four Small Dishes, one by one, mostly ignoring the small bowl of rice by his side. Lacke leaned forward and said in a low voice:

"Mind if I take the rice?"

"Hell, no. Want some sauce?"

"No, I just want a little soy."

Larry looked up over his copy of *Expressen,* made a face when Lacke took the bowl of rice and poured soy sauce over it with a glug-glug-glug and started to eat as if he had never seen food before. Larry motioned at the deep-fried shrimp that were heaped on Morgan's plate.

"You could offer to share, you know."

"Oh, sure. Sorry. You want a shrimp or something?"

"No, my stomach can't take it. But Lacke."

"You want a shrimp, Lacke?"

Lacke nodded and held out his bowl of rice. Morgan put two fried shrimp in the bowl with a grandiose flourish. Offered a little more. Lacke thanked him and dug in.

Morgan grunted and shook his head. Lacke had not been himself since Jocke disappeared. He had been hard up before but now he was drinking more and didn't have a cent left over for food. It was strange, this whole business with Jocke, but there was no reason for despair. Jocke had been missing for four days now and who really knew? He could have met a chick and gone to Tahiti, anything. He would turn up eventually.

Larry put down the paper, pushed his glasses up onto his head, rubbed his eyes and said: "Do you know where the nearest nuclear shelter is?"

Morgan guffawed. "What, are you planning to hibernate or something?"

"No, but this submarine. Hypothetically speaking, what if there was a full-scale invasion—"

"You're welcome to come over and use ours. I was down there a few years ago and checked it out when a guy from some defense something was there to run an inventory-check. Gas masks, canned food, Ping-Pong table, the whole deal. It's all there."

"Ping-Pong table?"

"Sure, you know. When the Russians land we just say 'Stop and take cover boys, put down your Kalashnikov-ies, we're going to determine this thing with a Ping-Pong match instead.' Then the generals go after each other by serving screwballs."

"Do the Russians even know how to play table tennis?"

"Nope. So we got this thing all sewn up. Maybe we'll even regain control of the Baltic territories."

Lacke wiped his mouth with exaggerated care on his napkin and said, "Anyway, it's all pretty strange."

Morgan lit up a John Silver. "What is?"

"This thing with Jocke. He would always tell us when he was going somewhere. You know. Even if he was just going to go see his brother on Väddö Island it was like a big event. Started talking about it a week before—what he was planning to bring, what they were going to do."

Larry put a hand on Lacke's shoulder.

"You're talking about him in the past tense."

"What? Oh, yeah. Anyway, I really think something's happened to him. I really think so."

Morgan downed a big mouthful of beer, burped.

"You think he's dead."

Lacke shrugged, looked beseechingly at Larry, who was studying the pattern printed on the paper napkins. Morgan shook his head.

"No way. We would have heard something. The cops said they would call you if they heard anything. Not that I trust cops but . . . you'd think we'd hear something."

"He should have called by now."

"Good grief, are you two married or something? Don't worry. He'll turn up soon. With roses and chocolates and promises neeeeeever to do anything like this again."

Lacke nodded despondently, sipping the beer Larry had bought him with the assurance that Lacke would return the favor when things looked up. Two more days, maximum. Then he would start looking himself. Call all the hospitals and morgues and whatever else you did. You didn't let down your best friend. If he was sick or dead or whatever. You didn't let him down.

†

It was half past seven and Håkan was starting to worry. He had wandered aimlessly around the Nya Elementar's Gymnasium and the Vällingby mall where the young people hung out. Various sport training sessions were underway, and the pool was open late, so there was no lack of potential victims. The problem was that most of them moved in groups. He had overheard a comment from one of three girls that her mother was "still completely psycho over this thing with the murderer."

He could of course have chosen to go further afield, to an area where his earlier act had less impact, but then he ran the risk of the blood going bad on the way home. And if he was going to go to the trouble of doing this again he wanted to give his beloved the best. The fresher it was, the closer to home, the better. That's what he had been told.

Last night the weather had turned and it had become very cold, the temperature falling below freezing. That meant the ski mask he was wearing, with holes for the eyes and mouth, did not attract undue attention.

But he couldn't sneak around here forever. Eventually someone would get suspicious.

What if he didn't manage to find anyone? If he came home without anything? His beloved wouldn't die, he was sure of that. A difference from the first time. But now there was another aspect, a wonderful one. A whole night. A whole night with the beloved body next to his. The tender, soft limbs, the smooth stomach to caress with his hand. A lighted candle in the bedroom whose light would flicker over silken skin, his for a night.

He rubbed his hand over his member that throbbed and cried out with longing.

Have to stay calm, have to . . .

He knew what he would do. It was insane but he would do it.

Go into the Vällingby Pool and find his victim there. It was probably fairly deserted at this time and now that he had decided he knew exactly what to do. Dangerous, of course. But possible.

If things went wrong he had his last resort. But nothing would go wrong. He saw the whole thing in detail now that he was walking briskly toward the entrance. He felt intoxicated. The cloth of the ski mask in front of his nose became wet with condensation as he panted.

This would be something to tell his beloved about tonight, something to tell while he caressed the firm, curved buttocks with his trembling hand, imprinting everything in his memory for all eternity.

He walked in the main entrance and felt the familiar mild chlorine smell. All the hours he had spent at the pool. With the others, or alone. The young bodies that glistened with sweat or water, at an arm's length, but unreachable. Only images that he could preserve and call forth when he lay in his bed with toilet paper in one hand. The smell of chlorine was comforting, home-like. He walked up to the cashier.

"One, please."

The woman at the cash register looked up from her magazine. Her eyes widened a little. He gestured to his head, to the mask.

"It's cold."

She nodded, uncertainly. Should he remove the mask? No. He didn't know how to do so without raising suspicion.

"Do you want a locker?"

"A private changing cabin, please."

She stretched out the key to him and he paid. He removed the mask as he moved away from her. Now she had seen him take it off, but without seeing his face. It was brilliant. He walked over to the changing area at a rapid clip, looking down at the floor in case he encountered anyone.

✝

Welcome to my humble abode. Come in."

Tommy walked past Staffan into the hallway; behind him he heard a clicking sound when his mom and Staffan kissed. Staffan said in a low voice "Have you? . . ."

"No, I thought . . ."

"Mmm, we'll have to . . ."

The clicking sound again. Tommy looked around the apartment. He had never been in a cop's home before and was, a little against his will, curious. What were they like?

But even out in the hall he realized Staffan could hardly be a satisfactory representative of the whole police corps. He had imagined something . . . yes, something like in detective novels. A little run-down and barren. A place where you came to sleep when you weren't out chasing bad guys.

Guys like me.

Nope. Staffan's apartment was . . . frilly. The hall entrance looked like it had been decorated by someone who bought *everything* from those little catalogues that came in the mail.

Here a velvet painting of a sunset, there a little alpine cottage with an old woman on a stick leaning out of the door. Here a lace doily on the telephone table, next to the telephone a ceramic figurine with a dog and a child. On the base a pithy inscription: DON'T YOU KNOW HOW TO TALK?

Staffan lifted the figurine.

"Nifty little thing, isn't it? It changes color depending on the weather."

Tommy nodded. Either Staffan had borrowed the apartment from his old mother, for the purposes of this visit, or else he was genuinely sick in the head. Staffan put the figurine back with care.

"I collect these kind of things, you see. Objects that tell you about the weather. This one, for example."

He poked the old woman peeking out of the alpine cottage. She swung back into the cottage and an old man came out instead.

"When the old lady looks out that means bad weather, and when the old man looks out—"

"It'll be even worse."

Staffan laughed, sounding slightly forced.

"It doesn't work so well."

Tommy looked back at his mom and was almost scared by what he saw. She stood there with her coat still on, her hands gripped tightly together, and a smile on her face that could have sent a horse bolting. Panic-stricken. Tommy decided to make an effort.

"Kind of like a barometer, you mean."

"Yes, exactly. That was what I started with, actually. Barometers. Collecting, I mean."

Tommy pointed to a little wooden cross with a silver Jesus hanging on the wall.

"Is that also a barometer?"

Staffan looked at Tommy, at the cross, then back at Tommy. Was suddenly serious.

"No, it's not. It's Christ."

"The one in the Bible."

"Yes, that's right."

Tommy pushed his hands into his pockets and walked into the living room. Yes, the barometers were in here. About twenty, in various shapes and sizes, hanging on the wall that ran the long length of the room, behind a gray leather couch with a glass coffee table in front of it.

They were not particularly consistent in their readings. Many of the hands were pointing to different numbers; it looked like a wall of clocks where each showed the time in a different part of the world. He knocked on the glass of one of the instruments and the needle jumped a little. He didn't know what it meant, but for some reason people always tapped barometers.

In a corner cabinet with glass doors there were a whole lot of small trophies. Four larger trophies were arranged along the top of a piano next to the cabinet. On the wall over the piano there was a large painting of the Virgin Mary with the baby Jesus in her arms. She nursed him with a vacant expression in her eyes that seemed to say, "What have I done to deserve this?"

Staffan cleared his throat when he came into the room.

"Well, Tommy. Is there anything you'd like to ask me about?"

Tommy understood full well what he was expected to ask.

"What trophies are these?"

Staffan gestured with an arm toward the goblets on top of the piano.

"These, you mean?"

No, you dumb bastard. The trophies down at the clubhouse by the soccer field, of course.

"Yes."

Staffan pointed to a silver-colored statue, some twenty centimeters tall, on a stone base, positioned between two trophies on the piano. Tommy had thought it was just a sculpture, but no, it was actually a prize. The human figure was standing wide-legged, arms straight, taking aim with a revolver.

"Pistol shooting. This is for first prize in the district championships, that one third prize at the national level in forty-five caliber, standing . . . and so on."

Tommy's mom came in and joined them.

"Staffan is one of Sweden's top five pistol shooters."

"Does it come in handy?"

"What do you mean?"

"You know, for when you shoot people."

Staffan ran his finger along the base of one of the trophies and then looked at it.

"The whole point of police work is to avoid shooting at people."

"Have you ever had to?"

"No."

"But you'd like to, wouldn't you?"

Staffan pointedly drew a deep breath, exhaled in a long sigh.

"I'm going to go . . . check on the food."

The gasoline . . . see if it's on fire.

He walked out to the kitchen. Tommy's mom grabbed him by the elbow and whispered,

"Why do you say things like that?"

"I was just wondering."

"He's a good person, Tommy."

"Yes, he must be. I mean, with prizes for pistol shooting and the Virgin Mary. Could it get any better?"

†

Håkan didn't bump into a single person on his way through the building. As he had thought, there were not very many people still here at this time. Two men his own age were putting their clothes on in the changing room. Overweight, shapeless bodies. Shriveled genitals under hanging bellies. The embodiment of ugliness.

He found his private changing cabin and locked the door behind him. Good. The initial preparations were completed. He put his ski mask back on, just in case, took off the halothane canister, hung his coat up on a hook. Opened his bag and took out his tools: knife, rope, funnel, container. He had forgotten to bring the raincoat. Damn. He would have to remove his clothes instead. The risk of getting splashed with blood was great but then he could conceal the stains *under* his clothes when he was done. Yes. And this was a pool, after all. Nothing strange about not having any clothes on in here.

He tested the strength of the other hook by grabbing it with both hands and lifting both feet from the floor. It held. It would easily hold a body most likely thirty kilos lighter than his own. Height might be a problem. The head was not likely to hang freely over the floor. He might have to fix the ropes by the knees. There was enough wall space between the hook and the top of the cabin wall to make sure the feet wouldn't stick up over it. *That* would attract suspicion.

The two men seemed about to leave. He heard their voices.

"And work?"

"The usual. No openings for someone from Malmberget."

"Did you hear this one: The question is not was it the Finns' oil but whether the oil was Finn's?"

"Yeah, that's a good one."

"Finn's a slippery guy."

Håkan giggled; something in his head was accelerating. He was too excited, was breathing too rapidly. His body consisted of butterflies that wanted to fly off in different directions at once.

Easy, easy.

He took deep breaths until he started to feel dizzy and then he undressed. Folded his clothes and put them into his bag. The two men left the changing area. Silence fell. He climbed onto the bench in order to peek over the top. Yes, his eyes just managed to clear the edge. Three boys around thirteen, fourteen years old came in. One used his towel to snap the rear end of the other one.

"Stop that, damn it!"

Håkan bent his head. Further down he felt his erection push into the corner of the booth as if between two hard, wide-opened buttocks.

Easy does it.

He peeked over the edge again. Two of the boys had taken off their Speedos and were bending forward into their lockers to take out their clothes. His groin area contracted in a single cramplike movement and the sperm shot out into the corner, spilling onto the bench he was standing on.

Calm down now.

Yes, he felt better. But the sperm was bad. A trace.

He took his socks out of his bag, wiped the corner and the bench clean, as best he could. Put the socks back in the bag, and adjusted the ski mask while he listened to the boys' conversation.

". . . new Atari. Enduro. Want to come over and try it out?"

"No, I have some stuff I have to . . ."

"How about you?"

"OK, do you have two joysticks?"

"No, but . . ."

"We can go home and get mine on the way. Then we can both play."

"OK. See you, Mattias."

"See you."

Two of the boys appeared to be on their way out. Perfect. One would be left behind without the others waiting around for him. He risked peeking out over the edge again. Two of the boys were leaving. The last one was putting on his socks. Håkan ducked down, remembering he still had the ski mask on. Lucky they hadn't seen him.

He picked up the halothane canister, put his finger on the trigger. Should he keep the mask on? *If* the kid got away, *if* someone came into the changing room. *If . . .*

Damn, it had been a mistake to take off all his clothes. If he needed to make a quick getaway. There was no time to think. He heard the boy close his locker and start toward the exit. In five seconds he would pass by the cabin door. No time to reconsider.

In the gap between the door and the wall he saw an approaching shadow. He blocked out all thoughts, unlocked the door, threw it open, and lunged.

Mattias turned around and saw a large, white naked body with a ski mask over its head come bearing down on him. Only one thought, one single word had time to flash through his consciousness before his body instinctively pulled back.

Death.

He was recoiling before Death, who wanted to take him. In one hand

Death was holding something black. This black object flew up toward his face and the boy drew in breath to scream.

But before the scream had time to escape, the black thing was over him, over his mouth, his nose. One hand gripped the back of his head, pressing his face into the black softness. The scream turned into a choked whimper and while he howled his mutilated scream he heard a hissing sound as if from a smoke machine.

He tried to scream again but when he drew in breath something happened with his body. A numbness spread to all his limbs and his next scream was just a squeak. He breathed again and his legs gave way, many-colored veils fluttering in front of his eyes.

He didn't want to scream anymore. Didn't have the energy. The veils now covered his entire field of vision. He didn't have a body any longer. The colors danced. He melted into the rainbow.

†

Oskar held the piece of paper with the Morse code in one hand and tapped letters into the wall with the other. Tapping his knuckles for a dot, slapping the wall with the flat of his hand for a dash, like they had agreed.

Knuckle. Pause. Knuckle, palm, knuckle, knuckle. Pause. Knuckle, knuckle. (E.L.I)

G.O.I.N.G. O.U.T.

The answer came after a few seconds.

I. M. C.O.M.I.N.G.

They met outside the entrance to her building. In one day she had . . . changed. About a month ago a Jewish woman had come to his school, talked to them about the Holocaust and shown them slides. Eli was looking a little bit like the people in those pictures.

The sharp light from the fixture above the door cast dark shadows on her face, as if the bones were threatening to protrude through the skin, as if the skin had become thinner. And . . .

"What have you done with your hair?"

He had thought it was the light that made it look like that, but when he came closer he saw that a few thick white strands ran through her hand. Like on an old person. Eli ran a hand over her head. Smiled at him.

"It'll go away. What should we do?"

Oskar made the few coins in his pocket jangle.

"Tjorren?"

"What?"

"The kiosk. The newspaper stand."

"OK. Last one there is a rotten egg."

An image flickered to life in Oskar's head.

Black-and-white kids.

Then Eli took off and Oskar tried to catch her. Even though she looked so sick she was much faster than him, flew gazelle-like over the stones on the path, had crossed the street in a couple of strides. Oskar ran as well as he could, distracted by the thought.

Black-and-white kids?

Of course. He was running down the hill past the Gummy Bear factory when he got it. Those old movies that were shown at Sunday matinees. Like *Anderssonskans Kalle. Last one there is a rotten egg.* That was the kind of thing they said in those films.

Eli was waiting for him down by the road, twenty meters from the kiosk. Oskar jogged over to her, tried not to pant. He had never been down to the kiosk with Eli before. Should he tell her that thing? Yes.

"Do you know it's called The Lover's Kiosk?"

"Why?"

"Because . . . that is, I heard it at a parents meeting . . . there was someone who said—not to me of course, but—I heard it. He said that the one who has it, that he . . ."

Now he was sorry he had brought it up. It was stupid. Embarrassing. Eli waved her arms around.

"What?"

"Uh, the guy who has it . . . that he invites *ladies* into the kiosk. You know, when he . . . when it's closed."

"Is it true?" Eli looked at the kiosk. "Do they have enough room in there?"

"Disgusting, isn't it?"

"Yes."

Oskar walked down toward the kiosk. Eli took a few quick steps to pull up alongside him, whispered "They must be *skinny!*"

Both of them giggled. They stepped into the circle of light from the kiosk. Eli rolled her eyes meaningfully at the kiosk owner, who was inside the kiosk watching a little TV.

"Is that him?" Oskar nodded. "He looks like a monkey."

Oskar cupped a hand around Eli's ear, whispered, "He escaped from the zoo five years ago. They're still looking for him."

Eli giggled and cupped her hand around Oskar's ear. Her warm breath flowed into his head.

"No they're not. They locked him up here instead!"

They both looked up at the kiosk owner and burst out laughing, imagining the stern kiosk owner as a monkey in a cage surrounded by candy. At the sound of their laughter the owner turned to them and frowned with his enormous eyebrows so that he looked even more like a gorilla. Oskar and Eli laughed so hard they almost fell over, pressed their hands over their mouths and tried to regain seriousness.

The owner leaned through the window.

"What do you want?"

Eli quickly became serious, removed her hand from her mouth, walked over to the window, and said, "I'd like a banana, please."

Oskar chuckled and pressed his hand harder against his mouth. Eli turned around with her index finger in front of her lips and shushed him with feigned severity. The owner was still looking out of the window.

"I don't have any bananas."

Eli pretended disbelief.

"No banaaaanas?"

"No. Anything else?"

Oskar's jaws were cramping because of his repressed laughter. He teetered away from the kiosk, ran a few steps toward the mailbox, leaned on it, and let it out, convulsing with laughter. Eli came up to him, shaking her head.

"No bananas."

Oskar managed to get out: "He must have . . . eaten them . . . all himself."

Then he pulled himself together and forced his mouth shut. He took out his four kronor and went up to the window.

"A bag of mixed candy, please."

The owner gave him a disapproving look but started picking out an assortment of candy with long tongs from the plastic bins, dropping them one by one into a small paper bag. Oskar glanced to the side to make sure Eli heard him, then said "Don't forget the bananas."

The owner stopped short.

"I don't *have* any bananas."

Oskar pointed to one of the plastic containers.

"I mean the candy foam bananas."

He heard Eli giggle, and put his finger to his lips just like she had done earlier and shushed her. The owner snorted, put a few candy foam bananas in the bag, and handed it to Oskar.

They walked back. Before Oskar had even had any himself he held the bag out to Eli. She shook her head.

"No thanks."

"Don't you eat candy?"

"I can't."

"No candy?"

"Nope."

"What a drag."

"Yes, no. I don't know what it tastes like."

"You haven't even tasted it."

"No."

"Then how do you know that . . ."

"I just know, that's all."

This happened sometimes. They would be talking about something, Oskar would ask her a question, and it would end with a "that's just the way it is" or "I just know, that's all." No further explanation. That was one of the things that was a little strange about Eli.

It was too bad he couldn't offer her any candy. That was what he had been planning. To be generous, offer her as much as she wanted. And then it turned out she didn't even eat candy. He popped a candy banana in his mouth and snuck a peek at her.

She really didn't look healthy. And those white strands in her hair . . .
In some story Oskar had read, a person's hair went white after he had a
big scare. Is that what had happened to Eli?

She glanced to the side, folded her arms around her body, and looked
really little. Oskar wanted to put his arm around her but didn't dare.

In the covered entrance leading to the courtyard Eli stopped and
looked at her window. It was dark. She stopped with her arms wrapped
around her body and stared at the ground.

"Oskar? . . ."

He did it. Her whole body was asking for it and from somewhere he
got the courage to do it. He hugged her. For a terrifying second he
thought he had done the wrong thing, her body was stiff, locked. He was
about to let go when she relaxed into his embrace. The knot loosened and
she coaxed her arms out, put them around his back and leaned trembling
against him.

She leaned her head against his shoulder and they stood like that. Her
breath against his shoulder. They held each other without saying anything. Oskar closed his eyes and knew: this was big. Light from the outside lamp filtered in through his closed eyelids and created a red
membrane in front of his eyes. The biggest.

Eli nuzzled her head in closer toward his neck. The heat from her
breath grew more intense. Muscles in her body that had been relaxed grew
tense again. Her lips nudged his throat and a shiver ran through his body.

Suddenly she shuddered and broke away, took a step back. Oskar let
his arms fall. Eli shook her head as if to free herself from a nightmare,
turned, and started walking to her door. Oskar stayed put. When she
opened the front door he called out to her.

"Eli?" She turned. "Where's your dad?"

"He was going to . . . bring me food."

She doesn't get enough to eat. That's what it is.

"You can have dinner with us if you like."

Eli let go of the door and walked back over to him. Oskar quickly
started to plan things out. He *did not* want his mom to meet Eli. Not the
other way around either. Maybe he could make a few sandwiches and take
them back to her place. Yes, that would be best.

Eli stopped in front of him, looking at him earnestly.

"Oskar, do you like me?"

"Yes. A lot."

"If I turned out not to be a girl . . . would you still like me?"

"What do you mean?"

"Just that. Would you still like me even if I wasn't a girl?"

"Yes . . . I guess so."

"Are you sure?"

"Yes. Why do you ask?"

Someone was struggling with a stuck window, then it opened. Over the top of Eli's head Oskar could see his mom poke her head out of his bedroom window.

"Ooooskar!"

Eli quickly drew in toward the wall. Oskar balled his hands into fists and ran up the hill, stopping underneath his window. Like a little kid.

"What is it?"

"Oh! Are you down there? I thought—"

"What is it?"

"It's about to start."

"I *know*."

His mother was about to add something, but shut her mouth and just looked at him standing there under the window with his hands still held in tight fists, his body tense.

"What are you doing?"

"I'll be right there."

"It's just . . ."

His eyes were starting to get watery from rage and he hissed "Go back in! Close the window. Go back!"

His mother stared at him for another second, then something changed in her face and she slammed the window shut, walked away. Oskar would have wanted . . . not to shout for her to come back . . . but to send her a thought. To explain quietly and calmly how it was. That she wasn't allowed to do that, because he . . .

He ran back down the hill.

"Eli?"

She wasn't there. She couldn't have gone inside because he would have noticed her. She must have left to take the subway to that aunt she had in the city where she went after school. That seemed likely.

Oskar went and stood in the dark corner where she had ducked in when his mom opened the window. Turned with his face toward the wall. Stood there for a while. Then he went inside.

†

Håkan dragged the boy inside the changing room and locked the door behind him. The boy had hardly made a noise. The only thing that could alert someone's attention now was the hissing noise from the gas bottle. He would have to work quickly.

It would have been so much easier to be able to attack directly with a knife. But no. The blood had to come from a living body. Another aspect that he had had explained to him. Blood from the dead was worthless, harmful even.

Well, the boy was alive. His chest rose and sank as he inhaled the stupifying gas.

He tightened the rope around the boy's legs, right above his knees, slung both ends above the hook, and started to pull. The boy's legs were lifted from the ground.

A door opened, voices rang out.

He held the rope in place with one hand and turned off the gas with the other, removing the mask from the boy's face. The anesthetic would hold for a few minutes. He would have to keep working, as silently as he could, regardless of the fact that there were people in the room.

There were several men out there. Two, three, four? They were talking about Sweden and Denmark. Some tournament. Handball. While they talked Håkan raised the boy's body. The hook squeaked, the weight fell differently than when he had tested it. The men stopped talking. Had they heard anything? He froze, hardly breathing. Held the body still, suspended with the head barely off the ground.

No, just a lull in the conversation. They continued.

Keep talking, keep talking.

"Sjögren's penalty was completely . . ."

"What you don't have in your arms you'd better have in your head."

"He's pretty good at getting them in, you have to give him that."

"That spin. Don't know how he does it."

The boy's head cleared the floor by a few decimeters. Now . . .

How could he secure the ends of the rope? The spaces between the planks were too narrow for the rope to fit through. And he couldn't very well work with one hand while the other was holding onto the rope. Wouldn't have the strength. He stood with the rope in his tightly knit hands, sweating. The ski mask was hot; he should take it off.

Later. When I'm done.

The other hook. Just had to make a loop first. Sweat ran into his eyes as he lowered the boy's body in order to create slack in the rope to allow him to form a loop. Pulled the boy back up and tried to get the loop on the hook. Too short. He lowered the boy again. The men stopped talking.

Leave! Just leave!

In the silence he made another hook further along the rope, waited. They started to talk again. Bowling. The Swedish women's successes in New York. Strikes and blocks, and the sweat stung his eyes.

Warm. Why does it have to be so warm.

He managed to get the loop onto the hook and exhaled. Couldn't they just leave?

The boy's body was suspended in the right position and now all he had to do was get to work before he woke up—and couldn't they just leave? But they went on sharing bowling memories and how people used to play in the olden days and someone who got his thumb stuck in the bowling ball and had to be taken to the hospital to get it out.

It couldn't be helped. Håkan put the funnel in the plastic jug and placed it next to the boy's neck. Took out the knife. When he turned around to start bleeding the boy the conversation out there had died down again. And the boy's eyes were open. Wide open. The pupils were wandering around as he hung there, upside down, trying to find a mental foothold, comprehension. They fixed on Håkan as he stood there, naked, with the knife in his hand. For a short moment, they gazed at each other.

Then the boy opened his mouth and screamed.

Håkan staggered back, hitting the changing room wall with a moist smack. His sweaty back slipped along the wall and he almost lost his balance. The boy screamed and screamed. The sound echoed in the dressing area, bouncing off the walls, was strengthened so that Håkan was deafened. His hand hardened around the knife handle and the only thought in his head was that he had to find a way to stop the boy's screams. Cut off his head so it stopped screaming. He bent over toward the boy.

Someone banged on the door.

"Hey! Open up!"

Håkan dropped the knife. The clang as the metal hit the floor was barely noticeable between the banging on the door and all the screaming. The door was rattling in its hinges from the blows.

"Open up, I said, or I'll knock the door down!"

Over. It was all over. There was only one thing left. The noises around him disappeared, his field of vision narrowed to a tunnel as he turned back to his bag. Through the tunnel he saw his hand reach down into the bag and take out the jam jar.

He sat down hard on his backside with the jar in his hand, unscrewed the lid.

When they got the door open. Before they managed to pull his hood off. His face.

Through all the screaming and blows to the door he thought about his beloved. The time they had had together. He conjured up the image of his beloved as an angel. A boy angel flying down from heaven, spreading his wings, who was going to pick him up. Carry him off. Take him to a place where they would always be together. For ever.

The door flew open and banged into the wall. The boy continued to scream. There were three men standing outside, more or less dressed. They stared uncomprehendingly at the scene in front of them.

Håkan nodded slowly, accepting it.

Then he shouted:

"Eli! Eli!"

and poured the concentrated acid over his face.

†

Rejoice! Rejoice!

Rejoice in your Lord and God!

Rejoice! Rejoice!

Honor your King and God!"

Staffan accompanied himself and Tommy's mom on the piano. From time to time they looked at each other, smiled and sparkled. Tommy sat in the leather sofa and suffered. He had found a little hole in one of the armrests and while Staffan and his mom sang he worked at making it bigger. His index finger dug around in the stuffing and he wondered if Staffan and his mom had ever done it on this sofa. Under the barometers.

The dinner had been OK, some kind of marinated chicken with rice. After dinner Staffan had showed Tommy the safe where he kept his pistols. He stored it under the bed and Tommy had wondered the same thing in there. Had they slept with each other in this bed? Did his mom think about Dad when Staffan was touching her? Did Staffan get turned on by the thought of the guns he kept under the bed? Did she?

Staffan played the final chord, allowed the sound to die away. Tommy pulled his finger out of the by-now substantial hole in the sofa. His mom nodded to Staffan, took his hand, and sat down on the piano bench next to him. From where Tommy was sitting it looked like the picture of the Virgin Mary was positioned exactly above their heads, almost as if they had rehearsed it in advance.

His mom looked at Staffan, smiled, and turned to Tommy.

"Tommy. There's something we'd like to share with you."

"Are you getting married?"

His mom hesitated. If they had rehearsed this with staging and all, then clearly this line had not been included.

"Yes. What do you think?"

Tommy shrugged.

"OK. Go ahead."

"We were thinking . . . maybe next summer."

His mom looked at him as if to see if he had a better suggestion.

"Yeah, whatever. Sure."

He put his finger in the hole again, let it stay there. Staffan leaned forward.

"I know that I can't . . . replace your dad. In any way. But I hope that you and I can . . . get to know each other and, well, become buddies."

"Where are you going to live?"

His mom suddenly looked sad.

"We, Tommy. This is about you too, you know. We don't know yet. But we were thinking of getting a house in Ängby. If we can."

"Ängby."

"Yes. What do you think?"

Tommy looked at the glass table in which his mom and Staffan were reflected, half-transparent, like ghosts. He squirmed his finger around in the hole, managed to pull off some foam.

"Expensive."

"What is?"

"A house in Ängby. It's expensive. Costs a lot of money. Do you have a lot of money?"

Staffan was about to answer when the phone rang. He stroked Tommy's mother on the cheek and walked out to the phone in the hall. His mom sat down next to Tommy on the sofa and asked, "Don't you like it?"

"I love it."

Staffan's voice came from the hall. He sounded agitated.

"That's . . . yes, I'll be there on the double. Should we . . . no, I'll go straight there. OK."

He came back out into the living room.

"The killer is at the Vällingby swimming pool. They don't have enough people down at the station so I have to . . ."

He disappeared into the bedroom and Tommy could hear the safe being opened and closed. Staffan changed in there and after a while he emerged in full police regalia. His eyes looked slightly crazed. He kissed Tommy's mother on the mouth and slapped Tommy's knee.

"Have to go right away. Don't know when I'll be back. We'll talk more later."

He hurried out into the hall and Tommy's mom followed after him.

Tommy heard something about "be careful" and "I love you" and "staying?" while he went up to the piano and, without knowing exactly why, stretched out his arm and picked up the shooting trophy. It was heavy, at least two kilos. While his mom and Staffan were saying good-bye to each other—*they're getting off on this. The man heading into battle. The woman who pines for him*—he walked out onto the balcony. He sucked the cold night air into his lungs and he felt like he could breathe for the first time in hours.

He leaned over the balcony railing, saw that thick bushes were growing underneath. He held the trophy out over the railing, let it go. It fell into the bushes with a rustling sound.

His mom came out on the balcony and stood next to him. After a few seconds the door to the building opened below them and Staffan came out, half-running to the parking lot. His mom waved, but Staffan didn't look up. Tommy giggled as he jogged past the balcony.

"What is it?" his mom asked.

"Nothing."

Just a little kid with a gun hiding in the bushes and taking aim at Staffan. That's all.

Tommy felt pretty good, all things considered.

✝

They had strengthened the gang with Karlsson, the only one among them with a "real" job, as he himself put it. Larry had taken early retirement, Morgan worked off and on at an auto scrap yard, and Lacke you didn't know exactly what he did for a living. Sometimes he turned up with a few bucks.

Karlsson had a full-time job at the toy store in Vällingby. Had owned it once upon a time but been forced to sell due to "financial difficulties." The new owner had eventually employed him because—as Karlsson put it—one couldn't deny the fact that "after thirty years in the business you get a certain amount of experience."

Morgan leaned back in his chair, let his legs flop to either side, and knit his hands together behind his head, his gaze fixed on Karlsson. Lacke and Larry exchanged a look. Now came the usual.

"So, Karlsson. What's new in the toy business? Thought of new ways of cheating kids out of their allowance?"

Karlsson snorted.

"You don't know what you're talking about. If anyone is being cheated it's me. You can't imagine the pervasiveness of the shoplifting. The kids . . ."

"Yes, yes, yes. But all you've got to do is buy some plastic doodad from Korea for two kronor and sell it for a hundred and you've covered your loss."

"We don't carry those kind of items."

"Sure you don't. What did I see in the store window the other day? Something with Smurfs? What was that? A quality product made in Bengtfors—?"

"I think this is remarkable coming from a man who sells cars that only run if you strap them to a horse."

And so on. Larry and Lacke listened, laughed from time to time, made a few comments. If Virginia had been here the stakes would have been raised a notch and Morgan would not have backed down until Karlsson was thoroughly pissed off.

But Virginia wasn't here and neither was Jocke. The evening didn't have the right feeling and it had already started to wind down when the door opened slowly at half past eight.

Larry looked up and saw a person he never thought would set foot here: Gösta. The Stinkbomb, as Morgan called him. Larry had sat on the bench outside the apartment buildings and talked to him before but he had never seen him in here.

Gösta looked shaken. He walked as if he was made of different pieces that were only poorly glued together and that could fall apart if he made the wrong move. He squinted and shook his head from side to side. He was either drunk out of his mind, or sick.

Larry waved to him. "Gösta! Come sit down!"

Morgan turned his head, checked him out, and said, "Oh, shit."

Gösta maneuvered himself over to their table as if traversing a minefield. Larry pulled out the chair next to him, made an inviting gesture.

"Welcome to the club."

Gösta didn't seem to hear him, but shuffled over to the chair. He was dressed in a worn suit with a waistcoat and bow tie, his hair combed flat with water. And he stank. Piss and piss and more piss. Even when you sat with him outside you could smell it, but it was bearable. Inside in the warmth, the stench of old urine was so overpowering you had to breathe through your mouth to stand it.

All of the guys, even Morgan, made an effort not to show on their faces what they felt. The waiter approached their table, stopped short when he caught a whiff of Gösta, and said:

"Can I . . . get you anything?"

Gösta shook his head, but without looking at the waiter. The waiter frowned and Larry signaled, "It's OK, we'll take care of it." The waiter left and Larry put his hand on Gösta's shoulder.

"So to what do we owe this honor?"

Gösta cleared his throat and with his gaze directed at the floor he said, "Jocke."

"What about him?"

"He's dead."

Larry heard Lacke catch his breath. He kept his hand on Gösta's shoulder, encouraging. Felt it was needed.

"How do you know?"

"I saw it. When it happened. When he was killed."

"When?"

"Last Saturday. Night."

Larry removed his hand. "Last Saturday? But . . . have you talked to the cops?"

Gösta shook his head.

"I haven't been able to make myself. And I . . . didn't exactly see it. But I know."

Lacke had his hands over his face, whispering, "I knew it. I knew it."

Gösta told his story. The child who had taken out the streetlight nearest the underpass by throwing a rock at it, then hidden inside and waited. Jocke, who had gone in and never come out again. The faint imprint of a body in the dead leaves the following morning.

When he was done, the waiter had for some time been making angry gestures at Larry, pointing at Gösta and then at the door. Larry put his hand on Gösta's arm.

"What do you say. Shall we go have a look?"

Gösta nodded and they stood up. Morgan downed the last of his beer, grinning at Karlsson, who took the newspaper, folded it, and slid it into his coat pocket like he always did, the cheap bastard.

Only Lacke was still sitting at the table, fiddling with some broken toothpicks. Larry bent down.

"Coming?"

"I knew it. I felt it."

"Yes. Aren't you going to come along?"

"Yes, of course. You go ahead. I'm coming."

Gösta calmed down when they were out in the cool evening air. He started walking so quickly that Larry had to ask him to slow down, his heart couldn't take it. Karlsson and Morgan walked side by side behind them, Morgan waiting for Karlsson to say something stupid that he could jump all over. That would feel good. But even Karlsson seemed absorbed by his thoughts.

The broken streetlight had been replaced and it was surprisingly light in the underpass. They stood grouped around Gösta, who pointed to the piles of dead leaves and talked. They stamped their feet to stay warm. Bad circulation. It echoed under the bridge like a marching army. When Gösta had finished Karlsson said:

"But you have no *proof* of any kind, do you?"

This was the kind of thing Morgan had been waiting for.

"You heard what he said, man, do you think he's making it all up?"

"No," Karlsson said, as if talking to a child, "but I don't think the police are going to be as prepared to believe his story as much as we do if there's no evidence to back it up."

"He's a *witness* for godssake."

"You think that's enough?"

Larry waved his hand at the piles of leaves.

"The question is where his body is now, if we assume it happened like this."

Lacke came walking along the footpath, walked up to Gösta, and pointed to the ground.

"There?"

Gösta nodded. Lacke pushed his hands into his pockets and stood there for a long time staring at the irregular arrangement of leaves as if it were all a gigantic puzzle he had to solve. His jaw clenched, relaxed, then clenched again.

"Well, what do you say?"

Larry took a few steps toward him.

"I'm sorry, Lacke."

Lacke waved his hand defensively, kept Larry at a distance.

"What do you say? Are we gonna get the guy who did this or not?"

The others looked anywhere but at Lacke. Larry was about to say something, that it was going to be difficult, probably impossible, but stopped himself. Finally Morgan cleared his throat, went over to Lacke, and put an arm around his shoulders.

"We'll get him, Lacke. Of course we will."

✝

Tommy looked out over the railing, thought he caught a glimpse of shiny metal down there. Looked like one of those things Huey, Dewey, and Louie came home with after their competitions.

"What are you thinking about?" his mom asked.

"Donald Duck."

"You don't like Staffan so much, do you?"

"It's OK, Mom."

"Is it?"

Tommy looked out toward the center of town. Saw the large red V in the neon sign that slowly rotated high above everything. Vällingby. Victory.

"Has he shown you his pistols?" he asked.

"Why do you want to know something like that?"

"Just wondering. Has he?"

"I don't understand."

"It's not that hard, Mom. Has he opened the safe, taken out the guns, and shown them to you?"

"Yes. Why?"

"When did he do it?"

His mom brushed something from her blouse, then rubbed her arms.

"I'm cold," she said.

"Do you think about Dad?"

"Yes, of course I do. All the time."

"All the time?"

His mom sighed, bending over a little to be able to look him in the eye.

"What are you implying?"

"What are *you* implying?"

Tommy's hand was on the railing; she put hers on top. "Will you come with me to see Dad tomorrow?"

"Tomorrow?"

"Yeah, it's All Saints or something."

"That's the day after. And yes, I will."

"Tommy."

She peeled his hands from the railing, turned him toward her. Hugged him. He stood there stiffly for a moment, then freed himself and walked back in.

While he was putting his coat on he realized he needed his mom to come back inside if he was going to be able to go look for the statuette. He called out to her and she quickly came back in, hungry for words.

"Yeah, . . . uh, give my regards to Staffan."

She lit up.

"I will. You're not staying?"

"No, I . . . it could take all night."

"Yes, I'm a little worried."

"You shouldn't be. He knows how to shoot. Bye."

"Good-bye . . ."

The front door slammed shut.

". . . honey."

✝

There was a muffled bang from deep inside the Volvo as Staffan drove it up over the curb at high speed. His upper and lower teeth slammed together with such force it almost sounded like a bell rang out in his head. He went blind for a second and almost ran over an older man who was about to join the group of onlookers that had gathered around the police car by the main entrance.

Larsson, a new police recruit, was in the patrol car talking on the radio. Probably calling for backup or an ambulance. Staffan drove up behind the patrol car in order to leave clearance for any other vehicles that might be on their way, jumped out and locked his car. He always locked his car, even if he was only going to be gone for a minute. Not because he was afraid it would get stolen but in order to keep the habit alive, so he would never forget to lock a *patrol car* for godssake.

He walked up the steps to the main entrance and made an effort to walk with authority in front of his onlookers; he knew he had an appearance that inspired confidence, at least with most people. Many of the people who were gathered probably saw him and thought: "Aha, here comes the guy who's going to clear up this whole thing."

Shortly inside the front doors there were four men in swimming trunks with towels wrapped around their shoulders. Staffan walked past them, toward the changing rooms, but one of the men called out, "Hello, excuse me," and ran over to him in bare feet.

"Yes, sorry, but . . , our clothes."

"What about them?"

"When can we get them?"

"Your clothes?"

"Yes, they're still in the changing rooms and we're not allowed in there."

Staffan opened his mouth and was about to say something sharp about the fact that their clothes were hardly the highest priority right now, but just then a woman in a white T-shirt came walking toward the men with a bunch of white robes in her arms. Staffan gestured to her and then continued on his way.

In the corridor he met another woman in a white T-shirt walking a boy of twelve or thirteen toward the entrance. The boy's face was a deep red against the white robe he was wrapped in; his eyes were devoid of expression. The woman turned to Staffan with a look that was almost accusatory.

"His mother's coming to pick him up."

Staffan nodded. Was this boy . . . the victim? He had wanted to ask this, but in his haste couldn't think of a reasonable way to put the question. Had to assume Holmberg had taken the boy's name and other information, judged it best to let his mother come in and take over, accompanying him to the ambulance, crisis intervention, therapy.

Protect these Thy smallest.

Staffan kept going down the corridor, ran up the steps while inside his head he recited a prayer of thanks for the Lord's mercy and for strength to meet the challenges ahead.

Was the murderer really still in the building?

Outside the changing rooms, under a sign with the single word MEN, there were, appropriately enough, three men talking to constable Holmberg. Only one of the three was fully dressed. The other two both lacked some item of clothing: one had no pants, the other had no shirt.

"I'm glad you got down here so fast," Holmberg said.

"Is he still here?"

Holmberg pointed at the changing room door.

"In there."

Staffan gestured at the three men.

"Are they? . . ."

Before Holmberg had time to say anything, the man without pants on took a half step forward and said—not without some pride—"We're witnesses."

Staffan nodded and looked inquiringly at Holmberg.

"Shouldn't they? . . ."

"Yes, but I thought I'd wait until you got down here. Apparently he's not violent." Holmberg turned kindly to the men and said, "We'll be in touch. The best thing you can do now is go home. Oh, and one more thing. I understand this may not be easy but try not to discuss this among yourselves."

The man without pants on half-smiled, nodding in agreement.

"Someone could overhear us, you mean."

"No, but you could start to imagine that you have seen something that you didn't really see, only because someone else did."

"Not me. I saw what I saw and it was the most hellish . . ."

"Believe me. It happens to the best of us. And now you'll have to excuse us. Thank you for you help."

The men walked off down the corridor, mumbling. Holmberg was good at this kind of thing. Talking to people. That was what he did most. Went around in schools and talked drugs and police work. Wasn't pulled into this kind of thing very often nowadays.

A metallic noise, as if a sheet of metal had fallen to the ground, came from inside the changing room. Staffan flinched and listened intently.

"Not violent, you said?"

"Badly injured, apparently. Poured some kind of acid onto his face."

"Why did he do that?"

Holmberg's face became blank; he turned to the door.

"I guess we'll have to go in and ask."

"Armed?"

"Probably not."

Holmberg pointed to a large kitchen knife with a wooden handle on a nearby window ledge.

"I didn't have a bag on me. And anyway the guy without pants had managed to stand there handling it for a while before I came. We'll have to deal with it later."

"Are we just going to let it stay there?"

"Got a better idea?"

Staffan shook his head and in the ensuing silence he perceived two different things. A soft, irregular blowing sound coming from inside the changing room. Wind whistling through a chimney. A cracked flue. That, and a smell. Something that he had at first assumed to be a part of the ubiquitous chlorine scent that permeated the whole building. But this was different. A sharp, stinging smell in his nostrils. Staffan wrinkled his nose.

"Should we? . . ."

Holmberg nodded but didn't make a move. Married, with children. Sure. Staffan pulled his gun from the holster, let his other hand rest on the door handle. It was the third time in his twelve years of service that he was entering a room with his weapon drawn. Didn't know if he was doing the right thing but no one would be likely to criticize him. A child killer. Cornered, perhaps desperate, no matter how injured.

He gave Holmberg a sign and opened the door.

The fumes overwhelmed him.

They stung so much his eyes started to water. He coughed. Took a handkerchief out of his pocket and held it over his nose and mouth. A few times when he had been assisting the fire department at a fire he had experienced something similar. But here there was no smoke, only a light mist suspended in the air.

Good God, what is this?

The repetitive, hacking sound could still be heard from the other side of the row of changing lockers in front of them. Staffan signalled for Holmberg to go around the lockers from the other side so they would be approaching from two directions. Staffan went up to the edge of the locker row and peeked around the corner with his gun held down along his side.

He saw a metal trash can kicked over on its side and next to it a prone, naked body.

Holmberg appeared on the other side, signalled to Staffan to take it easy, there didn't appear to be any immediate danger. Staffan felt a twinge of irritation that Holmberg was trying to take over command of the situation now that it didn't appear dangerous any longer. He breathed in through his handkerchief, took it away from his mouth, and said loudly,

"This is the police. Can you hear me?"

The man on the floor gave no sign of comprehension, just kept on making that repetitive noise with his face turned down into the ground. Staffan took a few steps forward.

"Put your hands where I can see them."

The man didn't move. But now that Staffan was closer he could see that the body was twitching all over. That part about the hands was unnecessary. One arm lay curled over the trash can, the other sprawled over the floor. The palms were swollen and cracked.

Acid . . . what does he look like . . .

Staffan held the handkerchief in front of his mouth again and walked up to the man while putting his gun back in his holster, trusting the fact that Holmberg would cover him if something happened.

The body twitched spasmodically and produced a soft smacking sound every time bare skin pulled free from the tile and then reattached itself. The hand lying on the floor flopped around like a flounder on a rock. And all the time this sound issued from the mouth, directed into the floor,

". . . eeiiieeeeiii . . ."

Staffan indicated to Holmberg to keep his distance, and crouched down next to the body.

"Can you hear me?"

The man stopped making noise. Suddenly the whole body writhed spasmodically and rolled over.

His face.

Staffan jumped back, lost his balance, and landed on his tailbone. He clenched his teeth not to cry out when the pain fanned out into his lower back. He squeezed his eyes shut. Opened them again.

He has no face.

Staffan had once seen a drug addict who, during a hallucination, had repeatedly smashed his face against a wall. He had seen a man who had welded near a gas tank without emptying it first. It had exploded into his face.

But nothing approached this.

The man's nose had completely burned away leaving only two holes in his head. The mouth had melted together, the lips sealed with the exception of a small opening in one corner. One eye had melted down over what had been his cheek, but the other . . . the other was wide open.

Staffan stared into that eye, the only thing that was still recognizeably human in this unshapely mass. The eye was red and when it tried to blink there was only a thread of skin that fluttered down and up again.

Where the rest of the face should have been there were only pieces of cartilage and bone sticking out between irregular shreds of flesh and blackened slivers of fabric. The naked, glistening muscles contracted and relaxed, contorting as if the head had been replaced by a mass of freshly killed and butchered eels.

The whole face, what had been the face, had its own life.

Staffan felt a retching in his throat and would probably have thrown up if his own body had not been so preoccupied with pumping pain into his lower back. Slowly he pulled his legs back in under him, stood up, leaning on the lockers for support. The red eye stared at him the whole time.

"What the . . ."

Holmberg stood with hanging arms and stared at the deformed body on the floor. It wasn't just the face. The acid had also run down onto the chest. The skin over the collarbone on one side was gone and a piece of the bone stuck out, glowing white like a piece of chalk in a meat stew.

Holmberg shook his head, raised and lowered one hand halfway up and down, up and down. Coughed.

"What the . . ."

†

It was eleven o'clock and Oskar lay in his bed. Slowly tapped out the letters against the wall.

E . . . L . . . I . . .

E . . . L . . . I . . .

No answer.

Friday

The boys in 6B stood lined up outside the school and waited for their gym teacher, Mr. Ávila, to give them the go-head. Everyone had some kind of gym bag in his hands because God save you if you forgot your gym clothes or didn't have an acceptable reason to sit out gym class.

They stood at arm's length from each other like the teacher had told them on the first day in fourth grade when he had taken over the responsibility of their physical education from their home room teacher.

"A straight line! Arm's length distance!"

Mr. Ávila had been a fighter pilot in the war. He had entertained the boys a few times with stories about airborne skirmishes and emergency landings in fields of wheat. They were impressed. They had respect for him.

A class that was considered difficult and unruly now stood lined up in a neat row an arm's length from each other even though the teacher was out of sight. If the line didn't meet his expectations he made them stand there an extra ten minutes or canceled a promised volleyball game in favor of pull-ups and sit-ups.

Like the rest of them, Oskar had a healthy respect for his gym teacher. With his stubbly gray hair, eagle nose, a still-impressive physique, and iron grip, Mr.Ávila was hardly predisposed to love or sympathize with a meek, somewhat chubby, and bullied boy. But order ruled during his class period. Neither Jonny, Micke, nor Tomas dared to do anything while Mr. Ávila was around.

Now Johan stepped out of line, threw a quick glance up at the school building, then gave a heil Hitler salute, and said with a feigned Spanish accent:

"Straight lines! Today fire drill! With ropes!"

Some pupils laughed nervously. Mr. Ávila had a fondness for fire drills. Once every semester he had his students practice lowering themselves out of the windows with ropes while he timed the whole procedure with a stopwatch. If they managed to beat the previous best time they would be allowed to play The Whole Sea is Raging in their next lesson. If they deserved to.

Johan quickly got back in line. He was lucky because, a few seconds later, Mr. Ávila came out of the front entrance and walked briskly to the gym. He was looking straight ahead without giving the class so much as a look. When he was halfway across the school yard he made a *follow me!* gesture with one hand without breaking his stride, without a backward glance.

The line started moving, all the while trying to retain the arm's length distance between people. Tomas, who was behind Oskar, stepped on Oskar's heel so the shoe slid off in the back. Oskar kept on walking.

Since the incident with the whips the day before yesterday they had left him alone. Not that they had gone so far as to apologize or anything, but the wound on his cheek was very visible and they probably felt it was enough. For now.

Eli.

Oskar bunched his toes up inside his shoe in order to keep it on, marching toward the gym. Where was Eli? Oskar had kept a lookout from his window last night to see if Eli's dad made it home. Instead he had seen Eli slip out around ten o'clock. Then he had had hot cocoa and rolls with his mom and maybe he had missed seeing her come home. But she had not answered any of the messages he tapped into the wall.

The class lumbered into the changing room and the line dissolved. Mr. Ávila stood waiting for them with crossed arms.

"Well, well. Today physical training, with bar, pommel horse and jump rope."

Groans. Mr. Ávila nodded.

"If it is good, if you work hard, next time we can play *spöck*-ball. But today: physical training. Get a move on!"

No room for discussion. You had to make do with the promise of ghost-ball, and the class hurried up and changed. As usual Oskar made sure he had his back turned to the others as he changed his pants. The Pissball made his underpants look a little strange.

Up in the gym hall the others were busy putting out the pommel horses and lowering the bars. Johan and Oskar carried out mats. When everything was arranged to his liking Mr. Ávila blew his whistle. There were five stations, so he divided them into five groups of two.

Oskar and Staffe were grouped together, which was good since Staffe was the only kid in the class who was worse at gym than Oskar. He had raw strength but was clumsy. Chubbier than Oskar. Even so, no one teased him. There was something about the way Staffe carried himself that told you if you messed with him something bad would happen to you.

Mr. Ávila blew his whistle again and everyone set to work.

Pull-ups on the bar. Chin over the bar, then down, then up again. Oskar managed two. Staffe did five, then gave up. Whistle. Sit-ups. Staffe just lay on the mat and stared at the ceiling. Oskar did cheater sit-ups until the next whistle. Jump rope. Oskar was good at this. He kept jumping while Staffe got tangled up in his rope. Then regular push-ups. Staffe could do these till the cows came home. Then the pommel horse, the damned pommel horse.

It was a relief to be paired with Staffe. Oskar snuck a peek at Micke and Jonny and Olof, how they flew over the horse via the springboard. Staffe geared up, ran, bounced so hard off the springboard that it creaked and still he didn't make it up onto the horse. He turned to walk back. Mr. Ávila came up to him.

"Up on pommel."

"Can't do it."

"Then you do ov*er*."

"What?"

"Do ov*er*. *Do over.* Go jump! Jump!"

Staffan grabbed the pommel horse, heaved himself up onto it and slid like a slug down the other side. Mr. Ávila waved *go!* and Oskar ran.

Somewhere during his run up to the pommel he made up his mind. He would try.

Once, Mr. Ávila had told him not to be afraid of the pommel horse, that everything hung on his attitude. Normally he didn't jump from the springboard with full force, afraid of losing his balance or of hitting something. But now he was going to go all out, *pretend* as if he could do it. Mr. Ávila was watching and Oskar ran with full force toward the springboard.

He hardly thought of the jump off the springboard, so focused was he on the aim of clearing the pommel horse. For the first time, he pushed his feet into the springboard with full force, without braking, and his body took off by itself, his hands stretched out to steady himself and steer his body on. He flew over the horse with such force that he lost his balance and tumbled headfirst when he landed on the other side. But he had cleared it!

He turned and looked at his teacher, who was definitely not smiling, but who nodded encouragingly.

"Good, Oskar, but more balance."

Then Mr. Ávila blew his whistle and they were allowed to rest for a minute before trying again. This time Oskar managed both to clear the pommel horse and keep his balance when he landed.

Mr. Ávila ended the lesson and went to his office while they put the equipment away. Oskar folded out the wheels under the pommel horse and wheeled it into the storage room, patting it like a good horse that had finally allowed itself to be tamed. He put it up against the wall and then walked to the changing room. There was something he wanted to talk to Mr. Ávila about.

He was stopped halfway to the door. A noose made from a jump rope went over his head and landed around his stomach. Someone held him in place. Behind him he heard Jonny's voice saying, "Giddy up, Piggy!"

Oskar turned so that the loop slid over his stomach and lay against his back. Jonny was standing in front of him with the ends of the jump rope in his hands. He waved them up and down.

"Giddy up, giddy up."

Oskar grabbed the rope with both hands and pulled the ends out of Jonny's grip. The jump rope clattered onto the floor behind Oskar. Jonny pointed to the rope.

"Now *you* have to pick it up."

Oskar picked up the jump rope in the middle and started to swing it above his head so the handles rattled against each other, yelled, "here it comes" and let go. The jump rope flew off and Jonny instinctively put his hands up to shield his face. The jump rope fluttered over his head and smacked against the wall bars behind him.

Oskar walked out of the gymnasium and ran down the stairs, the sound of his heart hammering in his ears. It had begun. He took the stairs three at a time, landing with both feet on the landings, walked through the changing rooms and into the teacher's office.

Mr. Ávila was sitting there in his gym clothes, talking on the phone in a foreign language, probably Spanish. The only word Oskar could make out was "perro," which he knew meant "dog." Mr. Ávila made a sign for him to sit down in the chair opposite his desk. Mr. Ávila kept talking, repeating "perro" a few more times. Oskar heard Jonny walk into the changing room and start talking in a loud voice.

The changing room had emptied out before Mr. Ávila was done talking about his dog. He turned to Oskar.

"So, Oskar. What do you want?"

"Yes, well, I . . . about these training sessions on Thursday."

"Yes?"

"Can I go to them?"

"You mean the strength training class at the swimming pool?"

"Yes, those. Do I have to sign up or . . ."

"No need to sign up. Just come. Thursdays at seven o'clock. You want to do it?"

"Yes, I . . . Yes."

"That is good. You train. Then you can do pull-up bar . . . fifty times."

Mr. Ávila mimed pulling up on a bar in the air. Oskar shook his head.

"No. But . . . yes, I'll be there."

"Then I see you Thursday. Good."

Oskar nodded, about to leave, then he said:

"How is your dog?"

"Dog?"

"Yes, I heard you say 'perro' on the phone just now. Doesn't that mean dog?"

Mr. Ávila thought for a moment.

"Ah. Not 'perro.' Pero. That means 'but' in Spanish. As in 'but not me.' That is pero no yo. Understand? You want to join the Spanish class too?"

Oskar smiled and shook his head. Said the strength training would do for now.

The changing room was empty except for Oskar's clothes. Oskar pulled off his gym clothes and stopped short. His pants were gone. Of course. That he hadn't thought of this in advance. He checked everywhere in the changing room, in the toilets. No pants.

†

The chill nipped his legs as he walked home in his gym shorts. It had started to snow during gym class. The snowflakes fell and melted on his legs. In his yard he stopped under Eli's window. The blinds were drawn. No movement inside. Large snowflakes carressed his upturned face. He caught some on his tongue. They tasted good.

†

Look at Ragnar."

Holmberg pointed in the direction of Vällingby plaza, where the falling snow was covering the cobblestones in gossamer. One of their regular alcoholics sat on a bench in the square without moving, wrapped in a large coat, while the snow slowly made him into a poorly proportioned snowman. Holmberg sighed.

"We'll have to go take a look if he doesn't move soon. How are you doing?"

"So so."

Staffan had put an extra cushion on his chair in order to assuage the pain in his lower back. He would rather be standing, or most of all, lying in his bed, but the report of last night's events had to be entered into the homicide register before the weekend.

Holmberg looked down at his pad and tapped his pen on it.

"Those three who were in the changing room. They said that the guy, the killer, before he poured the acid over his face, that he had shouted 'Eli, Eli,' and now I'm wondering . . ."

Staffan's heart leaped in his chest and he leaned across the desk.

"He said that?"

"Yes, do you know what . . ."

"Yes."

Staffan sat back suddenly and the pain shot up like an arrow all the way to the root of his hair. He grabbed the edge of the desk, straightened up, and put his hands over his face. Holmberg looked closely at him.

"Damn, have you seen a doctor?"

"No, it's just . . . it'll be fine in a minute. Eli, Eli."

"Is that a name?"

Staffan nodded slowly. "Yes . . . it means . . . God."

"I see, he was calling out to God. Do you think he was heard?"

"What?"

"God. Do you think God heard him? When you consider the circumstances it seems a little . . . unlikely. But you're the expert. Hm."

"They are the final words that Christ uttered on the cross. My God, my God, why hast Thou forsaken me? *Eli, Eli, lema sabachthani*?"

Holmberg blinked and looked down at his notes.

"Yes, that's right."

"According to the gospels of Matthew and Mark."

Holmberg nodded and sucked on the end of his pen.

"Should we include this in the report?"

†

When Oskar got home from school he put on a pair of new pants and went down to the Lover's kiosk to get himself a newspaper. There had been talk of the killer getting caught and he wanted to know everything. Clip articles for his scrapbook.

There was something that felt slightly different when he went down to the kiosk, something that wasn't how it normally was, even if you overlooked the snow.

On his way home with the newspaper he suddenly thought of it. He wasn't keeping a lookout. He just walked. He had walked all the way down to the kiosk without keeping an eye out for someone who would be able to hurt him.

He started to run. Ran home all the way with the paper in his hand while the snowflakes licked his face. Locked the front door from the inside. Went to his bed, lay down on his stomach, tapped on the wall. No reply. He would have wanted to talk to Eli, tell her.

He opened the newspaper. The Vällingby Pool. Police cars. Ambulance. Attempted murder. The man's injuries had made identification difficult. A picture of Danderyd where the man had been hospitalized. A run-down on the first murder. No comments.

Then submarine, submarine, submarine. The military on high alert.

The door bell rang.

Oskar jumped off his bed, walked quickly into the hall.

Eli, Eli, Eli.

He hesitated with his hand on the door handle. What if it was Jonny and the others? No, they would never come to his house like this. He opened. Johan was outside.

"Hey there."

"Yeah . . . hey there."

"Want to do something?"

"Sure . . . like what?"

"I don't know. Something."

"OK."

Oskar put on his shoes and coat while Johan waited for him on the stairs.

"What Jonny did back there was pretty shitty. In the gym."

"He took my pants, right?"

"Yeah, I know where they are."

"Where?"

"Back there. Behind the pool. I'll show you."

Oskar thought—but didn't say out loud—that in that case Johan could have made the effort to bring him the pants when he came over. But Johan's generosity did not extend that far. Oskar nodded and said, "Great."

They walked over to the pool and got the pants, which were hanging

on a bush. Then they walked around and checked things out. Made snow-
balls and tried to hit a specific target on a tree. In a container they found
some old electric cables that they could cut and use as slingshots. Talked
about the murderer, about the submarine, and about Jonny, Micke, and
Tomas who Johan thought were dumb.

"Completely retarded."

"But they don't do anything to you."

"No, but still."

They walked to the hotdog stand by the subway station and bought
two *luffare* each. One *krona* apiece; a grilled hot dog bun with only mus-
tard, ketchup, hamburger dressing, and raw onion inside. It was starting
to get dark. Johan talked to the girl in the hot dog stand and Oskar looked
at the subway trains that came and went, thinking about the electric wires
that ran above the tracks.

They started walking toward the school where they would go their
separate ways, their mouths reeking of onion. Oskar said:

"Do you think people kill themselves by jumping onto those wires
above the tracks?"

"Don't know. I guess so. My brother knows someone who went down
there and pissed on a live track."

"What happened?"

"He died. The current went up through the piss into his body."

"No way. So he *wanted* to die?"

"Nah. He was drunk. Shit. Think about it . . ."

Johan mimed taking out his dick, peeing, and then starting to con-
vulse. Oskar laughed.

Down by the school they said good-bye, waved. Oskar walked home-
ward with his newly recovered pants tied around his waist, whistling the signature melody to *Dallas*. It had stopped snowing but a white film covered
everything. The large frosted windows of the swimming pool were brightly
lit. He would go there Thursday evening. Start training. Get strong.

✝

Friday evening at the Chinese restaurant. The round, steel-rimmed clock
on one wall looks completely out of place among the rice paper lamps

and golden dragons. It says five to nine. The guys are leaning over their beers, losing themselves in the landscapes depicted on the placemats. The snow continues to fall outside.

Virginia stirs her San Francisco a little and sucks on the end of the stirrer, which has a little Johnnie Walker figure on the end.

Who was Johnnie Walker? Where was he walking with such determination?

She taps her glass with the stirrer and Morgan looks up.

"Giving a toast?"

"Someone should."

They had told her about it, everything that Gösta had said about Jocke, the underpass, the child. Then they had sunk into silence. Virginia let the ice cubes in her glass clink, looked at how the dimmed ceiling lights reflected in the half-melted cubes.

"There's one thing I don't get. If all this that Gösta says really happened, where *is* he? Jocke, I mean."

Karlsson brightened, as if this was an opportunity he had been waiting for.

"Exactly what I have been trying to say. Where is the body? If you're going . . ."

Morgan held up a finger in front of Karlsson.

"You do not refer to Jocke as 'the body,' understood?"

"Well, what do I call him? *The deceased?*"

"You don't call him anything, not until we know for sure."

"That's exactly what I've been trying to say. As long as we don't have a b—. . . as long as they haven't . . . found him, we can't."

"Who's 'they'?"

"Who do you think? The helicopter division in Berga? The police, of course."

Larry rubbed one eye, making a low clucking sound.

"That's a problem. As long as they haven't found him they aren't interested and as long as they aren't interested they won't find him."

Virginia shook her head. "You have to go to the police and tell them what you know."

"Oh yeah, and what exactly do you think we should tell them?" Morgan chuckled. "Hey, lay off all this shit with the child murderer, the submarine, and everything, because we're three merry alcoholics and one of our drinking buddies has disappeared and now another of our drinking buds tells us that one night when he was really high he saw . . . does that sound good?"

"But what about Gösta? He was the one who saw it. He's the one who . . ."

"Sure. But he's so damned unstable/insecure. Shake a uniform at him and he'll collapse, ready to be admitted to Beckis. He can't take it. Interrogations and shit." Morgan shrugged. "No chance there."

"But do we really do *nothing*?"

"Well, what the hell do you suggest?"

Lacke, who had had time to down his beer while the conversation was going on, said something too low for them to hear what it was. Virginia leaned toward him and put her head on his shoulder.

"What did you say?"

Lacke stared into the foggy ink-drawn landscape on his placemat and whispered: "You said that we would get him."

Morgan thumped the table with his hand so the beer glasses jumped. Held out his hand like a claw.

"And we will. But we need something to go on first."

Lacke nodded like a somnabulist and started to get up.

"Just have to . . ."

His legs gave way and he fell headfirst across the table. The loud crash of falling glass made all eight restaurant patrons turn and stare. Virginia grabbed hold of Lacke's shoulders and helped him up in the chair again. Lacke's eyes were far away.

"Sorry, I . . ."

The waiter hurried over to their table while frenetically rubbing his hands on his apron. He bent down to Lacke and Virginia and whispered furiously: "This is a restaurant not a pig sty!"

Virginia gave him the widest smile she could muster while she helped Lacke get to his feet.

"Come on, Lacke. We're going to my place."

With an accusing look at the other men, the waiter quickly walked around Lacke and Virginia, and supported Lacke on the other side in order to show his patrons he was just as concerned as they that this disturbing element be removed.

Virginia helped Lacke put on his heavy overcoat, elegant in an old-fashioned way—which he inherited from his father who had died a few years earlier—and ferried him to the door.

Behind her she heard a few meaningful whistles from Morgan and Karlsson. With Lacke's arm over her shoulder she turned to them and made a face. Then she pulled open the front door and walked out.

The snow was falling in large, slow flakes, creating a space of cold and silence for the two of them. Virginia's cheeks turned pink as she led Lacke down the park path. It was better like this.

†

Hi. I was going to meet my dad, but he didn't show up . . . may I come in and use the phone?"

"Of course."

"May I come in?"

"The telephone is over there."

The woman pointed further into the hallway; a gray telephone stood on a little table. Eli remained where she was outside the door; she hadn't yet been invited in. Right next to the door there was a cast iron hedgehog shoe wiper with prickles made of piassava fibers. Eli wiped off her shoes in order to cover her inability to enter.

"Are you sure it's alright?"

"Of course. *Come in, come in.*"

The woman made a tired gesture; Eli was invited. The woman seemed to have lost interest and walked into the living room, where Eli could hear the static whining of a TV. A long yellow silk ribbon tied around the woman's graying hair ran down her back like a pet snake.

Eli walked into the hall, took off her shoes and jacket, lifted the telephone receiver. Dialed a number at random. Pretended to talk to someone. Put the receiver down.

Drew air in through her nose. Cooking smells, cleaning agents, earth, shoe polish, winter apples, damp cloth, electricity, dust, sweat, wallpaper glue, and . . . cat urine.

Yes. A soot-black cat stood in the doorway to the kitchen, growling, the ears pulled back, fur standing on end, back arched. It had a red band around its neck with a little metal cylinder on it, probably containing a slip of paper with the owner's name and address.

Eli took a step toward the cat and it bared its teeth, hissing. The body was tensed for attack. One more step.

The cat retreated, pulling itself backward while continuing to hiss, maintaining eye contact. The hate pulsating through its body caused the metal cylinder to tremble. They took measure of each other. Eli moved slowly forward, forcing the cat back until it was in the kitchen, and then she closed the door.

The cat continued to growl and mew angrily on the other side. Eli walked into the living room.

The woman was sitting in a leather couch so well-polished the light from the TV was reflected in it. She sat bolt upright, staring unstintingly at the blue flickering screen. She had a yellow bow on one side of her head. On the other side the bow had pulled loose into a hanging length of ribbon. On the coffee table in front of her there was a bowl of crackers and a cutting board with three cheeses. An unopened bottle of wine and two glasses.

The woman did not seem to note Eli's presence; she was completely absorbed by what she saw on the screen. A nature program. Penguins at the South Pole.

"*The male carries the egg on his feet so it will not come in contact with the ice.*"

A caravan of penguins swaying from side to side moved across an ice desert. Eli sat down on the sofa, next to the woman. She sat stiffly, as if the TV was a disapproving teacher who was telling her off.

"*When the female returns after three months the male's layer of fat has been all but used up.*"

Two penguins rubbed their beaks together, greeting each other.

"Are you expecting someone?"

The woman flinched and stared without comprehension into Eli's eyes for a few seconds. The yellow bow accentuated how ravaged her face looked. She shook her head quickly.

"No, help yourself."

Eli didn't move. The picture on the TV screen changed to a panorama of the southern parts of Soviet Georgia, set to music. In the kitchen the tone of the cat's meows had turned into something . . . beseeching. There was a chemical smell in the room. The woman was exuding a hospital smell.

"Is anyone going to come over?"

Again the woman flinched as if she had been woken up, turned to Eli. This time she looked irritated, with a sharp furrow between her eyebrows.

"No. No one's coming. Eat if you like." She pointed with a stiff finger at the cheeses. "Camembert, Gorgonzola, and Roquefort. Eat. Eat."

She looked sternly at Eli, and Eli helped herself to a cracker, put it in her mouth, and started to chew slowly. The woman nodded and turned her gaze back to the screen. Eli spit the chewy mass of crackers into her hand and dropped it onto the floor behind the armrest.

"When are you leaving?" the woman asked.

"Soon."

"Stay as long as you like. It's all the same to me."

Eli moved a little closer, as if to be able to see the TV better, until their arms touched. Something happened to the woman. She trembled and sank together, softened like a punctured coffee packet. Now when she looked over at Eli it was with a mild, dreamy gaze.

"Who are you?"

Eli's eyes were only a few decimeters from hers. The hospital smell wafted from the woman's mouth.

"I don't know."

The woman nodded, reached for the remote control on the coffee table, and turned off the sound.

"*In the spring, southern Georgia blooms with a barren beauty . . .*"

The cat's beseeching meows could now be heard very clearly, but the woman didn't seem to care. She pointed to Eli's lap. "May I . . ."

"Of course."

Eli shifted slightly away from the woman, who pulled up her legs and rested her head on Eli's lap. Eli slowly stroked her hair. They sat like that for a while. The shimmering backs of whales broke the surface of the water, spurted out a fountain, disappeared.

"Tell me a story," said the woman.

"What do you want to hear?"

"Something beautiful."

Eli tucked a tendril of hair behind the woman's ear. She breathed slowly now and her body was completely relaxed. Eli spoke in a low voice.

"Once upon a time . . . a long, long time ago, there was a poor farmer and his wife. They had three children. A boy and a girl both old enough to work together with the adults. And then a little boy, only eleven years old. Everyone who saw him said he was the most beautiful child they had ever seen.

"The father was in villeinage to the lord who owned the land, and had to work many days for him. Therefore, it often fell to the mother and her two oldest to look after the house and garden. The youngest boy wasn't good for much.

"One day the lord announced a competition that all of the families who worked his land had to enter. Everyone who had a boy between the ages of eight and twelve. No reward was promised, no prize. Even so, it was called a competition.

"On the day of the competition the mother took her youngest to the lord's castle. They were not alone. Seven other children accompanied by one or both parents had gathered in the courtyard of the castle. Three more came. Poor families, the children dressed in the best clothes they had.

"They waited all day in the courtyard. When it was starting to get dark a man came out of the castle and told them they could come in."

Eli listened to the woman's breathing, deep and regular. She slept. Her breath was warm against Eli's knee. Right below her ear Eli could discern the pulse ticking under loose, wrinkled skin.

The cat was quiet.

The credits for the nature program rolled on the TV. Eli put a finger on the woman's throat artery. It felt like a beating bird heart under her fingertip.

Eli braced herself against the back of the couch and carefully pushed the woman's head forward so it leaned on Eli's knees. The sharp smell of Roquefort cheese drowned out the other smells. Eli pulled out a blanket from the back of the couch and draped it over the cheeses.

A soft squeaky sound, the woman's breathing. Eli leaned over and held her nose close to the woman's artery. Soap, sweat, the smell of old skin . . . and that hospital smell . . . something else that was the woman's own smell. And beneath all this: the blood.

The woman moaned when Eli's nose brushed against her throat, started to turn her head, but Eli gripped the woman's arms and chest with one hand, held the other one firmly around her head. Opened her mouth as much as she could, brought it down to the woman's throat until her tongue pressed against the artery and bit down. Locked her jaws.

The woman jerked as if she had received an electric shock. Her limbs flung out and her feet hit the armrest with such force that the woman pushed away and Eli ended up with her back across her knees.

The blood spurted rhythmically out of the open artery and splashed against the brown leather of the couch. The woman screamed and waved her hands in the air, pulling the blanket down from the table. A waft of blue cheese filled Eli's nostrils as she threw herself over the woman, pushing her mouth against her throat and drinking deeply. The woman's screams pierced her ears and Eli let go with one arm in order to be able to place a hand over her mouth.

The screams were muffled but the woman's free hand went out to the coffee table, grabbed the remote control, and banged it into Eli's head. The sound of plastic breaking as the sound of the TV came on again.

The signature melody of *Dallas* floated out into the room and Eli tore her head away from the woman's throat.

The blood tasted like medication. Morphine.

The woman stared up at Eli with wide eyes. Now Eli perceived yet another flavor. A rotten taste that combined with the smell of the blue cheese.

Cancer. The woman had cancer.

Her stomach turned with revulsion. She had to sit up and let go of the woman in order not to vomit.

The camera flew over Southfork while the music approached its crescendo. The woman wasn't screaming anymore, just lay still on her back while the blood pumped out of her in weaker and weaker spurts, streaming down behind the sofa cushions. Her eyes were damp and remote as she met Eli's gaze and said, "please . . . please . . ."

Eli held back her impulse to be sick, leaned forward over the woman. "Excuse me?"

"Please . . ."

"Yes, what is it you want?"

". . . please . . . please."

After a while the woman's eyes changed, stiffened. Became unseeing. Eli closed them. They opened again. Eli took the blanket from the floor and covered her face with it, sat up straight in the couch.

The blood was palatable even though it tasted bad, but the morphine . . .

There was a skyscraper of mirrors on the TV. A man dressed in a suit and a cowboy hat got out of his car, walked toward the skyscraper. Eli tried to get up out of the couch. She couldn't. The skyscraper started to lean, to turn. The mirrors reflected clouds that floated across the sky in slow motion, taking on the shape of animals, plants.

Eli burst out laughing when the man in the cowboy hat sat down behind a desk and started to speak in English. Eli understood what he was saying, but it was meaningless. Eli looked around. The whole room had started to lean in such a funny way it was strange the TV hadn't started to roll away. The cowboy-man's words echoed in her head. Eli looked for the remote control but it lay in pieces strewn across the table and floor.

Have to get the cowboy-man to stop talking.

Eli slid to the floor, crawling on all fours over to the TV with the morphine rushing through her body, laughing at the figures that dissolved into colors, colors. Didn't have the energy. Sank onto her stomach in front of the TV with the colors dancing in front of her eyes.

†

A few children were still sliding on their Snow Racers down the hill between Björnsonsgatan and the little field next to the park road. Death Hill, it was called for some reason. Three shadows started out at the same time from the top and some loud swearing was heard, when one of the shadows was forced off course into the forest, as well as laughter from the other two as they continued down the slope, flew up from the dip at the bottom, and came to rest with a muffled clatter.

Lacke stopped, looked down into the ground. Virginia tried carefully to shove him onward with her. "Come on, Lacke."

"It's just so damned hard."

"I can't carry you, you know."

A snort that was probably a laugh, that became a cough. Lacke dropped his arm from her shoulders, stood there with arms hanging, and turned his head toward the sledding hill.

"Damn it, here there are kids sledding, and there . . ." He gestured vaguely in the direction of the underpass that started at the far end of the hill that the slope was on. ". . . that's where Jocke was murdered."

"Don't think about that anymore."

"How can I stop? Maybe it was one of those kids who did it?"

"I don't think so."

She took his arm in order to put it around her neck again, but Lacke pulled away. "No, I can walk on my own."

Lacke started gingerly down the path. The snow crunched under his feet. Virginia stood still and watched him. There he was, the man she loved and whom she could never live with.

She had tried.

It was during a time eight years ago when Virginia's daughter had just moved away from home. Lacke had moved in. Then as now Virginia worked at a local grocery store, ICA, on Arvid Mörnes Road above China Park. She lived in a one-bedroom apartment about three minutes' walk from the store.

During the four months that they lived together Virginia never managed to figure out what Lacke actually *did*. He knew something about electrical wiring and put in a dimmer on the lamp in the living room. He knew something about cooking: surprised her several times with well-made fish-based creations. But what did he do?

He sat in the apartment, went for walks, talked to people, read a lot of books and newspapers. That was all. For Virginia, who had worked since she left school, it was an incomprehensible way to live. She had asked him:

"So Lacke, I don't mean this . . . but what is it you *do*? Where do you get your money?"

"I don't have any."

"But you do have a *little* money."

"This is Sweden. Carry out a chair and put it on the sidewalk. Sit there in that chair and wait. If you wait long enough someone will come out and give you money. Or take care of you somehow."

"Is that how you see me?"

"Virginia. When you say 'Lacke, please leave.' Then I'll leave."

It had taken a month before she said it. Then he had stuffed his clothes into a bag, his books into another. And left. She hadn't seen him for six months. During that time she had started to drink more, alone.

When she saw Lacke again he had changed. More sad. During those six months he had lived with his father, who was wasting away with cancer somewhere in a house in Småland. When his father died Lacke and his sister had inherited the house, sold it, and split the money. Lacke's share had been enough to get him a small condo with a low monthly fee in Blackeberg and now he was back for good.

In the years that followed they met more and more frequently at the Chinese restaurant, where Virginia had started to go more often in the evenings. Sometimes they left together, made love in a subdued way and—by silent agreement—Lacke made sure he was gone by the time Virginia came home from work the following day. They were a couple in the loosest sense of the word—sometimes a few months went by without them sharing their bed and this arrangement suited them.

They walked past the ICA store with its advertisement about cheap ground beef and its exhortation to "Live, drink, and be happy." Lacke stopped, waited for her. When she reached him he held an arm out to her. Virginia put her arm through his. Lacke nodded at the store.

"Good old work, huh?"

"The usual," Virginia said. "I did that one."

It was a sign that said CRUSHED TOMATOES. THREE CANS, 5 KRONOR.

"Nice job."

"Do you really think so?"

"Sure I do. Gives you a real craving for crushed tomatoes."

She jabbed him in the side, carefully. Felt her elbow make contact with a rib. "You don't even remember what real food tastes like."

"You certainly don't need to . . ."

"I know, but I'm going to anyway."

†

Eeeeli . . . Eeeeliii . . ."

The voice coming from the TV was familiar. Eli tried to back away from it, but her body wouldn't obey her. Only her hands moved around on the floor, in slow motion, searching for something to hold onto. Found a cord. Squeezed it hard with one hand as if it were a lifeline out of the tunnel that ended in the TV that was talking to Eli.

"Eli . . . where are you?"

Her head felt too heavy to lift from the floor; the only action Eli managed was to raise her eyes to the screen and of course it was . . . Him.

The blond tendrils from his wig made of human hair fanned out over the silk robe and made the effeminate face look even smaller than it was. The thin lips were pressed together, drawn into a lipsticked smile that looked like a knife gash in the pale powdered face.

Eli managed to raise her head slightly and saw His whole face. Blue, childishly large eyes, and above his eyes . . . the air came out of Eli's lungs in ragged spurts, and her head fell heavily to the ground, causing a crunching noise in her nose. Funny. He was wearing a cowboy hat on His head.

"Eeeliii . . ."

Other voices. Children's voices. Eli raised her head again, trembling like a baby. Drops of the sick blood ran from Eli's nose down to her mouth. The man had opened his arms in a gesture of welcome, revealing the red lining of his robe. The lining billowed out; it was swarming, made up of lips. Hundreds of children's lips that writhed painfully, whispering their story, Eli's story.

"Eli . . . come home . . ."

Eli sobbed, shut her eyes. Waited for the cold grip around the neck. Nothing happened. Opened her eyes again. The picture had changed. Now you could see a long line of children in poor clothes wandering over a snowy landscape, waddling in the direction of a castle of ice on the horizon.

This isn't happening.

Eli spit blood out of her mouth, toward the TV. Red dots punctured the white snow, ran down over the ice castle.

It isn't real.

Eli pulled on the lifeline, tried to pull herself out of the tunnel. A clicking was heard as the plug was pulled from the socket, and the TV turned off. Viscous strands of blood-tinged saliva ran down the darkened screen, dropping down onto the floor. Eli rested her head against her hands, disappearing into a dark red whirlpool.

✝

Virginia put on a quick pot of stew beef, onions, and crushed tomatoes while Lacke was showering. He was taking a long time. When the food was ready she went into the bathroom. He was sitting in the tub, his head between his knees, the detachable shower head resting against one shoulder, his vertebrae a string of Ping-Pong balls under the skin.

"Lacke? The food is ready."

"Great, that's great. Have I been in here long?"

"Not really. But the water company just called and said their wells are going dry."

"What?"

"Come on, up you go." She lifted her bathrobe up off its hook and held it out to him. He stood up by steadying himself with one hand on each side of the tub. Virginia winced as she noticed his emaciated body. Lacke saw her reaction and said: "Thus he rose from his bath, like a god, beautiful to behold."

Then they had dinner, splitting a bottle of wine. Lacke did not manage to get much down, but at least he was eating. They split another bottle of wine in the living room, then went to bed. Lay for a while next to each other, looking into each other's eyes.

"I've stopped taking the Pill."

"I see. We don't have to . . ."

"I didn't mean it like that. It's just I don't need them anymore. Menopause."

Lacke nodded. Thought about it. Stroked her cheek.

"Does that make you sad?"

Virginia smiled.

"You must be the only man I know who would think of asking me that. Yes, a little bit actually. It's as if . . . the part that makes me a woman. It doesn't apply to me anymore."

"Mmmm. Good enough for me, though."

"Really?"

"Yes."

"Come here."

He did as he was told.

†

Gunnar Holmberg was dragging his feet in the snow in order not to leave any footprints behind that would make things harder for the forensic technicians. He stopped and looked back at the traces that led away from the house. Light from the fire made the snow glow orange and the heat was intense enough that beads of sweat had formed along his hairline.

Holmberg had been teased many times for his naïve belief in the basic goodness of young people. That was what he tried to support through his frequent school visits, through his many and long conversations with youngsters who had made bad choices, and that was one reason why he was so affected by what he now saw in front of him.

The footprints in the snow had been made by *small* shoes. Not even what you would call a "young person," no, these tracks had been made by a child. Small, neat imprints spaced at a remarkable distance from each other. Someone had run here. Fast.

In the corner of his eye he saw Larsson, an officer-in-training, approaching.

"Drag your feet, for heaven's sake."

"Oh, sorry."

Larsson started wading through the snow, stopping next to Holmberg. Larsson had large bulging eyes with a constant expression of amazement that was now directed at the tracks in the snow.

"Damn."

"Couldn't have said it better myself. Made by a child."

"But . . . they are so . . ." Larsson followed the tracks for a while with his gaze. "Like a triple jump."

"Spaced widely, yes."

"More than 'widely,' it's . . . it's unbelievable. It's so far."

"What do you mean?"

"I run a lot and I wouldn't be able to run like this. More than for . . . two steps at least. And this goes on the whole way."

Staffan came jogging along past the houses, made his way through the group of curious onlookers who had gathered around the property, and walked up to the little group in the middle, which was just overseeing some paramedics who were maneuvering a covered female corpse on a stretcher into an ambulance.

"How did it go?" Holmberg asked.

"Uh . . . went out onto . . . Bällstavägen and then . . . can't follow them . . . any further . . . all the cars . . . we'll have to . . . put the dogs on it. . . ."

Holmberg nodded, half his attention claimed by a conversation nearby. A neighbor who was witness to part of the events was being questioned.

"At first I thought it was some kind of fireworks or something, you know. Then I saw the hands. Her hands were waving in the air. And then she came out like this . . . through the window . . . she came out."

"So the window was open?"

"Yes, it was open. And she came out of it . . . and then the house burned down. Of course. I saw it then. That it was all burning up behind her . . . and she came out . . . oh, shit. She was on fire, her whole body. And then she walked away from the house—"

"Excuse me. Walked? She wasn't running?"

"No, that's what was so damned . . . she was walking. Waved her arms around like this in order to . . . I don't know. And then she *stopped*. Follow me? She stopped. Her whole body on fire. Stopped like this. And *looked around*. As if . . . calmly. And then she started walking again. And then it was as if . . . as if it ended, you know? No sign of panic or anything, she . . . uh, damn . . . she wasn't *screaming*. Not a sound. She just collapsed like this. Fell to her knees. And then . . . boom. Down on the snow.

"And then it was as if . . . I don't know . . . it was so damned strange, all of it. That was when I . . . when I ran in and got a blanket, two blankets, and then I ran back out and . . . put it out. Shit, you know . . . when she was lying there, it was . . . no, shit."

The man put two sooty hands up to his face, sobbing. The police officer put a hand on his shoulder.

"We can maybe put together a more official version of this tomorrow. But you didn't see anybody else leaving the house?"

The man shook his head and the officer scribbled something on his pad.

"As I said, I'll be in touch with you tomorrow. Do you want me to ask a medic to give you something, to help you sleep, before they leave?"

The man rubbed the tears from his eyes. His hands left damp streaks of soot in his face.

"No, that's . . . I have something if I need it."

Gunnar Holmberg looked again at the burning house. The firefighters had been effective and now you could hardly see any flames. Only a giant pillar of smoke that rose into the night sky.

†

While Virginia was opening her arms to Lacke, while the crime technicians were making imprints of the tracks in the snow, Oskar stood by his window and looked out. The snow had blanketed the bushes under the window and made a white surface so thick you would have thought you could slide down it.

Eli hadn't come by this evening.

Oskar had stood, walked, waited, swung, and frozen down there on the playground between half past seven and nine o'clock. No Eli. At nine he had seen his mom standing in the window and he had gone inside, filled with anxiety. *Dallas* and hot chocolate and cinnamon rolls and his mom asking questions and he almost spilled the beans, but didn't.

Now it was a little after midnight and he stood next to his window with a hole in his gut. He cracked the window, breathing in the cold night air. Was it really for her sake that he had decided to fight back? Wasn't this really about him?

Yes.

But for her sake.

Unfortunately. That's how it was. If they went after him on Monday he wouldn't have the energy, the desire to stand up to them. He knew it. Wouldn't show up for the training session on Thursday. No reason.

He left the window cracked with the vague hope that she would come back in the night. Call his name. If she could go out in the middle of the night she could come back in the middle of the night.

Oskar undressed and went to bed. Tapped on the wall. No answer. He pulled the blankets over his head and kneeled in the bed. He intertwined his hands and pressed his forehead to them, whispering:

"Please, dear God. Let her come back. You can have whatever you like. All my magazines, all my books, my things. Whatever you want. But just make it so she comes back. To me. Please, please God."

He lay there curled up under the blankets until he was so hot he was sweating. Then he poked his head out again and rested it on the pillow. Assumed the fetal position. Closed his eyes. Images of Eli, of Jonny and Micke, Tomas. Mom, Dad. He lay there for a long time conjuring up the images he wanted to see, then they started to take on a life of their own as he slid off into sleep.

†

Eli and he were sitting in a swing that was going higher and higher until it loosened from its chains and flew up into the sky. They were holding on tight to the edge of the swing, their knees pressed against each other, and Eli whispered,

"Oskar. Oskar . . ."

He opened his eyes. The light inside the globe was turned off and the moonlight made everything blue. Gene Simmons looked at him from the wall across from the bed, sticking out his long tongue. He curled up, shut his eyes. Then he heard the whisper again.

"Oskar . . ."

It was coming from the window. He opened his eyes, looked over. He saw the contour of a little head on the other side of the glass. He pulled off the covers but before he managed to get out of bed Eli whispered,

"Wait there. Stay in bed. Can I come in?"

Oskar whispered: "Yes . . ."

"Say that I can come in."

"You can come in."

"Close your eyes."

Oskar shut his eyes tightly. The window opened and a cold draft blew into the room. The window was carefully closed. He heard how Eli breathed, whispered: "Can I look now?"

"Wait."

The sofa bed in the other room creaked. His mom had gotten up. Oskar was still keeping his eyes shut as the blanket was pulled off and a cold, naked body crept in beside him, pulled the covers back over them both, and curled up into a ball behind his back.

The door to his room opened.

"Oskar?"

"Mmm."

"Is that you talking?"

"No."

His mom stayed in the doorway, listening. Eli lay completely still behind his back, pushing her forehead in between his shoulder blades. Her breath ran warmly down the small of his back.

His mom shook her head.

"It must be those neighbors." She listened for another moment, then said, "Good night, sweetheart," and closed the door.

Oskar was alone with Eli. He heard a whisper behind his back.

"Those neighbors?"

"Shhhh."

There was a creaking sound as his mom got back into the sofa bed. He looked up at the window. It was closed.

A cold hand crept over his stomach and found its way to his chest, over his heart. He put both his hands over it, warming her hand. Eli's other hand worked its way under his armpit then up over his chest and in between his hands. Eli turned her head and laid her cheek between his shoulder blades.

A new smell had entered the room. The faint smell of his dad's moped when it was fully tanked. Gasoline. Oskar bent his head down and smelled her hands. Yes, the smell was coming from her hands.

They lay like that for a long time. When Oskar could tell from his mom's breathing that she had fallen asleep again, when the lump of their hands was warmed through and starting to get sweaty, he whispered:

"Where have you been?"

"Getting some food."

Her lips tickled his shoulder. She loosened her hands from his, rolled over on her back. Oskar stayed in the same position for a moment and looked into Gene Simmons' eyes. Then he turned onto his stomach. Behind her head he imagined the tiny figures in the wallpaper eyeing her with curiosity. Her eyes were wide open, blue-black in the moonlight. Oskar got goosepimples on his arms.

"What about your dad?"

"Gone."

"Gone?" Oskar couldn't help raising his voice.

"Shhh. It doesn't matter."

"But . . . what . . . is he—?"

"It. Doesn't. Matter."

Oskar nodded, signaling that he wasn't going to ask her any more questions, and Eli put both her hands under her head, staring up at the ceiling.

"I was feeling lonely. So I came here. Was that OK?"

"Yes. But . . . you don't have any clothes on."

"I'm sorry. Is that disgusting?"

"No. But aren't you freezing?"

"No, no."

The white strands in her hair were gone. Yes, she looked altogether healthier than when they met yesterday. Her cheeks were rounder, the dimples more pronounced, when Oskar joked and asked:

"You didn't happen to walk past the Lover's kiosk or anything?"

Eli laughed, then made her voice very serious and said with a ghostly voice:

"Yes, I did and you know what? He poked his head out and said: 'Coooome . . . coooom . . . I have candy and . . . banaaaanas. . . .'"

Oskar buried his face in the pillow. Eli turned her head toward his and whispered in his ear: "Cooome . . . jelly beans . . ."

Oskar shouted: "No, no!" into the pillow. They kept doing this for a while. Then Eli looked at the books in his bookcase and Oskar gave a synopsis of his favorite: *The Fog* by James Herbert. Eli's back glowed white like a sheet of paper in the dark as she lay there on her stomach in bed and studied the bookcase.

He held his hand so close to her skin that he could feel the warmth from it. Then he contracted his fingers and walked them down her back whispering, "Bulleribulleri bock. How many horns are sticking . . . up?"

"Mmm. Eight?"

"Eight you say and eight there are, bulleribulleribock."

Then Eli did the same to him but he was not at all as good at telling how many fingers there were as she was. On the other hand, he was much better at rock, paper, scissors. Seven to three. Then they played again. He won nine to one. Eli started to get a little irritated.

"Do you *know* what I am going to pick?"

"Yes."

"How?"

"I just know, that's all. It happens all the time. I get a picture in my head."

"One more time. I won't think this time, just choose."

"You can try."

They played again. Oskar won easily with eight-two. Eli pretended to be enraged, turned to the wall.

"I'm not playing with you. You cheat."

Oskar looked at her white back. Did he dare? Yes, now that she wasn't looking at her he could do it.

"Eli. Will you go out with me?"

She turned around, pulled the covers up to her chin.

"What does that mean?"

Oskar stared at the spines of the books in front of him, shrugged.

"That . . . you would want to be together with me."

"What do you mean 'together'?"

Her voice sounded suspicious, hard. Oskar hurriedly said: "Maybe you already have a guy at your school."

"No, I don't . . . but Oskar, I can't. I'm not a girl."

Oskar snorted. "What do you mean? You're a *guy*?"

"No, no."

"Then what are you?"

"Nothing."

"What do you mean, 'nothing'?"

"I'm nothing. Not a child. Not old. Not a boy. Not a girl. Nothing."

Oskar pulled his finger down the spine of *The Rats*, pinched his lips together and shook his head. "*Will* you go out with me or not?"

"Oskar I'd really like to but . . . can't we just be together like we already are?"

". . . yes."

"Are you sad? We can kiss, if you like."

"No!"

"You don't want to?"

"No, I don't!"

Eli frowned.

"Do you do anything in particular with someone you're going out with?"

"No."

"It's just like normal?"

"Yes."

Eli looked suddenly happy, folded her arms over her stomach, and gazed at Oskar.

"Then we can go out. We can be together."

"We can?"

"Yes."

"Good."

With a quiet happiness in his belly, Oskar kept studying the titles of the books. Eli lay still, waiting. After a while she said:

"Is there anything else?"

"No."

"Can't we lie down together again like we did before?"

Oskar rolled around so his back was against her. She put her arms around him and he took her hands. They lay like that until Oskar started to get sleepy. His eyes felt sandy; it was hard to keep them open. Before he slid off into sleep he said:

"Eli?"

"Mmm?"

"I'm glad you came over."

"Yes."

"Why . . . do you smell like gasoline?"

Eli's hands gripped more tightly around his hands, against his heart. Hugged. The room grew larger all around Oskar, the walls and ceiling softened, the floor fell away, and when he felt the whole bed floating in the air he knew he was asleep.

𝕾𝖆𝖙𝖚𝖗𝖉𝖆𝖞

3 1 OCTOBER

Night's candles are burnt out, and jocund day
Stands tiptoe on the misty mountain tops.
I must be gone and live, or stay and die.

——William Shakespeare, *Romeo and Juliet*, III:5

Gray. Everything was gray. His eyes wouldn't focus; it was like lying inside a rain cloud. Lying? Yes, he was lying down. There was pressure against his back, buttocks, heels. A hissing sound on his left side. The gas. The gas was on. No. It was turned off. Turned on. Something happened to his chest in time to the hissing sound. It filled and emptied in time to that sound.

Was he still at the pool? Was *he* hooked up to the gas? How could he, in that case, be awake? Was he even awake?

Håkan tried to blink. Nothing happened, almost nothing. Something jerked in front of his one eye, murkying his sight further. His other eye wasn't there. He tried to open his mouth. His mouth wasn't there. He conjured up an image of his mouth, as he had seen it in mirrors, tried . . . but it wasn't there. Nothing responded to his commands. Like trying to inject consciousness into a rock in order to get it to move. No contact.

A sensation of strong heat over his whole face. A dart of fear shooting into his stomach. His face was plastered with something warm, stiffening. Paraffin wax. A machine was doing his breathing because his whole face was covered in wax.

His thoughts stretched out toward his right hand. Yes. There it was.

He opened it, made a fist, felt the tops of his fingers against his palm. Touch. He sighed with relief, imagined a sigh of relief, since his chest didn't move according to his wishes.

He lifted his hand, slowly. A tightening sensation over his chest and shoulder. The hand entered his field of vision, a fuzzy lump. He moved it toward his face, stopped. There was a low beeping by his side. He carefully turned his head in its direction, felt something hard scrap against his chin. He moved his hand toward it.

A metal socket was implanted in his throat. A plastic tube fed into the metal socket. He followed the plastic tubing as far as he could, as far as a grooved metallic piece where the tube ended. He understood. This was what he should pull out when he wanted to die. They had set it up like this for him. He rested his fingers against the end of the tube.

Eli. The pool. The boy. Acid.

His memory stopped at the part where he unscrewed the lid. He must have poured it over himself, all according to the plan. The only miscalculation was that he was still alive. He had seen pictures. Women who had gotten acid thrown into their faces by jealous boyfriends. He didn't want to feel his face, even less see it.

His hold on the tube tightened. It didn't give way. Screwed in. He tried to turn the metal end and, as he had suspected, it turned. He kept unscrewing it. He searched for his left hand, but only sensed a prickling ball of pain where that hand should have been. With the tops of the fingers on his living hand he now felt a light, fluttering pressure. Air was starting to escape from around the seal. The hissing sound had changed slightly, become thinner.

The gray light around him was infiltrated by something blinking red. He tried to close his one eye. Thought about Socrates and the jar of poison. Because he had seduced the youth of Athens. Don't forget to offer a rooster to . . . what was he called? Archimandros? No . . .

A sucking sound as a door was pushed open and a white figure moved toward him. He felt fingers prying open his fingers, prying them from the metal end. A woman's voice.

"What are you doing?"

Asclepius. Offer a cock to Asclepius.

"Let go!"

A cock. To Asclepius. The god of healing.

A hissing sound when his fingers gave way and the tube was screwed back in place.

"We'll have to guard you from now on."

Offer it to him, do not forget.

†

Eli was gone when Oskar woke up. He lay with his face toward the wall. His back got cold. He drew himself up on one elbow and looked around the room. The window was open a crack. She must have let herself out that way.

Naked.

He rolled over in his bed, pressed his face against the place where she had slept, sniffed. Nothing. He moved his nose back and forth across the sheet trying to discern the tiniest glimmer of her presence, but nothing. Not even that smell of gasoline.

Had it really happened? He lay down on his stomach, thought about it.

Yes.

It was real. Her fingers on his back. The memory of her fingers on his back. Bulleribock. His mom had played it with him when he was little. But this was now. Not long ago. The hairs on his arms and on his neck stood up.

He got out of bed and started to pull his clothes on. When he had his pants on he walked up to the window. No snowfall. Four degrees below zero. Good. If the snow had started to melt it would be too slushy to set the bags of advertising down outside. He thought about crawling naked out of a window when it was four degrees below zero outside, down into snow-covered bushes, down into . . .

No.

He leaned forward, blinked.

The snow on the bushes was completely undisturbed.

Last night when he had stood there he had looked out onto a clean sweep of snow that ran down to the path. It looked exactly the same now. He opened the window a little more, stuck his head out. The bushes reached all the way up to the wall below his window, the snow cover as well. And it was undisturbed.

Oskar looked to the left, along the rough surface of the outside wall. Her window was three meters away.

Cold air swept over Oskar's naked chest. It must have snowed last night after she went back to her room. That was the only explanation. But anyway . . . now that he thought about it: how had she made it *up* to the window? Had she climbed up the bushes?

But then the snow couldn't look like this. And it hadn't been snowing when he went to bed. Neither her body nor her hair had been damp, so it couldn't have been snowing then. When did she go?

Some time between the time that she left and when she was here it must have snowed enough to cover the tracks of . . .

Oskar shut the window, continued to dress. It was unbelievable. He started thinking it was all a dream again. Then he saw the note. Folded and left under the clock on his desk. He took it out and unfolded it.

THEN WINDOW, LET DAY IN AND LET LIFE OUT.

A heart, and then:

SEE YOU TONIGHT, ELI.

He read the note five times. Then he thought about her, standing here by the desk as she wrote it. Gene Simmons' face on the wall, half a meter behind her, his tongue sticking out.

He leaned over the desk and took the poster down from the wall, crinkled it into a ball, and threw it into the trash.

Then he read the short note three more times, folded it, and put it in his pocket. Put on the last of his clothes. Today there could be five papers in each advertising packet as far as he was concerned. It would still be as easy as pie.

†

The room smelled of smoke and the dust particles danced in the rays of sunlight that filtered in through the blinds. Lacke had just woken up, was lying on his back in bed, coughing. Dust particles were doing a funny dance in front of his eyes. A smoker's cough. He turned, managed to get a hold of the lighter and cigarette packet that was on the nightstand next to an overflowing ashtray.

He helped himself to a cigarette—Camel lights, Virginia was starting to get health conscious in her old age—lit it, rolled over onto his back again with one arm behind his head, and reflected on the situation.

Virginia had left for work a few hours earlier, probably fairly tired. They had stayed awake for a long time after making love, talked and smoked. It was close to two in the morning when Virginia put out the last cigarette and said it was time to sleep. Lacke had slipped out of bed after a while, had drained the dregs of the bottle of wine, and smoked a few more cigarettes before he went back to bed. Maybe mostly because he liked this: crawling into bed next to a warm sleeping body.

Too bad he hadn't managed to arrange his life so he always had someone next to him. If there could have been someone, it would have been Virginia. Anyway . . . damn it, he had heard from others how things were for her. Rollercoaster times. Times when she drank too much in city pubs, dragged home any old guy. She didn't want to talk about that, but she had aged more than she needed to these past few years.

If he and Virginia could have . . . yes, what? Sell everything, buy a house in the country, grow their own potatoes. Sure, but it wouldn't last. After a month they would be getting on each others' nerves, and she had her mom here, her job, and he had . . . well, his stamps.

No one knew about that, not even his sister, and he had kind of a guilty conscience about that.

His dad's stamp collection, which had not been drawn up in the estate, was worth a small fortune as it turned out. He had raided it, a few stamps at a time, when he needed the cash.

Right now the market was at a low, and he didn't have many stamps left. But soon he would have to sell them anyway. Maybe sell those special ones, Norway number one, and buy a round of beer in return for all the beers he had gotten people to buy him the last while. That's what he should do.

Two houses in the country. Cottages. Close to each other. Cottages cost almost nothing. Then there was Virginia's mother. Three cottages. And then her daughter, Lena. Four. Sure. Buy a whole village while you're at it.

Virginia was only happy when she was with Lacke; she had said so herself. Lacke wasn't sure he had the capacity to be happy, but Virginia was the only person he liked being with. Why shouldn't they be able to make things work out somehow?

Lacke set the ashtray on his stomach, flicked the ash from the tip, put the cigarette in his mouth, and inhaled deeply.

The only person he liked being with these days. Since Jocke had . . . disappeared. Jocke had been good. The only one among all his acquaintances he counted as a friend. This thing about his body being missing was fucked up. It wasn't natural. There should be a funeral at least. A corpse that you can look at, that prompts you to say: yes, there you are, my friend. And you are dead.

Lacke's eyes teared up.

People always had so many damned friends, tossed the word around so lightly. He had had one, only one, and he happened to be the one who was taken from him by a cold-blooded mugger. Why the hell did that kid have to kill Jocke?

Somehow he knew that Gösta wasn't lying or making it up, and Jocke was gone, but it seemed so damned meaningless. The only reasonable explanation was that drugs were involved. Jocke must have been involved in some drug shit and double-crossed the wrong person. But why hadn't he said anything?

Before he left the apartment he emptied the ashtray, stowed the empty wine bottle on the floor of the pantry. Had to put it in upside down so it would fit with all the other bottles.

Yes, damn it. Two cottages. A potato patch. Earth on your knees and lark song in springtime. And so on. Some day.

He put on his coat and went out. When he walked past the ICA store he threw a kiss to Virginia, who was sitting at a register. She smiled and pouted at him.

On his way back to Ibsengatan he saw a young boy laden with two large paper bags. Someone who lived in his complex, but Lacke didn't know his name. Lacke nodded at him.

"Looks heavy, what you've got there."

"It's OK."

Lacke gazed after the boy struggling on with his bags in the direction of some nearby apartment buildings. Looked so damned happy. That's how you should be. Accept your burden and carry it, with joy.

That's how you should be.

Inside the courtyard he hung around hoping to bump into the guy who had bought him the whisky drinks. The man was sometimes up and walking around at this time. Walked in circles around the courtyard. But he hadn't seen him the last couple of days. Lacke peeked up at the covered windows to the apartment where he thought the man lived.

Probably in there drinking, of course. Could go ring the doorbell.

Maybe another day.

†

When it was starting to get dark Tommy and his mother went down to the graveyard. His dad's grave was just inside the dike that bordered Råcksta Lake. His mom was quiet until they reached Kanaanvägen, and Tommy had thought it was because she was grieving but when they walked onto the little road that ran parallel to the lake his mom coughed and said, "So you know, Tommy."

"What."

"Staffan says that something has gone missing from his apartment. Since we were there last."

"I see."

"Do you know anything about it?"

Tommy scooped up some snow with his hand, shaped it into a ball, and threw it at a tree. Bull's eye.

"Yeah. It's lying under his balcony."

"It's quite important to him because . . ."

"It's in the bushes under his balcony, I said."

"How did it end up there?"

A section of the snow-covered wall around the graveyard came into view. A soft red light illuminated the pine trees from below. The grave lantern that Tommy's mom was carrying made a clinking sound. Tommy asked: "Do you have a light?"

"Light? Oh yes. I have a lighter. How did it—"

"I dropped it."

Once he was inside the gate to the graveyard Tommy stopped and looked at the map; the different sections were marked with different letters. His dad was in section D.

If you thought about it, it was actually pretty sick. To do this. Burn people up, save the ashes, bury them in the ground, and then call the spot "Grave 104, section D."

Almost three years ago. Tommy had fuzzy memories of the funeral, or whatever it should be called. That thing with the coffin and a lot of people who alternated between crying and singing.

He remembered he had been wearing shoes that were too big for him, Daddy's shoes, that his feet had slipped around in them on the way home. That he had been afraid of the coffin, sat staring at it the whole time, sure his dad was going to get up out of it and come alive again, but . . . changed.

Two weeks after the funeral he had gone around with a total fear of zombies. Especially when it was dark, he looked in the shadows and thought he could make out the shrivelled being in the hospital bed, who was no longer his dad, coming at him with arms held out stiffly, like in those movies.

The terror had stopped after they interred the urn. It had only been him, Mom, a gravedigger, and a minister. The gravedigger had carried the urn and walked with a dignified stride while the minister comforted his mom. The whole thing was so fucking ridiculous. The little wooden box with a lid that a guy in carpenter overalls carried in front of him as he walked; that this had anything whatsoever to do with his dad. It was one big joke.

But the terror had lifted and Tommy's relationship to the grave had changed over time. Now he sometimes came here alone, sat a while by the gravestone, and ran his fingers across the carved letters that formed his father's name. That was what he came for. Not the box in the ground, but the name.

The distorted person in the hospital bed, the ashes in the box, none of that was Dad, but the name referred to the person he could remember and therefore he sometimes sat there and rubbed his finger over the depressions in the stone that formed the name MARTIN SAMUELSSON.

"How beautiful it is," his mom said.

Tommy looked out over the graveyard.

Small candles were lit all over. A city viewed from an airplane. Here and there dark figures moved among the gravestones. Mom walked in the direction of Dad's grave, the lantern dangling from her hand. Tommy looked at her thin back and was suddenly sad. Not for his sake, or his mom's sake, no: for everyone. For all the people walking here with their flickering lights in the snow. Themselves only shadows that sat next to the headstones, looked at the inscription, touching it. It was just so . . . stupid. *Dead is dead. Gone.*

Even so, Tommy walked over to his mom and crouched down next to his dad's grave while she lit the lantern. Didn't want to touch the letters in his name when she was there.

They sat like that for a while and watched the weak flicker make the shading in the marble block crawl and move. Tommy didn't feel anything except a certain embarrassment. To think he went along with this pretend play. After a minute he got up and started to head home.

His mom followed. A little too soon, in his opinion. As far as he was concerned, she could cry her eyes out, sit there all night. She caught up with him and carefully put her arm through his. He let her. They walked side by side and looked out over Råcksta Lake, where ice had started to form. If this cold snap kept up you'd be able to skate on it in a few days.

One thought kept going through his head like a stubborn guitar riff. *Dead is dead. Dead is dead. Dead is dead.*

His mom shivered, pressed up against him.

"It's awful."

"You think?"

"Yes, Staffan told me such an awful thing."

Staffan. Couldn't she keep herself from mentioning him, here of all . . .

"I see."

"Did you hear about that house that burned down in Ängby? The woman who . . ."

"Yes."

"Staffan told me that they did the autopsy on her. I think that kind of stuff is so awful. That they do those things."

"Yes. Sure."

A duck was walking on the thin ice toward the open water that had formed near a drain that let out into the lake. The small fishes you could catch in the summer smelled like sewage.

"Where does that drain lead from?" Tommy asked. "Does it come from the crematorium?"

"Don't know. Don't you want to hear about it? Do you think it's too awful?"

"No, no."

And then she told him while they were walking home through the woods. After a while Tommy got interested, started asking questions his mom couldn't answer; she just knew what Staffan had told her. In fact Tommy asked so much, became so interested, that his mom regretted having brought it up in the first place.

✝

Later that evening Tommy perched on a crate in the shelter, turning the small likeness of a man firing a pistol this way and that. He placed the statuette on top of three boxes containing cassette tapes, like a trophy. The cherry on top.

Stolen from a . . . policeman!

He carefully locked the shelter back up with the chain and padlock, put the key back in its hiding place, sat down in the clubhouse, and kept thinking about what his mother had told him. After a while he heard tentative steps walking down the corridor. A voice that whispered, "Tommy? . . ."

He got up out of the armchair, walked up to the door, and quickly opened it. Oskar was standing on the other side, looking nervous. He held out a bill.

"Here's your money."

Tommy took the fifty and stuffed it into his pocket, smiled at Oskar.

"You going to become a regular here? Come in."

"No, I have to . . ."

"Come in, I said. There's something I want to ask you."

Oskar sat down in the couch, hands clasped. Tommy flopped down in the armchair, looked at him.

"Oskar. You're a smart guy."

Oskar shrugged modestly.

"You know that house that burned down in Ängby? The granny who ran out into the garden in flames?"

"Yes, I've read about it."

"Thought you would. Have they written anything about the autopsy?"

"Not that I know of."

"No. Well, they've done one. An autopsy. And you know what? They didn't find any smoke in her lungs. Know what that means?"

Oskar thought about it.

"That she wasn't breathing."

"Right. And when do you stop breathing? When you're dead, right?"

"Yes," Oskar said eagerly. "I've read about that kind of stuff. That's why they always do an autopsy when there's been a fire. To make sure that there isn't . . . that no one started the fire to cover up the fact that they murdered the person who's in there. In the fire. I read about it in . . . well, *Hemmets Journal*, actually, about a guy from England who killed his wife and who knew about this so he had . . . before he started the fire he stuck a tube down her throat and . . ."

"OK, OK, so you know. Great. But in this case there wasn't any smoke in her lungs and even so the granny managed to get herself out into the garden and run around out there for a while before she died. How can that be?"

"She must have been holding her breath. No, of course not. You can't do that. I've read about that somewhere. That's why people always . . ."

"OK, OK. Explain this to me."

Oskar leaned his head in his hands, thought hard. Then he said: "Either they made a mistake or else she was running around like that even though she was dead."

Tommy nodded. "Exactly. And you know what? I don't think these dudes make those kind of mistakes. Do you?"

"No, but . . ."

"Dead is dead."

"Yes."

Tommy pulled a thread out of the armchair, rolled it up into a ball between his fingers, and then flicked it away.

"Yes. At least that's what we like to think."

Part Three

Snow, melting against skin

And after he had lain his hand on mine.
With joyful mien, whence I was comforted,
He led me in among the secret things.

— Dante Alighieri, *The Divine Comedy,*
Inferno, Canto III
[trans. Henry Wadsworth Longfellow]

"I'm not a sheet. I am a REAL ghost. BOO ... BOO ...
You're supposed to be scared!"
"But I'm not."

— Nationalteatern,* *Kåldolmar och kalsipper*

*Swedish rock/performance group

Thursday

Morgan's feet were freezing. The cold spell had arrived at about the same time as the submarine foundered, and it had only gotten worse during the past week. He loved his old cowboy boots but he couldn't fit thick socks in them. And anyway, there was a hole in one sole. Sure he could get some Chinese takeout for a hundred but he'd rather be cold.

It was nine-thirty in the morning and he was on his way home from the subway. He had been to the junkyard in Ulvsunda to see if they needed a hand, maybe make a couple of hundred, but business was bad. No winter boots this year either. He had had a cup of coffee with the guys in the office, which was overflowing with spare parts, catalogs, and pinup calendars, then headed to the subway.

Larry emerged from between the high-rises and, as usual, looked like he had just received a death sentence.

"Hey there, old man," Morgan yelled.

Larry nodded curtly, as if he had known from the moment he woke up this morning that Morgan would be standing here, then walked over to him.

"Hi. How's it going?"

"My toes are freezing, my car's at the junkyard, I have no work, and I'm on my way home to have a bowl of instant soup. How about you?"

Larry walked on in the direction of Björnsonsgatan, taking the path through the park.

"Thought I'd visit Herbert in the hospital. Coming?"

"Has his mind cleared up?"

"No, he's like he was before, I think."

"Then I'll pass. That kind of stuff gets me down. Last time he thought I was his mother, wanted me to tell him a story."

"And did you?"

"Sure. I told him the one about Goldilocks and the Three Bears. But no. I'm not in the mood today."

They kept walking. When Morgan saw that Larry was wearing a pair of thick gloves he realized his own hands were freezing and he pushed them—with some difficulty—into the narrow pockets of his denim jacket. The underpass where Jocke had disappeared came into view.

Maybe as a way to avoid talking about *that* Larry said:

"Did you see the paper this morning? Now Fälldin is saying that the Russians have nuclear weapons onboard."

"What did he think they had? Slingshots?"

"No, but . . . it's been there for a week now. What if it had blown up?"

"Don't worry about it. Those Russians know their stuff."

"You know I'm not a Communist."

"And I am?"

"Let's put it this way: who'd you vote for in the last election? The Liberals?"

"That doesn't mean I've pledged allegiance to Moscow."

They had been through this before. Now they took up the old routine in order not to see, not to have to think about *it* as they approached the underpass. But even so their voices died away as they walked under the bridge and came to a halt. Both of them had the impression it was the other guy who had stopped first. They looked at the piles of leaves that had turned into piles of snow, and that had taken on shapes that made them uneasy. Larry shook his head.

"What the hell do you do, you know?"

Morgan pushed his hands deeper into his pockets, stomping his feet to keep warm.

"Gösta's the only one who can do anything."

They both looked in the direction of Gösta's apartment. There were no curtains; the windowpane was streaked with dirt.

Larry held out a packet of cigarettes. Morgan took one, then Larry, who lit them both. They stood there smoking, contemplating the snowdrifts. After a while their thoughts were interrupted by the sound of children's voices.

A group of children carrying skates and helmets came streaming out of the school, led by a man with a military air. The children walked at intervals of a few meters from each other, almost in step. They passed Morgan and Larry. Morgan nodded at a kid he recognized from his building.

"Going off to war?"

The kid shook his head, was about to say something, but kept on marching, afraid of falling out of step. They kept on going toward the hospital; they were probably having a field trip of some sort. Morgan ground the cigarette under his foot, cupped his hands around his mouth, and shouted:

"Airborne attack! Take cover!"

Larry chuckled, extinguishing his cigarette.

"Jesus Christ. I didn't think that kind of teacher even existed anymore; the kind who wants even the coats to hang at attention. Are you going to come along?"

"No, not up for it today. But you run along. If you hurry you'll be able to fall in step with the rest."

"See you later."

"Will do."

They parted in the underpass. Larry left at a slow pace in the same direction as the children, and Morgan walked up the stairs. Now his entire body was freezing. Soup out of a packet wasn't so bad, particularly if you put a dash of milk in it.

†

Oskar was walking with his teacher. He needed to talk to someone and his teacher was the only one he could think of. Even so he would have switched groups given the chance. Jonny and Micke normally never chose the walking group when they had field trips, but they had today. They had whispered about something this morning, looking at him.

So Oskar walked with his teacher, not sure himself if it was for protection or because he needed to talk to a grown-up.

He had been going steady with Eli for five days now. They met every evening, outside. Oskar always told his mom he was going out to see Johan.

Yesterday evening Eli had come in through his window again. They had lain awake for a long time, told each other stories that started where the other person stopped. Then they had fallen asleep with their arms around each other and in the morning Eli was gone.

In his pocket, next to the old, well-thumbed, worn one there was now a new note that he had found on his desk this morning as he was getting ready to go to school.

I MUST BE GONE AND LIVE, OR STAY AND DIE. YOURS, ELI.

He knew it was a quote from *Romeo and Juliet*. Eli had told him that what she wrote in her first note came from there and Oskar had checked out the book from the school library. He liked it quite a bit, even though there were a lot of words he didn't understand. *Her vestal livery is but sick and green.* Did Eli understand all those words?

Jonny, Micke, and the girls were walking twenty meters behind Oskar and the teacher. They passed China Park where some daycare kids were sledding, their sharp cries slicing through the air. Oskar kicked at a clump of snow, lowered his voice and said:

"Marie-Louise?"

"Yes?"

"How do you know when you're in love?"

"Oh, I . . ."

His teacher pushed her hands into the pockets of her duffel coat and cast a glance at the sky. Oskar wondered if she was thinking of that guy that had come and waited for her at the school a few times. Oskar had not liked the look of him. He looked creepy.

"It depends on who you are, but . . . I would say that it's when you know . . . or at least when you really believe that this is the person you always want to be with."

"You mean, when you feel you can't live without that person."

"Yes, exactly. Two who can't live without the other . . . isn't that what love is?"

"Like *Romeo and Juliet*."

"Yes, and the bigger the obstacles . . . have you seen it?"

"Read it."

His teacher looked at him and gave him a smile that Oskar had always liked before but that he right now found a little disconcerting. He said quickly,

"What if it's two guys?"

"Then that's friendship. That's also a form of love. Or if you mean . . . well, two guys can also love each other in that way."

"How do they do it?"

His teacher lowered her voice.

"Well, not that there's anything wrong with it, but . . . if you want to. talk more about it we'll have to come back to it another time."

They walked a few paces in silence, arrived at the hill that led down to Kvarnviken Bay. Ghost Hill. His teacher drew the smell of pine forest deep into her lungs. Then she said:

"You form a covenant with someone, a union. Regardless of whether you're a boy or a girl you form a covenant saying that . . . that it's you and that person. Something just between the two of you."

Oskar nodded. He heard the girls' voices getting closer. Soon they would come and claim the teacher's attention. That's what normally happened. He was walking so close to his teacher that their coats touched, and he said:

"Can you be . . . both girl and boy at the same time? Or neither?"

"No, not people. There are some kinds of animals that . . ."

Michelle ran up to them and shouted in her squeaky voice: "Miss! Jonny put snow down my back!"

They were halfway down the hill. Shortly thereafter all the girls were there and told her what Jonny and Micke had done.

Oskar slowed down, fell back a few paces. He turned around. Jonny and Micke were at the top of the hill. They waved to Oskar, who didn't wave back. Instead he reached for a big branch on the side of the path, stripping the small twigs off it as he walked.

He passed the reputedly haunted house that gave the hill its name. A giant warehouse with walls of corrugated iron that looked completely out of place among the small trees. On the wall that faced the hill someone had sprayed in large letters:

CAN WE HAVE YOUR MOPED?

The girls and the teacher played tag, running down the path along the water. He was not planning to catch up to them. He knew Jonny and Micke were behind him. He gripped his stick more tightly, kept going.

It was nice out today. The ice had formed several days ago and now it was thick enough that the skating group could go out on it, led by Mr. Ávila. When Jonny and Micke said they wanted to join the walking group, Oskar had seriously thought about rushing home to grab his skates, switching groups. But he hadn't gotten new skates for two years, probably couldn't get his feet into the old ones anymore.

He was also scared of the ice.

Once when he was little he had been out with his dad in Södersvik, and his dad had gone out to check the fish traps. From his vantage point on the dock Oskar had seen his dad fall through the ice and how, for a terrifying second, his head had disappeared under the surface. Oskar was alone on the dock, started yelling for help at the top of his lungs. Fortunately his dad had an ice rescue pick in his pocket that he used to haul himself out of the water, but after that Oskar did not like to go out on the ice.

Someone grabbed him by his arms.

He quickly turned his head, saw that his teacher and the girls had disappeared down a curve in the path, behind the hill. Jonny said: "Piggy's going to take a bath."

Oskar grabbed the stick even more firmly, locking his hands around it. His only chance. They picked him up and started dragging him down to the ice.

"Piggy smells like shit and needs to wash."

"Let me go."

"Later. Take it easy. We'll let you go later."

Then they were on the ice. There was nothing for him to brace his feet against. They dragged him backwards, toward the sauna bathing hole. His heels made double tracks in the snow. In between them he dragged the stick, drawing a shallower line in the middle.

Far away on the ice he saw tiny moving figures. He screamed. Screamed for help.

"Holler away. Maybe they'll come in time to pull you out."

The open water gaped darkly only a few steps away. Oskar tensed all the muscles he could muster and flung himself to the side, twisting with a sudden wrenching motion. Micke lost his grip. Oskar dangled from Jonny's arms and swung the stick against his shin; it almost bounced out of his hand when wood met leg.

"Oww, damn!"

Jonny let go of him and Oskar fell to the ice. He got up at the edge of the hole in the ice, holding the stick in both hands. Jonny grabbed his shin.

"Fucking idiot. Now I'll fucking . . ."

Jonny approached him slowly, probably not daring to run because he was afraid of falling into the water himself if he pushed Oskar like that. He pointed at the stick.

"Put that down or I'll kill you. Get it?"

Oskar clenched his teeth. When Jonny was a little more than an arm's length away, Oscar swung the stick against his shoulder. Jonny ducked and Oskar felt a mute thwack in his hands when the heavy end of the stick struck Jonny square on the ear. He fell to the side like a bowling pin, landing outstretched on the ice, howling.

Micke, who had been a couple of steps behind Jonny, now started to back up, holding his hands in front of him.

"What the hell . . . we were just having some fun . . . didn't think . . ."

Oskar walked toward him, swinging the stick from side to side through the air with a low growl. Micke turned and ran back to shore. Oskar stopped and lowered his stick.

Jonny lay curled up on his side with his hand pressed against his ear. Blood was trickling out between his fingers. Oskar wanted to apologize. He hadn't meant to hurt him so bad. He crouched down next to Jonny, steadying himself on the stick, and he was about to say "sorry" but before he had a chance, he *saw* Jonny.

He was so small, curled up into a fetal position, whimpering "ow-owowow" while a thin trickle of blood ran down inside the collar of his coat. He was slowly turning his head back and forth.

Oskar looked at him in wonder.

That tiny bleeding bundle on the ice would not be able to do anything to him. Couldn't hit him or tease him. Couldn't even defend itself.

I could whack him a few more times and then it's all over.

Oskar stood up, leaned on the stick. The rush was ebbing away, replaced by a feeling of nausea that welled up from deep inside his stomach. What had he done? Jonny must be really hurt to be bleeding like that. What if he bled to death? Oskar sat down on the ice again, pulled off one shoe and removed his wool sock. He crawled over to Jonny on his knees, poked the hand that he was holding to his ear, and pushed the wool sock into it.

"Here. Take this."

Jonny grabbed the sock and pressed it to his wounded ear. Oskar looked up over the ice. He saw a person on skates approaching. A grown-up.

Shrill screams from far away. Children, screaming in panic. A single high, penetrating shriek that was joined by others after a few seconds. The person who had been on his way over, stopped. Stood motionless for a second, then turned and skated back.

Oskar was still kneeling beside Jonny, felt the snow melting, dampening his knees. Jonny had his eyes shut, whimpering from between clenched teeth. Oskar lowered his face closer to his.

"Can you walk?"

Jonny opened his mouth to say something and a yellow- and white-colored liquid gushed out from between his lips, coloring the snow. A little landed on one of Oskar's hands. He looked at the slimy drops that quivered on the back of his hands and became really scared. He dropped the stick and ran toward land to get some help.

The children's screams from next to the hospital had increased in volume. He ran toward them.

†

Mr. Ávila, Fernando Cristóbal de Reyes y Ávila, enjoyed ice skating. Yes. One of the things he most appreciated about Sweden was the long winters. He had participated in the Vasa cross-country ski race for ten consecutive years now, and whenever the waters of the outer archipelago froze solid he drove out to Gräddö Island on the weekends in order to skate out as far toward Söderarm as the ice cover allowed.

It was three years ago since the archipelago had frozen last, but an early winter such as this one gave him hope. Of course Gräddö Island would be crawling with skating enthusiasts if the waters froze, but that was in the daytime. Mr. Ávila preferred to skate at night.

With all due respect to the Vasa Race, it did make one feel like one of a thousand ants in a colony that had suddenly decided to emigrate. It was quite different to be on the open ice, alone in the moonlight. Fernando Ávila was only a lukewarm Catholic, but even he could feel in those moments that God was near.

The rhythmic scrape of the metal blades, the moonlight that gave the ice a leaden gleam, above him the stars vaulted in their infinity, the cold wind streaming over his face, eternity and depth and space in all directions. Life could not be bigger.

A little boy was tugging on his pant leg.

"Teacher, I have to pee."

Ávila woke from his skating dreams and looked around, pointed to some trees by the shore that grew out over the water; the bare network of branches fell like a shielding curtain toward the ice.

"You can pee there."

The boy squinted at the trees.

"On the ice?"

"Yes? What is wrong with that? Makes new ice. Yellow."

The boy looked at him as if he were crazy, but skated off toward the trees.

Ávila looked around and made sure none of the older ones had wandered too far. With a few quick strokes he took off to get an overview of the situation. Counted the children. Yes. Nine, plus the one who was peeing. Ten.

He turned the other way and looked in toward Kvarnviken, stopped.

Something was happening down there. A group of bodies approaching something that had to be an opening in the ice, the spot marked by small straggly trees. While he stood still, watching, the group broke up. He saw that one of them was holding a stick.

The stick was swung and one boy fell down. He heard a howl. Turning around, he checked his own group one last time, then set off swiftly toward the figures by the hole. One of them was now running toward land.

That was when he heard the scream.

The piercing scream of a child from his group. The snow spurted up around his blades as he made an abrupt halt. He had managed to ascertain that the kids by the hole were older. Maybe Oskar. Older boys. They would manage. His charges were younger.

The scream increased in intensity and when he turned and skated toward it he heard more voices join in.

Cojones!

Something happened in the exact moment when he was not there. Dear God, let the ice not have given way. He skated as fast as he could, the snow whirling around his blades as he sprinted toward the source of the scream. He saw now that many children had gathered, were standing and screaming hysterically in a choir of sorts, and more were on their way. He also saw that an adult was moving down toward the ice from up by the hospital.

With a few final strong pushes he arrived next to the children, and stopped so hard a fine ice-dust sprayed over the children's jackets. He did not understand. All the children were gathered next to the network of branches, looking down toward the ice, and shrieking.

He skated closer.

"What is it?"

One of the children pointed down toward the ice, to a lump that was frozen into it. It looked like a brown, frozen clump of grass with a red line on one side. Or a run-over hedgehog. He leaned down toward the clump and saw that it was a head. A human head frozen into the ice so that only the top of the head and forehead were visible.

The boy he had sent off to pee here was sitting on the ice a few meters away, sobbing.

"I—I—I ra-a-an into it."

Ávila straightened up.

"Get away! Everyone goes back onto land *now!*"

The children seemed as if they were also frozen in place in the ice; the little ones kept crying. He took out his whistle and blew into it sharply, twice. The screams stopped. He took a few pushes to position himself behind the children in order to herd them toward the shore. The children went. Only a fifth grader stayed where he was, leaning down toward the clump, full of curiosity.

"You too!"

Ávila gestured to him with his hand, indicating he should come over. Once they were on land he said to the woman who had come down from the hospital, "Call the police. An ambulance. There is a body frozen into the ice."

The woman ran back up to the hospital. Ávila counted the children on land, saw that one was missing. The boy who had run into the head was still sitting on the ice with his face in his hands. Ávila glided out to him and lifted him up by his armpits. The boy turned around and put his arms around Ávila, who lifted the boy as gently as if he were a fragile package and carried him to shore.

†

Can I talk to him?"

"He can't actually talk . . ."

"No, but he understands what is said to him."

"I would think so but . . ."

"Just for a little while."

Through the fog that clouded his vision Håkan saw a man in dark clothes pull up a chair and sit down next to his bed. He could not make out the man's features, but there was probably a serious expression on his face.

The last few days Håkan had been floating in and out of a red cloud scored through with lines as thin as hairs. He knew that they had anesthetized him a couple of times, operated on him. This was the first day he was fully conscious, but he did not know how many days had passed since he first came here.

Earlier this morning Håkan had been exploring his new face with the fingers on his feeling hand. A rubberlike bandage covered his whole face, but from what little he was able to make out after painfully exploring the contours protruding under the bandage with his fingertips, he concluded he no longer had a face.

Håkan Bengtsson no longer existed. All that was left of him was an unidentified body in a hospital bed. They would of course be able to connect him with the other murders, but not to his earlier or present life. Not to Eli.

"How are you feeling?"

Oh, very well, officer, thank you. Couldn't be better. It feels as if someone has applied burning napalm to my face but other than that I can't complain.

"Yes, I understand that you can't speak, but perhaps you can nod if you hear what I am saying? Can you nod?"

I can, but I don't want to.

The man next to his bed sighed.

"You tried to kill yourself by doing this, so clearly you are not completely . . . gone. Is it hard for you to raise your head? Can you lift your hand if you hear me? Can you lift your hand?"

Håkan disconnected himself from all thoughts of the policeman and instead started to think about the place in Dante's Hell, Limbo, where all the great souls from Earth without knowledge of Christ went after death. Tried to imagine the place in detail.

"We would like to know who you are, you see."

Which circle did Dante himself go to after death . . .

The policeman pulled his chair even closer.

"We'll find that out, you know. Sooner or later. You could save us some legwork by communicating with us now."

No one misses me. No one knows me. Go ahead, try.

A nurse came in. "There's a telephone call for you."

The policemanman stood up, walked over to the door. Before he walked out he turned around.

"I'll be back."

Håkan's thoughts now returned to more significant matters. Which circle was he destined for? The circle of child murderers? That was the seventh circle. On the other hand, maybe the first circle. Those who sinned for love's sake. Then, of course, the sodomites had their own circle. The most reasonable thing would be to assume you went to the circle that represented your worst crime. Therefore: if you had committed an absolutely terrible crime you could thereafter sin away all you liked with the crimes punished in higher circles. It couldn't get worse. Like murderers in the USA who were sentenced to three hundred years in prison.

The different circles whirled in their spiral patterns. The funnel of Hell. Cerberus with his tail. Håkan imagined the violent men, the bitter women, the proud ones in their boiling pots, in their fire rain, wandering among them, looking for their place.

One thing he was completely sure of. He would never end up in the lowest circle. The one where Lucifer himself chewed on Judas and Brutus, standing in a sea of ice. The circle of traitors.

The door opened again, with that strange, sucking sound. The policeman sat down next to the bed.

"Hello again. It seems like they've found another one, down by the lake in Blackeberg. Same rope, in any case."

No!

Håkan's body flinched involuntarily when the policeman said Blackeberg. The policeman nodded. "Apparently you can hear me. That's good. We can assume you live in the western suburbs then. Where? Råcksta? Vällingby? Blackeberg?"

The memory of how he had disposed of the man down by the hospital raced through his head. He had been sloppy. He had screwed up.

"OK, then I am going to leave you alone. You can think about if you want to cooperate. It'll be easier that way. Don't you think?"

The policeman stood up and left. In his place a nurse came in and sat down in the chair, keeping watch.

Håkan started to toss his head from side to side, in denial. His hand went out and started to tug on the tube to the respirator. The nurse quickly jumped up and tore his hand away.

"We'll have to tie you up. One more time and we'll tie you up. Understood? If you don't want to live that's your business but as long as you're here our job is to keep you alive. Regardless of what you have or haven't done. Got it? And we will do what we have to in order to get through this even if it means putting restraints on you. Do you hear me? Everything will be better for you if you cooperate."

Cooperate. Cooperate. Suddenly everyone wants to cooperate. I am no longer a person. I am a project. Oh my God. Eli, Eli. Help me.

†

Oskar heard his mom's voice as soon as he was in the stairwell. She was talking to someone on the phone, and she sounded angry. Jonny's mom? He stopped outside the door and listened.

"They're going to call me and ask me what I've done wrong . . . oh yes, they will, and what do I say? Sorry, but you see, my boy doesn't have a father and that . . . but live up to it then . . . no, you haven't . . . I think you should talk to him about this."

Oskar unlocked the door and stepped into the hall. His mom said, "That's him now" into the receiver and turned to Oskar.

"They called from school and I . . . you'll have to talk to your dad about this because I . . ." She talked into the receiver again. "Now you can . . . I am calm . . . it's easy for you to say, sitting out there . . ."

Oskar went into his room, lay down on his bed and put his hands over his face. It felt like his heart was beating in his head.

When he'd reached the hospital he had initially thought that all the people running around had something to do with Jonny. But it had turned out that wasn't it. Today he had seen a dead person for the first time in his life.

His mom opened the door to his room. Oskar removed his hands from his head.

"Your father wants to talk to you."

Oskar held the receiver to his ear and heard a distant voice reciting the names of lighthouses and wind strength, wind direction. He waited with the receiver to his ear without saying anything. His mom frowned and looked questioningly at him. Oskar put his hand over the earpiece and whispered: "the marine weather report."

His mom opened her mouth as if to say something, but only came out with a sigh and let her hands drop. She walked out into the kitchen. Oskar sat down on the chair in the hall and listened to the marine weather report along with his dad.

He knew his dad would remain distracted by what was said on the radio if Oskar tried to start a conversation now. The sea report was holy. Those times he was at his dad's, all activity in the house came to a stop at 16:45 and his dad sat down next to the radio while staring absently out over the fields, as if to check that what they were saying on the radio was true.

It was a long time since his dad had been at sea, but old habits died hard.

Almagrundet northwest eight, toward evening turning to the west. Good visibility. The Åland Sea and Archipelago area northwest ten, toward evening warning for gale-force winds. Good visibility.

There. The most important part of it was over.

"Hi Dad."

"Oh, it's you. Hi there. We're going to have gale-force winds here toward evening."

"Yeah, I heard."

"Hm. How are things?"

"Good."

"You know, your mom just told me about this thing with Jonny. That doesn't sound so good."

"No, I guess not."

"He got a concussion."

"Yeah, he threw up."

"That's a common side effect. Harry . . . yes, you've met him . . . he took the lead weight in the side of the head once and he . . . well, he lay there on deck and was sick as a calf after that."

"Was he OK?"

"Sure he was . . . well, he died last spring. But that wasn't anything to do with that. No. He got better real fast."

"Good."

"And we'll have to hope the same goes for this boy, too."

"Yes."

The voice on the radio kept reciting names of various sea regions: Bottenviken and all the rest. A couple of times he had sat at his dad's place with an atlas in front of him and followed all the lighthouses as they were named. For a while he knew all the places by heart, in order, but he had since forgotten them. His dad cleared his throat.

"Yes, your mom and I were talking about it . . . if you wanted to come out and see me this weekend."

"Mmmm."

"So we could talk more about this and about . . . everything."

"This weekend?"

"Yes, if you feel like it."

"I guess so. But I have a little . . . what about Saturday?"

"Or Friday night."

"No, but . . . Saturday. Morning."

"That sounds good. I'll take an eider duck out of the freezer."

Oskar pressed the mouthpiece closer and whispered: "Preferably without shot."

His dad laughed.

Last fall when Oskar had been out at his place he had broken a tooth on some shot left in a sea bird that they had eaten. He had told his mom it was a stone in a potato. Sea bird was Oskar's favorite food, but his mom thought it was "terribly cruel" to shoot such defenceless birds. If she knew he had broken a tooth on the instrument of murder itself it might lead to a moratorium on eating that kind of food altogether.

"I'll check extra carefully," his dad said.

"Is the moped running?"

"Yes, why?"

"No, I was just thinking."

"I see. Well, there's a fair amount of snow so we can probably make a round."

"Good."

"OK, I'll see you on Saturday. You'll take the ten o'clock bus."

"Yes."

"I'll come meet you. With the moped. The car is not completely functional."

"OK, great. Are you going to talk more to Mom?"

"Uh . . . no . . . you can tell her our plans, right?"

"Uh-huh. See you."

"That you will. Bye."

Oskar put the phone down. Sat there for a little while and imagined how it was going to be. Taking the moped out for a ride. That was fun. Oskar would strap on the mini-skis and they attached a rope to the moped carrier with a stick at the other end. Oskar held the tow rope with both hands and then he motored around the village like a snowborne waterskier. This as well as duck with rowanberry jelly. And only *one* night away from Eli.

He went to his room and packed up his workout gear, plus his knife, since he wasn't coming home before meeting Eli. He had a plan. When he was standing in the hall putting his coat on his mom came out of the kitchen and dried her floury hands on the apron. "So? What did he say?"

"I'm going to his place on Saturday."

"Fine, but what about the other thing?"

"I have to go work out now."

"He didn't say anything else?"

"Ye-es, but I have to go now."

"Where?"

"The pool."

"What pool?"

"The one next to our school. The little one."

"What are you doing there?"

"Working out. I'll be back around half past eight. Or nine. I'm meeting Johan afterwards."

His mom looked dismayed, didn't know what to do with her floury hands and stuck them both in the big pocket on the front of the apron.

"Yes, I see. Be careful. Don't trip on the side of the pool or anything. Do you have your hat with you?"

"Yes, yes."

"Well, put it on. When you've been in the water, because it's cold out and when your hair is wet and . . ."

Oskar took a step forward, kissed her lightly on the cheek and said: "good-bye," and left. When he came out of the front door to the building he glanced up at his window. His mom was standing there, with her hands still pushed into the big apron pocket. Oskar waved. His mom slowly lifted up a hand and waved back.

He cried half the way to the pool.

†

The gang stood assembled in the stairwell outside Gösta's door. Lacke, Virginia, Morgan, Larry, Karlsson. No one wanted to be the one to ring the doorbell, since this seemed to give the person who rang the responsibility to declare the reason for their visit. Even out in the stairwell you got a whiff of Gösta. Urine. Morgan poked Karlsson in the side and mumbled something. Karlsson lifted the earmuffs he wore instead of a hat and asked: "What?"

"I said, don't you think you can take those off for once? Makes you look like an idiot."

"That's your opinion."

But he removed the earmuffs, put them in the coat pocket and said:

"It'll have to be you, Larry. You're the one who saw it."

Larry sighed and rang the doorbell. An angry yowl from inside and then a soft thud as something landed on the floor. Larry cleared his throat. He didn't like this. Felt like a cop with the whole gang behind him; the only thing missing was the cocked pistols. Shuffled steps came from inside the apartment, then a voice.

"Are you alright, sweetheart?"

The door opened. A wave of urine-stench washed over Larry's face and he struggled for breath. Gösta was standing in the doorway, dressed in a worn shirt, vest, and tie. An orange- and white-striped cat was curled up under one arm.

"Yes?"

"Hi, Gösta. How's it going?"

Gösta's eyes roamed over their faces. He was pretty drunk.

"Fine."

"So, we're all here because . . . do you know what's happened?"

"No."

"Well, you see, they've found Jocke. Today."

"I see. Oh. Yes."

"And then . . . you know . . ."

Larry turned his head, seeking support from his delegation. The only thing he got was an encouraging gesture from Morgan. Larry couldn't handle standing out here like some official representative, presenting his ultimatum. There was only one way, however much he didn't like it. He asked: "Can we come in?"

He had anticipated some kind of resistance. Gösta was hardly used to five people dropping by to see him like this. But Gösta simply nodded and backed up a few steps in the hall to let them in.

Larry hesitated for a moment; the smell emanating from inside the apartment was unbelievable. It hovered in the air like viscous matter. During this moment of hesitation Lacke took a step inside, followed by Virginia. Lacke scratched the cat—still in Gösta's arms—behind the ears.

"Nice cat. What's its name?"

"It's a she. Thisbe."

"Nice name. Do you have a Pyramus as well?"

"No."

One by one they glided in through the door, tried to breathe through their mouths. After a minute everyone gave up the attempt to keep the stench at bay, relaxed, and got used to it. Cats were shooed out of the couch and armchair, a few chairs were carried out from the kitchen, vodka, grape tonic, and glasses appeared on the table, and after a few minutes of chitchat about cats and the weather Gösta said:

"So, they found Jocke."

Larry downed the last of his drink. His task felt easier with the warmth of the alcohol in his stomach. He poured himself a new glass and said, "Yes, down by the hospital. His body was frozen into the ice."

"In the ice?"

"Yes. Damned circus down there today. I was down there to see Herbert, don't know if you know him, anyway . . . when I came out there were cops everywhere and an ambulance and after a while the fire truck came."

"There was a fire?"

"No, but they had to hack him out of the ice. Well, at that point I didn't know it was him but then when they got him up on land I recognized the clothes, because the face . . . there had been ice all around it, so you couldn't . . . but the clothes . . ."

Gösta waved his hand in the air as if he was petting a big, invisible dog.

"Wait a minute now . . . so he drowned? . . . I mean, I don't understand . . ." Larry sipped his drink, wiped his hand over his mouth.

"No, that was what the cops thought at first too. At first. From what I understand. They were mostly standing around up there with their arms folded and the ambulance guys were all busy with some kid who turned up bleeding from his head, so there was . . ."

Gösta petted the invisible dog even more energetically, or he was trying to push it away. A little of his drink splashed out of his glass and landed on the rug.

"Hang on a minute . . . now I can't . . . bleeding from his head?"

Morgan put down the cat he had been holding on his lap, and brushed off his pants.

"That had nothing to do with it. Come on now, Larry."

"Yes, but then when they got him up on land. And I saw that it was him. And then you also saw that there was a rope like this, see. Tied up. And there were some kind of stones wrapped up in the rope like that. That got the cops going. Started talking into their radios and cordoning off the area with tape and shooing people away and all that. Got really interested all of a sudden. So that . . . well, turns out someone must have tried to dump his body there, pure and simple."

Gösta leaned back in the couch, holding his hand over his eyes. Virginia, who was sitting between him and Lacke, patted his knee. Morgan filled his glass and said: "The thing is they found Jocke, right? Want some tonic with that? Here. They found Jocke and now they know he was murdered. And that kind of changes things, don't you think?"

Karlsson cleared his throat, and said in a commanding tone:

"In the Swedish judicial system there's something called . . ."

"You shut up," Morgan interrupted. "Is it alright if I smoke?"

Gösta nodded feebly. While Morgan was taking out his cigarette and lighter Lacke leaned over in the sofa so he could look Gösta in the eye.

"Gösta. You saw what happened. That story should be told."

"Be told. How?"

"By going to the police and telling them what you saw. That's all."

"No . . . No."

The room got quiet.

Lacke sighed, poured himself half a glass of vodka and a little dash of tonic, took a big gulp, and closed his eyes as the burning cloud filled his stomach. He didn't want to force him.

Back at the Chinese restaurant Karlsson had ranted about the duty of a witness and legal responsibility but however much Lacke wanted the person who had done this to be caught he had no intention of sending the cops to a friend like some squealer.

A gray-speckled cat pushed its head against his shins. He picked it up into his lap and stroked it absently. *What does it matter?* Jocke was dead, he knew that now for sure. What did the rest matter, anyway?

Morgan got up, walked over to the window with the glass in his hand. "Was this where you were standing? When you saw it?"

". . . yes."

Morgan nodded, sipped the drink.

"Yes, I get it. You can see everything from here. Great place, actually. Nice view. Yes, I mean apart from . . . great view."

A tear ran quietly down Lacke's cheek. Virginia took his hand and squeezed it. Lacke took another big gulp to burn away the pain that was tearing at his chest.

Larry, who for a time had been watching the cats moving around the room in senseless patterns, drummed his fingers against his glass and said:

"What if we simply tipped them off? About the location, I mean. Maybe they can find some fingerprints and . . . whatever else it is they find."

Karlsson smiled.

"And how do we say we got this information? That we just know it? They're going to be pretty interested in how . . . in who we got this information from."

"We could make an anonymous call. Just to get the information out there."

Gösta mumbled something from the couch. Virginia leaned her head in toward him.

"What did you say?"

Gösta spoke in a very small voice as he stared into his drink.

"Please forgive me. But I'm too scared. I can't."

Morgan turned back from the window, held his arm out.

"That's how it is, then. Nothing more to talk about." He gave Karlsson a sharp look. "We'll have to think of an alternative. Do it some other way. Maybe make a sketch, call, whatever. We'll think of something."

He walked over to Gösta and nudged his foot with his own.

"Hey you, now. Pull yourself together. We'll take care of this thing anyway. Take it easy. Gösta? Can you hear me? We'll take care of this. Cheers!"

He stretched out his glass, clinked it against Gösta's and took a sip. "We'll fix this thing. Won't we?"

†

He had left the others outside the gymnasium and started to head home when he heard her voice coming from the school.

"Psst. Oskar!"

Footsteps on stairs and she emerged from the shadows. She had been sitting there, waiting. Then she heard him say good-bye to the others and how they answered as if he was a completely normal person.

The workout session had been good. He wasn't as weak as he had thought, was able to do more than a couple of the guys who had been there several times before. And his concern that Mr. Ávila would interrogate him about what had happened out there on the ice today turned out to be unfounded. Mr. Ávila had simply asked: "Do you want to talk about it?" and when Oskar shook his head they left it at that.

The gym was another world, separate from school. Mr. Ávila was less severe and the other guys left him alone. Micke hadn't been there, of course. Was Micke scared of him now? The thought was enough to make his head spin.

He walked over to meet Eli.

"Hi."

"Hey."

Without saying anything about it they had switched their words of greeting. Eli was wearing a checkered shirt that was much too big for her and she looked . . . shriveled again. Her skin was dry and her face thinner. Even yesterday Oskar had seen the first white hairs and tonight there were many more.

When she was healthy Oskar thought she was the cutest girl he had seen. But the way she looked right now she was . . . you couldn't compare her to anyone. No one looked like that. Dwarves, maybe. But dwarves weren't thin like that . . . nothing was. He was grateful she hadn't appeared in front of the others.

"How's it going?" he asked.

"So so."

"Want to do something?"

"Of course."

They walked home side by side. Oskar had a plan. They were going to enter into a pact together. If they entered into a pact together, Eli would become healthy. A magical thought, inspired by the books he had read. But magic . . . surely there was a little magic in the world. The people who denied the existence of magic, they were the ones that it went badly for.

They walked into the yard. He touched Eli's shoulder.

"Should we check the garbage room?"

"OK."

They walked in through Eli's front door and Oskar unlocked the door to the basement.

"Don't you have a basement key?" he asked.

"I don't think so."

It was pitch black in the basement entrance. The door slammed shut behind them with a heavy sound. They stood still, side by side, breathing. Oskar whispered:

"Eli, you know what? Today . . . Jonny and Micke tried to throw me into the water. Into a hole in the ice."

"No! You—"

"Wait. Do you know what I did? I had a stick, a big stick. I hit Jonny in the head with it so he started to bleed. He got a concussion, went to the hospital. I never ended up in the water. I . . . beat him."

Quiet for a few moments. Then Eli said:

"Oskar."

"Yes."

"Yippee."

Oskar stretched his hand to the light switch; he wanted to see her face. Turned it on. She was staring straight into his eyes and he saw her pupils. For a few moments before they got used to the light they looked like those crystals they talked about in physics class, what were they called . . . elliptical.

Like a lizard. No. Cats. Cats.

Eli blinked. Her pupils were normal again.

"What is it?"

"Nothing. Come on . . ."

Oskar walked over to the bulk item trash room and opened the door. The bag was almost full, hadn't been emptied for a while. Eli squeezed in beside him and they rummaged through the trash. Oskar found a bag with empty bottles that you could get a deposit back on. Eli found a plastic sword, waved it around, said:

"Should we check the one next door?"

"No, Tommy and those guys might be there."

"Who are they?"

"Oh, some older guys who use a basement storage unit . . . they hang out there in the evening."

"Are there a lot of them?"

"No, three. Most of the time it's just Tommy."

"And they're dangerous?"

Oskar shrugged. "Let's check it out, then."

They walked out through Oskar's building into the next basement corridor, all the way into Tommy's building. As Oskar stood there with a key in his hand, about to unlock the last door, he hesitated. If they were in there? If they caught sight of Eli? If they . . . it could turn into something he wasn't able to handle. Eli held the plastic sword in front of her. "What is it?"

"Nothing."

He unlocked the door. As soon as they walked into the corridor he heard music coming from the storage unit. As he turned to her he whispered: "They're here! Come on."

Eli stopped, sniffed.

"What's that smell?"

Oskar checked to make sure that nothing was moving around at the other end of the corridor, then sniffed the air. Couldn't smell anything except the usual basement air. Eli said, "Paint, glue." Oscar sniffed again. He couldn't smell it but he knew what it had to be. When he turned back to Eli to get her to follow him he saw that she was doing something with the lock.

"Come on. What are you doing?"

"I'm just . . ."

As Oskar was unlocking the door to the next basement corridor, their path of retreat, the door fell shut behind them. It didn't make the normal sound. No click, just a metallic clunk. On the way back to their basement he told Eli about glue-sniffing; how crazy those guys could get when they did that.

He felt safe again in his own basement. He knelt down and started to count the bottles in the bag. Fourteen beer bottles and a liquor bottle with no deposit value.

When he looked up to report this to Eli she was standing in front of him with the plastic sword held up as if about to attack. Used to sudden blows as he was, he flinched a little. But Eli mumbled something and lowered the sword against his shoulder and said, with as deep a voice as she could muster:

"I herewith dub you, Jonny's conqueror, knight of Blackeberg and all surrounding areas like Vällingby . . . um . . ."

"Råcksta."

"Råcksta."

"Maybe Ängby?"

"Ängby maybe."

Eli tapped him lightly on the shoulder for each new area. Oskar took his knife out of the bag, held it out, and proclaimed that he was the Knight of Ängby Maybe. Wanted Eli to be the Beautiful Maiden he would rescue from the Dragon.

But Eli was a terrible monster who ate beautiful maidens for lunch and she was the one he would have to fight. Oskar left the knife in his sheath as they fought, shouted, and ran around in the corridors. In the middle of their game they heard a scrape in the lock to the basement doors.

They quickly piled into a food cellar where they hardly had room to sit hip against hip, and breathed quickly and quietly. They heard a man's voice.

"What are you doing down here?"

Oskar and Eli held their breath as the man waited, listening. Then he said: "Damn kids" and left. They stayed in the food cellar until they were sure the man had gone, then they crawled out, leaned against the wooden wall, giggling. After a while Eli stretched out on the concrete floor and stared up at the ceiling.

Oskar touched her foot.

"Are you tired?"

"Yes. Tired."

Oskar pulled his knife out of the sheath, looked at it. It was heavy, beautiful. He carefully pressed his pointed finger against the tip, then removed it. A small red dot. He pressed again, harder. When he took his finger away a pearl-shaped drop of blood came out. But this wasn't the way to do it.

"Eli? Do you want to do something?"

She was still staring up at the ceiling.

"What?"

"Do you want to . . . enter into a pact with me?"

"Yes."

If she had asked him "how?" he would maybe have told her what he was thinking before he did it. But she simply said "yes." She wanted to do it, whatever it was. Oskar swallowed hard, gripped the knife so the edge was resting against the palm of his hand, shut his eyes, and pulled the blade out of his hand. A stinging, smarting pain. He caught his breath.

Did I do this?

He opened his eyes, opened his hand. Yes. A thin trickle of blood was revealed in his palm. The blood pushed out slowly, not as he had thought in a thin line but as a string of pearls that he stared at with fascination as they merged into a thicker, uneven mass.

Eli lifted her head.

"What are you doing?"

Oskar was still holding his hand in front of his face, staring at it, and said:

"It's easy, Eli, it wasn't even . . ."

He held his bleeding hand toward her. Her eyes widened. She shook her head violently while she crawled backward, away from his hand.

"No, Oskar . . ."

"What is it?"

"Oskar, no."

"It almost doesn't hurt at all."

Eli stopped backing up, staring at his hand while she kept shaking her head. Oskar was holding the knife by the blade in his other hand, held it out to her handle first.

"You only have to prick yourself in a finger or something. Then we'll mix our blood. And then we have our pact."

Eli did not take the knife. Oskar put it down on the floor so he could catch a drop of blood that fell from his wound.

"Come on. Don't you want to?"

"Oskar . . . we can't. You would be infected, you—"

"It doesn't feel like that, it . . ."

A ghost flew into Eli's face, distorting it into something so different from the girl he knew that he completely forgot about catching the blood that dropped from his hand. She now looked like the monster they had recently pretended that she was and Oskar jumped back while the pain in his hand intensified.

"Eli, what . . ."

She sat up, pulled her legs under her, crouched on all fours, and stared straight at his bleeding hand, took a step closer toward it. Stopped, clenched her teeth, and got out a gruff: "Leave!"

Tears of fear welled up in Oskar's eyes. "Eli, stop it. Stop playing. Stop it."

Eli crawled a bit closer, stopped again. She forced her body to contort itself so her head was lowered to the ground and screamed:

"Go! Or you'll die!"

Oskar got up, took a few steps back. His feet hit against the bag of bottles so it fell over, with a clinking sound. He flattened himself against the wall while Eli crawled over to the little smear of blood that had fallen from his hand.

Another bottle fell over and broke against the concrete floor while Oskar stood pressed against the wall and stared at Eli, who stretched out her tongue and licked the dirty concrete, whisked her tongue around on the place where blood had fallen.

A bottle clinked softly and stopped moving. Eli licked and licked the floor. When she lifted her face to him there was a gray smear of dirt on the tip of her nose. "Go . . . please . . . leave."

Then the ghost flew into her face again, but before it had time to take over she got up and ran down the corridor, opened the door to her stairwell, and disappeared.

Oskar stood there with the damaged hand tightly wrapped. Blood was starting to well out around the edges. He opened it, looked at the cut. It had gone deeper than he had intended, but it wasn't dangerous, he thought. Some blood was already starting to congeal.

He looked at the by-now pale splotch on the floor. Then he gingerly licked a little of the blood on his palm, spit it out.

†

Night lights.

Tomorrow they would operate on his mouth and throat, probably in the hopes that something would come out. His tongue was still there. He could move it around in the sealed cavity of his mouth, tickle his upper jaw with it. Maybe he would be able to talk again even though his lips were gone. But he did not intend to talk again.

A woman, he didn't know if she was from the police or a nurse, sat in the corner a few meters away, reading a book and keeping an eye on him.

They allot so much of their resources when a nobody decides his life is over?

He realized that he was valuable, that he meant a lot to them. Probably they were digging around in old records right now, cases they hoped to be able to solve with him as the perpetrator. A policeman had been in yesterday to take his fingerprints. He had not made any resistance. It didn't matter.

It was possible that the fingerprints would link him to the murders in both Växjö and Norrköping. He tried to remember how he had proceeded there, if he had left fingerprints or other traces. Probably.

The only thing that worried him was that by way of these events people could track down Eli.

People . . .

†

They had put notes in his mailbox, threatened him.

Someone who worked at the post office and who lived in the area had tipped off the other neighbors about what kind of mail, what kind of videos he received.

It took about a month before he was fired from his job at the school. You couldn't have someone like that working with children. He had walked away willingly, even though he could probably have brought it up with the union.

He hadn't actually done anything at the school; he wasn't that stupid. The campaign against him had increased in strength and finally one night someone had thrown a firebomb through his living room window. He had fled out onto the lawn in only his underpants, stood there and watched his life burn to the ground.

The crime investigation dragged on in time and therefore he didn't get the insurance money. With his meager savings he had taken the train, rented a room in Växjö. That's where he started working on trying to die.

He drank himself down to the level where he used whatever was at hand. Aco acne-solution, T-Röd denatured alcohol. He stole wine-making kits and Turbo yeast from hardware stores and drank everything before it was ready.

He was outside as much as possible. In some way he wanted "the people" to see him die, day for day.

In his drunken stupor he became careless, fondled young boys, got beaten up, ended up at the police station. Once he sat in jail for three days and puked his guts out. Was released. Kept drinking.

One evening when Håkan was sitting on a bench next to a playground with a bottle of half-yeasted wine in a plastic bag, Eli came and sat down beside him. In his drunkenness Håkan had almost immediately put a hand on Eli's thigh. Eli had let it stay there, taken Håkan's head between her hands, turned it toward her, and said: "You are going to be with me."

Håkan had mumbled something about how he couldn't afford such a beauty right now but when his finances allowed . . .

Eli had moved his hand from her thigh, leaned down, and taken his wine bottle, poured it out and said: "You don't understand. You're going to stop drinking now. You are going to be with me. You are going to help me. I need you. And I'm going to help you." Then Eli had held out her hand, Håkan had taken it, and they had walked away together.

He had stopped drinking and entered into Eli's service.

Eli had given him money to buy some clothes and to rent another apartment. He had done everything without wondering whether Eli was "evil" or "good" or anything else. Eli was beautiful and Eli had given him back his dignity. And in rare moments . . . tenderness.

†

The pages rustled when the night guard turned them in the book she was reading. Probably a dime store novel. In Plato's republic the "Guards" were supposed to be the most highly educated among the people. But this was Sweden, 1981, and they were probably reading Jan Guillou.

The man in the water, the man whose corpse he had sunk. That had been clumsy of him, of course. He should have done as Eli said and buried him. But nothing about the man would be traced back to Eli. The bite mark in his neck would be regarded as unusual, but they would think the blood had been washed away by the water. The man's clothes were . . .

Her top!

Eli's top, the one Håkan had found on the man's body when he first came to take care of it. He should have taken it home with him, burned it, anything.

Instead he had tucked it inside the man's coat. How would they interpret that? A child's top, spotted with blood. Was there a risk that someone had seen this shirt on Eli? Someone who would recognize it? If it were displayed in the paper, for example? Someone Eli had met before, someone who . . .

Oskar. The boy next door.

Håkan's body twisted restlessly in the bed. The guard put her book down and looked at him.

"Don't do anything stupid."

†

Eli crossed Björnsonsgatan, continued into the courtyard between the nine-story buildings, two monolithic lighthouses towering over the crouching three-story buildings scattered around. No one was outside, but there was light coming from the gymnasium and Eli slithered up the fire escape ladder, looked in.

Music was blaring out of a small tape player. Middle-aged women were jumping around in time to the music so the wooden floor shook. Eli curled up in the metal grating of the stairs, leaned her chin on her knees, and took in the scene.

Several of the women were overweight and their massive breasts were bouncing like cheery bowling balls under their T-shirts. The women jumped and skipped, lifting their knees so the flesh trembled in their too-tight workout pants. They moved in a circle, clapped their hands, jumped again. All the while the music kept going. Warm, oxygenated blood streaming through thirsty muscles.

But there were too many of them.

Eli jumped down from the fire escape, landed softly on the frozen ground underneath, continued around the back of the gym, and stopped outside the swimming pool.

The large frosted windows projected rectangles of light onto the snow cover. Over each large window there was a smaller, narrow window made of regular glass. Eli jumped up and hung from the edge of the roof with her hands, looked in. No one was inside. The surface of the pool glittered in the glow of the halogen lights. A few balls were floating in the middle.

Swim. Splash. Play.

Eli swayed back and forth, a dark pendulum. Looked at the balls, saw them flying through the air, thrown up again, laughter and screams and splashing water. Eli relaxed her hold on the edge of the roof, fell down, and consciously let herself land so hard that it hurt, then kept going over the school yard to the path through the park, stopping under a high tree hanging over the path. It was dark. No one around. Eli looked up into the top of the tree, along five six meters of smooth tree trunk. Kicked off her shoes. Thought herself new hands, new feet.

It hardly hurt at all anymore, just felt like a tingling, an electric current through her fingers and toes as they thinned out, took on a new shape. The bones crackled in her hands as they stretched out, shot out through the melting skin of the fingertips and made long, curved claws. Same thing with her toes.

Eli jumped a couple of meters up onto the trunk of the tree, dug in her claws, and climbed up to a thick branch that hung out over the path. Curled the claws on her feet around the branch and sat without moving.

A shooting sensation in her teeth as Eli thought them sharp. The enamel bulged out, was sharpened by an invisible file, became sharp. Eli carefully bit herself in her lower lip, a crescent-shaped row of needles that almost punctured the skin.

Now only the wait.

†

It was close to ten and the temperature in the room was approaching the unbearable. Two bottles of vodka had already been consumed, a new one had been taken out, and everyone agreed that Gösta was one hell of a guy and his kindness wouldn't count for nothing.

Only Virginia had been taking it easy, since she had to get up and work the next day. She also seemed to be the only one who was affected by the air in the room. The already damp smell of cat piss and stale air was now mixed with smoke, alcohol fumes, and the perspiration of six bodies.

Lacke and Gösta were still sitting on either side of her on the couch, now only half conscious. Gösta was petting a cat on his lap, a cat who was wall-eyed, something which had caused Morgan to have such fits of laughter that he had hit his head on the table and then had a shot of pure alcohol in order to dull the pain.

Lacke wasn't saying much. He mostly sat staring straight ahead, his eyes glazed over with haziness, then mist and fog. His lips moved soundlessly from time to time as if he were conversing with a ghost.

Virginia got up and walked over to the window. "Is it OK if I open this?"

Gösta shook his head.

"The cats . . . can . . . jump out."

"But I'll stand here and keep watch."

Gösta kept shaking his head mechanically and Virginia opened the window. Air! She greedily took a couple of lungfuls of fresh air and immediately felt better. Lacke, who had been starting to slip sideways in the couch since Virginia's support was no longer available, straightened up and said out loud:

"A friend! A real . . . friend!"

A mumble of agreement from around the room. Everyone knew he was talking about Jocke. Lacke stared into the empty glass in his hand and continued:

"You have one friend . . . who never lets you down. And that is worth *everything*. Do you hear that? *Everything*. And you have to get that me and Jocke were . . . like this!"

He made his hand into a tight fist, shook it in front of his face.

"And nothing can replace that. Nothing! You're all sitting here yammering about 'what a damn good guy' and all that but you . . . you're all empty. Hollow. I have nothing now that Jocke . . . is gone. Nothing. So don't talk about loss with me, don't talk about . . ."

Virginia stood next to the window, listening. She walked up to Lacke in order to remind him of her existence. Crouched down next to his knee and tried to catch his eye and said: "Lacke."

"No! Don't come here and . . . 'Lacke, Lacke' . . . this is just the way it is. You don't get it. You're . . . cold. You go downtown and pick up some damn truck driver or whatever, take him home, and let him screw you when you get down. That's what you do. Damn . . . trucking caravan is what you have going on. But a friend . . . a friend . . ."

Virginia stood up with tears in her eyes, slapped Lacke, and ran out of the apartment. Lacke lost his balance in the couch and hit Gösta in the shoulder. Gösta mumbled: "The window . . . the window."

Morgan closed it and said: "Well done, Lacke. That was a good one. You probably won't see any more of her."

Lacke stood up and walked with unsteady legs over to Morgan, who cast an eye out the window. "What the hell, I didn't mean to . . ."

"No, of course not. Go tell her instead."

Morgan nodded down at the ground where Virginia had just come out of the front door of the building, and was walking rapidly with a lowered gaze toward the park. Lacke heard what he had said. His last words to her stuck inside his head like an echo. Did I say that? He turned on his heel and hurried to the door.

"I just have to . . ."

Morgan nodded. "Hurry up. And give her my regards."

Lacke threw himself down the stairs as fast as his trembling legs could carry him. The speckle-patterned stairs were nothing but a shimmer before his eyes and the banister slid so quickly through his hand it started to sting from the heat of the friction. He tripped on a landing, fell, and hit his elbow hard. The arm filled with heat and became sort of paralyzed. He got up and stumbled on down the stairs. He was rushing to help save a life. His own.

✝

Virginia walked away from the building, down to the park, and did not turn around.

Her body was wracked with sobs, half-running as if to outrun the tears. But they followed her, forced themselves into her eyes, and fell in big drops down her cheeks. Her heels cut through the snow, clicking against the asphalt of the path, and she wound her arms around herself, hugging herself.

There was no one to be seen so she gave in freely to her sobs as she made her way home, pressed her arms against her stomach; the pain lodged in there like an ill-tempered fetus.

Let a person in and he hurts you.

There was a reason why she kept her relationships brief. Don't let them in. Once they're inside they have more potential to hurt you. Comfort yourself. You can live with the anguish as long as it only involves yourself. As long as there is no hope.

But with Lacke she had held out hope. That something would slowly grow up between them. And in the end. One day. *What?* He accepted her food and her warmth but in reality she meant nothing to him.

She walked huddled-up along the path, doubled over with sorrow. Her back was stooped and it was as if a demon sat there whispering terrible things in her ear.

Never again. Nothing.

Just as she was starting to imagine what this demon looked like, it landed on top of her.

A heavy weight struck her in the back and she fell helplessly to the side. Her cheek met snow and the film of tears was transformed into ice. The weight remained.

For one second she really believed it was the sorrow-demon who had taken a physical form and thrown itself on top of her. Then she felt the searing pain in her throat as sharp teeth penetrated the skin. She managed to get back on her feet, spinning around and trying to get rid of the thing that was on top of her.

There was something chewing on her neck, her throat; a stream of blood ran down between her breasts. She screamed at the top of her lungs and tried to shake off the creature on her back, kept screaming as she fell again onto the snow.

Until something hard was laid over her mouth. A hand.

Against her cheek there were claws digging into the soft flesh . . . all the way in until they reached the cheekbone.

The teeth stopped chewing and she heard a sound like the one you make with a straw as you suck up the dregs in the glass. Liquid flowed over one eye and she didn't know if it was tears or blood.

✝

When Lacke came out of the apartment building Virginia was nothing more than a dark shape moving down the path toward Arvid Mörnes. His chest was hurting from sprinting down the stairs and his elbow sent waves of pain toward the shoulder. In spite of all this, he ran. He ran as fast as he could. His head was starting to clear in the cool air, and fear of losing her drove him on.

When he reached the bend in the path where "Jocke's path"—as he had started to call it—met "Virginia's path" he stopped, drew as much air into his lungs as he could in order to shout out her name. She was walking up ahead only fifty meters away.

Just as he was about to call out her name he saw a shadow fall from a tree above Virginia, land on her, and knock her to the ground. His scream turned into a hiss, and he sped up. He wanted to shout something but there was not enough air to both run and shout.

He ran.

In front of him Virginia got to her feet with a large lump on her back, spun around like a crazed hunchback, and fell down again.

He had no plan, no thoughts. Nothing except this: to get to Virginia and get rid of whatever that was on her back. She lay in the snow next to the path with that black mass crawling on her.

When he reached her he directed all of his force into a kick at the black thing. His foot made contact with something hard and he heard a sharp crack, as when ice breaks up. The black thing was thrown from Virginia's back and landed in the snow next to her.

Virginia lay completely still; there were dark stains on the white ground. The black thing sat up.

A child.

Lacke stood there staring into the prettiest little child's face imaginable, framed by a veil of black hair. A pair of enormous dark eyes met his.

The child got up on all fours, cat-like, preparing to lunge. The face changed as the child drew back its lips and Lacke could see the rows of sharp teeth glow in the dark.

They remained like this for a few panting breaths, the child on all fours, and Lacke could now see that its fingers were claws, sharply defined against the snow.

Then a grimace of pain contorted the child's face, she got up on two legs and ran off in the direction of the school with long rapid steps. A few seconds later she reached the shadows and was gone.

Lacke stood where he was and blinked away the sweat running into his eyes. Then he threw himself down next to Virginia. He saw the wound. Her whole throat was ripped up. Dark strands of blood ran all the way up into her hair, down her back. He stripped off his jacket, pulled off the sweater he was wearing underneath, bunched it up into a ball, and pressed it against the wound.

"Virginia! Virginia! My darling, beloved . . ."

At last he was able to get the words out.

SATURDAY 7 NOVEMBER

On his way to Dad's house. Every bend in the road familiar; he had taken this route . . . how many times? Alone, maybe only ten or twelve, with his mom maybe another thirty, at least. His mom and dad had divorced when he was four, but Oskar and his mom had kept coming out on weekends and holidays.

The last three years he had been allowed to take the bus by himself. This time his mom hadn't even come with him to the Tekniska Högskolan stop where the buses left. He was a big boy now, had his own book of pre-paid tickets to the subway in his wallet.

Actually the main reason he had the wallet was to have a place to keep the prepaid tickets but now there was also twenty kronor to buy sweets and such, as well as the notes from Eli.

Oskar fiddled with the Band-Aid on his palm. He didn't want to see her anymore. She was scary. What happened in the basement was—

She showed her true face.

—there was something in her, something that was . . . Pure Horror. Everything you were supposed to watch out for. Heights, fire, shards of glass, snakes. Everything that his mom tried so hard to keep him safe from.

Maybe that was why he hadn't wanted Eli and his mom to meet. His mom would have recognized it, forbidden him to get near it. Near Eli.

The bus exited the freeway and turned down toward Spillersboda. This was the only bus that went to Rådmansö Island. That was why it had to wind its way up and down all the roads—in order to drive through as many settlements as possible. The bus drove past the mountainous land-scape of piled timber at the Spillersboda Sawmill, made a sharp turn and almost slid on its back down toward the pier.

He had not waited for Eli Friday evening.

Instead he had taken the Snow Racer and gone by himself to Ghost Hill. His mom had protested since he had stayed home from school that day with a cold, but he said he felt better.

He walked through China Park with the Snow Racer on his back. The sledding hill started a hundred meters past the last park lights, a hundred meters of dark forest. The snow crunched under his feet. There was a soft soughing from the forest, like breathing. The moonlight filtered through the trees and the ground between them turned into a woven tapestry of shadows where figures without faces waited, swaying to and fro.

He reached the place where the path started to bear down strongly toward Kvarnviken Bay, and climbed onto his Snow Racer. The Ghost House was a black wall next to the hill, a reprimand: *You are not allowed to be here in the dark. This is our place now. If you want to play here, you'll have to play with us.*

At the bottom of the hill he could see the occasional light shining

from the Kvarnviken boat club. Oskar inched himself forward a few centimeters, the incline took over, and the Snow Racer started to glide. He
squeezed the steering wheel, wanted to close his eyes but didn't dare to
because then he could veer off the road and down the steep slope toward
the Ghost House.

He shot down the hill, a projectile of nerves and tensed muscles.
Faster, faster. Formless, snow-covered arms stretched out from the Ghost
House, grabbing for his hat, brushing against his cheek.

Maybe it was only a sudden gust of wind but at the very bottom of the
hill he drove into a viscous, transparent, filmy barrier stretched out over
the path that tried to stop him. But his speed was too great.

The Snow Racer drove into the filmy barrier and it glued itself onto
his face and body, was stretched until it burst, and then he was through.

The lights were glittering over Kvarnviken Bay. He sat on his Snow
Racer and stared out over the spot where he had knocked down Jonny
yesterday morning. Turned around. The Ghost House was an ugly shack
of sheet metal.

He pulled the Snow Racer up the hill again. Slid down. Up again.
Down again. Couldn't stop. And he went on. Went on until his face was a
mask of ice.

Then he walked home.

†

He had only slept four or five hours, afraid that Eli was going to come. Of
what he would be forced to say, to do if she did that. Push her away.
Therefore he fell asleep on the bus to Norrtälje and didn't wake up until
they were there. On the Rådmansö bus he had kept himself awake, made
a game out of trying to remember as much as possible along the way.

Soon there will be a yellow house with a windmill on the lawn.

A yellow house with a snowy windmill on the lawn passed by outside
the window. And so on. In Spillersboda a girl got on the bus. Oskar
gripped the back of the seat in front of him. She looked a little like Eli. Of
course it wasn't her. The girl sat down a few seats in front of him. He
looked at her neck.

What's wrong with her?

The thought had come to him even as he was in the cellar gathering the bottles together and wiping the blood away with a piece of cloth from the garbage: that Eli was a vampire. That explained a lot of things.

That she was never out in the daytime.

That she could *see in the dark*; he had come to understand that she could.

Plus a lot of other things: the way she talked, the cube, her flexibility, things that of course could have a natural explanation . . . but then there was also the way that she had licked his blood from the floor, and what really made him shiver was when he thought about the:

"Can I come in? Say that I can come in."

That she had needed an invitation to come into his room, to his bed. And he had invited her in. A vampire. A being that lived off other peoples' blood. Eli. There was not *one* person who he could tell. No one would believe him. And if someone did believe him, what would happen?

Oskar imagined a caravan of men walking through Blackeberg, in through the covered entrance where he and Eli had hugged, with sharpened stakes in their hands. He was afraid of Eli now, didn't want to see her anymore, but he didn't want *that*.

Three quarters of an hour after he had boarded the bus in Norrtälje he arrived in Södersvik. He pulled on the string and the bell rang up front by the driver. The bus pulled over right in front of the store and he had to wait for an old lady, whom he recognized but didn't know the name of, to get off.

His dad was standing below the stairs, nodded and said "hum" to the old lady. Oskar climbed off the bus, stood still for a second in front of his dad. This last week things had happened that had made Oskar feel bigger. Not adult. But bigger, at any rate. All that fell away as he stood in front of his father.

His mom claimed his dad was childlike, in a bad way. Immature, couldn't handle responsibility. Oh, she said some nice things about him too, but that was what she always came back to. The immaturity.

For Oskar, his dad was the very image of an adult as he now stretched out his broad arms and Oskar fell into them.

His dad smelled different from all the people in the city. In his torn Helly Hansen vest fixed with Velcro there was always the same mixture of wood, paint, metal, and above all, oil. These were the smells but Oskar didn't think of them in that way. It was all simply "Dad's smell." He loved it and drew a deep breath through his nose as he pressed his face against his dad's chest.

"Well hey there."

"Hi Dad."

"Your trip go OK?"

"No, we ran into an elk."

"Oh no. That must have been something."

"Just joking."

"I see. I see. But you know, I remember a time . . ."

As they walked toward the store, Dad started telling a story about how once a truck he was driving had collided with an elk. Oskar had heard the story before and looked around, humming from time to time.

The Södervik store looked as trashy as ever. Signs and streamers that had been allowed to stay up in anticipation of next summer made the whole store look like an oversized ice cream stand. The large tent behind the store, where they sold garden tools, soil, outdoor furniture, and such, was tied up for the season.

In summer the population of Södervik increased four-fold. The whole area down toward Norrtäljeviken Bay, Lågarö, was an unruly con-glomeration of summer houses, and even though the mailboxes down to-ward Lågarö were hung in double rows of thirty, the mailman almost never had to go there at this time of year. No people, no mail.

Just as they reached the moped his dad finished the story with the elk.

". . . and then I had to hit him with a crowbar that I had for opening drawers and that kind of thing. Right between the eyes. He twitched like this and . . . yes. No, it wasn't so nice."

"No, of course not."

Oskar jumped up on the trailer, pulling his legs in under him. His dad dug around in a pocket on the vest and pulled out a cap.

"Here. It'll get cold around your ears."

"No, I have one."

Oskar took out his own cap and put it on. Dad put the other one away.

"What about you? It'll get cold around your ears."

Dad laughed.

"No, I'm used to it."

Of course Oskar knew that; he was just teasing. He couldn't remember ever seeing his dad in a wool cap. If it got really cold and windy he put on a kind of bearskin hat with ear flaps that he called his "inheritance," but that was the limit.

His dad kick-started the moped and it roared like an electric chain saw. He shouted something about the idling and put it in first. The moped jumped forward, almost causing Oskar to fall backwards; his dad yelled something about the gears and then they were off.

Second, third gear. The moped flew through the town. Oskar sat with his legs crossed in the clattering trailer. He felt like a king of the world and would have been able to keep going like this forever.

†

A physician had explained it to him. The fumes he had inhaled had burned away his vocal chords and he would probably never be able to speak normally again. A new operation would be able to give him a rudimentary ability to produce vowels, but since even his tongue and lips were badly injured there would have to be additional operations to enable the possibility of uttering consonants.

As a former Swedish teacher Håkan could not help but be fascinated at the thought: to create speech by surgical means.

He knew quite a bit about phonemes and the smallest components of language, common across many cultures. He had never reflected much over the actual tools of production—the roof of the mouth, lips, tongue, vocal chords—in this way. To coax speech from this shapeless raw material with a scalpel.

But it was meaningless anyway. He did not intend to speak. In addition, he suspected that the doctor was talking that way for a special reason. He was considered suicide-prone. Therefore it was important to imprint him with a linear sense of time. To recreate the feeling of life as a project, a dream of future conquests.

He didn't buy it.

If Eli needed him he could consider living. Otherwise he could not. Nothing indicated that Eli needed him.

But how would Eli be able to contact him in this place? From the tree tops outside his window he sensed that he was high up. And furthermore, he was well-guarded. In addition to the doctors and nurses there was always at least one policeman nearby. Eli could not reach him and he could not reach Eli. The thought of escaping, of getting in touch with Eli one last time had gone through his head. But how?

The throat operation had made him capable of breathing on his own again. He no longer had to be attached to a respirator. But he could not get down food in the normal way (even this would be repaired, the doctor had assured him). The feeding tube dangled constantly at the edge of his vision. If he pulled it out an alarm would go off somewhere, and anyway he couldn't see very well. To escape was basically unthinkable.

A plastic surgeon had taken the opportunity to transplant a piece of skin from his back to his eyelid so he could shut his eye.

He shut his eye.

The door to his room opened. It was time again. He recognized the voice. The same man as before.

"Well, well," said the man. "They tell me there won't be any talking in the near future. That's too bad. But I have this stubborn thought that we could still manage to communicate with each other, you and me, if you're up for it."

Håkan tried to remember what Plato said in *The Republic* about murderers and violent offenders, what you were supposed to do with them.

"I see you can shut your eye now. That's good. You know what? I'll try to make this a little more concrete for you. Because it struck me that maybe you don't believe we're going to identify you. But we will. I'm sure you remember you had a wristwatch. Luckily it was an older watch with the manufacturer's initials, serial number, and everything. We're going to trace it within a couple of days, in one way or another. A week maybe. And there are other things.

"We'll find you, that's a certainty.

"So . . . Max. I don't know why I want to call you Max, it is entirely provisional. Max? You maybe want to help us out a little here. Otherwise we'll have to take a picture of you and send it to the papers and . . . well, you see. It will be . . . complicated. Much easier if you talk . . . or something . . . with me now.

"You had a piece of paper with the Morse code in your pocket. Do you know the Morse code? Because in that case we can talk by tapping."

Håkan opened his eye, looked in the direction of the two dark spots in the white, blurry oval that was the man's face. The man clearly chose to interpret this as an invitation. He continued.

"This man in the water. It wasn't you who killed him, was it? The pathologists say that the bite marks in his neck were probably made by a child. And now we've had a report that I unfortunately can't give any details of, but . . . I think you are protecting someone. Is this correct? Lift your hand if this is correct."

Håkan shut his eye. The policeman sighed.

"OK, then we'll let the machine keep working. Is there anything else you would like to tell me before I go?"

The man was about to get up when Håkan lifted one hand. The policeman sat down again. Håkan lifted the hand higher. And waved.

Good-bye.

The policeman let out a snorting sound, got up, and left.

†

Virginia's injuries had not been life-threatening. On Friday afternoon she was discharged from the hospital with fourteen stitches and a large bandage on her neck, a smaller one on her cheek. She had refused Lacke's offer to stay with her, live with her, until she felt better.

She had gone to bed Friday evening convinced that she would get up and go to work Saturday morning. Couldn't afford to stay home.

It had been hard to fall asleep. Memories of the attack kept returning, and she couldn't get settled. Thought she saw black lumps emerge out of the shadows of her room and fall down on her as she lay in bed with her eyes wide open. Her wound itched under the bandage on her throat. Around two o'clock in the morning she got hungry, went out into the kitchen, and opened the refrigerator.

Her stomach had felt empty, but as she stood there and looked at all the food, there was nothing she felt she wanted. From habit, she had still taken out the bread, butter, cheese, and milk and set them on the kitchen table.

She made herself a cheese sandwich and poured milk into a glass. Then she sat at the table and looked at the white liquid in the glass, the brown piece of bread with its yellow slice of cheese. It looked revolting. She didn't want it. She threw it out, pouring the milk down the drain. There was a half-full bottle of white wine in the fridge. She poured out a glass, brought it to her lips. But when she smelled the wine she lost interest.

With a feeling of failure she poured herself a glass of water from the tap. She hesitated as she brought it to her mouth. Surely you could always drink *water*? . . . Yes. She could drink the water. But it tasted . . . stale. As if everything good in the water had been removed and only left the flat dregs.

She went back to bed, shifting restlessly for a few more hours then finally falling asleep.

✝

When she woke up it was half past ten. She threw herself out of bed, pulled on some clothes in the dimly lit bedroom. Good heavens. She should have been at the store at eight. Why hadn't they called?

Oh, but wait. She had heard the phone ring. It had rung in her last dream before she woke up, then stopped. If they hadn't called she would still be sleeping. She buttoned her blouse and walked over to the window, pulled up the blinds.

The light struck her face like a physical blow. She staggered backward, away from the window, and dropped the cords to the blinds. They slipped down again with a clattering sound, stopping at a crooked angle. She sat down on the bed. A single beam of sunlight came in through the window, shining on her naked foot.

A thousand pinpricks.

As if her skin were being twisted in two directions at once.

What is this?

She moved her foot away, pulled on her socks. Moved her foot back into the sunlight. Better. Only a hundred pinpricks. She stood up to go to work then sat down again.

Some kind of . . . shock.

The sensation when she pulled up the blinds had been ghastly. As if the light were heavy matter flung at her body, pushing her away. It had been the worst in the eyes. Two strong thumbs pressing on them, threatening to gouge them out of her head. They were still stinging.

She rubbed her eyes with the palms of her hands, took her sunglasses out of the bathroom cabinet and put them on.

Hunger raged in her body but all she had to do was think of the contents of the refrigerator and pantry to make all thoughts of eating breakfast disappear. And anyway she had no time. She was almost three hours late.

She went out, locked the door, and walked down the stairs as fast as she could. Her body was weak. Maybe it was a mistake to go to work today. Well, the store would only be open four more hours and it was *now* the Saturday customers started to come in.

She was so preoccupied with these thoughts that she did not hesitate before opening the front door of the building.

The light was there again.

Her eyes hurt despite the sunglasses, boiling water was poured over her hands and face. She gave a little scream. Pulled her hands into her coat, bent her face to the ground and ran. She could not protect her neck and scalp and they stung like they were on fire. Luckily it was not far to the store.

When she was safely inside, the stinging and pain quickly lifted. Most of the store windows were covered in advertising and protective plastic film so that the sunlight wouldn't affect the goods. She took off her sunglasses. It hurt a little, but that could be because a little bit of sunlight came in the spaces between the advertising posters. She put her sunglasses in her pocket and walked out to the office.

Lennart, the store manager and her boss, was there filling out forms, but he looked up when she came in. She had expected some kind of reprimand but he simply said. "Hi, how's it going."

"Oh . . . fine."

"Shouldn't you be at home getting some rest?"

"No, I thought . . ."

"You didn't need to, you know. Lotten will fill in for you today. I tried to call you earlier, but when you didn't pick up . . ."

"Isn't there anything for me to do, then?"

"Check with Berit in the meat department. And Virginia . . ."

"Yes."

"I'm sorry about what happened. I don't know exactly how to say it, but . . . I feel badly about it. And I completely understand if you need to take it easy for a while."

Virginia couldn't get her head around it. Lennart was not the kind of person who looked kindly on sick leave, or for that matter, any kind of problem that other people might have. And to hear him extend his *personal sympathies* was something completely new. She must look pretty terrible with her swollen cheek and her bandages.

Virginia said: "Thanks. I'll think it over," and went to the meat department.

She looped over past the checkout registers in order to say hi to Lotten. Five people were lined up at her register and Virginia thought she should open another one after all. But the question was if Lennart even wanted her to sit at a checkout register looking as she did.

When she walked into the light from the horrible window behind the checkout registers it got like that again. Her face tightened, her eyes ached. It wasn't as bad as the direct sunlight out on the street, but it was bad enough. She would not be able to sit there.

Lotten caught sight of her, waved in between two customers.

"Hi, I read . . . How are you doing?"

Virginia held up her hand, wiggled it from side to side: so so.

Read?

She nabbed the *Svenska Dagbladet* and *Dagens Nyheter*, took them with her over to the meat department, quickly eyed the first page news. Nothing there. That would have been a reach.

The meat department was at the very back of the store, beside the milk products, strategically planned so that you had to walk through the whole store in order to get there. Virginia stopped next to the shelves with canned food. She was trembling with hunger. She looked carefully at all the cans.

Crushed tomatoes, mushrooms, mussels, tuna, ravioli, Bullen's beer sausage, pea soup . . . no. She felt nothing but revulsion.

Berit saw her from the meat counter, waved. As soon as Virginia had come around the back of the counter Berit hugged her, and carefully touched the bandage on her cheek.

"Ugh. Poor you."

"Oh, it's . . ."

Fine?

She retreated to the little storage room behind the meat counter. If she let Berit get started she would be subject to a long harangue about people's suffering in general and the evils of today's society in particular.

Virginia sat down on a chair between the scales and the door to the freezer room. It was an area of only a few square meters but it was the most comfortable place in the store. No sunlight. She flipped through the papers and found a small article in the *Dagens Nyheter* domestic news section. She read:

Woman attacked in Blackeberg

A fifty-year-old woman was attacked and assaulted Thursday night in the Stockholm suburb of Blackeberg. A passerby intervened and the perpetrator, a young woman, immediately fled the scene. The motive of the assault is unknown. The police are now investigating a possible connection to other violent incidents in the western suburbs during the past few weeks. The fifty-year-old woman's injuries were described as minor.

Virginia lowered the paper. So strange to read about yourself in that way. "Fifty-year-old woman," "passerby" "minor injuries." Everything that was concealed by those words.

"Possible connection?" Yes, Lacke was convinced that she had been attacked by the same child who killed Jocke. He had had to bite his tongue not to say this at the hospital, some time on Friday morning, to the female police officer and the doctor who examined her wounds.

He was planning to talk to the police, but wanted to inform Gosta first, thought Gösta would see the whole thing from a new perspective now that even Virginia had been involved.

She heard a rustling sound and looked around. It took a few seconds before she realized that it was the newspaper shaking in her own hands that was making the noise. She set the newspapers on the shelf above the white coats and went out to join Berit.

"Anything I can do?"

"Do you really think it's a good idea, hon?"

"Yes, it's better for me to be doing something."

"I see. You can portion out the shrimp, in that case. Five hundred gram bags. But shouldn't you? . . ."

Virginia shook her head and walked back to the storage room. She put on a white coat and hat, took a case of shrimp out of the freezer, pulled a plastic bag over her hand, and started to weigh them out. Dug around in the carton with the hand that had the plastic bag over it, portioned them out into bags, weighed them on the scales. A boring, mechanical job, and her right hand felt frozen already on her fourth bag. But she was doing something, and it gave her an opportunity to think.

That night at the hospital Lacke had said something really strange: that the child who attacked her had not been a human being. That it had had fangs and claws.

Virginia had dismissed this as a drunken hallucination.

She didn't remember much from the attack. But she could accept this: the thing that had jumped on top of her had been much too light to be an adult, almost too light to be a child, even. A very small child in that case. Five or six maybe. She recalled that she had stood up with the weight on her back. After that everything was black until she woke up in her apartment with all the guys except Gösta gathered around her.

She put a tie around a finished bag, took out the next one, dropped in a few handfuls. Four hundred and thirty grams. Seven more shrimp. Five hundred and ten.

Our treat.

She looked down at her hands, which were working independently of her brain. Hands. With long nails. Sharp teeth. What was that called? Lacke had said it out loud. A vampire. Virginia had laughed, carefully, so that the stitches in her cheek wouldn't come out. Lacke had not even smiled.

"You didn't see it."

"But Lacke . . . they don't really exist."

"No. But what was it then?"

"A child. Living out a strange twisted fantasy."

"Who grew out her nails? Filed her teeth down? I'd like to see the dentist who . . ."

"Lacke, it was dark. You were drunk, it—"

"It was, and I was. But I saw what I saw."

It burned and felt tight under the bandage on her cheek. She removed the plastic bag from her right hand, put her hand over the bandage. It was ice cold and that felt good. But she was weak; it felt as if her legs weren't going to carry her much longer.

She would finish this carton and then go home. This wasn't going to work. If she could rest over the weekend she would probably feel better on Monday. She put the plastic bag back on and started in on the work again with a spark of anger. Hated being sick.

A sharp pain in her index finger. Damn it. That's what happens if you don't concentrate. The shrimp were sharp when they were frozen and she had pricked her finger. She pulled off the plastic bag and looked at the finger. A smallish cut with a little blood welling out of it.

She automatically popped it into her mouth to suck the blood away.

A warm, healing, delicious spot radiating out from the place where her fingertip met her tongue, started to spread. She sucked harder on the finger. All good tastes concentrated into one filled her mouth. A shiver of well-being went through her body. She sucked and sucked, giving in to the pleasure until she realized what she was doing.

She pulled the finger out of her mouth, stared at it. It was shiny with saliva and the tiny amount of blood that now welled out was immediately thinned out by the wetness, like an overly diluted watercolor. She looked at the shrimp in the carton. Hundreds of pink bodies, covered with frost. And eyes. Black pinheads dispersed in the white and pink, an upside-down starry sky. Patterns, constellations started to dance in front of her eyes.

The world spun on its axis and something hit her in the back of the head. In front of her eyes there was a white surface with cobwebs in the corners. She understood that she was lying on the floor but had no strength to do anything about it.

In the distance she heard Berit's voice: "Oh my God . . . Virginia . . ."

†

Jonny liked to hang out with his older brother. At least when none of his sketchy buddies were around. Jimmy knew some guys from Råcksta that

Jonny was pretty scared of. One evening a few years ago they had come by to talk to Jimmy, hanging around outside but without ringing the buzzer. When Jonny told them Jimmy wasn't home they asked him to deliver a message.

"Tell your brother that if he doesn't get us the dough by Monday we'll put his head in a vice . . . you know what that is? . . . OK . . . and turn it like this until the dough runs out of his ears. Can you tell him that? OK, great. Jonny's your name? Good-bye then, Jonny."

Jonny had delivered the message and Jimmy had simply nodded, said he knew. Then some money had disappeared from Mom's wallet and then there had been an angry scene.

Jimmy was not home as often nowadays. There was sort of no room for him anymore since their youngest little sister was born. Jonny already had two younger siblings and there weren't supposed to be any more. But then Mom had met some guy and . . . well . . . that's how it went.

At least Jonny and Jimmy had the same dad. He worked on an oil rig off the coast of Norway and not only had he started sending regular child support, he was also sending a little extra just to make up for before. Mom blessed him, and when she was drunk she had even cried over him a few times and said she would never again meet a man like that. So for the first time in as long as Jonny could remember a lack of money was not the constant topic of conversation.

Now they were sitting in the pizzeria on the main square in Blackeberg. Jimmy had been home in the morning, argued a bit with Mom, and then he and Jonny had gone out. Jimmy heaped condiments on his pizza, folded it up, picked up the large roll with both hands, and started to eat. Jonny ate his pizza in the usual way, thinking that next time he ate pizza without Jimmy he would eat it like that.

Jimmy chewed, nodded his head at the bandage over Jonny's ear. "Looks like hell."

"Yes."

"Does it hurt?"

"It's OK."

"Mom said it's damaged for life. That you won't be able to hear anything."

"They don't know yet. Maybe it'll be alright."

"Hm. Let me get this straight. The guy just picked up some big branch and bashed it into your head."

"Mm."

"Damn. What are you going to do about it?"

"Don't know."

"Need any help?"

". . . No."

"What? Me and a few of my pals can take him out."

Jonny pulled off a big piece with shrimp, his favorite, put it in his mouth and chewed. No. Better not drag Jimmy's friends into this, then it would get out of hand. Nonetheless Jonny smiled at the thought of how scared shitless Oskar would be if he appeared at his house with Jimmy and, say, those guys from Råcksta. He shook his head.

Jimmy put his pizza roll down and looked seriously at Jonny.

"OK, but I'm just saying. *One* more thing, and then . . ."

He snapped his fingers hard, then made a fist.

"You're my brother and no little shit is going to come and . . . *One* more thing, then you can say whatever you like. Then I'm going after him. OK?"

Jimmy held out his fist across the table. Jonny also made a fist and bumped Jimmy's with it. It felt good. That there was someone who cared. Jimmy nodded.

"Good. I have something for you."

He bent down under the table, took out a plastic bag that he had been carrying all morning. He drew a thin photo album out of the bag. "Dad came by last week. He's grown a beard, almost didn't recognize him. He had this with him."

Jimmy held the album out to Jonny, who wiped his fingers on a napkin and opened it.

Pictures of children. Of Mom. Maybe ten years ago. And a man he recognized as his father. The man was pushing the kids on swings. In one picture he was wearing a much-too-small cowboy hat. Jimmy, maybe nine years old, was standing next to him with a plastic rifle in his hands and a grim expression. A little boy who had to be Jonny sat on the ground nearby and looked wide-eyed at them.

"He loaned me this till next time. He wants it back, said it was . . . yeah, what the fuck was it . . . 'my most valuable possession,' I think he said. Thought it might interest you too."

Jonny nodded without looking up from the album. He had only met his dad two times since he left when Jonny was four. At home there was one picture of him, a pretty bad one where he was sitting around with some other people. This was something completely different. Here you could kind of construct a real image of him.

"One more thing. Don't show it to Mom. I think Dad kind of swiped it when he left and if she sees it . . . well, he wants it back, as I told you. Promise. Don't show Mom."

Still with his nose buried in the album, Jonny made a fist and held it out over the table. Jimmy laughed and then Jonny felt Jimmy's knuckles against his. Promise.

"Hey, you check it out later. Take the bag too."

Jimmy held out the bag and Jonny reluctantly folded up the album, put it in the bag. Jimmy was done with his pizza, leaned back in his chair, and patted his stomach.

"So. How are things on the chick front?"

†

The village flew by. Snow that was kicked up by the wheels of the moped trailer was sprayed back and peppered Oskar's cheeks. He gripped the towrope with both hands, shifted his weight to the side, swinging out of the snow cloud. There was a sharp scraping sound as the skis sliced through the loose snow. The outer ski nudged an orange reflector where the road split in two. He wobbled, then regained his balance.

The road down to Lågarö and the summer houses wasn't plowed. The moped left three deep tracks in the untouched snow cover, and five meters behind it came Oskar on skis, making two additional tracks. He drove zigzag over the moped tracks, stood on one ski like a trick skier, crouched down into a little ball of speed.

When his dad slowed down on the long hill heading down to the old steamship pier, Oskar was going faster than the moped and he was forced to brake a little in order not to let too much slack into the line, which would then result in a strong jerk when the hill leveled off and the moped picked up speed again.

The moped got all the way down to the pier and his dad switched down out of gear and stood on the brake. Oskar was still traveling at full throttle and for a short moment he thought about *dropping the rope and keeping going* . . . Out over the end of the pier, down into the black water. But he angled the mini-skis out, braked a couple of meters from the edge.

He stood panting for a while, looked out over the water. Thin sections of ice had started to form, bobbed up and down in the small waves by the shores. Maybe there was a chance of real ice this year. So you could walk across to Vätö on the other side. Or did they keep a channel in to Norrtälje open? Oskar couldn't remember. It was several years since there had been ice like that.

When Oskar was out here in the summer he would fish for herring from this pier. Loose hooks on the line, a lure on the end. If he found a school he could end up with a couple of kilos if he had the patience, but mostly he ended up with ten or fifteen fish. That was enough for dinner for him and his dad; the smallest ones went to the cat.

Dad came up and stood behind him.

"That went well, it did."

"Mmm. But I went all the way through the snow a couple of times."

"True, the snow is a little loose. If we could pack it tighter, somehow. If we could . . . maybe take a particleboard and hitch it up, put some weight on it. You know, if you put the board and the weight down, then . . ."

"Should we do it?"

"No, it'd have to be tomorrow, at any rate. It's getting dark now. We'll have to get home and work on that bird a little if there's going to be any dinner."

"OK."

His dad looked out over the water, stood there quietly for a while.

"You know, I've been thinking about something."

"Yes?"

It was coming now. Mom had told Oskar that she let Dad know *in no uncertain terms* that he had to talk to him about what happened with Jonny. And actually Oskar wanted to talk about it. Dad was at a secure distance from it all, wouldn't interfere in any way. His dad cleared his throat, gathered himself. Breathed out. Looked over the water. Then he said: "Yes, I was thinking . . . do you have any ice skates?"

"No, none that fit me."

"No, no. No. Well, if we get ice this winter and it looks like . . . then it would be fun to have some, wouldn't it. I have some."

"They probably won't fit."

His dad snorted, a kind of chuckle.

"No, but . . . Östen's boy has some he's grown out of. Thirty-nines. What size do you wear?"

"Thirty-eight."

"Yes, but with woolen socks you'd . . . I'll ask him if you can have them."

"Great."

"Then it's settled. Good. Should we get going, then?"

Oskar nodded. Maybe it would come later. And the part about the skates was good. If they could manage it tomorrow then he could bring them back with him.

He walked on his mini-skis over to the end of the towrope, backed up until the line was taut, signaled his dad that he was ready. His dad started the moped. They had to go up the hill in first gear. The moped roared so that it frightened some crows out of the top of a pine tree.

Oskar glided slowly up the hill like he was going up a rope tow, stood straight with his legs pressed together. He wasn't thinking about anything except trying to keep his skis in the old tracks in order to avoid cutting through the snow layer to the ground. They made their way home as twilight was falling.

†

Lacke walked down the stairs from the main square with a box of Aladdin chocolates tucked inside the top of his pants. Didn't like to steal, but he had no money and he wanted to give Virginia something. Should have brought roses as well, but try swiping anything at a florist.

It was already dark and when he reached the bottom of the hill toward the school he hesitated. Looked around, scraped the snow with his foot, and uncovered a rock the size of a fist that he kicked loose and slipped in his pocket, squeezing his hand around it. Not because he thought it would help against what he had seen but the stone's weight and cold offered a bit of comfort.

†

His asking around in the various apartment courtyards had not yielded any results other than guarded, suspicious looks from parents who were out building snowmen with their youngsters. Dirty old man.

It was only when he opened his mouth to talk to a woman who was beating rugs that he realized how unnatural his behavior must appear. The woman had paused in her task, turned to him with the stick in her hand like a weapon.

"Excuse me," Lacke said, ". . . yes, I was wondering . . . I'm looking for a child."

"Really?"

He heard himself how it sounded, and it made him even more unsure of himself. "Yes, she has . . . disappeared. I was wondering if someone had seen her around here."

"Is it your child?"

"No, but . . ."

Apart from a couple of teenagers, he had given up talking to people he didn't know. Or at least recognized. He bumped into some acquaintances, but they hadn't seen anything. Seek and thou shalt find, sure. But then you probably also had to know exactly what you were looking for.

†

He came down the path through the park leading to the school and glanced over at Jocke's underpass.

The news had made quite a splash in the papers yesterday, mostly because of the macabre way in which the body had been discovered. A murdered alcoholic was normally nothing noteworthy but there had been salacious interest in the children watching, the fire department who had to saw into the ice, etc. Next to the text there was a passport photo of Jocke in which he looked like a mass murderer, at the very least.

Lacke continued on past the Blackeberg school's dour brick façade, the wide high steps, like the entrance to the National Courts, or to hell. On the wall next to the lowest step someone had spray painted the words "Iron Maiden," whatever that meant. Maybe some group.

He walked past the parking lot, out onto Björnsonsgatan. Normally he would have taken a short cut across the back of the school but there it was . . . dark. He could very easily imagine that creature curled up in the shadows. He looked up into the tops of the tall pine trees that bordered the path. A few dark clumps in among the branches. Probably bird nests.

It wasn't just what the creature looked like, it was also the way in which it attacked. He would maybe, *maybe*, have been able to accept the idea that the teeth and claws had some natural explanation, if it hadn't been for the jump from the tree. Before carrying Virginia back he had looked up at the tree. The branch that the creature had jumped from was maybe five meters above the ground.

To fall five meters onto someone's back—if you added "circus artist" to the other things to arrive at a "natural explanation," then maybe. But all things considered it was as improbable as what he had said to Virginia, which he now regretted.

Damn it . . .

He pulled the box of chocolates from his pants. Maybe his body heat had already melted the chocolates? He shook the box gently. No. It made a rattling sound. The chocolates had not run together. He continued along Björnsonsgatan, past the ICA store.

CRUSHED TOMATOES. THREE CANS 5 KRONOR.

Six days ago.

Lacke's hand was still wrapped around the stone. He looked at the sign, could imagine Virginia's concentration in order to make the even, straight letters. Wouldn't she have stayed home to rest today? It would be just like her to stumble in to work before the blood even had a chance to congeal.

When he reached the front door of her building he looked up at her window. No light. Maybe she was with her daughter? Well, he had to at least go up and leave the chocolates on her door handle if she wasn't home. It was pitch black inside the stairwell. The hair on the back of his neck stood up.

The child is here.

He stood frozen in place, then threw himself on the shining red button of the light switch, pushing it in with the back of the hand carrying the box of chocolates. The other hand squeezed tightly around the stone in his pocket.

A soft clonking from the relay in the cellar as the light was turned on. Nothing. Virginia's stairwell. Yellow vomit-patterned concrete stairs. Wood doors. He breathed deeply a few times and started up the steps.

Only now did he realize how tired he was. Virginia lived all the way up on the third floor, and his legs were dragging him up there, two lifeless planks attached to his hips. He was hoping Virginia was home, that she was feeling good, that he could sink down into her armchair and simply rest in the place he most wanted to be. He let go of the rock in his pocket and rang the bell. Waited a while. Rang it again.

He had started trying to balance the box of chocolates on the door handle when he heard creeping steps from within the apartment. He backed away from the door. On the inside, the steps came to a halt. She was standing next to the door, on the other side.

"Who is it?"

Never, ever had she asked this question before. You rang the bell, you heard her steps, swish swish, and then the door opened. Come in, come in. He cleared his throat.

"It's me."

Pause. Could he hear her breath or was it his imagination?

"What do you want?"

"I wanted to see how you were doing, that's all."

Another pause.

"I'm not feeling so good."

"Can I come in?"

He waited. Held the box of chocolates in front of him in both hands, feeling silly. A bang as she turned the first lock, the rustle of keys as she unlocked the dead bolt. Another rustle as she took the chain off the door. The door handle was pushed down and the door opened.

He involuntarily took half a step back, the small of his back hitting against the stair railing. Virginia was standing in the doorway. She looked like she was dying.

Besides the swollen cheek, her face was covered with tiny little boils and her eyes looked like she had the hangover of the century: a network of red lines in the whites and the pupils so tightly contracted they had almost disappeared. She nodded. "I look like hell."

"No, no. I only . . . I thought maybe . . . can I come in?"

"No. I don't have the energy."

"Have you been to the doctor?"

"I will. Tomorrow."

"Good. Well, I . . ."

He handed her the box of chocolates that he had been holding in front of him the whole time like a shield. Virginia accepted it. "Thank you."

"Virginia. Is there anything I can—?"

"No. It'll be alright. I just need some rest. Can't stand here any longer. We'll be in touch."

"Yes, I'll come by . . ."

Virginia closed the door.

". . . tomorrow."

The rustling of locks and chains again. He stood there outside her door with his arms hanging by his sides. Walked up to the door and put his ear to it. He heard a cabinet opened, slow steps inside the apartment.

What should I do?

It was not his place to force her to do something she didn't want, but he would have preferred to bring her to the hospital now. Well. He would come back here tomorrow morning. If there was no improvement he would bring her in to the hospital whether she wanted to or not.

Lacke walked down the stairs, one step at a time. So tired. When he reached the last flight of stairs before the door to the outside, he sat down on the highest step and leaned his head in his hands.

I am . . . responsible.

The light went off. The tendons in his neck tensed; he drew a ragged breath. Only the relay. On a timer. He sat on the steps in the dark, carefully taking the rock out of his pocket, resting it in both hands and staring out into the dark.

Come on, then, he thought. *Come on.*

✝

Virginia closed the door on Lacke's pleading face, locked it, and put the chain on. Didn't want him to see her. Didn't want to see anyone. It had cost her a great effort to say those few words, to act according to some basic form of normality.

Her condition had deteriorated rapidly after she got home from the ICA store. Lotten had helped her home and in her dazed state she had simply put up with the pain of daylight on her face. Once she was home she had looked in the mirror and seen the hundreds of tiny blisters on her face and hands. Burn marks.

She had slept for a few hours, woken up when it got dark. Her hunger had then changed in nature, been transformed into anxiety. A school of hysterically wriggling little fish now filled her circulatory system. She could neither lie down, nor sit, nor stand. She walked around and around the apartment, scratched her body, took a cold shower to dampen the jumpy, tingling feeling. Nothing helped.

It defied description. It reminded her of when she was twenty-two and had been informed that her father had fallen from the roof of their summer cottage and broken his neck. That time she had also walked around and around as if there was not a single place on earth where her body could rest, where it didn't hurt.

Same thing now, except worse. The anxiety did not let up for a moment. It forced her around the apartment until she couldn't stand it any longer, until she sat down on a chair and banged her head into the kitchen table. In desperation she took two sleeping pills and washed them down with a couple of mouthfuls of wine that tasted like dishwater.

Normally one was all she needed to fall asleep as if she had been hit in the head. The only effect on her now was that she became intensely nauseated and after five minutes vomited green slime and both of the half-dissolved tablets.

She kept walking around, ripped a newspaper into tiny pieces, crawled on the floor and whimpered. She crawled into the kitchen, pushed the bottle of wine from the table so it fell to the ground and broke in front of her eyes.

She picked up one of the broken shards.

Didn't think. Just pressed it into the palm of her hand and the pain felt good, felt right. The school of fish in her body rushed toward the point of the pain and blood welled out. She pressed the palm to her mouth and licked it, and the anxiety gave way. She cried with relief while she punctured her hand in a new place and kept sucking. The taste of blood mingled with the taste of tears.

Curled up on the kitchen floor, with her hand pressed against her mouth, greedily sucking like a newborn child that finds its mother's breast for the first time, she felt—for the second time on this terrible day—calm.

About half an hour after she had stood up from the floor, swept the shards up from the floor, and put on a Band-Aid, the anxiety had started to return. That was when Lacke had rung the bell.

When she had sent him away and locked the door she walked out into the kitchen and put the box of chocolates in the pantry. She sat down on a kitchen chair and tried to understand. The anxiety would not let her. Soon it would force her to her feet again. The only thing she knew was that no one could be with her here. Particularly not Lacke. She would hurt him. The anxiety would drive her to it.

She had contracted some kind of disease. There were medicines for diseases.

Tomorrow she would consult a doctor, someone who could examine her and say that: Well, this was simply an attack of X. We'll have to put you on Y and Z for a couple of weeks. That'll clear it right up.

She walked to and fro in the apartment. It was starting to get unbearable again.

She hit her arms, her legs, but the small fish had come back to life and nothing helped. She knew what she had to do. She sobbed from fear of the pain but the actual sensation was so brief and the relief so great.

She walked out into the kitchen and got a sharp little fruit knife, went back out and sat down in the couch in the living room, rested the blade against the underside of her arm.

Only to get her through the night. Tomorrow she would seek help. It was self-evident she couldn't keep going like this. Drink her own blood. Of course not. There would have to be a change. But for now . . .

The saliva rose up in her mouth, wet anticipation. She cut into herself. Deeply . . .

Saturday

Oskar cleared the table and his dad did the dishes. The eider duck had been delicious, of course. No shot. There was not much to wash off the plates. After they had eaten most of the bird and almost all of the potato they had sopped up the remains on their plates with white bread. That was the best part. Pour out gravy on the plate and sop it up with porous bits of white bread that half-dissolved in the gravy and then melted in your mouth.

His dad wasn't a great cook or anything, but three dishes—*pytt-i-panna*, fried herring, and roasted seabird—he made so often that he had mastered them. Tomorrow they would have *pytt-i-panna* made from the leftovers.

Oskar had spent the hours before dinner in his room. He had his own room at his dad's house that was bare compared to his room in town, but he liked it. In town he had posters and pictures, a lot of things; it was always changing.

This room never changed and that was exactly what he liked about it.

It looked the same now as when he was seven years old.

When he walked into the room, with its familiar damp smell that lingered in the air after a rapid heating job in anticipation of his visit, it was as if nothing had happened for . . . a long time.

Here were still the Donald Duck and Bamse comic books bought during the many summers of years past. He no longer read them when he was in town, but here he did. He knew the stories by heart but he read them again.

While the smells filtered in from the kitchen he lay on his bed and read an old issue of Donald Duck. Donald, his nephews, and Uncle Scrooge were traveling to a distant country where there was no money and the cap tops of the bottles containing Uncle Scrooge's calming tonic became the currency.

When he had finished reading he busied himself with the assortment of lures and sinkers that he kept in an old sewing kit his dad had given him. Tied a new line with loose hooks, five of them, and attached the lures for summertime herring fishing.

Then they ate, and when his dad was done with the dishes they played tic-tac-toe.

Oskar liked sitting like that with his dad; the graph paper on the thin table, their heads leaning over the page, close to each other. The fire crackled in the fireplace.

Oskar was crosses and his dad circles, as usual. His dad never let Oskar win purposely and so until a few years ago his dad had always won easily, even if Oskar got lucky now and again. But now it was more even. Maybe it had to do with him practicing so much with the Rubik's Cube.

The matches could go on over half the page, which was to Oskar's advantage. He was good at keeping in mind places with holes that could be filled if Dad did this or that, mask an offensive as a defense.

Tonight it was Oskar who won.

Three matches in a row had now been encircled and marked with an "O" in the middle. Only a little one, where Oskar had been thinking of something else, had a "P" on it. Oskar filled in a cross and got two open fours where his dad could only block one. His dad sighed and shook his head.

"Well, Oskar. Looks like I've met my match."

"Seems like it."

For the sake of the game, his dad blocked the one four and Oskar filled in the other. His dad closed one side of the four and Oskar put a fifth cross on the other side, drew a circle around the whole thing, and wrote a neat "O." His dad scratched his beard and pulled out a new sheet of paper. Held his pen up.

"But this time I'm going to . . ."

"You can always dream. You start."

✝

Four crosses and three circles into the match there was a knock at the front door. Shortly thereafter it opened and Oskar could hear thuds from someone stamping the snow off their feet.

"Hello, hello!"

Dad looked up from the paper, leaned back in the chair, and looked out into the hall. Oskar pinched his lips together.

No.

His dad nodded at the new arrival. "Come in."

"Thank you."

Soft thumps from someone walking through the hall with woolen socks on their feet. A moment later Janne came into the kitchen, said: "Oh I see. Well aren't you two having a cozy evening."

Dad gestured toward Oskar. "You've met my boy."

"Sure," Janne said. "Hi Oskar, how's it going?"

"Fine."

Until now. Go away.

Janne thudded over to the kitchen table; the woolen socks had slid down his heels and were fluttering out in front of his toes like deformed flippers. He pulled out a chair and sat down.

"I see you're playing tic-tac-toe."

"Yes, but the boy is too good for me. I can't beat him anymore."

"No. Been practicing in town? Do you dare play against me, then, Oskar?"

Oskar shook his head. Didn't even want to look at Janne, knew what he would see there. Watery eyes, a mouth pulled into a sheep-grin; yes, Janne looked like an old sheep and the blond curly hair only strengthened the impression. One of Dad's "friends" who was Oskar's enemy.

Janne rubbed his hands together, producing a sound like sandpaper, and in the backlight from the hall Oskar could see small flakes of skin fall to the floor. Janne had some kind of skin disease that flared up in the summer that made his face look like a rotten blood orange.

"Well, well. It sure is cozy in here."

You always *say that. Go away with your revolting face and your old stale words.*

"Dad, aren't we going to keep playing?"

"Of course, but now that we have a guest . . ."

"Go on, play."

Janne leaned back in his chair and looked like he had all the time in the world. But Oskar knew he had lost the battle. It was over. Now it would turn out like always.

Most of all he wanted to scream, break something, most of all Janne, when Dad walked over to the pantry and brought out the bottle, picked up two shot glasses and put them on the table. Janne rubbed his hands so the flakes danced.

"Well, well. What have we here . . ."

Oskar looked down at the paper with its unfinished game.

He was going to put his cross there.

But there would be no more crosses tonight. No circles. Nothing.

There was a light gurgling sound as Dad poured out the shots. The delicate upside-down cone of glass was filled with transparent liquid. It was so little and fragile in Dad's hand. It almost disappeared.

And still it ruined everything. Everything.

Oskar crinkled up the unfinished game and put it in the woodstove. Dad made no protests. He and Janne had started talking about some acquaintance who had broken his leg. Went on to talk about other cases of broken bones that they had experienced or heard about, refilled their glasses.

Oskar stayed where he was in front of the stove, with the doors open, looking at the paper that burst into flames, blackened. Then he got the other games and put them in the fire as well.

Dad and Janne took the glasses and the bottle and moved to the living room. Dad said something to Oskar about "come and talk a little" and Oskar said "later, maybe." He sat there in front of the stove and stared into the fire. The heat caressed his face. He got up, got the graph paper from the kitchen table, tore unused pages out of it and put them in the fire.

When the whole pad with cover and all was blackened he took the pencils and threw them into the fire as well.

†

There was something uncanny about the hospital at this time of night. Maud Carlberg sat in the reception and looked out over the almost empty entrance hall. The cafeteria and kiosk were closed; only the occasional person came through, like a ghost under this high ceiling.

Late at night like this she liked to imagine that it was she and only she who was guarding this enormous building that was Danderyd Hospital. It wasn't true, of course. If there was any kind of a problem she only had to push a button and a night guard would turn up within three minutes.

There was a game she liked to play to get these late-night hours to pass.

She thought of a profession, a place to live, and the basic outline of a person's background. Perhaps an illness. Then she applied all this in her mind to the next person who approached her at the desk. Often the result was . . . amusing.

For example, she could imagine a pilot who lived on Götgatan and had two dogs that a neighbor took care of when the pilot was away on his or her flights. The neighbor was secretly in love with the pilot, whose biggest problem was that he or she saw little green men with red caps swimming around in the clouds when he or she was out flying.

OK. Then all she had to do was wait.

Maybe after a while a woman with a ravaged appearance turned up. A female pilot. Had been drinking too much on the sly from those tiny liquor bottles they give you on the planes, had seen the little green men, had been fired. Now she sat at home with her dogs all day. The neighbor was still in love with her, however.

Maud kept going like that.

Sometimes she lectured herself about her game, because it prevented her from taking people seriously. But she couldn't help herself. Right now she was waiting for a minister whose passion was expensive sports cars and who loved picking up hitchhikers with the motive of trying to convert them.

Man or woman? Old or young? How would someone like that look?

Maud rested her chin in her hands and looked toward the front doors. Not a lot of people tonight. Visiting hours were over and new patients who turned up with Saturday-night injuries—mostly alcohol-related in one way or another —were brought to the emergency room.

The revolving doors started to turn. The sports car minister, perhaps.

But no, this was one of those cases where she had to give up. It was a child. A waif-like little . . . girl, about ten or twelve years old. Maud started to imagine a chain of events that would eventually lead this child to become that minister, but quickly stopped herself. The girl looked unhappy.

She walked over to the large map of the hospital with the color-coded lines marking the routes you had to take to go to this or that place. Few adults could make sense of that map, so how would a child be able to?

Maud leaned forward and said in a low voice: "Can I help you?"

The girl turned to her and smiled shyly, went over to the reception. Her hair was wet, the occasional snowflake that had not yet melted shone white against the black. She didn't keep her gaze glued to the floor as children often did in a foreign environment. No, the dark sad eyes stared straight into Maud's as she walked over to the counter. A thought, as clear as though it were audible, flashed through Maud's head.

I have to give you something. But what?

In her mind, stupidly, she quickly went through the contents of her desk drawers. A pen? A balloon?

The child stopped in front of the counter. Only her neck and head reached over the top of it.

"Excuse me . . . I'm looking for my father."

"I see. Has he been admitted here?"

"Yes, although, I don't know for sure . . ."

Maud looked past her at the doors, looked quickly around the hall, and then fixed on the girl in front of her, who was not even wearing a jacket. Only a black knitted turtleneck where drops of water and snowflakes glittered in the light of the reception area.

"Are you all alone here, dear? At this hour?"

"Yes, I . . . just wanted to know if he is here."

"Let's see about that then, shall we? What's his name?"

JOHN AJVIDE LINDQVIST   254

"I don't know."

"You don't know?"

The girl bent her head, seemed to be looking for something on the ground. When she straightened her head again the large dark eyes were wet with tears and her lower lip trembled.

"No, he . . . But he is here."

"But my dear . . ."

Maud felt as if something in her chest were breaking and tried to take refuge in action; she bent down and took out her roll of paper towels from the lowest desk drawer, pulled off a piece, and handed it over to the girl. At last she was able to give her something, if only a piece of paper.

The girl blew her nose, and dried her eyes in a very . . . adult way.

"Thank you."

"But then I don't know . . . so what's wrong with him?"

"He is . . . the police took him."

"But then you'd better turn to them."

"Yes, but they're keeping him here. Because he's sick."

"Well, what kind of illness does he have?"

"He . . . I just know that the police have him here. Where is he?"

"Probably on the top floor, but you can't go up there if you haven't . . . made an appointment with them ahead of time."

"I just wanted to know which window was his so I could . . . I don't know."

The girl started to cry again. Maud's throat got so tight it hurt. The girl wanted to know this so she could stand outside the hospital in the snow . . . and look up toward her father's window. Maud swallowed.

"I can call them if you like. I'm sure that you can—"

"No, it's fine. Now I know. Now I can . . . Thanks, thanks a lot."

The girl turned away and walked back to the revolving door.

My Lord, all these broken families.

The girl walked out the doors and Maud kept staring at the place where the girl had disappeared.

Something was wrong.

In her mind Maud went over what the girl had looked like, how she had moved. There was something that didn't match up, something you . . . It took Maud half a minute to remember what it was. The girl had not been wearing any shoes.

Maud jumped up and ran to the doors. She was only allowed to leave the reception desk unattended under very special circumstances. She decided that this counted as one of them. She trotted through the revolving doors impatiently *hurry hurry hurry* and then out into the parking lot. The girl was nowhere in sight. What should she do? The social welfare people would have to be brought in; no one had checked to make sure there was someone to look after the girl. That was the only explanation. Who was her father?

Maud looked around the parking lot without finding the girl. She ran down one side of the hospital, in the direction of the subway. No girl. On her way back to the reception she tried to figure out who she should call, what she should do.

✝

Oskar lay in bed, waiting for the Werewolf. He felt the inside of his chest churning with rage, despair. From the living room he heard his dad's and Janne's loud voices, mixed with music from the tape recorder. The Deep Brothers. Oskar could not actually make out the words but he knew the song by heart.

> "We live in the country, and soon we realized
> we're country fellas and then it hit us
> We needed something for the barn
> We sold the china, all nice and fine
> and bought ourselves a great big swine . . ."

At this point the whole band started to imitate different farm animals. Normally he thought the Deep Brothers were funny. Now he hated them. Because they were part of this. Singing their idiotic songs for Dad and Janne while they got packed.

He knew exactly how it was going to go.

In an hour or so the bottle would be empty and Janne would go home.

Then Dad would pace up and down in the kitchen for a while, and finally decide he needed to talk to Oskar.

He would come into Oskar's room and he would no longer be Dad. Just an alcohol-stinking, clumsy mess, all sentimental and needy. Would want Oskar to get out of bed. Needed to talk for a while. About how he still loved Mom, how he loved Oskar, did Oskar love him back? Slurring about all the wrongs he had ever experienced, and in the worst case scenario get himself worked up, become angry.

He never got violent or anything. But what Oskar saw in his eyes at those times was the absolutely scariest thing he had ever seen. Then there was no trace of Dad left. Just a monster who had somehow crawled into his dad's body and taken control of it.

The person his dad became when he drank had no connection to the person he was when he was sober. And so it was comforting to think about Dad being a werewolf. That he in fact contained a whole other person in his body. Just as the moon brought out the wolf in a werewolf, so alcohol brought this creature out of his dad.

Oskar picked up a Bamse comic, tried to read but couldn't concentrate. He felt . . . forlorn. In an hour or so he would find himself alone with the Monster. And the only thing he could do was wait.

He threw the Bamse comic at the wall and got out of bed, went to get his wallet. One pack of prepaid subway tickets and two notes from Eli. He put Eli's notes side by side on the bed.

THEN WINDOW, LET DAY IN, AND LET LIFE OUT.

A heart.

SEE YOU TONIGHT. ELI.

And then the second.

I MUST BE GONE AND LIVE, OR STAY AND DIE. YOURS, ELI.

There are no vampires.

The night was a black cover over the window. Oskar shut his eyes and thought about the route to Stockholm, raced past the houses, the farms, the fields. Flew into the courtyard in Blackeberg, in through her window, and there she was.

He opened his eyes, stared at the black rectangle of the window. Out there.

The Deep Brothers had started a song about a bicycle that got a flat tire. Dad and Janne laughed much too loudly at something. Something fell over.

Which monster do you choose?

Oskar put Eli's notes back in his wallet and put his clothes on. Sneaked out into the hall and put on his shoes, his coat, and hat. He stood still in the hall a few seconds, listening to the sounds from the living room.

He turned to go, saw something, stopped.

On the shoe rack in the hall were his old rubber boots, the ones he had worn when he was four or five. They had been there as long as he could remember, even though there was no one who could use them. Next to them were his dad's enormous Tretorn boots, one of them with a patch on the heel like the kind you use to fix bicycle tires.

Why had he kept them?

Oskar knew why. Two people grew up out of the boots with their backs to him. His dad's broad back, and next to it Oskar's thin one. Oskar's arm upstretched, his hand in Dad's. They walked in their boots up over a boulder, maybe on their way to pick raspberries.

He suppressed a sob, tears rising in his throat. He stretched out his hand to touch the small boots. A salvo of laughter came from the living room. Janne's voice, distorted. Probably imitating someone, he was good at that.

Oskar's fingers closed over the top of the boots. Yes. He didn't know why but it felt right. He carefully opened the front door, closed it behind him. The night was icy cold, the snow a sea of tiny diamonds in the moonlight.

He started to walk up to the main road, with the boots tightly clasped in his hands.

✝

The guard was sleeping, a young policeman who had been brought in after the hospital staff had protested against having one of them constantly assigned to guard Håkan. The door was, however, secured with a coded lock. That was probably why he had dared to snooze.

Only a night lamp was on and Håkan was studying the blurry shadows on the ceiling the way a healthy man might lie in the grass looking at clouds. He was looking for shapes, figures in the shadows. Didn't know if he would be able to read, but longed to do so.

Eli was gone and everything that had dominated his old life was coming back. He would get a long prison sentence and he would devote that time to read everything he had not yet read and also to reread everything he had promised himself to reread.

He was going over all the books by Selma Lagerlöf when a scraping sound interrupted him. He listened. More scraping. It was coming from the window.

He turned his head as far as he could, looked in that direction. Against the dark sky there was a lighter oval, lit by the night lamp. A pale little blob appeared beside the oval, moving back and forth. A hand. Waving. The hand pulled along the window and that scraping, screeching sound came again.

Eli.

Håkan was grateful for the fact that he was not connected to an EKG machine as his heart began to race, fluttering like a bird in a net. He imagined his heart bursting out of his chest, crawling over the floor to the window.

Come in, my beloved, come in.

But the window was locked and even if it had been open his lips could not form the words that would allow Eli to enter the room. He could perhaps make a gesture that meant the same thing, but he had never really understood all that.

Can I?

Tentatively he pulled one leg down off the bed, then the other. Put both feet on the floor, tried to stand. His legs did not want to carry his weight after lying in bed for ten days. He steadied himself against the railing, was about to fall to one side.

The IV tube was stretched taut, tugging on the skin where it entered his body. Some kind of alarm was connected to the IV, a thin electric wire ran along the length of it. If he pulled the tube out at either end the alarm would go off. He moved his arm in the direction of the IV stand creating more slack, then turned to the window.

Have to.

The IV stand had wheels, the batteries to the alarm were screwed in a little ways under the bag. He reached for the stand, grabbed hold of it. With the stand as support he stood up, slowly, slowly. The room swam around in front of his one eye as he took a tentative step, stopped, listened. The guard's breathing was still calm and regular.

He shuffled through the room at a snail's pace. As soon as one of the wheels squeaked he stopped and listened. Something told him this was the last time he would see Eli and he didn't intend to . . .

. . . *blow it.*

His body was as exhausted as after a marathon when he finally reached the window and pressed his eye against it so the gelatinous membrane on his face was plastered onto the glass and his skin started to burn again.

Only a few centimeters of double-paned glass separated his eye from his beloved. Eli moved her hand across the window as if to caress his deformed face. Håkan held his eye as close to Eli's as he could and still his sight was distorted: Eli's black eyes dissolved, became fuzzy.

He had assumed his tear canal had burned away like everything else, but this wasn't the case. Tears welled up in his eye and blinded him. The provisional eyelid could not blink them away and so he carefully wiped his eye with his uninjured hand while his body shook with silent sobs.

His hand fumbled for the window lock. Turned it. Snot ran out of the hole that had been his nose, dripping down onto the window sill as he opened the window.

Cold air rushed into the room. Only a matter of time before the guard woke up. Håkan reached his arm, his healthy hand, through the window toward Eli. Eli pulled herself up onto the window ledge, took his hand between hers and kissed it. Whispered: "Hello, my friend."

Håkan nodded slowly to let her know he could hear her. Took his hand out of Eli's and stroked her over the cheek, Her skin like frozen silk. Everything came back.

He wasn't going to rot in some jail cell surrounded by meaningless letters. Harassed by other prisoners for having committed the—in their eyes—worst of all crimes. He would be with Eli. He would . . .

Eli leaned close to him, curled up on the windowsill.

"What do you want me to do?"

Håkan moved his hand from her cheek and pointed to his throat.

Eli shook her head.

"That would mean I'd have to kill you . . . after."

Håkan took his hand from his throat, brought it back to Eli's face. Rested a finger for a moment on her lips. Then pulled it back.

Pointed once more at his throat.

†

His breath came out in white clouds but he wasn't cold. After ten minutes Oskar had reached the store. The moon had followed him from his dad's house, played hide-and-seek behind the spruce tops. Oskar checked the time. Half past ten. He had seen on the bus schedule in the hall that the last bus from Norrtälje left around half past twelve.

He crossed the open space in front of the store, lit up by the lights of the gas pumps, walked out toward Kapellskärsvägen. He had never hitched a ride before and his mom would go crazy if she knew. Climbing into a complete stranger's car . . .

He walked faster, past a few lit-up houses. People were sitting in there having a good time. Kids sleeping in their beds without having to worry about their parents coming and waking them up to talk a lot of nonsense.

This is Dad's fault, not mine.

He looked down at the boots he was still carrying in his hands, threw them into the ditch, stopped. The boots came to rest there, two dark splotches against the snow in the moonlight.

Mom will never let me come out here again.

Dad would realize he was gone in maybe . . . one hour. Then he would go outside and look for him, shout out his name. Then he would call Mom. Would he? Probably. To see if Oskar had called her. Mom would realize Dad was drunk when he told her about Oskar being gone and then it would be . . .

Wait. Like this.

When he got to Norrtälje he would call his dad from a pay phone and tell him he had gone back to Stockholm, that he was going to spend the night at a friend's house and then go back to Mom's tomorrow morning and not say anything about it.

Then Dad would get his lesson without turning it into a catastrophe. *Great. And then . . .*

Oskar walked down into the ditch and picked up the rubber boots, crumpled them up into his pockets, and kept walking along the road. Now everything was good. Now Oskar was the one who decided where he was going and the moon shone kindly down on him, lighting up his way. He lifted his hand in greeting and started to sing.

"Here comes Fritjof Andersson, it's snowing on his hat . . ."

Then he didn't know any more of the lyrics so he hummed instead.

After a couple hundred meters, a car came. He heard it from far away and slowed down, holding out a raised thumb. The car drove past him, stopped, and backed up. The door to the passenger side opened; there was a woman in the car, a little younger than Mom. Nothing to be afraid of.

"Hello. Where are you headed?"

"Stockholm. Well, Norrtälje."

"I'm also on my way to Norrtälje, so . . ."

Oskar leaned into the car.

"Oh my, do your mom and dad know you're here?"

"Yes, but Dad's car has broken down and . . . well . . ."

The woman looked at him, seemed to be thinking something over.

"OK, why don't you get in."

"Thanks."

Oskar slid into the seat, closed the door behind him. They drove off.

"Do you want to be dropped off at the bus stop?"

"Yes, please."

Oskar sat back in the seat, enjoying the warmth rising in his body, especially across his back. Must be one of those electric chairs. To think it was this easy. Lit-up houses flickered by.

Go on, sit there.

And with a song, with a game we go to Spain and . . . somewhere.

"Do you live in Stockholm?"

"Yes. In Blackeberg."

"Blackeberg . . . that's somewhere to the west, isn't it?"

"I think so. They call it the Western Suburbs, so it must be."

"I see. Is there something important waiting for you?"

"Yes."

"Must be something extra special for you to set off like this."

"Yes. It is."

†

It was cold in the room. His joints felt stiff after having rested so long in an uncomfortable position. The guard stretched and his joints creaked. He glanced at the hospital bed and was suddenly wide awake.

Gone . . . the cold . . . damn!

He got to his feet unsteadily, looked around. Thank God. The man had not escaped. But how the hell had he managed to get over to the window? And . . .

What is that?

The murderer stood leaning against the windowsill with a black lump on one shoulder. His naked backside was visible under the hospital gown. The guard took a step toward the window, stopped, caught his breath.

The lump was a head. A pair of dark eyes met his.

He fumbled for his weapon, realized he wasn't carrying one. For security reasons. The nearest weapon was kept in the safe out in the corridor. And anyway, this was just a child, he saw that now.

"You there! Keep absolutely still!"

He ran the three paces to the window and the child's head rose up from the man's throat.

At the same moment the guard reached them the child jumped from the windowsill and disappeared upward. The feet dangled for a moment in the upper corner of the window before they vanished.

Bare feet.

The guard stuck his head out the window, managed to catch sight of a body making its way across the roof, out of sight. The man by his side wheezed.

God almighty. Fuck it.

In the weak light he could see the man's shoulder and back were darkly stained. The man's head was hanging down and there was a fresh wound on his neck. Up on the roof he heard the light thuds of feet making their way across the sheet metal. He stood up, paralyzed.

Priorities. What were the priorities?

He could not remember. Save life first. Yes. But there were others who could . . . he ran to the door, punched in the combination and ran slip-sliding out into the corridor, shouting:

"Nurse! Nurse! Come here! This is an emergency!"

He ran to the fire stairs while the night nurse came out of her office, jogging in the direction of the room he had just left. When they passed each other she asked: "What is it?"

"Emergency. It's an . . . emergency. Get people in here, there's been a . . . murder."

The words didn't want to come. He had never experienced anything like this before. He had been assigned to this boring guard duty because he was inexperienced. Replaceable, so to speak. As he ran to the stairs he pulled out his radio and alerted the station, called for reinforcements.

✝

The nurse tried to prepare for the worst: a body lying on the floor in a pool of blood. Hanging by a sheet from a hot water pipe. She had seen both.

When she walked into the room she saw only an empty bed. And something by the window. At first she thought it was a heap of clothes laid on the windowsill. Then she saw it was moving.

She rushed over to the window in order to stop him, but the man had gotten too far. He was already up on the windowsill, halfway out the window, when she started to run. She got there in time to catch a corner of his hospital gown before the man rolled his body off the sill, the IV pulling out of his arm. The sound of ripping fabric and then she stood there with a piece of blue cloth in her hand. After a couple of seconds she heard a distant, dull thud when the body hit the ground. Then the high-pitched alarm from the IV stand.

✝

The taxi driver pulled around in front of the emergency room entrance. The older man in the back seat who, during the whole trip from Jakobsberg had entertained him with his medical history of heart trouble, opened the door and remained seated, expectantly.

OK, OK.

The driver opened his door, walked around the side, and put out his arm to support the old man. Snow fell inside the collar of his jacket. The old one was about to take his arm but his gaze fixed on a point somewhere in the sky, and froze.

"Come on. I'll help you."

The old man pointed up. "What is that?"

The driver looked where he was pointing.

A person was standing on the roof of the hospital. A small person. With a bare chest, arms held tightly along the side.

Alert someone.

He should send out an alert via the radio. But he just stood there, unable to move. If he moved some kind of balance would be upset and the little person would fall.

There was a pain in his hand where the old one gripped him with claw-like fingers, digging his nails into his palm. But still he didn't move.

The snow fell into his eyes and he blinked. The person on the roof spread his or her arms, brought them up overhead. Something was suspended between the arms and the body, some kind of membrane . . . webbing. The old man pulled on his hand, got up out of the car, and stood next to him.

At the same time as the old man's shoulder touched his, the little person . . . the child . . . fell straight out. He gasped and the old one's fingers again dug into his hand. The child fell straight at them.

Instinctively they both ducked, putting their arms up over their heads. Nothing happened.

When they looked up again the child was gone. The driver looked around, but all they could see around them was the falling snow in the glow of the street lamps. The old man drew a rattling breath.

"It was the angel of death. The angel of death. I will never leave this place alive."

Saturday

Habba-Habba-soudd-soudd!"

The very vocal group of boys and girls had gotten on at Hötorget. They were maybe Tommy's age. Drunk. The guys howled from time to time, fell on top of the girls, and the girls laughed, beating them off. Then they sang again. The same song, over and over. Oskar looked at them in secret.

I'm never going to be like that.

Unfortunately. He would have liked to. It looked like fun. But Oskar would never manage to be like that, do what the guys did. One of them stood up on his seat and sang loudly: "A-Huleba-Huleba, A-ha-Huleba . . ."

An old man who was dozing in a handicapped seat at one end of the subway car shouted out: "Keep it down, will you? I'm trying to sleep."

One of the girls gave him the finger.

"You can sleep at home."

The whole gang laughed and started in on the song again. A few seats away there was a man reading a book. Oskar craned his neck so he could read the title, but could only see the name of the author: Göran Tunström. Nobody he had ever heard of.

In the nearest block of two-seaters facing each other there was an old woman with a handbag on her lap. She was talking to herself in a low voice, gesturing to an invisible interlocutor.

He had never taken the subway this late before. Were these the same people who in the daytime sat quietly and stared in front of them, or read newspapers? Or was this a special group that only appeared at night?

The man with the book turned the page. Strangely enough Oskar had no book with him. Too bad. He would have wanted to be like that man, reading a book, oblivious to everything around him. But he only had his Walkman and the Cube. Had been planning to listen to the KISS tape he had gotten from Tommy, had tried it a little on the bus but got sick of it after only a couple of songs.

He took his Cube out of his bag. Three sides were solved. Only an insignificant amount needed to be done on the fourth. Eli and he had spent one evening working on it together, talked about how you could do it and since then Oskar had become better. He looked at all sides and tried to think up a strategy but couldn't get past thinking of Eli's face.

What will she look like?

He wasn't afraid. He was in a state of . . . yes . . . he could not be here, at this time, could not be doing what he was doing. It didn't exist. It wasn't him.

I don't exist and no one can do anything to me.

He had called his dad from Norrtälje and his dad had cried on the phone. Said he would call for someone to go and pick up Oskar. It was the second time in his life Oskar heard his father cry. For a moment Oskar was about to give in. But when his dad had gotten worked up and started yelling about how he had to have his own life and be allowed to do as he damn well pleased in his own house, Oskar had hung up on him.

That was when it had really started, that feeling that he didn't really exist.

The group of boys and girls got off at Ängbyplan. One of the guys turned around and shouted into the subway car:

"Sweet dreams, my . . . my . . ."

He couldn't think of the word and one of the girls pulled him back with her. Just before the doors closed he tore himself away and ran over to them, holding one open and shouting:

". . . fellow passengers! Sweet dreams, my fellow passengers!"

He let go of the door and the subway car started to go. The reading man lowered his book and looked at the young people on the platform. Then he turned to Oskar and looked him in the eyes. And smiled. Oskar smiled back briefly, then pretended to turn his attention back to the Cube.

In his chest a feeling of having . . . passed muster. The man had looked at him and transmitted the thought, *You're alright. What you're doing is good.*

He didn't dare look up at the man anymore. He felt like the man *knew*. Oskar turned the Cube one click, then turned it back.

†

With the exception of Oskar, two people got off at Blackeberg, from other subway cars. An older guy he didn't recognize and then a rockabilly guy who appeared very drunk. The rockabilly guy walked up to the older guy and shouted:

"Hey man, spare a cigarette?"

"Sorry, don't smoke."

The rockabilly guy didn't appear to hear more than the negative, because he drew a ten kronor note from his pocket and waved it around. "I got ten! One stick is all I need, man."

The guy shook his head and walked away. The rockabilly guy stood still, swaying, and when Oskar walked past he lifted his head and said: "You!" But his eyes narrowed, he focused them on Oskar, and then he shook his head. "No. Nothing. Go in peace, brother."

Oskar kept going up the stairs, up into the subway station. Wondered if the rockabilly guy was planning to pee on the electric rail. The older guy went out through the exit doors. Except for the ticket collector in his booth, Oskar was alone in the station.

Everything was so different at night. The photo shop, florist, and clothing store in the station were dark. The ticket collector sat with his feet up on the counter, reading something. So quiet. The clock on the wall said a few minutes past two. He should be lying in bed now. Sleeping. Should at the very least be sleepy. But no. He was so tired his body felt hollow, but it was a hollowness filled with electricity. Not sleepiness.

A door down by the platform was thrown open and he heard the rockabilly guy's voice from down there: "And bow down, you officers in your helmets and batons . . ."

Same song he had been singing. He chuckled and started to run. Ran out the doors, down the hill toward the school, past it and the parking lot. It had started to snow again and the large flakes squelched the heat in his face. He looked up as he was running. The moon was still there, peeking out between the houses.

Once he was in the courtyard he stopped, caught his breath. Almost all the windows were dark, but wasn't there a faint light coming from behind the blinds of Eli's apartment?

What will she look like?

He walked up the sloping yard, glancing at his own dark window. The normal Oskar was lying in there, sleeping. Oskar . . . pre-Eli. The one with the Pissball in his underpants. That was something he had done away with, didn't need any longer.

Oskar unlocked the door to his building and walked through the basement corridor over to hers, did *not* stop to see if the stain was still on the floor. Just walked past it. It didn't exist any longer. He had no mom, no dad, no earlier life, he was simply . . . here. He walked through the door, up the stairs.

Stood there on the landing, looking at the worn wooden door, the empty name plate. *Behind that door.*

He had imagined he was going to dash up the stairs, make a dive for the bell. Instead he sat down on the next to last step, next to the door.

What if she didn't want him to come?

After all, she was the one who had run away from him. She would maybe tell him to go away, that she wanted to be left alone, that she . . .

The basement storage room. Tommy's gang.

He could sleep there, on the couch. They weren't there at night, were they? Then he could see Eli tomorrow evening, like normal.

But it won't be like normal.

He stared at the doorbell. Things would not simply return to normal. Something big had to be done. Like running away, hitchhiking, making your way home in the middle of the night to show that it was . . . important. What he was scared of was *not* that maybe she was a creature who

LET THE RIGHT ONE IN ✤ 269

survived by drinking other people's blood. No—it was that she might push him away.

He rang the bell.

A shrill sound rang out inside the apartment, stopped abruptly when he let go of the button. He stood there, waiting. Rang it again, longer this time. Nothing. Not even a sound.

She wasn't home.

Oskar sat still on the step while disappointment sank like a stone to his stomach. And he suddenly felt so tired, so very tired. He got up slowly, walked down the stairs. Halfway down he had an idea. Stupid, but why not. Walked up to her door again and with short and long tones of the doorbell he spelled out her name in Morse code.

Short. Pause. Short, long, short, short. Pause. Short, short. E . . . L . . . I . . .

Waited. No sound from the other side. He turned to leave when he heard her voice.

"Oskar? Is that you?"

And so it was, after all; joy exploded inside his chest like a rocket blasting off through his mouth with an altogether too-loud:

"Yes!"

✝

In order to have something to do, Maud Carlberg got herself a cup of coffee from the room behind the reception desk, sat down at the darkened counter. She should have finished her shift an hour ago but the police had asked her to wait.

A couple of men—not dressed like police officers—were painstakingly brushing a kind of powder onto the floor where the little girl had walked in her bare feet.

The policeman who had questioned her about what the girl had said, done, what she looked like, had not been friendly. The whole time Maud got the impression from the tone in his voice that she had done the wrong thing. But how could she have known?

Henrik, one of the security guards, whose shift often overlapped with hers, came over to the reception desk and pointed at her cup of coffee.

"For me?"

"If you like."

Henrik picked up the cup, took a sip, and looked out into the hall. Apart from the men who were brushing the floor for prints there was also a uniformed policeman who was talking to a taxi driver.

"A lot of people tonight."

"I don't understand any of it. How did she get up there?"

"No idea. They're working on it. Looks like she climbed up the walls."

"But surely that's not possible."

"No."

Henrik took a bag of licorice boats out of his pocket and held them out to her. Maud shook her head and Henrik took three boats, put them in his mouth, and shrugged apologetically.

"I stopped smoking. Put on four kilos in two weeks." He made a face. "Christ. You should have seen him."

"Him . . . the murderer?"

"Yes. It had splattered . . . over the whole wall. And his face . . . shit. If I ever have to kill myself it'll be pills. Just think about the guys who do the autopsy. To have to—"

"Henrik."

"Yes?"

"Stop."

✝

Eli was standing in the open door. Oskar was sitting on the step. In one hand he was squeezing the handle of the bag, like he was prepared to leave at any moment. Eli pushed a tendril of hair behind her ear. She looked completely healthy. A little girl, unsure of herself. She looked down at her hands, said in a low voice: "Are you coming?"

"Yes."

Eli nodded almost imperceptibly, fidgeting with her fingers. Oskar was still sitting on the step.

"Can I . . . come in?"

"Yes."

The devil flew into him. He said: "Say that I can come in."

Eli lifted her head, made an attempt to say something, but didn't. She started to close the door a little, stopped. Shifted her weight between her bare feet, then said:

"You can come in."

She turned and walked into the apartment, Oskar followed, closing the door behind him. He put the bag down in the hall, took off his jacket and hung it on the hat shelf with little hooks underneath where, he noted, nothing else was hanging.

Eli was standing in the door to the living room with her arms limp at her sides. She was wearing panties and a red T-shirt with the words IRON MAIDEN on it, over a picture of the skeleton monster they had on their albums. Oskar thought he recognized it. Had seen it in the trash room at some point. Was it the same one?

Eli was studying her dirty feet.

"Why did you say that?"

"You said it."

"Yes. Oskar . . ."

She hesitated. Oskar stayed in the same position, with his hand on the jacket he had just hung up. He looked at the jacket as he asked:

"Are you a vampire?"

She wrapped her arms around her body, slowly shook her head.

"I . . . live on blood. But I am not . . . that."

"What's the difference?"

She looked him in the eyes and said somewhat more forcefully:

"There's a very big difference."

Oskar saw her toes tense, relax, tense. Her naked legs were very thin, where the T-shirt stopped he could see the edge of a pair of white panties. He gestured to her. "Are you kind of . . . *dead*?"

She smiled for the first time since he had arrived.

"No. Can't you tell?"

"No, but . . . I mean . . . did you die once, a long time ago?"

"No, but I've lived for a long time."

"Are you *old*?"

"No. I'm only twelve. But I've been that for a long time."

"So you are old, inside. In your head."

"No, I'm not. That's the only thing I still think is strange. I don't understand it. Why I never . . . in a way . . . get any older than twelve."

Oskar thought about it, stroking the arm of his jacket.

"Maybe that's just it, though."

"What do you mean?"

"I mean . . . you can't understand why you're only twelve years old, because you *are* twelve years old."

Eli frowned. "Are you saying I'm stupid?"

"No, just a bit slow. Like kids are."

"I see. How are you doing with the Cube?"

Oskar snorted, met her gaze, and remembered that thing about her pupils. Now they looked normal but they had looked really strange before, hadn't they? But still . . . it was too much. Couldn't believe it.

"Eli. You're just making all this up, aren't you?"

Eli stroked the skeleton monster on her belly, let her hand stop right over the monster's gaping mouth.

"Do you still want to be blood brothers?"

Oskar took half a step back.

"No."

She looked up at him. Sad, almost accusing.

"Not like *that*. Don't you understand . . . that . . ."

She stopped. Oskar finished her sentence for her.

"That if you had wanted to kill me you would have done it a long time ago."

Eli nodded. Oskar took another half step back. How quickly could he get out the door? Should he leave the bag behind? Eli didn't seem to notice his anxiety, his impulse to flee. Oskar stayed put, his muscles tensed.

"Will I get . . . infected?"

Still looking down at the monster on her T-shirt, Eli shook her head. "I don't want to infect anyone. Least of all you."

"What is it then? This alliance."

She lifted her head to the point where she thought his face would be, saw that he was no longer there. Hesitated. Then walked up to him, took his head between her hands. Oskar let her do it. Eli looked . . . blank. Distant. But no hint of that face he had seen in the cellar. Her fingertips brushed against his ears. A sense of calm welled up quietly inside of his body.

Let it happen.

No matter what.

Eli's face was twenty centimeters from his own. Her breath smelled funny, like the shed where his dad kept metal scraps and parts. Yes. She smelled . . . rusty. The tip of her finger stroked his ear. She whispered:

"I'm all alone. No one knows. Do you want to?"

"Yes."

She quickly brought her face up to his, sealed her lips over his upper lip, held it firm with a light, steady pressure. Her lips were warm and dry. Saliva started in his mouth and when he closed his own lips around her lower one it moistened it, softened. They carefully tasted each others' lips, let them glide over each other, and Oskar disappeared into a warm darkness that gradually lightened, became a large room, a large room in a castle with a table in the middle laden with food, and Oskar . . .

. . . runs up to the delicacies, starts to eat from the platters with his hands. Around him there are other children, big and small. Everyone eats from the table. At the far end of the table there is a . . . man? . . . woman . . .

. . . person wearing what has to be a wig. An enormous mane of hair covers the person's head. The person is holding a glass filled with a dark red liquid, comfortably reclining in the chair, sipping from the glass and nodding encouragingly to Oskar.

They eat and eat. Farther away, against a wall, Oskar can see people in poor clothes anxiously following the events at the table. He sees a woman with a brown shawl over her head and her hands clamped tight over her stomach and Oskar thinks, "Mama."

Then there is the ding of a glass and all attention is directed toward the man at the far end of the table. He stands up. Oskar is afraid of him. His mouth is small, thin, unnaturally red. His face is chalk white. Oskar feels saliva run out the corner of his mouth; a little flap of flesh has loosened from the inside of his cheek towards the front; he runs his tongue over it.

The man is holding up a suede bag. With an elegant motion he opens the hand holding the bag shut and then out roll two large white dice. It echoes in the large room when the two dice roll, come to a stop. The man takes up the dice in his hand, holds them out to Oskar and the other children.

*The man opens his mouth to say something but at that moment the lit-
tle flap of flesh falls out of Oskar's mouth and . . .*

✝

Eli's lips left his. She let go of his head, took a step back. Even though it
scared him, Oskar tried to hold onto the image of the castle room again,
but it was gone. Eli scrutinized him. Oskar rubbed his eyes, nodded.

"It really happened, didn't it?"

"Yes."

They stood there for a while, not saying anything. Then Eli said: "Do
you want to come in?"

Oskar didn't reply. Eli pulled on her T-shirt, lifted her hands, let them
fall.

"I'm never going to hurt you."

"I know that."

"What are you thinking about?"

"That T-shirt. Is it from the trash room?"

". . . yes."

"Have you washed it?"

Eli didn't answer.

"You're a little gross, you know that?"

"I can change, if you like."

"Good. Do that."

✝

He had read about the man on the gurney, under the sheet. The Ritual
Killer.

Benke Edwards had wheeled all sorts through these corridors, to cold
storage. Men and women of all ages and sizes. Children. There was no
particular gurney for children and few things made Benke feel as uncomfortable as seeing the empty spaces left over on the trolley when he was
transporting the body of a child; the little figure under the white cover,
pushed up against the headboard. The whole lower half empty, the sheet
smooth. That flat sheet was death itself.

But now he was dealing with a grown man, and not only that, a celebrity.

He guided the gurney through the silent corridors. The only sound was the squeak of the rubber wheels against the linoleum floor. There were no colored markings on this floor. On the few occasions they ever had a visitor here they were always accompanied by a member of the staff.

Benke had waited outside the hospital while the police took photographs of the body. A few members of the press had been standing around with their cameras, outside the restricted area, taking pictures of the hospital with their powerful flashes. Tomorrow the pictures would be in the papers, complete with a dotted line showing how the man had fallen.

A celebrity.

The lump under the sheet gave no indication of any such thing. A lump of flesh like any other. He knew the man looked like a monster, that his body had exploded like a water balloon when he hit the ground, and he was thankful for the cover. Under the cover we are all alike.

Even so, many people were probably grateful that this particular lump of no-longer-living flesh was now being wheeled into cold storage, awaiting later transport to the crematorium when the police pathologists were done with it. The man had a wound in his throat that the police photographer had been particularly interested in getting on film.

But did it matter?

Benke saw himself as a philosopher of sorts. Probably came with the job. He had seen so much of what people really were, when you got down to it, and he had developed a theory and it was relatively uncomplicated.

"Everything is in the brain."

His voice echoed in the empty corridors as he stopped the gurney in front of the doors to the morgue, entered in the code, and opened the door.

Yes. Everything is in the brain. From the beginning. The body is sim ply a kind of service unit that that brain is forced to be burdened with in order to keep itself alive. But everything is there from the beginning, in the brain. And the only way to change someone like this man under the sheet would be to operate on the brain.

Or turn it off.

The lock that was programmed to keep the door open for ten seconds after the code had been entered had still not been repaired and Benke was

forced to hold the door open with one hand as he grabbed the head of the
gurney with the other and guided it into the room. The trolley bumped
against the door post and Benke swore.

If this had been the OR, it would have been fixed in five seconds flat.

Then he noticed something unusual.

On the sheet, to the left of and slightly underneath the raised area that
was the man's face, there was a brownish stain. The door locked behind
them as Benke bent down to take a closer look. The stain was slowly
growing.

He's bleeding.

Benke was not one to be easily shaken. This kind of thing had been
known to happen before. Probably an accumulation of blood in the skull
that had been jolted and started to drain when the trolley hit the door post.

The stain on the sheet grew larger.

Benke went over to a first aid cabinet and took out surgical tape and
gauze. He had always thought it was funny that there was one in a place
like this, but of course the supplies were here in case a living person injured themselves, got their finger caught on a gurney or some such thing.

With his hand on the sheet slightly above the stain he steeled himself.
He was, of course, not afraid of dead bodies but this one had looked pretty
bad. And now Benke had to bandage him up. He was the one who would
get in trouble if a bunch of blood spilled and messed up the floor in here.

So he swallowed, and folded the sheet down.

The man's face defied all description. Impossible to imagine how he
had lived for a whole week with this face. Nothing there that looked even
remotely human with the exception of an ear and an . . . eye.

Couldn't they have . . . taped it shut?

The eye was open. Of course. There was hardly any eyelid to close it.
And the eye itself was so badly damaged it looked as if scar tissue had
formed in the eyeball.

Benke tore himself away from the dead man's gaze and concentrated
on the task at hand. The source of the stain looked to be that wound on his
throat.

He heard a soft dripping sound and quickly looked around. Damn.
He must be a little on edge after all. Another drip. That came from his

feet. He looked down. A drop of water had fallen from the gurney and landed on his shoe. Plop.

Water? ·

He examined the wound on the man's throat. The liquid had formed a small pool underneath it and was spilling out over the metal rim of the stretcher.

Plop.

He moved his foot. Another drop fell onto the tile floor.

Plip.

He stirred the pool of liquid with his index finger, then rubbed his finger and thumb together. It wasn't water. It was some slippery, transparent fluid. He smelled his hand. Nothing he recognized.

When he looked down at the white floor he saw a veritable puddle had formed down there. The liquid was not transparent after all; it had a pink tinge. It reminded him of when blood separates in transfusion bags. The stuff that is left over when the red blood cells sink to the bottom.

Plasma.

The man was bleeding plasma.

How that was possible was a question the experts would have to deal with tomorrow, or rather, later today. His job was simply to patch it so it didn't make a mess. Wanted to go home now. To crawl into bed beside his sleeping wife, read a few pages of *The Abominable Man From Säffle*, and then sleep.

Benke folded the gauze into a thick compress and pushed it up against the wound. How the hell was he supposed to secure it with tape? Even the rest of the man's throat and neck was so damaged as to offer almost no area of undamaged skin to attach the tape to. But what did he care. He wanted to go home now. He pulled off long strips of the adhesive, weaving them this way and that across the neck, an arrangement he would probably be criticized for later, but what the hell.

I'm a janitor, not a surgeon.

When the compress was in place he wiped off the stretcher and mopped the floor. Then he rolled the corpse into room four, rubbed his hands together. Mission accomplished. A job well done and a story to tell in the future. While he made a last check and turned off the light he was already working on his formulations.

You know that murderer who fell from the top floor? Well, I was in charge of him later and when I wheeled him down to the morgue I saw something strange . . .

He took the elevator up to his room, washed his hands thoroughly, changed, and threw his coat into the laundry on his way out. He walked down to the parking lot, got into his car, and smoked a single cigarette before he started the engine. After he stubbed it out in the ashtray—which really needed to be emptied—he turned the key in the ignition.

The car was resisting as it always did when it was cold or damp. It always started in the end, though. You only had to keep at it. As the *wah-wah* sound on the third attempt transformed into a hacking engine roar he suddenly thought of it.

It doesn't coagulate.

No. The stuff seeping out of the man's neck was not going to coagulate under the compress. It would soak through and then spill onto the floor . . . and when they opened the door in a few hours . . .

Shit!

He pulled the key out of the ignition, thrust it angrily into his pocket, got out of the car, and headed back to the hospital.

†

The living room was not as empty as the hall and the kitchen. Here there was a sofa, an armchair, and a large coffee table with a lot of little things on it. A lone floor lamp sent a soft yellow glow over the table. But that was all. No carpets, no pictures, no TV. Thick blankets had been draped over the windows.

It looks like a prison. A big prison cell.

Oskar whistled, tentatively. Yes. There was an echo, but not too much. Probably because of the blankets. He put his bag down next to the armchair. The click when the bottom of it landed on the hard cork flooring was amplified, sounded desolate.

He had started to look at the things on the table when Eli came out of the next room, now wearing her too-big checkered shirt. Oskar waved his arm, indicating the living room.

"Are you two moving?"

"No. Why?"

"I was just thinking."

You two?

Why didn't he think of it before? Oskar let his gaze travel over the things on the table. Looked like toys, every last one of them. Old toys.

"That old man who was here before. That wasn't your dad, was it?"

"No."

"Was he also? . . ."

"No."

Oskar nodded. Looked around the room again. Hard to imagine anyone could live like this. Except if . . .

"Are you sort of . . . poor?"

Eli walked over to the table, picked up a box that looked like a black egg, and handed it to Oskar. He leaned over, held it under the lamp in order to see better.

The surface of the egg was rough and when Oskar looked more closely he saw hundreds of complex strands of gold thread. The egg was heavy, as if the whole thing was made of some kind of metal. Oskar turned it this way and that, looked at the gold threads embedded on the egg's surface. Eli stood next to Oskar. He smelled it again . . . the smell of rust.

"What's it worth, do you think?"

"Don't know. A lot?"

"There are only two of them in the world. If you had both of them you could sell them and buy yourself . . . a nuclear power plant, maybe."

"Nooo? . . ."

"Well, I don't know. What does a nuclear power plant cost? Fifty million?"

"I think it would cost . . . billions."

"Really? In that case I guess you couldn't."

"What would you do with a nuclear power plant?"

Eli laughed.

"Put it between your hands. Like this. Cup them. And then you let it roll back and forth."

Oskar did as Eli said. Rolled the egg gently back and forth in his cupped hands and felt the egg . . . crack, collapse between his palms. He gasped and removed the upper hand. The egg was now just a heap of hundreds . . . thousands of tiny slivers.

"Gosh, I'm sorry. I *was* careful, I—"

"Shhh. It's supposed to be like that. Make sure you don't drop any of it. Pour them out onto this."

Eli pointed to a piece of white paper on the table. Oskar held his breath as he gently let the glittering shards fall out of his hand. The individual pieces were smaller than drops of water and Oskar had to use his other hand to wipe his palm free of every last one.

"But it broke."

"Here. Look."

Eli pulled the lamp closer to the table, concentrated its dim light on the heap of metal slivers. Oskar leaned over and looked. One piece, no bigger than a tick, lay on its own to one side of the stack, and when he looked very closely he could see that it had indentations and notches on a few sides, almost microscopic light bulb-shaped protrusions on the other. He got it.

"It's a puzzle."

"Yes."

"But . . . can you put it together again?"

"I think so."

"It must take forever."

"Yes."

Oskar looked at more pieces that were spread out next to the pile. They looked to be identical to the first, but when he looked closer he saw there were subtle variations. The notches were not in exactly the same place; the protrusions were at another angle. He also saw a piece was all smooth sided, except for a gold border a hair's width across. . . . A piece of the outside.

He slouched down into the armchair.

"It would drive me crazy."

"Think about the guy who *made* it."

Eli rolled her eyes and stuck her tongue out so she looked like the dwarf Dopey. Oskar laughed. Ha-ha. When he stopped the sound still vibrated in the walls. Desolate. Eli sat down on the couch and crossed her legs, looking at him with . . . anticipation. He looked away and looked at the table, and the toys that made a landscape of ruins.

Desolate.

All at once he felt tired in that way again. She wasn't "his girl," couldn't be that. She was . . . something else. There was a big distance between them that couldn't be . . . he shut his eyes, leaned back in the armchair, and the black behind his eyelids was the space that separated them.

He dozed off, gliding into a momentary dream.

The space between them was filled with ugly, sticky insects that flew at him and when they got closer he saw they had teeth. He waved his hand to get rid of them, and woke up. Eli was sitting on the couch watching him.

"Oskar. I'm a person, just like you. It's just that I have . . . a very unusual illness."

Oskar nodded.

A thought wanted to get out. Something. A context. He didn't catch hold of it. Dropped it. But then that other thought came out, the terrible, frightening one. That Eli was just *pretending*. That there was an ancient person inside of her, watching him, who knew everything, and was smiling at him, smiling in secret.

But that can't be.

In order to have something to do, he dug around in his bag for the Walkman, took out the tape that was in it, read the title *KISS: Unmasked*, turned it over, *KISS: Destroyer*, put it back.

I should go home.

Eli leaned forward.

"What's that?"

"This? It's a Walkman."

"Is it for . . . listening to music?"

"Yes."

She doesn't know anything. She's superintelligent but she doesn't know anything. What does she do all day? Sleep, of course. Where does she keep the coffin? That's right. She never slept those times she came over. She simply lay there in my bed and waited for the sun to come up. I must be gone . . .

"Can I try it?"

Oskar held it out to her. She took it and looked like she didn't know what to do with it, but then put the headphones on and looked inquiringly at him. Oskar pointed at the buttons.

"Press the one that says 'play.'"

Eli read the top of the buttons, selected play. Oskar felt a calm settle over him. This was normal; playing your music for a friend. He wondered what Eli would think of KISS.

She pushed in the button, and even from his armchair Oskar could hear the whispery, noisy jangle of guitar, drums, and vocals. She had ended up in the middle of one of the heavier songs.

Eli's eyes opened wide, she screamed in pain, and Oskar was so shocked he was thrown back in the armchair. It tipped back, almost falling over while he watched Eli tear the headphones off so violently that the cables became detached, threw them down, pressed her hands against her ears, whimpering.

Oskar gaped, staring at the headphones that had hit the wall. He got to his feet, picked them up. Completely destroyed. Both of the cords had been torn out of the earpieces. He put them on the table and sank down into the armchair again.

Eli removed her hands from her ears.

"Sorry, I . . . it hurt so much."

"Don't worry about it."

"Was it expensive?"

"No."

Eli took down the highest moving box, reached into it, and fished out a couple of banknotes, holding them out to Oskar.

"Here."

He took them, counted them out. Three thousand kronor bills and two one hundreds. He felt something akin to fear, looked at the carton she had taken the money from, back at Eli, back at the money.

"I . . . it cost fifty kronor."

"Take it anyway."

"No, but, it . . . it was only the headphones that broke and they . . ."

"But you can have it. Please?"

Oskar hesitated, then crumpled the notes into his pants pocket while he mentally calculated their worth in advertising flyers. Around one year of Saturdays, maybe . . . twenty-five thousand delivered flyers. One hundred and fifty hours. More. A fortune. The bills in his pocket rubbed uncomfortably against him.

"Thanks."

Eli nodded, picked something up off the table that looked like a knot of wires but that was probably a brain teaser. Oskar looked at her as she fiddled with the knots. Her neck bent, her long thin fingers that flew over the wires. He went over everything she had told him. Her dad, the aunt who lived in the city, the school she went to. Lies, all of it.

And where had she gotten the money from? Stolen?

He was so unaccustomed to the feeling he didn't even know what it was at first. It started like a kind of tingle in his head, continued into his body, then made a sharp, cold arc back from his stomach to his head. He was . . . angry. Not desperate or scared. Angry.

Because she had lied to him and then . . . and who had she stolen the money from anyway? From someone she had? . . . He crossed his arms over his stomach, leaned back.

"You kill people."

"Oskar . . ."

"If this is true then you must kill people. Take their money."

"I've been *given* the money."

"You're just lying. The whole time."

"It's true."

"What part is true? That you're lying?"

Eli put down the tangle of knots and looked at him with wounded eyes, threw her arms out. "What do you want me to do?"

"Prove it to me."

"Prove what?"

"That you are . . . who you say you are."

She looked at him for a long time. Then she shook her head.

"I don't want to."

"Why not."

"Guess."

Oskar sank deeper into the armchair. Felt the small wad of bills in his pocket. Saw the bundles of advertising flyers in his mind. That had arrived this morning. That had to be delivered before Tuesday. Gray fatigue in his body. Tears in his head. Anger. "Guess." More games. More lies. Wanted to leave. To sleep.

The money. She gave me money so I would stay.

He got up out of the armchair, took out the crumpled bills from his pocket, laid everything except a hundred kronor note on the table. Put it back in his pocket and said: "I'm going home."

She leaned over, grabbed his wrist. "Stay. Please."

"Why? All you do is lie."

He tried to move away from her, but her grip on his wrist hardened. "Let me go!"

"I'm not some freak from the circus!"

Oskar clenched his teeth, said calmly: "Let me go."

She did not let go. The cold arc of anger in Oskar's chest started to vibrate, sing, and he threw himself on top of her. Landed on top of her and pressed her backwards into the couch. She weighed almost nothing and he had her pinned up against the armrest, sat down on her chest while the arc bent, shook, made black dots in front of his eyes as he raised his arm and hit her in the face as hard as he could.

A sharp slapping sound bounced between the walls and her head jerked to the side, drops of saliva flew out of her mouth, and his hand burned. The arc cracked, fell to pieces, and his anger dissolved.

He sat on her chest, looked bewildered at her little head that lay turned in profile against the black leather of the couch as a flush bloomed on the cheek he had struck. She lay still, her eyes open. He rubbed his hands over his face.

"Sorry. Sorry. I . . ."

Suddenly she turned around, threw him off her chest, pushed him up against the back of the couch. He tried to get a grip on her shoulders, but missed, got ahold of her hips, and she landed with her belly right over his face. He threw her off, twisted around, and both of them tried to get ahold of the other.

They rolled around on the couch, wrestling. With tensed muscles and utter concentration. But with care, so that neither would hurt the other. They snaked around each other, bumped against the table.

Pieces of the black egg fell to the floor with the sound of raindrops on a metal roof.

†

He didn't bother going up to his room to get his coat. His shift was over.

This is my time off, and this is something I'm doing for the sheer pleasure *of it.*

He could help himself to a spare pathologist's coat in the morgue if it was really . . . messy. The elevator came and he walked in, pushed the button for lower level two. What would he do in that case? Call the ER and see if someone could come down and sew him up? There was no protocol for this kind of situation.

Probably the bleeding, or whatever it was called, had already ended, but he had to make sure. Would not be able to sleep otherwise. Would lie there and hear the dripping.

He smiled to himself as he got out of the elevator. How many normal people would be prepared to take care of this kind of thing without batting an eye? Not many. He was pretty pleased with himself for . . . well, for doing his duty. Taking responsibility.

I'm not completely normal.

And he couldn't deny it: there was something in him that was actually hoping that . . . that the bleeding had continued, that he would have to call the ER, that there would be a hoopla. However much he wanted to go home and sleep. Because it would make a better story, that's why.

No, he was not completely normal. He had no problems with the corpses: organic machines with the brains turned off. But what could make him a little paranoid were all these corridors.

Simply the thought of this network of tunnels ten meters underground, the large rooms and offices in some kind of administrative department in Hell. So large. So quiet. So empty.

The corpses are a picture of health by comparison.

He punched in the code, automatically put his finger on the opener, which only answered with a helpless click. Pushed the door open manually and walked into the morgue, pulled on a pair of rubber gloves.

What was this?

The man he had left covered in a sheet now lay fully exposed. His penis was erect, pointing to one side. The sheet lay on the floor. Benke's smoke-damaged airways squeaked as he gasped for breath.

The man wasn't dead. No. He couldn't be dead . . . since he was moving.

Slowly, in an almost dream-like way, the man turned over on the gurney. His hands fumbled for something and Benke instinctively took a step back as one of them—it didn't even look like a hand—swept past his face. The man tried to get up, fell back onto the metal stretcher. The lone eye stared straight ahead without blinking.

A sound. The man was uttering a sound.

"Eeeeeeeeee . . ."

Benke rubbed his face. Something had happened to his skin. His skin felt . . . he looked at his hand. Rubber gloves.

Behind his hand he saw the man make another attempt to get up.

What the hell do I do?

Again the man fell down onto the gurney with a moist boom. A few drops of that fluid splattered onto Benke's face. He tried to wipe it away with the rubber glove but only managed to smear it around.

He took up a corner of his shirt and wiped himself with it.

Ten stories. He fell ten stories.

OK, OK, you've got a situation here. Deal with it.

If the man wasn't dead, he was surely in the process of dying. Needed care.

"Eeeee . . ."

"I'm here. I'll help you. I'm going to bring you to the emergency room. Try to lie still, I will . . ."

Benke walked over and put his hands on the man's struggling body. The man's un-deformed hand shot out and grabbed Benke's wrist. Damn, he was strong. Benke had to use both hands to free himself from the man's grip.

The only thing at hand to put over the man to warm him was the standard-issue morgue sheet. Benke took three of them and spread them over the man, who was writhing like a worm on a hook, still making that sound. He leaned down over the man, calmer now since Benke had covered him with the sheets.

"I'll take you down to the emergency room, OK? Try to keep still."

He pushed the stretcher to the door and, despite the situation, he remembered that the door opener wasn't working. He walked over to the head of the gurney and opened the door, looked down at the man's head. Immediately wished he hadn't done so.

The mouth, which was not a mouth, was opening.

The half-healed wound tissue came apart with a sound like when you skin a fish; single strips of pink skin refused to tear, stretched out when the hole in the lower half of the face widened, kept widening.

"AAAAAA!"

The howl echoed through the empty corridors and Benke's heart was beating faster.

Keep still! Be quiet!

If he had had a hammer in his hand in that moment there would have been a great likelihood that he would have smashed it right into that revolting, quivering mass with that staring eye, those strips of skin over the mouth hole that now snapped like overstretched rubber bands, and Benke could see the man's teeth glow white in all that reddish brown fluid that was his face.

Benke walked back to the foot end of the gurney again, started to push it through the corridors, toward the elevator. He half-ran, afraid that the man was going to twist so much he fell off.

The corridors stretched out endlessly before him, like in a nightmare. Yes. It was like a nightmare. All thoughts of a "good story" were gone. He wanted to come up to the surface where there were other people, living people who could rescue him from this monster who was screaming on the gurney.

He reached the elevator and pressed the button that would get it to come, visualizing the route to the ER. Five minutes and he would be there.

Already up on the ground floor there would be other people who could help him. Two minutes and he would be back in real life.

Come on, damn you!

The man's healthy hand was waving.

Benke looked at it and closed his eyes, opened them again. The man was trying to say something, softly. He was indicating for Benke to come closer. He was clearly conscious.

Benke stepped next to the gurney, bent down over the man. "Yes, what is it?"

The hand suddenly grabbed hold of his neck, pulled his head down. Benke lost his balance, fell down over the man, the grip on his neck iron-hard as the hand pulled him down to that . . . hole.

He tried to grab hold of the metal bars at the top end of the stretcher in order to resist, but his head twisted to the side and his eyes ended up only a few centimeters from the wet compress on the man's neck.

"Let go of me, for . . ."

A finger pushed into his ear and he *heard* the bones in the ear canal crackle and give way as the finger forced itself in, further in. He kicked out with his legs and when his shin hit the metal bars under the gurney he finally screamed.

Then teeth clamped down on his cheek and the finger in his ear reached a point where it turned something off, something turned off and . . . he gave up.

The last thing he saw was how the wet compress in front of his eyes changed color and grew pink as the man chewed on his face.

The last thing he heard was a

pling

as the elevator arrived.

†

They lay next to each other on the couch, sweating, panting. Oskar was sore all over, exhausted. He yawned so wide his jaws cracked. Eli also yawned. Oskar turned his head to her.

"Give it up."

"Excuse me?"

"You aren't really sleepy, are you?"

"No."

Oskar made an effort to keep his eyes open, was talking almost without moving his lips. Eli's face was starting to appear foggy, unreal.

"What do you do? To get blood."

Eli looked at him. For a long time. Then she seemed to make up her mind about something and Oskar saw how something moved inside her cheeks, lips, as if she was swirling her tongue around in there. Then she parted her lips, opened wide.

And he saw her teeth. She closed her mouth again.

Oskar turned away and looked up at the ceiling, where a thread of dusty cobwebs stretched down from the unused overhead light. He didn't even have the energy to be surprised. Oh. She was a vampire. But he already knew that.

"Are there a lot of you?"

"What do you mean?"

"You know."

"No, I don't."

Oskar's gaze roamed the ceiling, trying to locate more cobwebs. Found two. Thought he saw a spider crawling on one of them. He blinked. Blinked again. Eyes full of sand. No spider.

"What do I call you, then? This thing that you are."

"Eli."

"Is that really your name?"

"Almost."

"What's your real name?"

A pause. Eli shifted away from him, against the back of the couch, turned around onto her side.

"Elias."

"But that's a . . . boy's name."

"Yes."

Oskar closed his eyes. Couldn't take any more. His eyelids had glued themselves shut onto his eyeballs. A black hole was growing, enveloping his whole body. There was a faint impression somewhere far away at the very back of his head that he should say something, do something. But he didn't have the energy.

The black hole exploded in slow motion. He was sucked forward, inward, turned a slow somersault in space, into sleep.

Far away he felt someone stroke his cheek. Didn't manage to articulate the thought that, because he felt it, it must be his own. But somewhere, on a planet far far away, someone gently stroked someone's cheek.

And that was good.

Then there were only stars.

Part Four

WE ARE THE TROLL COMPANY

We are the troll company,
we don't let anyone go free!
—Rune Andréasson, *Bamse in the Magic Forest*
[popular Swedish children's comic book]

𝔖𝔲𝔫𝔡𝔞𝔶

8 NOVEMBER

The Traneberg Bridge. When it was unveiled in 1934 it was hailed as a minor miracle of engineering. The longest concrete single-span bridge *in the world*. One single mighty arc that soared between Kungsholmen and the western suburbs, which at that time consisted of the little garden cities of Bromma and Äppelviken. The single-family-house movement's prefabricated prototypes were in Ängby.

But the modern was already on its way. The first real suburbs of three-story apartment buildings were already finished in Traneberg and Abrahamsberg, and the state had bought up large areas further west in order to start constructing everything that would one day become Vällingby, Hässelby and Blackeberg.

To all this, the Traneberg Bridge was the link. Almost everyone who traveled to or from the western suburbs used the Traneberg Bridge.

Already in the 1960s reports had started to come in about how the bridge was slowly disintegrating as a result of the heavy traffic it was subjected to. It was renovated and reinforced from time to time but the large-scale renovation and new construction that came up in talks was still a thing of the future.

So on the morning of the eighth of November 1981 the bridge looked tired. A life-weary senior, sorrowfully pondering the days when the heavens were brighter, the clouds lighter, and when it was still the longest single-span concrete bridge *in the world*.

The snow had started to melt toward morning and snow-slush ran down into cracks in the bridge. The city didn't dare to salt it because it could eat away further at the aging concrete.

There wasn't much traffic at this time of day, particularly not on a Sunday morning. The subway had stopped running for the night and the occasional drivers who passed by were either longing for their beds or to return to their beds.

Benny Molin was an exception. Sure, he was looking forward to his bed at home but he was probably too happy to be able to sleep.

Eight times now he had met with various women through the personal ads, but Betty, whom he had arranged to meet on Saturday night was the first . . . that he had clicked with.

This was going to be something. Both of them knew it.

They had doubled over with laughter at how ridiculous it sounded: "Benny and Betty." Like a comedic duo, but what can you do? And if they had kids, what would they call them? Lenny and Netty?

Yes, they had had a lot of fun together. They had sat in her place in Kungsholmen, talking about their worlds, trying to fit their puzzle pieces together, with pretty good results. Toward morning there were sort of only two alternatives for what to do next.

And Benny had chosen what he thought was the right one, even though it was hard. He had said good-bye, with the promise of meeting up again Sunday night, then got into his car and driven home to Bromma while he sang "Can't Help Falling in Love" out loud.

So Benny was not someone who had any energy to spare for complaining about, or even noticing, the miserable state of the Traneberg Bridge this Sunday morning. For him it was simply the bridge to paradise, to love.

He had just arrived at the end of the bridge on the Traneberg side and started in on the refrain for perhaps the tenth time when a blue figure turned up in the beam of his headlights, in the middle of the road.

He had time to think: *Don't jump on the brakes!* before he took his foot off the accelerator and jerked the steering wheel to the side, swerving to the left when there were only about five meters between him and the person. He caught a glimpse of a blue coat and a pair of white legs before the corner of the car banged into the concrete barrier between the lanes.

The scraping sound was so loud it deafened him as the car was pressed up against and forced down along the barrier. The side view mirror was torn off and fluttered away, and the car door on his side was pushed in until it touched his hip before the car was flung out into the middle of the road again.

He tried to ward it off, but the car skidded over to the other side and hit the railing of the pedestrian walkway. The other side view mirror was knocked off and flew away over the bridge railing, reflecting the lights of the bridge up into the sky. He braked carefully and the next skid was less violent; the car only nudged up against the concrete barrier.

After approximately a hundred meters he managed to stop the car. He exhaled, sat still with his hands in his lap and the engine running. He had a bloody taste in his mouth, had bitten his lip.

What kind of lunatic was that back there?

He looked up into the rearview mirror and in the yellowish light of the street lamps he could see the person stagger on down in the middle of the lane as if nothing had happened. That made him angry. A nutcase, sure, but there were limits, damn it.

He tried to open the door on his side, but couldn't. The lock must have gotten smashed in. He took off his seat belt and crawled over onto the passenger side. Before he wriggled out of the car he turned on the hazard lights. He stood next to the car, his arms folded, waiting.

Saw that the person making his way across the bridge was dressed in some kind of hospital gown and nothing more. Bare feet, bare legs. Would have to see if it was possible to talk any sense into him.

Him?

The figure got closer. The slush splashed up around the bare feet; he walked as if he had a thread attached to his chest, inexorably pulling him along. Benny took a step toward him and stopped. The person was maybe ten meters away now and Benny could clearly see his . . . face.

Benny gasped, and steadied himself against the car. Then he quickly wriggled back into it through the passenger side, put the car in first gear and drove away so fast the slush sprayed out from his back wheels and probably hit . . . that thing on the road.

Once he was back in his apartment, he poured himself a good-sized whisky, drank about half. Then he called the police. Told them what he had seen, what had happened. When he had drunk the last of the whisky and started to lean towards hitting the hay after all, the mobilization was in full swing.

✝

They were searching all of Judarn forest. Five police dogs, twenty officers. Even one helicopter, unusual for this type of search.

One wounded, dazed man. A single canine unit should have been able to track him down.

But the stakes were raised in part because of the high media profile of the case (two officers had been assigned simply to handle all the reporters crowding around Weibull's nursery next to the Åkeshov subway station) and they wanted to demonstrate that the police were putting in the maximum effort even on a Sunday morning.

And in part it was because they had found Benke Edwards.

That is to say, they assumed it was Benke Edwards, since they had found a wedding band with the name Gunilla engraved on it.

Gunilla was Benke's wife; his coworkers knew that. No one could bring themselves to call her. Tell her that he was dead, but that they still could not be completely sure it was him. Ask her if she knew of any defining bodily characteristics on, say . . . the lower half of his body?

The pathologist who had arrived at seven o'clock in the morning in order to work on the body of the ritual killer found himself with a new case. If he had been presented with Benke Edwards' remains without knowing any of the circumstances he would have guessed that the body had lain outside for one or two days in severe cold, during which time it would appear the body had been mutilated by rats, foxes, perhaps wolverines and bears—if "mutilate" is even the appropriate word to use in the context of animals. At any rate, larger predators could have torn off pieces of flesh in this way, and rodents could have been responsible for damage to protrusions such as nose, ears, and fingers.

The pathologist's hasty, preliminary assessment that went out to the police was the other reason for the considerable mobilization on their part. The offender was determined to be extremely violent, in official terms.

Completely fucking crazy, in other words.

That the man was still alive was nothing short of a miracle. Not a miracle of the kind the Vatican would want to wave their incense at, but a miracle nonetheless. He had been a vegetable before the fall from the tenth story. Now he was up and walking and worse.

But he couldn't exactly be in great shape. The weather was a little milder now, of course, but it was only a few degrees above freezing and the man was dressed in a hospital gown. He had no accomplices as far as the police knew, and it was simply not possible for him to remain hidden in the forest for more than a few hours.

The telephone call from Benny Molin had come in almost an hour after he had seen the man on the Traneberg Bridge. But a few minutes later they had received an additional call from an older woman.

She had been out for a morning walk with her dog when she had spotted a man in a hospital gown in the vicinity of the Åkeshov stables where the King's sheep were housed in the winter. She had immediately gone home and called the police, thinking the sheep were potentially in danger.

Ten minutes later the first patrol car had turned up and the first thing the officers did was check the stables, nervous, their guns out and ready.

The sheep had become restless and before the officers were done combing the building the whole place was a seething mass of anxious, woolly bodies, loud bleating, and an inhuman screeching that drew even more police.

During their search of the sheep pen, a number of sheep escaped into the walkway in the middle, and when the police finally determined that the place was clean and left the building—their ears ringing—a ram managed to slip out the front door. An older officer with farmers in the family threw himself over the ram and grabbed him by his horns, dragging him back to the pen.

It was only after he had finished coaxing the animal back that he realized some of the bright flashes he had seen out of the corner of his eye during his quick action had been photoflashes. He had made the erroneous assumption that the matter was too serious for the press to want to use such a picture. Shortly thereafter, however, they managed to erect a base for the media, outside the perimeter of the search area.

It was now half past seven in the morning and dawn was creeping in under dripping trees. The search for the lone lunatic was well-organized and in full swing. The police felt assured of a resolution before lunchtime.

Another couple of hours would go by with negative results from the infrared camera of the helicopter, and from the secretions-sensitive noses of the dogs, before the speculation started that the man was no longer alive. That they were searching for a corpse.

†

When the first pale dawn light trickled in through the tiny gaps in the blinds and struck Virginia's palm like a burning hot light bulb, she only wanted one thing: to die. Even so she instinctively pulled her hand away and crawled further back into the room.

Her skin was cut in more than thirty places. There was blood all over the apartment.

Several times during the night she had sliced her arteries in order to drink but had not had time to suck or lick everything that ran out. It had landed on the floor, on the table, chairs. The large rug in the living room looked like someone had butchered a deer on it.

The degree of satisfaction and relief lessened each time she opened a new wound, each time she drank a mouthful of her own rapidly thinning blood. Towards morning she was a whimpering mass of abstinence and anguish. Anguish because she knew what had to be done if she was to live.

The realization had come to her gradually, grown to certainty. Another person's blood would make her . . . healthy. And she couldn't manage to take her own life. Probably it was not even possible; the cuts she made in her skin with the fruit knife healed with unnatural swiftness. However hard and deep she cut, the bleeding stopped within a minute. After an hour the scar tissue was already visible.

And anyway . . .

She had sensed something.

It was toward morning, when she was sitting on a kitchen chair and sucking blood from a cut in the crook of her arm—the second one in the same spot—that she was suddenly pulled into the depths of her body and caught sight of it.

The infection.

She didn't really *see* it, of course, but suddenly she had an ever-increasing perception of what it was. It was like being pregnant and getting an ultrasound, looking at the screen showing you how your belly was filled with, in this case, not a child but a large, writhing snake. That this was what you were carrying.

Because what she had realized at that moment was that the infection had its own life, its own force, completely independent of her body. That the infection would live on even if she did not. The mother-to-be could die of shock at the ultrasound but no one would notice anything because the snake would take control of the body instead.

Suicide would make no difference.

The only thing the infection seemed to fear was sunlight. The pale light on her hand had hurt more that the deepest cut.

For a long time she sat curled up in a corner of the living room, watching how the dawn light through the slats of the blinds laid a grate over the soiled rug. Thought about her grandson Ted. How he had crawled over to that place where the afternoon sun shone in onto the floor and fallen asleep in the pool of sunlight with his thumb in his mouth.

The naked, soft skin, the tender skin that you would only have to . . .

What am I thinking!

Virginia flinched, staring vacantly into space. She had seen Ted, and she had imagined that she . . .

No!

She hit herself in the head. Hit and hit until the picture was crushed. But she would never see him again. Could never see anyone she loved ever again.

I am never again to see anyone I love.

Virginia forced her body to straighten up, crawled slowly over to the sun-grate. The infection protested and wanted to pull her back, but she was stronger, still had control over her own body. The light stung her eyes, the bars of the grate burned her corneas like glowing-hot steel wire.

Burn! Burn up!

Her right arm was covered in scars, dried blood. She stretched it into the light.

She could not have imagined it.

What the light had done to her on Saturday was a caress. Now a blow-torch started up, directed at her skin. After one second the skin was chalk-white. After two seconds it started to smoke. After three seconds a blister formed, blackened, and burst with a hiss. The fourth second she pulled her arm back and crawled sobbing into the bedroom.

The stench of burnt flesh poisoned the air. She didn't dare look at her arm as she slithered up into her bed.

Rest.

But the bed . . .

Even with the blinds drawn there was too much light in the bedroom. Even if she pulled the covers over her she felt too exposed on the bed. Her ears perceived every smallest morning noise coming from the house around her, and every noise was a potential threat. Someone walked over a floor above her. She flinched, turned her head in the direction of the sound, listened. A drawer was pulled out, the clinking of metal one floor up.

Coffee spoons.

She knew from the delicateness of the sound that it was . . . coffee spoons. Saw before her the velvet-clad case with silver coffee spoons that had been her grandmother's and that she had been given when her mother moved into the nursing home. How she had opened that case, looked at the spoons, and realized that *they had never been used.*

Virginia thought about that now as she slid down out of bed, pulled the covers off with her, crawled over to the double closet, opened its doors. On the floor of the closet there was an extra duvet and a couple of blankets.

She had felt a kind of sadness, looking at the spoons. Spoons that had been lying in their case for perhaps sixty years without anyone ever pick-ing them up, holding them, using them.

More sounds around her, the building coming to life. She didn't hear them anymore when she pulled out the duvet and the blankets and wrapped them around her, crawled into the closet and shut the doors. It was pitch black in there. She pulled the duvet and blankets over her head, curling up like a caterpillar in a double cocoon.

Never ever.

On parade, standing at attention in their velvet bed, waiting. Fragile little coffee spoons of silver. She rolled over with the fabric of the blankets tight over her face.

Who will get them now?

Her daughter. Yes. Lena would get them, and she would use them to feed Ted. Then the spoons would be happy. Ted would eat mashed potatoes from the spoons. That would be good.

She lay completely still, like a stone, calm spreading through her body. She had time to formulate one last thought before she sank into rest. *Why isn't it hot?*

With the blankets over her face, wrapped in heavy cloth, it should be hot and sweaty around her head. The question floated sleepily around a large black room, finally landing on a very simple answer.

Because I have not been breathing for several minutes.

And not even now, when she was conscious of the fact, did she feel any need to. No feeling of suffocation, no lack of oxygen. She didn't need to breathe anymore. That was all.

†

The mass started at eleven o'clock but Tommy and his mom, Yvonne, were already on the platform in Blackeberg at a quarter past ten, waiting for the subway.

Staffan, who was singing in the choir, had already informed Yvonne what the theme of today's mass was going to be. Yvonne had told Tommy about it, cautiously asking if he wanted to go and to her surprise he had accepted.

The theme was about the youth of today.

Taking their starting point from a place in the Old Testament that described the Israelites' exodus from Egypt, the ministers had—with Staffan's help—crafted a series of texts around the idea of *guiding stars*. Something a young person in today's society could, so to speak, hold up before him, something he could use to guide him through his desert wanderings, and so forth.

Tommy had read this particular passage in the Bible and then said he was happy to attend.

So when the subway came thundering out of the tunnel from Iceland

Square this morning, propelling a pillar of air in front of it that caused Yvonne's hair to fly around, she was completely happy. She looked at her son, who was standing next to her with his hands pushed deep into the pockets of his jacket.

It's going to be alright.

Yes. Simply the fact that he was willing to come to church with her was big enough. But this also pointed to the fact that he had accepted Staffan, didn't it?

They got on the subway car and sat down next to an old man, across from each other. Before they got on the train they had been talking about what they had heard on the radio this morning: the search for the ritual killer in the Judarn forest. Yvonne leaned forward to Tommy.

"Do you think they're going to catch him?"

Tommy shrugged.

"Probably. But it's a big forest and all that . . . have to ask Staffan."

"I just think the whole thing is so horrible. What if he comes here?"

"What would he do here? But, sure. What's he going to do in Judarn? He might as well come here."

"Ugh."

The older man stretched, made a movement like he was shaking something off his shoulders, said: "You have to ask yourself if someone like that is even human."

Tommy looked up at the man. Yvonne said, "Hm," and smiled at him, which the man clearly took as an encouragement.

"I mean . . . first those terrible . . . deeds, and then . . . in that condition, a fall of that magnitude. No, I tell you: he can't be human, and I hope the police shoot him on sight."

Tommy nodded, pretending to agree.

"Hang him in the nearest tree."

The man was getting excited.

"Exactly. That's what I've been saying this whole time. They should have given him a lethal injection or something while he was in the hospital, like you do with crazy dogs. Then we wouldn't have to be sitting here in a state of constant terror and be witness to this panicky search paid for with the taxpayer's money. A helicopter. Yes, I went by it on the train right by Åkeshov and they had a helicopter up there. Oh, they can afford that alright. But when it comes to paying out pensions large enough to live on, after a lifetime of service to society, that they can't do. But to send a helicopter up there circling around, scaring the animals out of their wits . . ."

The monologue continued all the way to Vällingby where Yvonne and Tommy got off, while the man stayed on. The train was going to turn here, so he was probably going back the way he came in order to get yet another glimpse of the helicopter, maybe continue his monologue with a different audience.

Staffan was waiting for them outside the brick heap that was the St. Thomas church.

He was wearing a suit and a pale yellow-striped tie that made Tommy think of the picture from the war: "A Swedish Tiger." Staffan's face lit up when he saw them, and he walked forward to greet them. He embraced Yvonne and held his hand out to Tommy, who shook it.

"I'm so glad both of you wanted to come. Especially you, Tommy. What made you decide? . . ."

"I just wanted to see what it was like."

"Mm. Well, I hope you'll like it. That we'll get to see you here again."

Yvonne stroked Tommy's shoulder.

"He read that part in the Bible . . . the passage you're going to be talking about."

"Has he, indeed? Well, that's very impressive . . . by the way, Tommy. I haven't found that trophy yet. But . . . I think maybe we should just write it off, what do you say?"

"Mmm."

Staffan waited for Tommy to say something, but when he didn't, Staffan turned back to Yvonne.

"I should be out in Åkeshov right now, but . . . I didn't want to miss this. But as soon as it's over I'll have to go, so we'll have to . . ."

Tommy walked into the church.

There were only a few older people, with their backs to him, sitting in the pews. To judge by their hats they were all old ladies.

The church was lit up by a yellow light coming from lamps that were suspended along either wall. In the walkway down between the pews there was a red carpet all the way to the altar, woven with geometric figures; a stone bench with some flower arrangements. Above all that there was a large wooden cross with a modernist Jesus. His facial expression could easily be interpreted as a taunting smile.

At the very back of the church, by the entrance where Tommy was, there was a stand with brochures, a box to put money in, and a christening font. Tommy walked up to the font and looked in.

Perfect.

When he first saw it he thought it looked too good to be true, that it was probably filled with water. But it wasn't. The whole christening font was carved out of one large piece of stone that reached up to Tommy's waist. The bowl part was dark gray, had a rough surface and did not have a single drop of water in it.

OK, let's do it.

He pulled out a two-liter plastic bag from his pocket, filled with a white powder. Looked around. No one even looking in his direction. He made a hole in the bag with his finger and let its contents run down into the christening font.

Then he tucked the empty bag back in his pocket and walked back out, while he tried to figure out a good explanation for why he didn't want to sit up next to his mom in church, why he wanted to sit way back, next to the christening font.

Could say he wanted to be able to leave without disturbing anyone, if it got too boring. That was good. That sounded . . .

Perfect.

†

Oskar opened his eyes and was filled with anxiety. He didn't know where he was. The room around him was only dimly lit and he didn't recognize the bare walls.

He was lying on a couch, a blanket pulled over him that smelled a little.

The walls floated in front of his eyes, swimming freely in the air while he tried to put them in their place, organize them so they made a room he recognized. He couldn't.

He pulled the blanket up to his nose. A mildewy smell filled his nostrils and he tried to calm down, stop working on the room and *remember* instead.

Yes, now he remembered.

Dad. Janne. Hitching a ride. Eli. The couch. Cobwebs.

He stared up at the ceiling. The dusty cobwebs were still up there, hard to discern in the half-light. He had fallen asleep with Eli next to him on the couch. How long ago was that? Was it morning?

The windows were covered in blankets, but in the corners he could make out a faint outline of gray light. He pulled off the blanket and walked over to the balcony window, lifted the corner of the blanket. The blinds were drawn. He angled them open and yes, it was morning out there.

His head ached and the light stung his eyes. He drew his breath in sharply, dropped the blanket, and felt his neck with both hands. No. Of course not. She had said she would never . . .

But where is she?

He looked around the room; his eyes stopped at the closed door to the room where Eli had changed her shirt. He took a few steps toward the door, stopped himself. The door lay in shadow. He balled his hands up, sucked on a knuckle.

What if she really . . . sleeps in a coffin.

Silly. Why would she do that? Why do vampires do that anyway? Because they're dead. And Eli said she wasn't . . .

But what if . . .

He sucked on his knuckle, ran his tongue over it. Her kiss. The table with food in his vision. Just the fact that she could make him see that. And . . . her teeth. A predator's teeth.

If only it wasn't so dark in here.

The switch for the overhead lamp was next to the door. He pushed on it, thinking nothing would happen, but yes, it went on. He screwed up his eyes in the strong light, let his eyes get used to it before he turned to the door, rested his hand on the door handle.

The light didn't help at all. In fact it was only more horrible now that the door was only a normal door. Like the door to his own room. Exactly the same. The door handle felt the same. What if she was lying in there? Maybe her arms neatly folded across her chest?

I have to look.

He pushed the handle down, tentatively; it only offered light resistance. The door must not be locked, then it would only have glided down.

He pushed it down all the way and the door opened, the gap widened. The room inside was dark.

Wait!

Would she be hurt by the light if he opened the door?

No, yesterday she had sat next to the floor lamp without it seeming to bother her. But the overhead light was stronger and perhaps there was a . . . special kind of bulb in the floor lamp, a light that . . . vampires could withstand.

Ridiculous. The specialty store for vampire lamps.

And why would she have let the overhead light remain in place if it could be . . . harmful to her?

Even so, he opened the door cautiously, allowing the cone of light to slowly widen into the room. It was as sparsely furnished as the living room. A bed and a pile of clothes, nothing more. The bed only had a sheet and a pillow. The blanket he had slept with on the couch must have come from there. There was a note taped to the wall next to the bed.

The Morse code.

So it was here she had been lying when she . . .

He drew a deep breath. He had managed to forget it.

My room is on the other side of this wall.

Yes, he was two meters from his own bed, from his own normal life.

He lay down on the bed, had the impulse to tap out a message on the wall. To Oskar. On the other side. What should he say?

W.H.E.R.E. A.R.E. Y.O.U.

He sucked on his knuckle again. He was here. It was Eli who was gone.

He felt dizzy, confused. Let his head flop down onto the pillow, his face turned out facing the room. The pillow smelled funny. Like the blanket, but stronger. A stale, greasy smell. He looked at the pile of clothes a few meters from the bed.

It's so repulsive.

He didn't want to be here anymore. It was completely quiet and empty in the apartment, and everything was so . . . abnormal. His gaze traveled over the pile of clothes, stopped at the closets that covered the whole length of the opposite wall, all the way to the door. Two double closets, one single.

There.

He pulled his legs up against his stomach, staring at the closed closet doors. He didn't want to. His stomach hurt. A shooting pain in his lower belly.

Had to pee.

He stood up from the bed, walked to the door with his eyes glued to the closet doors. He had the same kind of closets in his room and knew she could easily fit inside. That's where she was and he didn't want to see anymore.

Even the light in the hall worked. He turned it on and walked along the short corridor to the bathroom. The door to the bathroom was locked. The colored strip above the handle was red. He knocked on the door.

"Eli?"

Not a sound. He knocked again.

"Eli? Are you in there?"

Nothing. But when he said her name aloud he remembered that it was wrong. That was the last thing she had said as they lay together on the couch. That her real name was . . . Elias. *Elias*. A boy's name. Was Eli a boy? They had . . . kissed and slept in the same bed and . . .

Oskar pressed his hands against the bathroom door, rested his forehead against his hands. He tried to think. Hard. And he didn't get it. That he could somehow accept that she was a *vampire*, but the idea that she was somehow a *boy*, that that could be . . . harder.

He knew the word. Fag. Fucking fag. Stuff that Jonny said. To think it was worse to be gay than to be a . . .

He knocked on the door again.

"Elias?"

A weird feeling in his stomach as he said it. No, he wasn't going to get used to it. She . . . His name was Eli. But it was too much. Regardless of what Eli was, it was too much. He just couldn't. Nothing about her was normal.

He lifted his forehead from his hands, held the pee back firmly.

Steps outside in the stairwell and shortly thereafter a sound of the mailbox opening, a thud. He walked out there and looked at what it was. Advertising.

Ground beef. 14:90 per kilo.

Garish red letters and numbers. He picked up the advertisements in his hand with dawning comprehension; pressed his eyes against the keyhole while footsteps echoed in the stairwell; more bangs as additional mail flaps were opened and shut.

After half a minute his mom passed by the keyhole, on her way down. He only managed to catch a glimpse of her hair, the collar of her coat, but he knew it was her. Who else would it be?

Delivering the advertising packets in his absence.

With the flyers clenched in his hand, Oskar sank down into a crouch by the front door, leaned his forehead against his knees. He didn't cry. The need to pee was like a stinging nest of ants in his groin that in some way prevented him.

But the thought ran through his head over and over:

I don't exist. I don't exist.

†

Lacke had spent the night worrying. Ever since he left Virginia, a sneaking anxiety had been intent on gnawing a hole in his stomach. He had spent about an hour with the regulars at the Chinese restaurant Saturday night, trying to share his concerns, but the others wanted none of it. Lacke had sensed things could get out of hand, that there was a danger he would get really ticked off, so he left.

Those guys weren't worth shit.

Sure, it wasn't exactly news to him, but he had thought that . . . well, what the hell had he thought?

That we were all in on it.

That at least one other person also had the feeling that something damn creepy was going on. There was so much talk, big words, especially from Morgan, but when it came down to it, no one had the gumption to lift a finger to actually *do* something.

Not that even Lacke knew what to do, but he was at least worried about it. If that helped. He had lain awake most of the night, tried to read a little from Dostoevsky's *The Demons* but kept forgetting what happened on the previous page, the previous sentence, and he gave up.

But the night brought something good with it; he had made up his mind about something.

Sunday morning he had gone over to Virginia's place, knocked on the door. No one opened and he had assumed that . . . hoped that she had gone to the hospital. On his way back home he walked past two women who were talking, heard something about a murderer that the police were searching for in the Judarn forest.

There's a murderer behind every damn bush these days, for god's sake. Now the papers have something else to jump all over.

About ten days had gone by since they captured the Vällingby killer and the newspapers had grown tired about speculating about his identity and possible motive.

In the articles that mentioned him there had been a strong streak of . . . ghoulish delight. With painstaking care they had described the murderer's present condition and how he was unlikely to leave his hospital bed for six months. A separate factual box about hydrochloric acid and what it could do to the body, so you could really revel in how much it must hurt.

No, Lacke took no pleasure in that kind of thing. Just thought it was creepy how people got all worked up about someone getting their "just deserts" and all that. He himself was absolutely anti-death penalty. Not because he had some "modern" sense justice, no. More like a premodern one.

His reasoning went something like this: if someone kills my child, then I kill that person. Dostoevsky talked a lot about forgiveness, mercy. Sure. From society's perspective, absolutely. But as a parent to the child it is my moral right to end the life of the one who did it. That society in turn gives me eight years in jail or something is a different matter.

That wasn't what Dostoevsky meant, and Lacke knew it. But he and Fyodor simply didn't see eye to eye on this point.

Lacke thought about these things as he walked home to Ibsengatan. Once he was home he realized he was hungry and cooked up a batch of quick macaroni, ate them from the pan with a spoon, squeezed some ketchup on them. While he was pouring water into the pan to make it easier to wash up later he heard something in the mail slot.

Advertisements. He didn't care about that, had no money anyway.

No, that was just it.

He wiped off the kitchen table with the dishrag, went and got his dad's stamp collection from the sideboard, which he had also inherited from his father, and that had been hell to transport back to Blackeberg. He put the album down on the kitchen table, opened it.

There they were. Four unmarked specimens of the first stamp ever to be issued in Norway. He leaned over the album and squinted at the lion, raised up on its hind legs against a light blue background.

Incredible.

They had cost four shillings when they were issued in 1855. Now they were worth . . . more. That they were connected in two pairs made them even more valuable.

That was what he had made up his mind about last night, while he tossed and turned between his smoke-saturated sheets; that it was time. This thing with Virginia had been the last straw. Then, on top of that, the complete incomprehension on the part of the guys, his realization that: you know, these are not people worth hanging around with.

He was going to leave this place, and so was Virginia.

Depressed market or not, he would get about three hundred thousand for the stamps, plus two hundred for the apartment. Then they would get a house in the country. Or alright: two houses. A little farm. There was enough money for that and it would work out. As soon as Virginia had recovered he would present her with the idea, and he thought that . . . he was almost certain that she would agree to it, would love it in fact.

So that was how it was going to be.

Lacke felt calmer now. He saw everything clearly. What he would do today, and in the future. It would all work out.

Filled with pleasant thoughts, he wandered into the bedroom, lay down on top of the bed to rest for five minutes, and fell asleep.

†

We see them on streets and squares and we find ourselves standing in before them at a loss, saying to ourselves: what can we do?"

Tommy had never been this bored in his whole life. The service had only been going for half an hour and he thought he would have had more fun if he had sat in a chair staring at the wall.

"Blessed be" and "Hallelujah!" and "Joy of the Lord," but why did they all sit there staring in front of them like they were watching a qualifying match between Bulgaria and Romania? It didn't *mean* anything to them, that stuff they read in the book, that they sang about. Didn't seem to mean anything to the minister either. Just something he had to get through in order to collect his paycheck.

Now the sermon was underway, at least.

If the minister mentioned that place in the Bible, that stuff Tommy had read, then he would do it. Otherwise he wouldn't.

Let him decide.

Tommy checked his pocket. Everything was ready and the christening font was only three meters behind him from where he sat in the back row. His mom was sitting in the very front, no doubt so she could twinkle at Staffan as he sang his meaningless songs with his hands loosely clasped in front of his police dick.

Tommy clenched his teeth. He hoped the minister was going to say it.

"We see a lost look in their eyes, the look of someone who has wandered astray and is unable to find his way back home. When I see a young person like this, I always think about the Israelites' exodus from Egypt."

Tommy stiffened. But maybe the minister was not going to mention that exact place. Maybe it would be something about the Red Sea. Still, he took the stuff out of his pocket; a lighter and a small tinder cube. His hands were trembling.

"For it is thus we have to view these young people who sometimes leave us so perplexed. They are wandering in a desert of unanswered questions and unclear future prospects. But there is a great difference between the people of Israel and the young people of today. . . ."

Go on, say it . . .

"The people of Israel had someone leading them. You are probably familiar with the words of the Scripture. 'And the Lord went before them, by day in a pillar of cloud, to lead them along the way, and by night in a pillar of fire to give them light.' It is this cloud, this fire that the young people of today lack and . . ."

The minister looked down into his papers.

Tommy had already set fire to the tinder cube, holding it between thumb and forefinger. At the top end of it there was a pure blue flame trying to reach down toward his fingers. When the minister looked down at his papers, he took the chance.

He crouched down, took a long step out of the pew, stretched his arm out as far as he could, and dumped the tinder cube into the christening

font, pulled himself quickly back into the pew. No one had noticed anything.

The minister looked up again.

". . . and it is our responsibility as adults to be this cloud, this guiding
star for young people. Where else will they find one? And the strength for
this we can get from the works of the Lord."

A white smoke rose up from the christening font. Tommy already had
a whiff of the familiar sweet smell.

He had done this a bunch of times: burned saltpeter and sugar. But
rarely in this quantity, and never inside. He was excited to find out what
the effect would be without a wind to disperse the fumes. He interlaced
his fingers, pressing his hands hard together.

†

Bror Ardelius, temporary minister of the Vällingby parish, was the first
to notice it. He took it for what it was: smoke from the christening font.
He had been waiting for a sign from the Lord his whole life and it was un-
deniably the case that when he saw the first pillar of smoke he thought for
a moment,

Oh, My Lord. At last.

But the thought did not last long. That the feeling of it being a miracle left him so quickly, he took as a proof that it was indeed no miracle,
no sign. It was simply this: smoke from the christening font. But why?

The janitor, whom he was not on particularly good terms with, had decided to play a practical joke. The water in the font had started to . . . boil.

The problem was that he was in the middle of a sermon and could not
spend a long time thinking about these questions. So Bror Ardelius did
what most people do in these situations: he carried on as if nothing had
happened and hoped the problem would resolve itself on its own. He
cleared his throat and tried to remember what he had just said.

*The works of the Lord. Something about seeking strength in the works of
the Lord. One example.*

He glanced down at the notes on his paper. He had written: Barefoot.

*Barefoot? What did I mean by that? That the people of Israel walked
barefoot or that Jesus . . . wandered for a long time . . .*

He looked up and saw that the smoke had thickened, formed a pillar that rose up from the font to the ceiling. What was the last thing he had said? Yes, now he remembered. The words were still hanging in the air.

"And the strength for this we can take from the works of the Lord."

That was an acceptable conclusion. Not great, not what he had been planning, but acceptable. He gave the congregation a somewhat bewildered smile and nodded to Birgit, who led the choir.

The choir, eight people, stood up as one and walked up to the podium. When they turned to the congregation he could tell by their expressions that they also saw the smoke. Blessed be the Lord; it had occurred to him that perhaps it was only he who could see it.

Birgit looked at him for guidance and he made a gesture with his hand: go on, get started.

The choir started to sing.

> *Lead me, God, lead me into righteousness.*
> *Let mine eyes behold Thy path . . .*

One of old Wesley's beautiful compositions. Bror Ardelius wished he had been able to enjoy the beauty of the song, but the pillar of cloud was starting to worry him. Thick white smoke was billowing up out of the christening font and something inside the basin itself was burning with a blue-white flame, smoking and sputtering. A sweetish smell reached his nostrils and the members of the congregation started to turn around in order to figure out where the crackling sound was coming from.

> *For only you, my Lord,*
> *offer my soul*
> *peace and security . . .*

One of the women in the choir started to cough. The members of the congregation turned their heads from the smoking font to Bror Ardelius in order to receive instruction from him as to how they should behave, if this was a part of the service.

More people started to cough, holding handkerchiefs or sleeves in front of their mouths, noses. A thin haze had started to form inside the church, and through this haze Bror Ardelius saw someone get up from the very last row and run out the door.

Yes, that is the only reasonable thing to do.

He leaned toward the microphone.

"Yes, well, there has been a small . . . mishap and I think it is best if we . . . clear the building."

Already at the word "mishap" Staffan left the podium and started walking toward the exit with quick, controlled steps. He got it. It was Yvonne's hopeless delinquent of a kid who had done this. Even now, as he was walking down from the podium he was trying to control himself, because he sensed that if he got hold of Tommy right now he would give him a good hiding.

Of course this was exactly what the young hooligan needed; it was exactly the kind of guidance he was lacking.

Pillar of cloud come help me. A good spanking is what this kid sorely needs.

But Yvonne wouldn't accept it, as things stood right now. Once they were married things would be different. Then he would, God so help him, take on the task of disciplining Tommy. But first and foremost he would get ahold of him right now. Shake him up a little bit, at the very least.

Staffan didn't get very far. Bror Ardelius' words from the podium had worked like a starting gun on the members of the congregation, who had only been waiting for his go-ahead in order to stampede out of the church. Halfway down the aisle Staffan found himself blocked by little old ladies who were hurrying toward the exit with grim determination.

His right hand flew to his hip but he stopped it halfway, clenched it into a fist. Even if he had had his baton this would hardly have been a good time to use it.

The smoke production in the font was starting to die down but the church was now full of a thick haze that smelled of candy and chemicals. The exit doors were wide open and through the haze you could see a strong rectangle of morning light.

The congregation moved toward the light, coughing.

†

There was a single wooden chair in the kitchen, nothing more. Oskar pulled it up to the sink, stood on it, and peed into the drain while he had water running out of the tap. When he was done he put the chair back. It looked strange in the otherwise empty kitchen. Like something in a museum.

What does she keep it for?

He looked around. Above the fridge there was a row of cabinets you could only reach by standing on the chair. He pulled it over and steadied himself by putting a hand on the refrigerator door handle. His stomach rumbled. He was hungry.

Without thinking more about it, he opened the fridge in order to see what there was. Not much. An open carton of milk, half a packet of bread. Butter and cheese. Oskar put his hand out for the milk.

But . . . Eli . . .

He stood there with the carton of milk in his hand, blinked. This didn't add up. Did she eat real food as well? Yes. She must. He took the milk carton out of the fridge and put it on the counter. In the kitchen cabinet above the counter there was almost nothing. Two plates, two glasses. He took a glass and poured milk into it.

And then it hit him. With the cold milk glass in his hand it finally hit him, with full force.

She drinks blood.

Yesterday evening, in his tangle of sleepiness and sense of detachment from the world, in the dark, everything had somehow felt possible. But now in the kitchen, where no blankets hung in the window and the blinds let in a weak morning light, with a glass of milk in his hand it seemed so . . . beyond anything he could comprehend.

Like: If you have milk and bread in your fridge you must be a human being.

He took a mouthful of milk and immediately spit it out. It was sour. He smelled the rest that was in the glass. Yes, definitely bad. He poured it out into the sink, rinsed the glass out, and then drank some water in order to get the taste out of his mouth. Looked at the date on the carton.

USE BY 28 OCTOBER.

The milk was ten days too old. Oskar had a realization.

The old guy's milk.

The refrigerator door was still open. The old guy's food.

Revolting. Totally revolting.

Oskar slammed the door shut. What had that old guy been here for anyway? What had he and Eli . . . Oskar shivered.

She has killed him.

Yes. Eli must have kept the old guy around in order to be able to . . . drink from him. To use him like a living blood bank. That's what she did. But why had the old guy agreed to it? And *if* she had killed him, where was the body? Oskar glanced up at the high kitchen cabinets. And suddenly he didn't want to be in the kitchen anymore. Didn't want to stay in the apartment at all. He walked out of the kitchen, through the hall. The closed bathroom door.

She's in there.

He hurried into the living room, collected his bag. The Walkman was on the table. He would have to buy new headphones, that was all. When he picked up the Walkman in order to put it into his bag he saw the note. It was lying on the coffee table, at the same height as his head had been resting.

Hi. Hope you've slept well. I'm also going to sleep now. I'm in the bathroom. Don't try to go in there, please. I'm trusting you. I don't know what to write. I hope you can like me even though you know what I am. I like you. A lot. You're lying here on the couch right now, snoring. Please. Don't be afraid of me.

Please please please don't be afraid of me.

Do you want to meet me tonight? Write so on this note if you do.

If you write No I'll move tonight. Probably have to do that soon anyway. But if you write Yes I'll hang around for a while longer. I don't know what I should write. I'm alone. Probably more alone than you can imagine, I think. Or perhaps you can.

Sorry I broke your music machine. Take the money if you want. I have a lot. Don't be afraid of me. There's no reason for you to be. Maybe you know that. I hope you know that. I like you so very much.

Yours,
Eli

P.S. Feel free to stay. But if you leave make sure the door locks behind you.

Oskar read the note several times. Then he picked up the pen next to it. He looked around the empty room, Eli's life. The bills she had tried to give him were still lying on the table, scrunched up. He took *one* thousand kronor bill, put it in his pocket.

He looked for a long time at the space on the page under Eli's name. Then he lowered the pen and wrote in letters as tall as the space

YES.

He put the pen down, got up, and slipped the Walkman into his bag. He turned around one last time and looked at the by-now upside-down letters.

YES.

Then he shook his head, dug the thousand kronor bill out of his pocket, and put it back on the table. When he was out in the stairwell he checked that the door had locked securely behind him. He pulled on it several times.

From the Daily Update, 16:45, Sunday 8 November 1981

The official search for the man who early Sunday morning escaped from Danderyd Hospital after having killed one person, has not yet yielded any results.

The police have searched all of Judarn forest in western Stockholm in the attempt to track down the man, who is assumed to be the so-called Ritual Killer. At the time of his escape the man was critically wounded and the police now suspect he had an accomplice.

Arnold Lehrman, of the Stockholm Police:

"Yes, that's the only logical explanation. There is no physical possibility that he would have been able to keep himself hidden this long in his . . . condition. We have had thirty officers out here, dogs, a helicopter. It's just not feasible, that's all."

"Will you keep searching Judarn forest?"

"Yes. The possibility that he remains in the area cannot be ruled out. But we will divert some of our forces from here in order to concentrate on . . . in order to investigate how he has been able to proceed."

The man is severely disfigured and was at the time of his escape dressed in a light blue hospital gown. The police ask that anyone with information regarding the disappearance contact them at the following number . . .

Sunday

Public interest in the police search of Judarn forest was at an all-time high. The evening news realized they would not be able to print the composite picture of the murderer one more time. They had been hoping for images of an apprehended suspect but in the absence of this both evening papers ran the sheep picture.

The *Expressen* even put it on the front page.

Say what you will, there was undeniable drama in that photograph. The police officer's face twisted by exertion, the splayed limbs and open mouth of the sheep. You could almost hear the panting, the bleating.

One of the papers had even tried to reach the royal court for comment, since it was the King's sheep that the officer was manhandling in this way. The King and Queen had only two days earlier informed the public that they were expecting their third child, and decided that that would have to do. The court offered no comment.

Of course several pages were devoted to maps of Judarn and the western suburbs. Where the man had been sighted, how the police search had been organized. But all this had been seen before, in other contexts. The sheep picture was something new and it was this that people remembered.

Expressen had even dared to try a little joke. The caption said, "Wolf in sheep's clothing?"

You had to laugh a little, and people needed this. They were scared. This same man had killed two people, almost three, and now he was once more on the loose and kids again were subject to a curfew. A school field trip to Judarn on Monday was canceled.

And running right through this there was an underlying anger at the fact that one person, one single person, could have the power to dominate so many people's lives simply through his evil and his . . . ability to stave off death.

Yes. Experts and professors who were called upon to comment in newspapers and TV all said the same thing: it was impossible that the man was still alive. In answer to a direct question they then went on to say in the next breath that the man's escape was just as impossible.

A professor of medicine at Danderyd made an unfavorable impression on the evening news when he said, in an aggressive tone of voice: "Until very recently the man was hooked up to a respirator. Do you know what that means? That means that you are not able to breathe on your own. Add to this a fall of about thirty meters . . ." The professor's tone implied that the reporter was an idiot and that the whole thing was an invention by the media.

So everything was a soup of guesses, impossibilities, rumors and—of course—fear. Not so strange then that one used the sheep picture in spite of everything. That at least was concrete. The photograph was disseminated throughout the land and found its way to people's eyes.

†

Lacke saw it when he bought a packet of Red Prince cigarettes in the Lover's newsstand, with his last few kronor, on his way over to Gösta's. He had been sleeping all afternoon and felt like Raskolnikov; the world was hazily uncertain. He glanced at the sheep photograph and nodded to himself. In his present state it did not seem strange to him that the police were apprehending sheep.

Only when he was halfway to Gösta's place did the image come back to him and he thought, "What the hell was that?" but didn't have the energy to pursue it. He lit a cigarette and kept going.

†

Oskar saw it when he came home after having spent the afternoon walking around Vällingby. When he got off the subway Tommy was getting on. Tommy looked jumpy and wound up and said he had done something "fucking hilarious" but didn't have time to say anything more before the doors closed. At home there was a note on the kitchen table; his mom was going to dinner with the choir tonight. There was food in the refrigerator, the advertising flyers had been delivered, hugs and kisses.

The evening paper was on the kitchen sofa. Oskar looked at the sheep on the front page and read everything about the search. Then he did something he had been lagging behind on: cut out and saved the articles about the Ritual Killer from the paper over the last few days. He took the pile of newspapers out from the cleaning closet, his scrapbook, scissors, paste, and got to work.

†

Staffan saw it about two hundred meters from where it had been taken. He had not been able to catch Tommy, and after a few brief words with a distraught Yvonne he had left for Åkeshov. Someone there had referred to a colleague he didn't know by the name of "the sheep man" but he hadn't gotten the joke until a few hours later when he had a chance to see the evening paper.

Police management was ticked off at the newspapers' indiscretion, but most officers in the field thought it was funny. With the exception of "the sheep man" himself, of course. For several weeks he had to endure the occasional "baaaaaa" and "nice sweater, is that sheep's wool?"

†

Jonny saw it when his four-year-old little brother—*half* little brother—Kalle came up to him with a present. A wooden block that he had wrapped in the first page of the evening paper. Jonny shooed him out of his room, said he wasn't in the mood, locked the door. Took up the photo album again, looking at pictures of his dad, his real dad, who was not Kalle's dad.

A little later he heard his stepfather yelling at Kalle because he had destroyed the paper. Jonny then unwrapped the present, turning the block in his fingers as he studied the close-up of the sheep. He chuckled, the skin pulled taut around his ear. He stowed the photo album in his gym bag—it would be safest to keep it at school—and from there his thoughts turned to what the hell he should do with Oskar.

†

The sheep picture would start a minor debate about the ethics of photo-journalism, but was nonetheless featured in both papers' end-of-year collage of the year's most unforgettable images. In the spring the tackled ram himself was let out into the Drottningholm summer pastures, forever oblivious to his fifteen minutes of fame.

†

Virginia rests rolled up in duvets and blankets. Her eyes are closed, the body completely still. In a moment she will wake up. She has been lying here for eleven hours. Her body temperature is down to twenty-seven degrees, which corresponds to the temperature inside the closet. Her heart rate is four faint beats a minute.

During these past eleven hours her body has changed irrevocably. Her stomach and lungs have adapted to a new kind of existence. The most interesting detail, from a medical point of view, is a still-developing cyst in the sinoatrial node of the heart, the clump of cells that controls the heart's contractions. The cyst has now grown to twice its former size. A cancer-like growth of foreign cells continues unhindered.

If one could take a sample of these cells, put the sample under a microscope, one would see something that all heart specialists would reject with the assumption that the sample had become contaminated, mixed. A tasteless joke.

Namely, the tumor in the sinoatrial node consists of brain cells.

Yes. Inside Virginia's heart a separate little brain is forming. This new brain has, during its initial stage of development, been dependent on the large brain. Now it is self-sufficient, and what Virginia during a terrible moment sensed is completely correct: it would live on even if her body died.

Virginia opened her eyes and knew she was awake. Knew it even though opening her eyelids made no difference. It was as dark as before. But her consciousness was turned on. Yes. Her consciousness came to life, and at the same time it was as if something else quickly withdrew.

Like . . .

Like coming to a summer cottage that has been empty all winter. You open the door, fumble for the light switch, and at that same moment you hear the rapid scuttling, the clicking of small claws against the floorboards, you catch a brief glimpse of the rat squeezing in under the kitchen counter.

An uncanny feeling. You know it's been living there in your absence. That it thinks of the house as its own. That it will come sneaking out again as soon as you turn out the light.

I am not alone.

Her mouth felt like paper. She had no feeling in her tongue. She continued to lie there, thinking of the cottage that she and Per, Lena's father, had rented a couple of summers when Lena was little. The rat's nest they found all the way in under the kitchen counter. The rats had chewed off small pieces of a milk carton and a packet of cornflakes, built what almost looked like a little house, a fantastic construction of multicolored cardboard.

Virginia had felt a certain kind of guilt as she vacuumed up the little house. No, more than that. A superstitious feeling of *transgression*. As she inserted the cold mechanical trunk of the vacuum cleaner into the delicate, fine construction the rat had spent the winter building it felt like she was casting out a good spirit.

And sure enough. When the rat was not caught in any of the traps but continued to eat their dry goods even though it was summer, Per had put out rat poison. They had argued about it. They had argued about other things. About everything. In July sometime the rat had died, somewhere inside the wall.

As the stench of the rat's dead, decomposing body spread through the house, their marriage slowly broke down that summer. They had gone home a week earlier than planned since they could no longer tolerate the stench or each other. The good spirit had left them.

What happened to that house? Does anyone else live there now?

She heard a squeaking sound, a hiss.

There IS a rat! Inside these blankets!

She was gripped by panic.

Still wrapped up, she threw herself to the side, hitting the closet doors so they flew open, and she tumbled out onto the floor. She kicked with her legs, waving her arms until she managed to free herself. Disgusted, she crawled up onto the bed, into a corner, pulling her knees under her chin, staring at the pile of blankets and duvets, waiting for a movement. She would scream when it came. Scream so the whole house came rushing with hammers and axes and beat the pile of blankets until the rat was dead.

The blanket on top was green with blue dots. Wasn't there a movement there? She drew a breath in order to scream, and she heard the squeaking, hissing again.

I'm . . . breathing.

Yes. That was the last thing she had determined before she fell asleep: that she wasn't breathing. Now she was breathing again. She drew the air in tentatively, and heard the squeaking, hissing. It was coming from her air passages. They had dried out as she was resting, were making these sounds. She cleared her throat and felt a rotten taste in her mouth.

She remembered everything. Everything.

She looked at her arms. Strands of dried blood covered them, but no cuts or scars were visible. She picked out the spot on the inside of her elbow where she knew she had cut herself at least twice. Maybe a faint streak of pink skin. Yes. Possibly. Except for that everything was healed.

She rubbed her eyes and checked the time. A quarter past six. It was evening, Dark. She looked down again at the green blanket, the blue dots.

Where is the light coming from?

The overhead light was off, it was evening outside, all the blinds were drawn. How could she possibly be seeing all the contours and colors so clearly? In the closet it had been pitch black. She hadn't seen anything there. But now . . . it was clear as day.

A little light always gets in.

Was she breathing?

She couldn't figure it out. As soon as she started to *think* about her breathing she also controlled it. Maybe she only breathed when she thought of it.

But that first breath, the one she had mistaken for the sound of a rat . . . she hadn't thought that one. But perhaps it had only been like a . . . like a . . .

She shut her eyes.

Ted.

She had been there when he was born. Lena had never met Ted's father again after the night when Ted was conceived. Some Finnish businessman in Stockholm for a conference and so on. So Virginia had been there for the birth, had nagged and pleaded her way there.

And now it came back to her. Ted's first breath.

How he had come out. The little body, sticky, purple, hardly human. The explosion of joy in her chest that changed to a cloud of anxiety when he didn't breathe. The midwife who had calmly picked up the little creature in her hands. Virginia had expected her to hold the little body upside down, slap him on the behind, but just as the midwife picked him up a bubble of saliva formed at his mouth. A bubble that grew, grew and . . . burst. And then came his cry, the first cry. And he breathed.

So?

Was that what Virginia's squeaky breath had been? A birth cry?

She straightened up, lying down on her back on the bed. Continued to replay the images of the birth. How she had washed Ted, since Lena had been too weak, had lost a lot of blood. Yes. After Ted had come out it had run over the edge of the birthing bed and the nurses had been there with paper, masses of paper. Finally it had stopped of its own accord.

The heap of blood-drenched paper, the midwife's dark red hands. Her calm, her efficiency in spite of all . . . the blood. All that blood.

Thirsty.

Her mouth was sticky and she replayed the sequence a number of times, zooming in on everything that had been covered in blood; the midwife's hands *to let my tongue glide over those hands, the blood-drenched paper on the floor, put them in my mouth, suck on them, between Lena's legs where the blood ran out in a thin rivulet, to . . .*

She sat up abruptly, ran doubled-over to the bathroom and threw open the lid to the toilet, leaned her head over the bowl. Nothing came. Just dry, convulsive heaves. She leaned her forehead against the edge of the bowl. The images of the birth started to well up again.

Don'twantdon'twantdon'twantdon'twa—

She banged her forehead hard against the porcelain and a geyser of icy clear pain spurted up in her head. Everything in front of her eyes turned bright blue. She smiled, and fell sideways to the floor, down onto the bathroom rug that . . .

Cost 14:90, but I got it for ten because a large piece of fuzz came off when the cashier pulled off the price tag, and when I came out onto the square from Åhlen's department store there was a pigeon pecking from a cardboard container where there were a couple of french fries and the pigeon was gray . . . and . . . blue . . . there was . . . a strong backlight . . .

She didn't know how long she had been gone. One minute, an hour? Maybe only a few seconds. But something had changed. She was calm.

The fuzz of the bathroom mat felt good against her cheek as she lay there and looked at the rusted pipe that ran down from the sink into the floor. She thought the pipe had a beautiful shape.

A strong smell of urine. She hadn't wet her pants, no, because it was . . . Lacke's urine she smelled. She bent her body, moved her head closer to the floor under the toilet, sniffed. Lacke . . . and Morgan. She couldn't understand how she knew that but she knew: Morgan had peed on the side.

But Morgan hasn't even been here.

No, actually. That evening when they had helped her home. The evening when she was attacked. Bitten. Yes, of course. Everything fell into place. Morgan had been here, Morgan had used the bathroom, and she had been lying out there on the couch after having been bitten and now she could see in the dark, was sensitive to light, and needed blood and—

A vampire.

That's how it was. She had not contracted some rare and unpleasant disease that was treatable at the hospital or in a psychiatric ward or with . . .

Photo-therapy!

She started to laugh, then coughed, turned over on her back, stared up at the ceiling, and went over everything. The cuts that healed so quickly, the effect of the sun on her skin, blood. She said it aloud:

"I am a vampire."

It couldn't be. They didn't exist. But even so something felt lighter. As if a pressure in her head eased. A weight lifted from her. It wasn't her fault. The revolting fantasies, the terrible things she had done to herself all night. It wasn't something she was responsible for.

It was simply . . . very natural.

She got up halfway, and started to run a bath, sat on the toilet and watched the running water, the bath as it slowly filled. The phone rang. She only registered it as an indifferent noise, a mechanical signal. It didn't mean anything. She couldn't talk to anyone anyway. No one could talk to her.

†

Oskar had not read Saturday's paper. Now it was spread out in front of him on the kitchen table. He had had it turned to the same page for a while and read the caption to the picture over and over again. The picture he couldn't let go of.

The text was about the man who had been found frozen into the ice down by the Blackeberg hospital. How he had been found, how the recovery work had been undertaken. There was a small picture of Mr. Ávila as he stood pointing out over the water, toward the hole in the ice. In the quote from Mr. Ávila, the reporter had smoothed out his linguistic eccentricities.

All this was interesting enough and worth cutting out to save, but that wasn't what he was staring at, couldn't tear himself from.

It was the picture of the shirt.

Stuffed inside the man's jacket there had been a child-sized blood-stained sweater, and it was reproduced here, laid out against a neutral background. Oskar recognized the sweater immediately.

Aren't you cold?

The text stated that the dead man, Joakim Bengtsson, was last seen alive Saturday the twenty-fourth of October. Two weeks ago. Oskar remembered that evening. When Eli had solved the Cube. He had stroked her cheek and she had walked out of the courtyard. That night she and . . . the old guy had argued and the old guy had left.

Was that the night that Eli had done it?

Yes, probably. The next day she had looked a lot healthier.

He looked at the photograph. It was in black and white but the caption said the sweater was light pink. The reporter speculated that the murderer might have yet another young victim on his conscience.

Hang on a minute.

The Vällingby murderer. In the article it said the police now had strong indications that the man in the ice had been killed by the so-called Ritual Killer, who had been captured at the Vällingby swimming pool about a week earlier, and who was now on the loose.

Was it . . . the old guy? But . . . the kid in the forest . . . why?

A lightbulb went on in his head. Understood everything. All of these articles he had cut out and saved, radio, TV, all the talk, the fear . . .

Eli.

Oskar didn't know what to do. What he should do. So he went to the fridge and took out the piece of lasagna his mom had saved for him. Ate it cold while he kept looking at the articles. When he was done eating he heard a tap on the wall. Closed his eyes so he could hear better. He knew the code by heart at this point.

I.A.M.G.O.I.N.G.O.U.T.

He quickly got up from the table, walked into his room, lay belly-down on his bed, and tapped out an answer.

C.O.M.E.O.V.E.R.

A pause. Then:

Y.O.U.R.M.O.M.

Oskar tapped a reply.

A.W.A.Y.

His mom wouldn't be back until around ten. They still had three hours. When Oskar had tapped the last message he rested his head on the pillow. For a moment he concentrated on formulating words that he had forgotten.

Her top . . . the paper.

He jumped, was about to get up in order to sweep up all the papers that lay out. She would see them . . . know that he . . .

Then he leaned his head back against the pillow, decided he didn't care.

A low whistle outside the window. He got up out of bed, walked forward, and leaned against the windowsill. She stood there below with her face turned up to the light. She was wearing the checkered shirt that was too big for her.

He made a gesture with his finger: Go to the door.

†

Don't tell him it was me, OK?"

Yvonne made a face, blew smoke out of the corner of her mouth in the direction of the half-open kitchen window, didn't reply.

Tommy snorted. "Why do you smoke like that, out the window?"

The ash pillar of her cigarette was so long it started to bend. Tommy pointed to it, made a *duht-duht* movement with his finger like he was flicking the ash off. She ignored him.

"Because Staffan doesn't like it, right? The smell of smoke."

Tommy leaned back in his kitchen chair, looked at the ash, and wondered what it actually consisted of that allowed it to get so long without breaking off, waved his hand in front of her face.

"I don't like the smell of smoke either. Didn't like it *at all* when I was little. But that didn't make you crack the window like this. Oh, see there it goes . . ."

The pillar of ash broke off and landed on Yvonne's thigh. She brushed it off and a gray streak was left on her pants. She raised the hand holding the cigarette.

"I did so. Most of the time, at least. There may have been times when I had people over or something, when I didn't . . . and who the hell are you to sit here lecturing me about not liking smoke."

Tommy grinned. "But you have to admit it was a little funny."

"No, it was not. Think about if people had panicked. If people had . . . and what about that basin, the . . ."

"Christening font."

"Yes, the christening font. The minister was in despair over it, there was like a . . . black crust over the whole . . . Staffan had to—"

"Staffan, Staffan."

"Yes, Staffan. He didn't say it was you. He said it to me, that it was hard for him, with his . . . faith to stand there lying to the minister's face but that he . . . to protect you . . ."

"But you get it, don't you?"

"Get what?"

"That he's really protecting himself."

"He is not, I—"

"Think about it."

Yvonne took a last long drag of her cigarette, put it out in the ashtray, and immediately lit another.

"It was an . . . antique. Now they have to send it off to be restored."

"And it was Staffan's stepson who did it. How would that look?"

"You are not his stepson."

"No, but you know. If I said to Staffan that I was going to go see the minister and tell him that it was me, and that my name is Tommy and Staffan is my . . . sort-of stepfather. Don't think he would like it."

"You should talk to him yourself."

"No, not today anyway."

"You don't dare."

"You sound like a little kid."

"And you're behaving like one."

"But it was a little funny, wasn't it?"

"No, Tommy. It wasn't."

Tommy sighed. He knew his mom would get pissed, but he had still thought she might be able to see something comical in it. But she was on Staffan's side now. Had to come to terms with it.

So the problem, the real problem, was finding somewhere to live. When they got married, that is. For now he could crash in the basement those evenings when Staffan came over. At eight he was going to finish his shift at Åkeshov and come straight out here. And Tommy had no intention of listening to some damn moralizing lecture from that guy. Not on his life.

So Tommy went to his room and got his blanket and pillow from his bed while Yvonne still sat there smoking, looking out of the kitchen window. When he was ready he stood in the kitchen door with his pillow under one arm, the rolled up blanket under the other.

"OK, I'm going now. I'd appreciate it if you didn't tell him where I am."

Yvonne turned to him. She had tears in her eyes. Smiled a little.

"You look like when . . . when you would come and ask . . ."

The words caught in her throat. Tommy stood still. Yvonne swallowed, cleared her throat, and looked at him with clear eyes, said quietly: "Tommy. What should I do?"

"I don't know."

"Should I? . . ."

"No, not for my sake. Things are what they are."

Yvonne nodded. Tommy felt that he was also going to get really sad, that he should go now before things went wrong.

"And you won't tell, that—"

"No, no. I won't."

"Good. Thanks."

Yvonne got up and went over to Tommy. Hugged him. She smelled strongly of cigarettes. If Tommy's arms had been free he would have hugged her back. But he didn't, so he just put his head on her shoulder and they stood like that for a while.

Then Tommy left.

Don't trust her. Staffan can start going off on some damn thing or other and . . .

In the basement he threw the blanket and pillow on the couch. Put in a wad of chewing tobacco and lay down to think things over.

It would be best if he got shot.

But Staffan probably wasn't the kind of guy who . . . no, no. Was more like the one who would plant a bull's-eye right in the killer's forehead. Get a box of chocolates from his police friends. The hero. Would turn up here later looking for Tommy. Maybe.

He fished out his key, walked out in the corridor and unlocked the shelter, took the chain in with him. With his lighter as a lamp he made his way through the short corridor with the two storage units on either side. In the storage units there were dry goods, cans of food, old games, a camp stove, and other things to make it through a siege.

He opened a door, threw in the chain.

OK, he had an emergency exit.

Before he left the shelter he took down the shooting trophy and weighed it in his hand. At least two kilos. Maybe he could sell it? The value of the metal alone. They could melt it down.

He studied the pistol shooter's face. Didn't he kind of look like Staffan? In that case melting it down was the right option.

Cremation. Definitely.

He laughed.

The absolutely best thing would be to melt everything down except the head and then give it back to Staffan. A solid pool of metal with only that little head sticking up. Was probably too hard to arrange. Unfortunately.

He put the trophy back in its place, walked out, and closed the door without turning the wheels of the lock. Now he would be able to slip in here if he had to. Which he didn't really think would happen.

But just in case.

†

Lacke let it ring ten times before hanging up. Gösta sat on the couch and stroked a striped orange cat over the head, didn't look up when he asked:

"No one home?"

Lacke rubbed his hand over his face, said with some irritation: "Yes, damn it. Didn't you hear us talking?"

"You want another one?"

Lacke softened, tried to smile.

"Sorry, I didn't mean to . . . sure, yes, what the hell, Thanks."

Gösta leaned over carelessly so the cat on his knee was squeezed. It hissed and slipped down onto the floor, sat down and stared accusingly at Gösta, who was pouring a touch of tonic and a good amount of gin in Lacke's glass, holding it out to him.

"Here. Don't worry, she's probably just . . . you know . . ."

"Admitted. Thanks. She's gone to the hospital and they've admitted her."

"Yes . . . that's right."

"Then say that."

"What?"

"Oh, nothing. Cheers."

"Cheers."

They both drank. After a while Gösta started to pick his nose. Lacke looked at him, and Gösta pulled his finger away, smiled apologetically. Not used to having people around.

A large gray and white cat was lying flat on the floor, looked like it barely had the energy to lift its head up. Gösta nodded at it. "Miriam is going to have babies soon."

Lacke took a big sip, made a face. For every drop of numbness the alcohol gave him, the smell of the apartment lessened.

"Whadya do with them?"

"What do you mean?"

"The kittens. What do you do with them? Let them live, do you?"

"Yes, but mostly they're dead. Nowadays."

"So that . . . what. That fat one, you said . . . Miriam? . . . that belly, it's just . . . a bag of dead kittens in there?"

"Yes."

Lacke drank the rest of the glass, put it on the table. Gösta gestured to the gin bottle. Lacke shook his head.

"No, I'm taking a little break."

He lowered his head. An orange carpet so full of cat hair it looked like it was made of it. Cats and cats all over. How many were there? He started to count. Got to eighteen. In this room alone.

"You've never thought about . . . having them fixed? Like castration, or whatever it's called . . . sterilizing? You could make do with one sex, you know."

Gösta looked at him uncomprehendingly.

"How would I go about doing that?"

"No, you're right."

Lacke imagined Gösta getting on the subway with maybe . . . twenty-five cats. In one box. No, in a bag, a sack. Go to the vet and just pour out all the cats. "Castration, please." He chuckled. Gösta put his head to one side.

"What is it?"

"I was just thinking . . . you could get a group discount."

Gösta did not appreciate the joke and Lacke waved his hands in front of him. "No, sorry. I was just . . . uh, I'm all . . . this thing with Virginia, you know. I . . ." He suddenly straightened up, slammed his hand on the table.

"I don't want to be here anymore!"

Gösta jumped in his spot on the couch. The cat in front of Lacke's feet snuck away, hid under the armchair. From somewhere in the room he heard a cat hiss. Gösta shifted his weight, wiggled his glass in his hand.

"You don't have to. Not for my . . ."

"No, not that. Here. The whole shebang. Blackeberg. Everything. These buildings, the walking paths, the spaces, people, everything is just . . . like a single big damn sickness, see? Something went wrong. They thought all this out, planned it to be . . . perfect, you know. And in some damn wrinkle it went wrong, instead. Some shit.

"Like . . . I can't explain it . . . like they had some idea about the angles, or fucking whatever, the angles of the buildings, in their relation to each other, you know. So it would be harmonious or something. And then they made a mistake in their measurements, their triangulation, whatever the hell they call it, so that it was all a little off from the start, and it went downhill from there. So you walk here with all these buildings and you just feel that . . . no. No, no, no. You shouldn't be here. This place is all *wrong*, you know?

"Except it isn't the angles, it's something else, something that just . . . like a disease that's in the . . . walls and I . . . don't want any part of it anymore."

A clinking when Gösta, unasked, poured Lacke another drink. Lacke took it gratefully. The outburst had caused a pleasant calm in his body, a calm that the alcohol now suffused with warmth. He leaned back in the chair, exhaled.

They sat quietly until the doorbell rang. Lacke asked: "Are you expecting anyone?"

Gösta shook his head while he heaved himself out of the couch.

"No. Damn central station here tonight."

Lacke grinned and raised his glass to Gösta as the latter walked past. Felt better now. Felt pretty OK actually.

The front door opened. Someone outside said something and Gösta answered:

"Please come in."

†

Lying there in the bathtub, in the warm water that grew pink as the dried blood on her skin dissolved, Virginia had made up her mind.

Gösta.

Her new consciousness told her it had to be someone who would let her in. Her old one said it couldn't be someone she loved. Or even liked. Gösta fit both descriptions.

She got up, dried herself, and put on pants and a blouse. It was only when she was down on the street that she realized she hadn't put on a coat. Even so she wasn't cold.

New discoveries all the time.

Below the tall building she stopped, looked up at Gösta's window. He was home. Was always home.

If he resists?

She hadn't thought about that. Only imagined the whole thing as her taking what she needed. But maybe Gösta wanted to live?

Of course he wants to live. He is a person, he has his pleasures, and think of all the cats that will . . .

She put the brakes on, willed the thought away. Put her hand over her heart. It had a rate of five beats a minute and she knew she had to protect it. That there was something to that thing with . . . stakes.

She took the elevator up to the second to last floor, rang the bell. When Gösta opened the door and saw Virginia his eyes widened to something that resembled horror.

Does he know? Can you see it?

Gösta said: "But . . . is it you?"

"Yes, can I? . . ."

She gestured into the apartment. Couldn't understand. Only knew intuitively that she needed an invitation, otherwise . . . otherwise . . . something. Gösta nodded, took a step back.

"Please come in."

She stepped into the hall and Gösta pulled the door shut, looked at her with watery eyes. He was unshaven, the droopy skin of his throat dirty with gray stubble. The stench in the apartment was worse than she remembered, clearer.

I don't want to—

Then the old brain was turned off, and hunger took over. She put her hands on his shoulders, saw her hands put on his shoulders. Allowed it to happen. The old Virginia now sat curled up somewhere at the back of her head, without control.

The mouth said: "Do you want to help me with something? Stand still."

She heard something. A voice.

"Virginia! Hi! I'm so glad to . . ."

†

Lacke flinched when Virginia's head turned toward him.

Her eyes were empty. As if someone had poked a needle into them and sucked out what had been Virginia and only left behind the expressionless gaze of an anatomical model. Plate number eight: Eyes.

Virginia stared at him for a second, then she let go of Gösta and turned to the door, pressed the handle down, but the door was locked. She turned the lock, but Lacke grabbed ahold of her, dragged her away from the door.

"You're not going anywhere until . . ."

Virginia fought his hold and he got her elbow against his mouth, his lip splitting against his teeth. He held her arms firmly, pressed his cheek against her back.

"Ginja, damn it. I have to talk to you. I've been so damn worried. Calm down, what is it?"

She jerked toward the door but Lacke held her fast, coaxing her in the direction of the living room. He made an effort to speak calmly and quietly, as if to a frightened animal, while he pushed her in front of him.

"Now Gösta is going to pour us a drink and then we'll sit down all calm and collected and talk about this, because I . . . I'm going to help you. Whatever it is, I'm going to help you. OK?"

"No, Lacke. No."

"Yes, Ginja. Yes."

Gösta pushed past both of them into the living room and poured Virginia a drink in Lacke's glass. Lacke managed to get Virginia in, let go of her, and placed himself in the doorway to the hall with his hands on the door posts, like a sentry.

He licked a little blood away from his lower lip.

Virginia was standing in the middle of the room, tensed. Looked around as if she were looking for a way out. Her eyes stopped at the window.

"No, Ginja."

Lacke prepared to run over to her, to grab her again if she tried something stupid.

What is it with her? She looks like the whole room is full of ghosts.

He heard a sound like when you crack an egg into a hot pan.

Then another.

And another.

The room was filled with more and more hissing, spitting.

All of the cats in the room had stood up, their backs curled and tails bushed out, looking at Virginia. Even Miriam got clumsily to her feet, her belly dragging on the floor, pulling her ears back and baring her teeth.

From the bedroom, kitchen, more cats streamed in.

Gösta had stopped pouring; stood there now with the bottle in his hand, staring wide-eyed at his cats. The hissing was a cloud of electricity in the room, increasing in strength. Lacke had to shout in order to make his voice carry above the din.

"Gösta, what are they doing?"

Gösta shook his head, sweeping his arm to the side and spilling a little gin from the bottle.

"I don't know . . . I've never . . ."

A little black cat jumped up onto Virginia's thigh, digging in her claws and biting down. Gösta brought the bottle down on the table with a bang, said: "Bad, Titania, bad!"

Virginia bent over, grabbed the cat by its back, and tried to pull it off. Two other cats used this as an opportunity to jump up on her back and neck. Virginia let out a scream and ripped the cat from her leg, throwing it from her. It flew across the room, hit the edge of the table, and fell down at Gösta's feet. One of the cats on Virginia's back climbed up onto her head and held itself in place with its claws while it made dives for her forehead.

Before Lacke got there three more cats had jumped up. They screeched at the top of their lungs while Virginia pummeled them with her fists. Even so they managed to hang on, ripping her flesh with their small teeth.

Lacke thrust his hands into the crawling, seething mass on Virginia's chest, grabbed skin that glided over tensed muscles, pulled off small bodies, and Virginia's blouse was ripped, she screamed and—

She's crying.

No; it was blood running down her cheek. Lacke grabbed the cat that was sitting on her head, but the cat dug its claws in even deeper, sat there like it was sewn on. Its head fit inside Lacke's hand and he yanked it from side to side until he—in the middle of all the noise—heard a

snap

and when he dropped the head it fell down lifeless on Virginia's head. A drop of blood trickled out of the cat's nose.

"Aaaaaah! My baby . . ."

Gösta reached Virginia and, with tears in his eyes, he started to stroke the cat that even in death stayed attached to Virginia's head.

"My baby, little darling . . ."

Lacke lowered his gaze and his eyes met Virginia's.

It was her again.

Virginia.

†

Let me go.

Through the double tunnel that was her eyes Virginia was looking out at everything that was happening with her body, Lacke's attempts to save her.

Let it be.

She wasn't the one fighting them off, her arms going out. It was that other thing that wanted to live, wanted that its . . . host should live. She had given up when she saw Gösta's throat, taken in the stench of the apartment. This was how it was going to be. And she didn't want a part of it.

The pain. She felt the pain, the cuts. But it would soon be over.

So . . . let it be.

†

Lacke saw it. But he didn't accept it.

The farm . . . two cottages . . . the garden . . .

In a panic he tried to tear the cats from Virginia. But they hung on, furry knots of muscles. The few he managed to get off took with them strips of her clothing, leaving deep cuts in the skin underneath, but most of them stayed put like leeches. He tried to hit them, he heard bones cracking, but if one came off another jumped on, because the cats were climbing over each other in their eagerness to . . .

Black.

Something hit him in the face and he stumbled back about one meter, almost falling, steadied himself against the wall, blinking. Gösta stood next to Virginia fists drawn, staring at him with tearful anger in his gaze.

"You are hurting them! You're *hurting* them!"

Next to Gösta, Virginia was a boiling mass of mewling, hissing fur. Miriam dragged herself across the floor, got up on her hind legs and bit Virginia in the calf. Gösta saw it, bent down, and shook his finger at her.

"You can't do that, little lady. That *hurts!*"

All sense of reason left Lacke. He took two steps, aimed a kick at Miriam. His foot sunk into her bloated belly and Lacke felt no revulsion, only satisfaction, when that sack of guts flew from his foot, was crushed against the radiator. He grabbed Virginia's arm—

Out, must get out of here

—and pulled her with him toward the door.

†

Virginia tried to resist. But Lacke and the will of her sickness were the same, and they were stronger than she. Through the tunnels in her head she saw Gösta fall to his knees on the floor, heard his howl of grief as he took a dead cat in his hands, caressing its back.

Forgive me, forgive me—

Then Lacke pulled her out with him, and her ability to see was blocked as a cat climbed up onto her face, bit her in the head, and all was pain, living needles puncturing her skin, and she found herself in a live iron maiden as she lost her balance, fell, felt herself dragged across the floor.

Let me go.

But the cat in front of her eyes changed position and she saw the apartment door opening in front of her, Lacke's hand, dark red, that pulled her along, and she saw the stairwell, the steps, she was up on her feet again, fighting her way along, in her own consciousness, taking control and—

†

Virginia pulled her arm free of his hand.

Lacke turned around to the crawling mass of fur that was her body in order get a hold of her again, in order to—

What? What?

Out. In order to get out.

But Virginia forced her way past him and for one second the trembling back of a cat was pressed against his face. Then she was out in the stairwell where the cats' hissing was amplified like excited whispers while she ran toward the edge of the landing and—

Nonono—

Lacke tried to reach her in time to stop her, but like someone convinced of a soft landing or someone who doesn't care if she crashes, Virginia relaxed and toppled forward, let herself fall down the stairs.

Cats that were caught underneath her howled as she rolled and bounced down the concrete steps. Damp crunching sounds as slender bones broke, heavier thuds that made Lacke cringe when Virginia's head—

Something walked across his foot.

A small gray cat that had something wrong with its hind legs dragged itself out into the stairwell, sat down on the top step, and howled sorrowfully.

Virginia came to rest at the bottom of the stairs. The cats that survived the fall left her and went back up the stairs. Went into the hall and started to groom themselves.

Only the little gray one stayed where it was, mourning the fact that it had not been able to take part.

†

The police held a press conference Sunday evening.

They had chosen a conference room at the police station with room for forty people, but it had turned out to be too small. A number of reporters from European newspapers and television stations turned up. The fact that the man had not been recaptured during the day made the news more sensational, and a British journalist gave the best analysis of why the whole thing had attracted such attention.

"It's a search for the archetypal Monster. This man's appearance, what he's done. He is The Monster, the evil at the heart of all fairy tales. And every time we catch it, we like to pretend it's over for good."

Already, a quarter of an hour before the appointed time, the air in the poorly ventilated room was warm and humid, and the only ones who did not complain were the Italian TV team who said they were used to worse conditions.

They moved the event to a larger room and at exactly eight o'clock, the Stockholm district's chief of police came in, flanked by the commissioner who was spearheading the investigation and who had questioned the Ritual Killer in the hospital, as well as the patrol leader who had directed operations in Judarn forest earlier that day.

They were not afraid of being torn limb from limb by the reporters, because they had decided to throw them a bone.

They had a photograph of the man.

†

The investigation of the watch had finally yielded results. On Saturday a watchmaker in Karlskoga had taken the time to go through his index file of outdated proof-of-insurance forms and had come across the number the police had asked him and other watchmakers to try to locate.

He called the police and gave them the name, address, and phone number of the man who was registered as the buyer. The Stockholm police entered the man's name into their register and asked the Karlskoga police to go to the address to see what they could find.

There was some excitement at the station when it turned out that the man had been prosecuted for attempted rape of a nine-year-old, seven years earlier. Had spent three years locked up in an institution, deemed mentally ill. Was thereafter determined to be recovered and subsequently released.

But the Karlskoga police found the man at home, in good health.

Yes, he had had a watch like that. No, he couldn't remember what had happened to it. It took a couple of hours of interrogation at the station in Karlskoga, reminders that there were conditions under which a psychiatric certificate of good health could be subject to reevaluation, before the man recalled who he had sold the watch to.

Håkan Bengtsson, Karlstad. They had met somewhere and done something, he couldn't remember what. He had sold him the watch, at any rate, but he had no address and could only give a vague description of him, and could he please be allowed to go home now?

There was nothing on Håkan Bengtsson in the police records. There were twenty-four Håkan Bengtssons in the Karlstad area. About half of them could immediately be disregarded because of age. The police started to call around. The search was simplified by the fact that the ability to speak immediately disqualified someone as a viable candidate.

Toward nine o'clock in the evening they were able to narrow the list to a single person. One Håkan Bengtsson who had been a Swedish teacher at the high school and who had left Karlstad after his house burned down under unclear circumstances.

They called the principal of the high school and were told that yes, there had been rumors about Håkan Bengtsson . . . liked children a little bit too much, you could say. They had the prinicipal go to the school on a Saturday evening and produce a photo of Håkan Bengtsson from the school archives, taken for the school catalogue in 1976.

A Karlstad police officer, who needed to be in Stockholm on Sunday anyway, faxed over a copy and then started driving up with the original late Saturday night. It reached the Stockholm headquarters at one o'clock Sunday morning, that is to say, about a half hour after the man in question had fallen from his hospital window and been declared dead.

Sunday morning was devoted to verifying through dental and medical records from Karlstad that the man in the snapshot was the same man who, until the preceding evening, had been bound to his hospital bed, and yes: it was him.

Sunday afternoon there was a meeting at the station. They had counted on slowly being able to unravel what the dead man had done since leaving Karlstad, see if his deeds were part of a larger context, if he had left more victims strewn in his wake.

But now the situation had changed.

The man was still alive, was on the loose, and the most important thing at this point appeared to be locating where the man had lived since there was a small chance he would try to return there. His movements toward the western suburbs seemed to indicate as much.

Therefore it was decided that if the man was not apprehended before the press conference one would turn to the somewhat unreliable but oh so many-headed hunting dog, The General Public.

It was possible that someone had seen him during the time when he still looked like he did in the photo and maybe had some sense of where he had lived. And anyway, of course it was only a secondary concern. One needed a bone to throw the media.

†

So now the three police officers were sitting there at the long table up by the podium, and a ripple went through the assembled journalists when the police chief—with the simple gesture that he well knew was the most effective, theatrically speaking—held up the enlarged school photo of Håkan Bengtsson, and said:

"The man we are looking for is called Håkan Bengtsson and before his face was damaged he looked . . . like this."

The police chief paused while the cameras clicked and the flashes transformed the room into a stroboscope for a while.

Of course there were copies of the grainy picture on hand to be passed out among the journalists but, above all, the foreign papers were most likely to prefer the more emotionally expressive staging of the police chief with the murderer—so to speak—in his hand.

When everyone had gotten their photos and the investigative team had reported on their activities, it was time for questions. The first one came from a reporter from *Dagens Nyheter*, the big morning paper.

"When do you expect to apprehend him?"

The police chief took a deep breath, decided to put his reputation on the line, and said:

"Tomorrow at the latest."

†

Hey there."

"Hi."

Oskar went in before her, straight to the living room in order to get the record he wanted. Flipped through his mom's thin record collection and found it. The Vikings. The whole group was assembled in something that looked like the skeleton of a Viking ship, misplaced in their shiny costumes.

Eli didn't come in. With the record in his hand he went back into the hall. She was still standing outside the front door.

"Oskar, you have to invite me in."

"But . . . the window. You have already . . ."

"This is a new entrance."

"I see. OK you can . . ."

Oskar stopped himself, licked his lips. Looked at the picture on the album cover. The picture had been taken in the dark, with a flash, and the Vikings glowed like a group of saints about to walk onto land. He stepped toward Eli, showed her the album.

"Check it out, they look like they're in the belly of a whale or something."

"Oskar . . ."

"Yes?"

Eli stood still, with her arms hanging by her side, and looked at Oskar. He smiled, went up to the door, waved his hand in the air between the door frame and the door jamb, in front of Eli's face.

"What? Is there something here or what?"

"Don't start."

"But seriously. What happens if I don't do it?"

"Don't. Start." Eli gave a thin smile. "You want to see? What happens? Do you? Is that what you want?"

Eli said it in a way that was clearly intended for Oskar to say no: the promise of something terrible. But Oskar swallowed and said: "Yes. I do. Show me."

"You wrote in the note that . . ."

"Yes, I know. But let's see it. What happens?"

Eli pinched her lips together, thought for a second, and then took a step forward, over the threshold. Oskar tensed his whole body, waiting for a blue flash, or for the door to swing forward through Eli and slam shut or something like that. But nothing happened. Eli went into the hallway, closed the door behind her. Oskar shrugged his shoulders.

"Is that all?"

"Not exactly."

Eli stood still, in the same way as she had outside the door, her arms along her sides and her eyes glued to Oskar's. Oskar shook his head.

"What? There's nothing . . ."

He stopped when he saw a tear come out of the corner of one of Eli's eyes; no, one in each eye. But it wasn't a tear, since it was dark. The skin in Eli's face started to flush, became pink, red, wine-red, and her hands tightened into fists as the pores in her face opened and tiny pearls of blood started to appear in dots all over her face and throat.

Eli's lips twisted in pain and a drop of blood ran out of the corner of her mouth, joined with the pearls emerging on her chin and, growing larger, trickled down to join the drops on her throat.

Oskar's arms became limp; he let them fall and the record fell out of its sleeve, bounced once with its edge against the floor, then fell flat onto the hall rug. His gaze went to Eli's hands.

The backs of her hands were damp with a thin covering of blood and more was coming out.

Again he looked Eli in the eyes, didn't find her. Her eyes looked like they had sunk into their sockets, were filled with blood flowing out, running along the bridge of her nose over her lips into her mouth, where more blood was coming out, two streams running out of the corners of her mouth down over her throat, disappearing under the collar of her T-shirt where dark spots were starting to appear.

She was bleeding out of all the pores in her body.

Oskar caught his breath, shouted: "You can come in, you can . . . you are welcome, you are . . . allowed to be here!"

Eli relaxed. Her clenched fists loosened. The grimace of pain disappeared. Oskar thought for a moment that even the blood would somehow dissolve, that it would all sort of not have happened once she was invited in.

But no. The blood stopped running, but Eli's face and hands were still dark red, and while the two of them were standing in front of each other without saying anything, the blood started to coagulate, form darker stripes and lumps in the places it had flowed, and Oskar picked up a faint hospital smell.

He picked the record up off the floor, put it back in its sleeve and said, without looking at Eli: "Sorry, I . . . I didn't think . . ."

"It's alright. I was the one who wanted to do it. But I think I should probably have a shower. Do you have a plastic bag?"

"Plastic bag?"

"Yes. For the clothes."

Oskar nodded, went out into the kitchen and dug a plastic bag with the logo ICA—EAT, DRINK, AND BE HAPPY on it from the recess down below the sink. He walked into the living room, put the record on the coffee table, and stopped, the bag crinkling in his hand.

If I hadn't said anything. If I had let her . . . bleed.

He scrunched the bag into a ball, let go of it, and the bag jumped out of his hand, fell to the floor. He picked it up, threw it into the air, caught it. The shower was turned on in the bathroom.

It's all true. She is . . . he is . . .

While he walked toward the bathroom he smoothed out the bag. Eat, drink and be happy. He heard splashing from behind the closed door. The lock showed white. He knocked gently.

"Eli . . ."

"Yes. Come in . . ."

"No, it's just . . . the bag."

"Can't hear what you're saying. Come in."

"No."

"Oskar, I—"

"I'm leaving the bag here for you!"

He laid the bag outside the door and fled to the living room. Took the record out of its sleeve, put it on the playing table, turned the record player on, and moved the needle to the third track, his favorite.

A pretty long intro, and then the singer's soft voice began rolling out of the speakers.

> The girl puts flowers in her hair
> as she wanders through the field.
> She will be nineteen this year
> and she smiled to herself as she walks.

Eli came into the living room. She had fastened a towel around her waist. In her hand she had the plastic bag with her clothes. Her face was clean now and her wet hair fell in tendrils over her cheeks, ears. Oskar folded his arms across his chest where he stood next to the record player, nodding to her.

> Why are you smiling, the boy asks then
> when they meet by chance at the gate
> I'm thinking of the one who will be mine
> says the girl with eyes so blue
> The one that I love so.

"Oskar?"

"Yes?" He lowered the volume, inclined his head toward the record player. "Silly, isn't it?"

Eli shook her head. "No, this is great. *This* I really like."

"You do?"

"Yes. But Oskar . . ." Eli looked like she was going to say more, but only added an "oh well" and undid the towel knotted around her waist. It fell to the floor at her feet and she stood there naked a few feet away from him. Eli made a sweeping gesture with her hand over her thin body, said: "Just so you know."

> . . . down to the lake, where they draw in the sand
> they quietly say to each other;

You my friend, it is you I want
La-lala-lalala . . .

A short instrumental section and then the song was over. A mild crackling from the speakers, as the needle moved toward the next song, while Oskar looked at Eli.

The small nipples looked almost black against her pale white skin. Her upper body was slender, straight, and without much in the way of contours. Only the ribs stood out clearly in the sharp overhead light. Her thin arms and legs appeared unnaturally long the way they grew out of her body. a young sapling covered with human skin. Between the legs she had . . . nothing. No slit, no penis. Just a smooth surface.

Oskar pulled his hand through his hair, let it rest cupped against his neck. He didn't want to say that ridiculous mommy-word, but it slipped out anyway.

"But you don't have a . . . willie."

Eli bent her head, looked down at her groin as if this was a completely new discovery. The next song started and Oskar didn't hear what Eli answered. He pushed back the lever that raised the needle so it lifted from the record.

"What did you say?"

"I said I've had one."

"What happened to it?"

Eli chuckled and Oskar heard himself what the question sounded like, blushing a little. Eli waved her arms to the side and pulled her lower lip over the upper one.

"I left it on the subway."

"Don't be stupid."

Without looking at Eli, Oskar went past her to the bathroom to check that there were no traces.

Warm steam hung in the air; the mirror was misted over. The bathtub was as white as before, just a faint yellow streak of old dirt near the edge that never went away. The sink, clean.

It hasn't happened.

Eli had simply gone into the bathroom for appearance's sake, dropped the illusion. But, no: the soap. He lifted it up. The soap was faintly

streaked with pink and in the little porcelain indentation under it, in the
water that collected there, there was a lump of something that looked like
a tadpole, yes: alive, and he flinched when it started to—

to swim

—to move, wag its tail and wriggle its way to the outlet of the indentation, ran down into the sink, getting stuck on the edge. But it didn't
move there, was not alive. He ran water out of the tap and splashed some
on it so it was flushed down the drain. He also rinsed off the soap and
washed out the indentation. Then he took his bathrobe from the hook,
went back into the living room, and held it out to Eli, who was still standing naked on the floor, looking around.

"Thanks. When will your mother be back?"

"In a couple of hours." Oskar held up the bag with her clothes.
"Should I throw these away?"

Eli pulled on the bathrobe, tied the belt around the middle.

"No. I'll get it later." She nudged Oskar's shoulder. "Oskar? You understand now that I'm not a girl. That I'm not . . ."

Oskar stepped away from her.

"You're like a goddamn broken record. I *got* it. You *told* me already."

"But I haven't."

"Of course you have."

"When?"

Oskar thought it over.

"I can't remember, but I knew about it at least. Have known it for a
while."

"Are you . . . disappointed?"

"Why would I be?"

"Because . . . I don't know. Because you think it's . . . complicated.
Your friends—"

"Cut it out! Cut it out! You're sick. Just lay off."

"OK."

Eli fiddled with the belt of the bathrobe, then walked over to the
record player and looked at the turning record. Turned around, looked
around the room.

"You know, it's been a long time since I was . . . just hanging out in
someone's home like this. I don't really know . . . What should I do?"

"I don't know."

Eli let her shoulders fall, pushed her hands into the pockets of the bathrobe, and watched the record's dark hole in the middle as if she were hypnotized. Opened her mouth as if to say something, closed it again. Took her right hand out of the pocket, stretched it out toward the record, and pushed her finger on it so it came to a stop.

"Watch it. It can get . . . damaged."

"Sorry."

Eli quickly pulled his hand back and the record sped up, kept turning. Oskar saw that his finger had left a damp imprint behind that could be seen every time the record spun through the strip of light from the overhead lamp. Eli put his hand back in the pocket, watching the record as if he were trying to listen to the music by studying the tracks.

"This sounds a bit . . . but . . ." the corners of Eli's mouth twitched, ". . . I haven't had a . . . normal friendship with anyone in two hundred years."

He looked at Oskar with a sorry-I'm-saying-such-silly-things smile. Oskar widened his eyes.

"Are you really that old?"

"Yes. No. I was born about two hundred and twenty years ago, but half the time I've slept."

"That's normal, I do that too. Or at least . . . eight hours . . . what does that make . . . one third of the time."

"Yes. But . . . when I say *sleep* I mean that there are months at a time when I don't . . . get up at all. And then a few months when I . . . live. But then I rest during the daytime."

"Is that how it works?"

"I don't know. That's how it is with me at any rate. And then when I wake up I'm . . . little again. And weak. That's when I need help. That's maybe why I've been able to survive. Because I'm small. And people want to help me. But . . . for very different reasons."

A shadow crossed Eli's cheek as he clenched his teeth, pushed his hands down into the pockets of the robe, found something, drew it up. A shiny, thin strip of paper. Something Oskar's mom had left there; she sometimes used Oskar's bathrobe. Eli gently laid the strip of paper back in the pocket as if it was something valuable.

"Do you sleep in a coffin?"

Eli laughed, shook his head.

"No, no, I . . ."

Oskar couldn't keep it in any longer. He didn't mean to, but it came out like an accusation when he said: "But you kill people!"

Eli looked back at him with an expression that looked like surprise, as if Oskar had forcefully pointed out that he had five fingers on each hand or some such equally self-evident fact.

"Yes. I kill people. Unfortunately."

"So why do you?"

A flash of anger from Eli's eyes.

"If you have a better idea I'd like to hear it."

"Yes, what . . . blood . . . there must be some way of . . . some way to . . . that you . . ."

"There isn't."

"Why not?"

Eli snorted, his eyes narrowed.

"Because I am like you."

"What do you mean like me? I . . ."

Eli thrust his hand through the air as if he was holding a knife, said:

"What are you looking at, idiot? Want to die, or something?"

Stabbed the air with his empty hand. "That's what happens if you look at me."

Oskar rubbed his lips together, dampening them.

"What are you saying?"

"It's not me that's saying it. It's you. That was the first thing I heard you say. Down on the playground."

Oskar remembered. The tree. The knife. How he had held up the blade of the knife like a mirror, seen Eli for the first time.

Do you have a reflection? The first time I saw you was in a mirror.

"I . . . don't kill people."

"No, but you would like to. If you could. And you would really do it if you had to."

"Because I hate someone. That's a very big . . ."

"Difference. Is it?"

"Yes? . . ."

"If you got away with it. If it just happened. If you could wish someone dead and they died. Wouldn't you do it then?"

". . . sure."

"Sure you would. And that would be simply for your own enjoyment. Your revenge. I do it because I have to. There is no other way."

"But it's only because . . . they hurt me, because they tease me, because I . . ."

"Because you want to *live*. Just like me."

Eli held out his arms, laid them against Oskar's cheeks, brought his face closer.

"Be me a little."

And kissed him.

†

The man's fingers are curled around some dice and Oskar sees that the nails are painted black.

Silence blankets the room like thick fog. The thin hand tips . . . slowly . . . and the dice fall out, onto the table . . . pa-bang. Hit against each other, spin around, stop.

A two. And a four.

Oskar feels a sense of relief . . . he doesn't know where it comes from . . . when the man walks around the table, stopping in front of the row of boys like a general in front of his army. The man's voice is tonelessly flat, neither low nor high, as he stretches out his long index finger and starts to count down the row.

"One . . . two . . . three . . . four . . ."

Oskar looks to the left, in the direction the man has started to count. The boys stand, relaxed, freed. A sob. The boy next to Oskar bends over, his lower lip trembling. Oh. He's the one who is . . . number six. Oskar now understands his own relief.

"Five . . . six . . . and . . . seven."

The finger points straight at Oskar. The man looks into his eyes. And smiles.

No!

That wasn't . . . Oskar tears his gaze away from the man, looks at the dice. They now show a three and a four. The boy next to Oskar looks around wildly, as if he has just woken up from a nightmare. For a second their eyes meet. Empty. Without comprehension.

Then a scream from next to the wall.

. . . mother . . .

The woman with the brown shawl runs toward him, but two men intervene, gripping her arms and . . . throwing her back against the stone wall. Oskar's arms fly out a little as if to catch when she falls and his lips form the word:

". . . Mama!"

But hands as strong as knots are laid over his shoulders and he is taken out of the line, led to a little door. The man in the wig is still holding out his finger, following him with it while he is pushed, pulled out of the room into a dark chamber that smells

. . . alcohol . . .

. . . then flickering, fuzzy images; light, dark, stone, bare skin . . .

until the picture stabilizes and Oskar feels a strong pressure against his chest. He cannot move his arms. His right ear feels as if it is going to burst, lies pressed against a . . . wooden plank.

Something is in his mouth. A piece of rope. He sucks on the rope, opens his eyes.

He is lying face down on a table. Arms bound to the legs of the table. He is naked. In front of his eyes are two figures: the man with the wig and another one. A little fat man who looks . . . funny. No. Who looks like someone who thinks he is funny. Always tells stories that no one laughs at. The funny man who has a knife in one hand, a bowl in the other.

Something is wrong.

The pressure against his chest, his ear. Against his knees. There should be pressure against his . . . willie as well. But it is as if there is a . . . hole in the table right there. Oskar tries to wriggle a little to check it out but his body is bound too hard.

The man in the wig says something to the funny man and the funny man laughs, nods. Then both of them crouch down. The wig man fastens his gaze on Oskar. His eyes are clear blue, like the sky on a cold autumn day. Looks as if he is taking a friendly interest. The man looks into Oskar's eyes as if he is searching for something wonderful in there, something he loves.

The funny man crawls in under the table with the knife and the bowl in his hands. And Oskar understands.

He also knows that if he can just . . . get this piece of rope out of his mouth he doesn't have to be here. Then he disappears.

Oskar tries to pull his head back, leave the kiss. But Eli, who was prepared for this reaction, cups one hand around the back of his head, pushing his lips against his, forcing him to stay in Eli's memories, continues.

The piece of rope is pressed into his mouth and there is a hissing, wet sound when Oskar farts with fear. The man in the wig scrunches up his nose and smacks his lips, disapprovingly. His eyes don't change. Still the same expression, as on a child opening a cardboard box he knows contains a puppy.

Cold fingers grasp Oskar's penis, pulling on it. He opens his mouth to scream "nooo!" but the rope prevents him from forming the word and all that comes out is "aaaaaaah!"

The man under the table asks something and the wig man nods without shifting his gaze from Oskar. Then the pain. A red hot iron forced into his groin, gliding up through his stomach, his chest corroded by a cylinder of fire that passes right through his body and he screams, screams so his eyes are filled with tears and his body burns.

His heart beats against the table like a fist against a door and he shuts his eyes tight, he bites the rope while at a distance he hears splashing, he sees . . .

. . . his mother on her knees at the stream rinsing the clothes. Mama. Mama. She drops something, a piece of cloth, and Oskar gets up, he has been lying on his stomach and his body is burning, he gets up, he runs toward the stream, toward the rapidly disappearing piece of cloth, he throws himself into the stream to put out his torched body, to save the piece of cloth, and he manages to get it. His sister's shirt. He holds it up to the light, to his mother, who is silhouetted on the shore, and drops fall from the cloth, glittering in the sun, falling splashing into the stream, in his eyes, and he cannot see clearly because of the water running into his eyes, over his cheeks as he . . .

. . . opens his eyes and sees the blond hair unclearly, the blue eyes like distant forest pools. Sees the bowl the man is holding in his hands, the bowl he brings to his mouth and how he drinks. How the man shuts his eyes, finally shuts them and drinks . . .

More time . . . Endless time. Imprisoned. The man bites. And drinks.
Bites. And drinks.

Then the glowing rod moves up into his head and everything turns pink
as he jerks his head up from the rope and falls . . .

†

Eli caught him when he fell backward from Eli's lips. Held him in his
arms. Oskar fumbled for whatever there was to grasp, the body in front of
him, and squeezed it hard, looked unseeing around the room.

Stay still.

After a while a pattern started to emerge before Oskar's eyes. Wallpaper. Beige with white, almost invisible roses. He recognized it. It was the
wallpaper in his living room. He was in the living room in his and his
mom's apartment.

And the person in his arms was . . . Eli.

A boy. My friend. Yes.

Oskar felt sick to his stomach, dizzy. He freed himself from Eli's arms
and sat down in the couch, looked around as if to reassure himself again
that he was back and not . . . there. He swallowed, noticing that he could
recall every detail of the place he had just been. It was like a real memory.
Something that had happened to him, recently. The funny man, the bowl,
the pain . . .

Eli kneeled on the floor in front of him, hands pressed against his
stomach.

"Sorry."

Just like . . .

"What happened to Mama?"

Eli looked uncertain, asked:

"Do you mean . . . my mother?"

"No . . ." Oskar grew silent, saw the image of Mama down by the
stream rinsing the clothes. But it wasn't his mother. They didn't look anything alike. He rubbed his eyes and said,

"Yes. Right. Your mother."

"I don't know."

"They weren't the ones who—"

"I don't know!"

Eli's hands squeezed so hard in front of his stomach that the knuckles whitened, his shoulders pulled up. Then he relaxed, said more gently: "I don't know. Excuse me. Excuse the whole . . . thing. I wanted you to . . . I don't know. Please excuse me. It was . . . stupid."

Eli was a copy of his mother. Thinner, smoother, younger but . . . a copy. In twenty years Eli would probably look just like the woman by the stream.

Except that he won't. He's going to look exactly like he looks now.

Oskar sighed, exhausted, leaned back in the couch. Too much. An incipient headache groped along his temples, found foothold, pressed in. Too much. Eli stood up.

"I'll go now."

Oskar leaned his head in his hand, nodded. Didn't have the energy to protest, think about what he should do. Eli took off the bathrobe and Oskar got another glimpse of his groin. Now he saw that in the midst of that pale skin there was a faint pink spot, a scar.

What does he do when he . . . pees? Or maybe he doesn't . . .

Couldn't muster the energy to ask. Eli crouched down next to the plastic bag, untied it, and started to pull out his clothes. Oskar said: "You can . . . take something of mine."

"It's OK."

Eli took out the checkered shirt. Dark squares against the blue. Oskar sat up. The headache whirled against his temples.

"Don't be silly, you can—"

"It's OK."

Eli started to put on the bloodstained shirt and Oskar said: "You're gross, don't you get it? You're gross."

Eli turned to him with the shirt in his hands. "Do you think so?"

"Yes."

Eli put the shirt back in the bag.

"What should I take then?"

"Something from the closet. Whatever you like."

Eli nodded, went into Oskar's room where the closets were while Oskar let himself slide sideways into the couch and pressed his hands against his temples to prevent them from cracking.

Mom, Eli's mom, my mom. Eli, me. Two hundred years. Eli's dad. Eli's dad? That old man who . . . the old man.

Eli came back into the living room. Oskar got ready to say what he was planning to say but stopped himself when he saw that Eli was wearing a dress. A faded yellow summer dress with small white dots. One of his mother's dresses. Eli stroked his hand over it.

"Is this alright? I took the one that looked the most worn."

"But it's . . ."

"I'll bring it back later."

"Yes, yes, yes."

Eli went up to him, crouched down, and took his hand.

"Oskar? I'm sorry that . . . I don't know what I should . . ."

Oskar waved with his other hand to get him to stop, said: "You know that that old guy, that he's escaped, don't you?"

"What old guy?"

"The old guy who . . . the one you said was your dad. The one who lived with you."

"What about him?"

Oskar shut his eyes. Blue lightning flashed inside his eyelids. The chain of events he had reconstructed from the papers flashed past and he got angry, loosening his hand from Eli's and making it into a fist, hitting against his own throbbing head. He said with his eyes still shut: "Cut it out. Just cut it out. I know all of it, OK. Quit pretending. Quit lying, I'm so damn tired of that."

Eli didn't say anything. Oskar pinched his eyes shut, breathed in and out.

"The old man has escaped. They've been looking for him the whole day without finding him. Now you know."

A pause. Then Eli's voice, above Oskar's head:

"Where?"

"Here. In Judarn. The forest. By Åkeshov."

Oskar opened his eyes. Eli had stood up, stood there with his hand over his mouth and large, frightened eyes above his hand. The dress was too big, hung like a sack over his thin shoulders, and he looked like a kid who had borrowed his mom's clothes without permission and was now awaiting his punishment.

"Oskar," said Eli. "Don't go out. After it gets dark. Promise me that."
The dress. The words. Oskar snorted, couldn't help saying it.
"You sound like my mom."

†

The squirrel darts down the trunk of the oak tree, stops, listens. A siren, in the distance.

†

On Bergslagsvägen an ambulance is going by with flashing blue lights, the sirens on.

Inside the ambulance there are three people. Lacke Sörensson is sitting on a folding seat and is holding a bloodless, lacerated hand belonging to Virginia Lind. An ambulance technician is adjusting the tube that administers saline solution to Virginia's body in order to give her heart something to pump around, now that she has lost so much blood.

†

The squirrel judges the sound to be not dangerous, irrelevant. It continues down the tree trunk. All day there have been people in the forest, dogs. Not a moment of calm and only now, when it is dark, does the squirrel dare come down out of the oak tree it has been forced to hole up in all day.

Now the dogs' barking and the voices have died down, gone away. The thundering bird that has been hovering over the tree tops also appears to have returned to its nest.

The squirrel reaches the foot of the tree, runs along a thick root. It docs not like to make its way over the ground in the dark, but hunger forces it on. It makes its way with alertness, stopping to listen, looking around every ten meters. Makes sure to steer clear of a badger den that has been inhabited as recently as this summer. He hasn't seen the family for a long time but you can never be too careful.

Finally the squirrel reaches its goal: the nearest of the many winter stores it has laid up in the fall. The temperature this evening has sunk below freezing and on top of the snow that has been melting all day there is now a thin, hard crust. The squirrel scratches with its claws through the crust, gets through, and moves down. Stops, listens, and digs again. Through snow, leaves, dirt.

Just as it picks up a nut between its paws it hears a sound.

Danger.

It takes the nut in its teeth and runs straight up into a pine tree without having time to cover over the store. Once in the safety of a branch it takes the nut into its paws again, tries to locate the sound. Its hunger is great and the food only some centimeters from its mouth but the danger must first be located, identified, before it is time to eat.

The squirrel's head jerks from side to side, his nose trembles as he looks down over the moon-shadowed landscape below and traces the sound to its source. Yes. Taking the long way around was worth it. The scratching, wet sound comes from the badger den.

Badgers can't climb trees. The squirrel relaxes a little and takes a bite of the nut while it continues to study the ground, but now more as a member of a theater audience, third balcony. Wants to see what will happen, how many badgers there are.

But what emerges from the badger's den is no badger. The squirrel removes the nut from its mouth, looks down. Tries to understand. Put what it sees together with known facts. Doesn't manage it.

Therefore takes the nut into its mouth again, dashes further up the trunk, all the way up into the very top.

Maybe one of those can climb trees.

You can never be too careful.

Sunday

8 NOVEMBER [EVENING/NIGHT]

It is half past eight, Sunday evening.

At the same time as the ambulance with Virginia and Lacke is driving over the Traneberg Bridge, the Stockholm district chief of police holds up a photograph for the image-hungry reporters, Eli chooses a dress out of Oskar's mother's closet, Tommy squeezes glue into a plastic bag and draws in the exquisite fumes of numbness and forgetfulness, a squirrel sees Håkan Bengtsson—as the first living creature in fourteen hours to have done so—and Staffan, one of the ones who has been searching for him, is pouring out a cup of tea.

He has not realized that a sliver is missing from the very front of the spout and a large quantity of tea runs along the spout, the teapot, down onto the kitchen counter. He mumbles something and tips the teapot at an even steeper angle so the tea comes splashing out and the lid tumbles off and into the cup. Scalding hot tea splashes onto his hands and he slams the teapot down, holding his arms stiffly at his sides, while in his head he starts to run through the Hebrew alphabet in order to quell his impulse to throw the teapot against the wall.

Aleph, Beth, Gimel, Daleth . . .

✝

Yvonne came into the kitchen, saw Staffan bent over the counter with closed eyes.

"How are you doing?"

Staffan shook his head. "It's nothing."

Lamed, Mem, Nun, Samesh . . .

"Are you sad?"

"No."

Koff, Resh, Shin, Taff. There. Better.

He opened his eyes, pointed at the teapot.

"That's a terrible teapot."

"It is?"

"Yes, it . . . spills when you try to pour the tea."

"I've never noticed."

"Well, it does."

"There's nothing wrong with it."

Staffan pinched his lips together, stretched out his scalded hand towards her with a gesture of *Peace. Shalom. Be quiet.* "Yvonne. Right now I feel such an . . . intense desire to hit you. So please, don't say any more."

Yvonne took half a step back. Something in her had been prepared for this. She had not admitted this insight into her conscious mind, but had still sensed that behind his pious façade Staffan stored some kind of . . . rage.

She crossed her arms, breathed in and out a few times, while Staffan stood still, staring at the teacup with the lid in it. Then she said: "Is that what you do?"

"What?"

"Hit. When something goes wrong."

"Have I hit you?"

"No, but you said—"

"I *said*. And you listened. And now it's alright."

"And if I hadn't listened?"

Staffan looked completely calm again and Yvonne relaxed, lowered her arms. He took both her hands in his, kissed the backs of them lightly.

"Yvonne. We *have* to listen to each other."

The tea was poured out and they drank it in the living room. Staffan made a mental note to buy Yvonne a new teapot. She asked about the search in Judarn forest and Staffan told her. She did her best to engage him in conversation on other topics but, finally, came the unavoidable question.

"Where's Tommy?"

"I . . . don't know."

"You don't know? Yvonne . . ."

"Well, at a friend's house."

"Hm. When is he coming home."

"I think he was . . . supposed to spend the night. Over there."

"There?"

"Yes, at . . ."

In her head Yvonne went through the names of Tommy's friends that she knew. Didn't want to tell Staffan that Tommy was gone for the night without knowing where. Staffan took this thing about a parent's responsibility very seriously.

". . . at Robban's."

"Robban. Is that his best friend?"

"Yes, I guess so."

"What is he called, more than Robban?"

". . . Ahlgren. Why? Is that someone you have . . ."

"No, I was just thinking."

Staffan took his spoon, hit it lightly against the teacup. A delicate ringing sound. He nodded.

"Great. You know . . . I think we're going to have to call this Robban and ask Tommy to come home for a while. So I can talk to him a little."

"I don't have the number."

"No, but . . . Ahlgren. You know where he lives, don't you? All you have to do is look it up in the telephone directory."

Staffan got up out of the couch and Yvonne bit her lower lip, felt how she was constructing a labyrinth that it was getting harder and harder to get out of. He got the local part of the telephone book and stopped in the middle of the living room, flipping through it and mumbling:

"Ahlgren, Ahlgren . . . Hm. Which street does he live on?"

"I . . . Björnsonsgatan."

"Björnsonsgatan . . . no. No Ahlgren there. But there is one here on Ibsengatan. Could it be him?"

When Yvonne didn't answer, Staffan put his finger in the phone book and said:

"Think I'll give him a try at any rate. It's Robban, right?"

"Staffan . . ."

"Yes?"

"I promised him not to tell."

"Now I don't understand anything."

"Tommy. I said I wouldn't tell you . . . where he is."

"So he is *not* at Robban's?"

"No."

"Where is he then?"

"I . . . I promised."

Staffan put the telephone book on the coffee table, went and sat down next to Yvonne on the couch. She took a sip of tea, held the teacup in front of her face as if to hide behind it while Staffan waited for her. When she put the cup down on the saucer she saw that her hands were shaking. Staffan put his hand on her knee.

"Yvonne. You have to understand that—"

"I promised."

"I only want to *talk* to him. Forgive me for saying this, Yvonne, but I think it is exactly this kind of inability to deal with a situation as it arises that is the reason . . . well, that they happen in the first place. In my experience, the faster young people have someone respond to their actions, the greater the chance that . . . take a heroin addict, for example. If someone takes action when he is only doing, say, hashish . . ."

"Tommy doesn't do things like that."

"Are you *completely* sure of that?"

Silence fell. Yvonne knew that for each second that went by, her "yes" in response to Staffan's question decreased in value. Tick-tock. Now she had already answered "no" without saying the word. And Tommy did act strange sometimes. When he came home. Something about his eyes. What if he . . .

Staffan leaned back in the couch, knew the battle was won. Now he was only waiting for her conditions.

Yvonne's eyes were searching for something on the table.

"What is it?"

"My cigarettes, have you—"

"In the kitchen. Yvonne—"

"Yes. Yes. You can't go to him now."

"No. You can decide. If you think—"

"Tomorrow morning. Before he goes to school. Promise me. That you won't go to him now."

"Promise. So. What kind of mysterious place is he holed up in any-way?"

Yvonne told him.

Then she went out into the kitchen and smoked a cigarette, blew the smoke out through the open window. Smoked one more, cared less about where the smoke went. When Staffan came out into the kitchen, demonstratively waved away the smoke with his hand, and asked where the cellar key was, she said she had forgotten for the moment but it would *probably* come back to her tomorrow morning.

If he was nice.

†

When Eli had gone, Oskar sat down at the kitchen table again looking through the displayed newspaper articles. The headache was starting to lessen now that the impressions were taking on more of a pattern.

Eli had explained that the old man had become . . . infected. And worse. The infection was the only thing in him that was alive. His brain was dead, and the infection was controlling and directing him. Toward Eli.

Eli had told him, *begged* him not to do anything. Eli would leave this place tomorrow as soon as it got dark, and Oskar had of course asked why not leave tonight already?

Because . . . I can't.

Why not? I can help you.

Oskar, I can't. I'm too weak.

How can that be? You've just . . .

I just am.

And Oskar had realized that he was the reason that Eli was weak. All the blood that had run out in the hall. If the old guy got ahold of Eli it would be all Oskar's fault.

The clothes!

Oskar got up so violently the chair tipped over backward and fell to the floor.

The bag with Eli's bloodied clothes was still sitting in front of the couch, the shirt half hanging out. He pressed it deeper into the bag and the sleeve was like a damn sponge when he pressed it down, tied the bag, and . . . He stopped, looked at the hand that had pressed the shirt down.

The cut he had made in his palm had a crust that had broken up a little, revealing the wound underneath.

. . . the blood . . . he didn't want to mix it . . . am I . . . infected now?

His legs carried him mechanically to the front door with the bag in his hand, listening for sounds outside. He didn't hear anyone and he ran up the stairs to the garbage chute, opened it. He pushed the bag in through the opening, held it fast for a moment, dangling in the dark.

A cold breeze whooshed through the chute, chilling his hand where he held it outstretched, squeezed around the plastic knot of the bag. The bag shone white against the black, slightly craggy walls of the duct. If he let go, the bag would not be sucked up. It would fall down. Gravity would pull it down. Into the big garbage sack.

In a few days the garbage truck would come and collect the sack. It came early in the morning. The orange, blinking lights would flash onto Oskar's ceiling at about the same time as he generally woke up and he would lie there in his bed and listen to the rumbling, masticating crunch as the garbage was crushed. Maybe he would get up and watch the men in their overalls who tossed the big bags with habitual ease, pressed the button. The jaws of the garbage truck closing and the men who then hopped into the truck and drove the short distance to the next building.

And it always gave him such a feeling of . . . warmth. That he was safe in his room. That things worked. Maybe there was also a longing. For those men, for the truck. To be allowed to sit in that dimly-lit coach, drive away . . .

Let go. I have to let go.

The hand was convulsively clenched around the bag. His arm was aching from having been held outstretched so long. The back of his hand was numb from the cold air. He let go.

There was a hissing sound as the bag slipped along the walls, a half second of silence as it fell freely, and then a thud when it landed in the sack below.

I'll help you.

He looked at his hand again. The hand that helped. The hand that . . .

I'll kill someone. I'll go in and get the knife and then I'll go out and kill someone. Jonny. I'll slit his throat and gather up his blood and then I'll bring it home for Eli because what does it matter now that I'm infected and soon I will . . .

His legs wanted to crumple up under him and he had to lean on the edge of the garbage chute not to fall over. He had thought it. For real. This wasn't like the game with the tree. He had . . . for a moment . . . really thought about doing it.

Warm. He was warm, like he had a fever. His body ached and he wanted to go lie down. Now.

I'm infected. I'm going to become a . . . vampire.

He forced his legs to move back down the stairs while he steadied himself with one hand—

the uninfected one

—on the railing. He managed to let himself back into the apartment, went into his room, lay down on his bed, and stared at the wallpaper. The forest. Quickly one of his figures appeared, looked him in the eyes. The little gnome. He stroked his finger over it while a completely ridiculous little thought appeared:

Tomorrow I have to go to school.

And there was a worksheet he hadn't filled out yet. Africa. He should get up now, sit down at his desk, light the lamp, and start to look up places in the geography book. Find meaningless names and write them down on the blank lines.

That was what he ought to do. He softly stroked the gnome's little cap, Then he tapped on the wall.

E.L.I.

No answer. Was probably out—

doing what we do.

He pulled the covers over his head. A fever-like chill coursed through his body. He tried to imagine it. How it would be. To live forever. Feared, hated. No. *Eli* wouldn't hate him. If they were . . . together. . . .

He tried to imagine it; he spun out a fantasy about it. After a while the front door was unlocked. His mom was home.

†

Pillows of fat.

Tommy stared blankly at the picture in front of him. The girl was pressing her breasts together with her hands so they stood out like two balloons, had pursed her mouth into a pout. It looked sick. He had thought he was going to jack off, but there must be something wrong with his brain, because he thought the girl looked like a freak.

He folded the magazine up with unnatural slowness, tucked it back in under the sofa cushions. Every little movement directed by conscious thought. Wasted. He was utterly wasted with glue fumes. And that was good. No world. Only the room he was in, and outside that . . . a billowing desert.

Staffan.

He tried to think about Staffan. Couldn't. Didn't get ahold of him. Only saw that cardboard cutout of the policeman up at the post office. Lifesize. To scare off any would-be robbers.

Should we rob the post office?

Man, you must be crazy! Can't you see the cardboard policeman is there?

Tommy giggled when the cardboard policeman's face took on Staffan's features. Assigned as punishment. To guard the post office. There was something written on the cutout as well, what was it?

Crime doesn't pay. No. The police are watching you. No. What the hell was it? Watch out! I'm a champion pistol-shooter!

Tommy laughed. Laughed more. Laughed until he shook and thought the naked bulb in the ceiling was swinging to and fro in time with his laughter. Giggled at it. Watch out! The cardboard policeman! With his cardboard gun! And his cardboard head!

There was a knock inside his head. Someone wanted to come into the post office.

The cardboard policeman pricks up his ears. There are two hundred cardboards at the post office. Undo the safety. Bang-bang.

Knock. Knock. Knock.

Bang.

. . . Staffan . . . Mom, shit . . .

Tommy stiffened. Tried to think. Couldn't. Just a ragged cloud in his head. Then he calmed down. Maybe it was Robban or Lasse. It could be Staffan. And he was made of cardboard.

Penis-dummy, cardboard-mummy.

Tommy cleared his throat, said thickly: "Who is it?"

"It's me."

He recognized the voice, couldn't place it. Not Staffan, at any rate. Not paper-Papa.

Barba-papa. Stop it.

"Who are you, then?"

"Can you open?"

"The post office is closed for the day. Come back in five years."

"I have money."

"Paper money?"

"Yes."

"That's good."

He got up out of the couch. Slowly, slowly. The contours of things didn't want to stay put. His head was full of lead.

Concrete cap.

He stood still for a few seconds, swaying. The concrete floor tilted dreamily to the right, to the left, like in the Funny House. He walked forward, one step at a time, lifted the latch, pushed open the door. It was that girl. Oskar's friend. Tommy stared at her without understanding what he was seeing.

Sun and surf.

The girl was wearing only a thin dress. Yellow, with white dots that absorbed Tommy's gaze, and he tried to focus on the dots but they started to dance, move around so he became sick to his stomach. She was maybe twenty centimeters shorter than him.

As cute as . . . a summer day.

"Is it summer now all of a sudden?" he asked.

The girl put her head to one side.

"What?"

"Well you're wearing a . . . what's it called . . . a sundress."

"Yes."

Tommy nodded, pleased that he had been able to think of the word. What had she said? Money. Yes. Oskar had said that . . .

"Do you . . . want to buy something?"

"Yes."

"What?"

"Can I come in?"

"Yes, sure."

"Say that I can come in."

Tommy made an exaggerated, sweeping gesture with his arm. Saw his own hand moving in slow-motion, a drugged fish swimming through the air.

"Step inside. Welcome to the . . . local branch."

He didn't have the energy to stay on his feet any longer. The floor wanted him. He turned around and flopped back on the couch. The girl walked in, closed the door behind her, put the latch back on. He saw her as an enormous chicken, giggling at his vision. The chicken sat down in an armchair.

"What is it?"

"No, it's just . . . you're so . . . yellow."

"I see."

The girl crossed her hands over a little purse in her lap. He hadn't noticed that she had one. No. No not a purse. More like a cosmetic bag. Tommy looked at it. You see a bag. You wonder what's inside.

"What do you have in there?"

"Money."

"Of course."

Nope. This is fishy. There's something strange about this.

"What do you want to buy, then?"

The girl unzipped the case and took out a thousand kronor note. One more. Then another. Three thousand. The bills looked ridiculously large in her small hands when she leaned forward and laid them on the floor.

Tommy chortled: "What's all this?"

"Three thousand."

"Yes. But what for?"

"For you."

"Give me a break."

"No, really."

"That must be some kind of damn . . . Monopoly money or something. Isn't it?"

"No."

"It isn't?"

"No."

"What's it for, anyway?"

"Because I want to buy something from you."

"You want to buy something for three thou . . . no."

Tommy stretched out one arm as far as he could, snapped up a bill. Felt it, crinkled it with his hand, held it up against the light and saw the watermark. Same king or whatever who was printed on the front. The real deal.

"You're not kidding, are you?"

"No."

Three thousand. Could . . . go somewhere. Fly somewhere.

Then Staffan and his mom could stand there and . . . Tommy felt his head clear a little. The whole thing was cuckoo but OK: three thousand. That was a fact. Now the only question was . . .

"What do you want to buy? For this you can have . . ."

"Blood."

"Blood."

"Yes."

Tommy snorted, shook his head.

"No, sorry. We're all sold out."

The girl sat still in the armchair, looking at him. Didn't even smile.

"No, but seriously," Tommy said. "I mean, what?"

"You'll get this money . . . if I get some blood."

"I don't have any."

"Yes, you do."

"No."

"Yes."

Tommy suddenly got it.

What the hell . . .

"Are you . . . serious?"

The girl pointed at the bills.

"It's not dangerous."

"But . . . what . . . how?"

The girl stuck her hand into the kit, fished something out. A small, white, square bit of plastic. Shook it. It rattled a little. Now Tommy saw what it was. A packet of razor blades. She put it into her lap, took out something else. A skin-colored rectangle. A large Band-Aid.

This is ridiculous.

"No, cut it out now. Don't you understand that . . . I could just take that money from you, you know. Put it in my pocket and say, What? Three thousand? Haven't seen it. It's a *lot* of money, don't you realize that? Where did you get it from?"

The girl shut her eyes, sighed. When she opened them again she didn't look as friendly.

"Do you want to or not?"

She means it. She really means it. No . . . no . . .

"What, are you, like, going to . . . swish, and then . . ."

The girl nodded, eagerly.

Swish? Wait a minute. Wait a little now . . . what was it . . . pigs . . .

He frowned. The thought bounced around inside his head like a rubber ball thrown hard inside a room, trying to find a resting place, to stop. And it stopped. He remembered something. Gaped. Looked her in the eyes.

". . . no . . ."

"Yes."

"This is some kind of joke, isn't it? You know what? Go. I want you to leave."

"I have an illness. I need blood. You can have more money if you want."

She dug around in the kit and took out two more thousand kronor notes, put them on the floor. Five thousand. "Please."

The murderer. Vällingby. His throat slit. But what the hell . . . this girl . . .

"What do you need it for . . . what the hell . . . you're just a kid, you . . ."

"Are you scared?"

"No, I can always . . . are *you* scared?"

"Yes."

"Of what?"

"Of you saying no."

"But I *am* saying no. This is completely . . . come off it. Go home."

The girl sat still in the chair, thinking. Then she nodded, got up, and picked the money up off the floor, put it back in the makeup kit. Tommy looked at the spot where it had been. Five. Thousand. A clink as the latch was lifted. Tommy turned over on his back.

"But . . . what . . . are you planning to slit my throat?"

"No, on the inside of your elbow. Only a little."

"But what will you do with it?"

"Drink it."

"Now?"

"Yes."

Tommy's mind turned inward and he saw that chart of the circulatory system projected over his skin like an overhead transparency. Felt, maybe for the first time in his life, that he had a circulatory system. Not just isolated points, wounds where one or more drops came out, but a large pumping tree of veins filled with . . . how much was it? . . . four or five liters of blood.

"What kind of *illness* is it?"

The girl didn't say anything, just stood there at the door with the latch in her hand, studying him, and then the lines of veins and arteries of his body, the chart, suddenly took on the character of a . . . butcher's chart. He pushed the thought away, and thought instead: *Become a blood donor. Twenty-five even and a cheese sandwich.* Then he thought:

"So give me the money."

The girl unzipped the case, took out the bills again.

"How about if I give you . . . three now. And two after?"

"Yeah, sure. But I could just . . . jump you and take the money anyway, don't you understand that?"

"No. You couldn't."

She held the three thousand out to him, between index and middle finger. He held each one of them up to the light, checking to make sure that they were genuine. Rolled them into a cylinder that he clenched his left hand around.

"OK. And now?"

The girl put the other two bills on the chair, crouched down next to the couch, dug out the white packet from the kit, shaking out a razor blade.

She's done this before.

The girl turned the razor blade to see which side was sharper. Then held it up next to her face. A little message, whose only word was: *Swish.* She said:

"You can't tell anyone about this."

"What happens if I do?"

"You cannot tell anyone about this. Ever."

"No." Tommy glanced at his outstretched arm, at the thousand kronor bills on the chair. "How much are you going to take?"

"One liter."

"Is that . . . a lot?"

"Yes."

"Is it so much that I . . ."

"No. You can handle it."

"Because it comes back."

"Yes."

Tommy nodded. Then watched with fascination as the razor blade, shining like a little mirror, was lowered against his skin. As if it was happening to someone else, somewhere else. Only saw the play of lines. The girl's jawbone, her dark hair, his white arm, the rectangle of the razor blade that pushed aside a thin hair on his arm and reached its goal, rested for a split second against the swelling of the vein, somewhat darker than the surrounding skin.

Then it pressed down, lightly, lightly. A point that sank down without puncturing it. Then—

Swish.

He had an involuntary reaction to pull away and Tommy gasped, squeezed his other hand tightly around the bills. A creaking inside his head as his teeth bit down, grinding against each other. The blood streamed out, pressed out in spurts.

The razor blade fell to the floor with a tinkle and the girl grabbed hold of his arm with both hands, pressing her lips against the inside of his arm.

Tommy turned his head away, only felt her warm lips, her tongue lapping against his skin, and again he saw that chart inside his head, the channels that the blood ran through, rushing toward that . . . opening.

It's running out of me.

Yes. The intensity of the pain increased. The arm was starting to feel paralyzed; he no longer felt the lips, he only felt the strong suction, how it was sucked out of him, how it was . . .

Flowing away.

He got scared. Wanted to put an end to it. It hurt too much. The tears came to his eyes, he opened his mouth to say something, to . . . couldn't. There were no words that would . . . He bent his free arm toward his mouth, pressed the clenched fist against his mouth. Felt the cylinder of paper that stuck out of it. Bit down on it.

21:17, SUNDAY EVENING, ÄNGBYPLAN:

A man is observed outside the hair salon. He presses his face and hands against the glass, and appears extremely intoxicated. The police arrive at the scene fifteen minutes later. The man has left by this point. The window does not appear damaged in any way, only the traces of mud or earth. In the lighted window display there are numerous pictures of young people, hair models.

†

Are you sleeping?"

"No."

A waft of perfume and cold as his mom came into his room, sat down on the bed.

"Have you had a good time?"

"Yes."

"What did you do?"

"Nothing in particular."

"I saw some papers. On the kitchen table."

"Mm."

Oskar pulled the covers more tightly around him, pretended to yawn.

"Are you sleepy?"

"Mm."

True and not true. He was tired, so tired his head was buzzing. Only wanted to roll himself up in his covers, seal the entrance, and not emerge again until . . . until . . . but sleepy, no. And . . . *could* he even sleep now that he was infected?

Heard his mother ask him something about his dad, and he said "fine" without knowing what he was answering. It got quiet. Then his mom sighed, deeply.

"Sweetheart, how are you doing, really? Is there anything I can do?"

"No."

"What is it?"

Oskar pressed his face into the pillow, breathing out so that his nose, mouth, and lips became hot and moist. He couldn't do it. It was too hard. Had to tell someone. Into the pillow he said: ". . . iemfecte . . ."

"What did you say?"

He lifted his mouth from the pillow.

"I'm infected."

His mom's hand stroked the back of his head, across his neck, continued, and the blankets came off a little.

"How do you mean, inf . . . but . . . you're still wearing all your clothes!"

"Yes, I . . ."

"Let me feel you. Are you hot?" She leaned her cold cheek onto his forehead. "You have a fever. Come on. You have to take your clothes off and get into bed properly." She stood up and gently shook his shoulder. "Come on."

She was breathing faster now, thinking something else. Said in a different tone of voice:

"Weren't you dressed warmly enough when you were at your dad's?"

"I was, it's not that."

"Were you wearing a hat?"

"Yes. It's not *that*."

"What is it then?"

Oskar pressed his face into the pillow again, squeezed it, and said: ". . . agoinbeahmpire . . ."

"Oskar, what are you saying?"

"I'm going to be a vampire!"

Pause. The soft rustling of his mother's coat as she crossed her arms over her chest.

"Oskar. Get up. And take your clothes off. And get into bed."

"I'm going to be a *vampire*."

His mom's breathing. Deliberate, angry. "Tomorrow I am going to throw away all of those books you're always reading."

The covers were pulled off him. He got up, slowly took his clothes off, avoided looking at her. Lay down in the bed again, and his mom tucked the covers in around him.

"Do you want anything?"

Oskar shook his head.

"Should we take your temperature?"

Oskar shook his head harder. Now he looked at her. She was leaning over the bed, hands on her knees. Searching, concerned eyes.

"Is there *anything* I can do for you?"

"No. Yes."

"What?"

"No, nothing."

"No, tell me."

"Could you . . . tell me a story?"

A string of different emotions crossed his mom's face: sadness, joy, worry, a small smile, a wrinkle of concern. All in a few seconds. Then she said: "I . . . don't know any fairy tales. But I . , , I can read one to you if you want. If we have some book . . ."

Her gaze went up to the bookcase by Oskar's head.

"No, don't bother."

"But I'm happy to do it."

"No, I don't want you to."

"Why not? You said—"

"Yes, I did, but . . . no. I don't want you to."

"Should I . . . should I sing something?"

"No!"

She pressed her lips together, hurt. Then she decided not to be, since Oskar was sick, said: "I guess I could think of something, if that is—"

"No, it's fine. I want to sleep now."

His mom eventually said good night, left the room. Oskar lay there, his eyes open, staring at the window. Tried to feel if he was in the process of . . . becoming. Didn't know what that felt like. Eli. How had that actually worked when he . . . was transformed?

To be separated from everything.

Leave. His mom, dad, school . . . Jonny, Tomas . . .

To be with Eli. Always.

He heard the TV go on in the living room, how the volume was quickly lowered. Distant clatter of the coffee pot from the kitchen. The gas stove being turned on, rattle of a cup and saucer. Cupboards opened.

The normal sounds. He had heard them a hundred times. And he felt sad. So very sad.

†

The wounds had healed. The only remaining traces of the lacerations on Virginia's body were white lines, here and there the remnants of scabs that had not yet fallen off. Lacke stroked her hand, pressed against her body with a leather strap, and yet another scab crumbled away under his fingers.

†

Virginia had resisted. Had made violent resistance when she came to her full senses and understood what was happening. She had torn out the catheter for the blood transfusion, screamed and kicked.

Lacke had not been able to watch as they struggled with her, how she seemed like a different person. Had gone down to the cafeteria and had a cup of coffee. Then another, and another. When he was in the process of pouring himself his fourth cup, the woman at the register had pointed out in a tired voice that he was only allowed *one* free refill. Lacke had then said that he was broke, felt like he was going to die tomorrow, could she make an exception?

She could. She even offered Lacke a dry *mazarin* cake that would have been thrown away the next day anyway. He had eaten it with a lump in his throat, thinking about people's relative goodness, relative evil. Then he went and stood out by the front doors and smoked the second to last cigarette in the packet before he went back up to Virginia.

They had tied her down with straps.

A nurse had received such a blow that her glasses had broken and a sliver had slashed an eyebrow. Virginia had been impossible to calm. They had not dared give her an injection because of her general state and therefore they had strapped her arms down with leather straps, mainly to prevent—as they put it—"to prevent her from injuring herself."

Lacke rubbed a scab between his fingers; a powder as fine as pigment colored the tops of his fingers red. A movement in the corner of his eye; the blood from the bag hanging from the stand next to Virginia's bed fell in drops down a plastic tube, and on down through the catheter into Virginia's arm.

Apparently, once they had identified her blood group, they had first given her a transfusion where they literally pumped in a quantity of blood, but now, when her condition had stabilized, she received it by the drop. There was a label on the half-full blood bag printed with incomprehensible markings, dominated with a capital A. The blood type, of course.

But . . . wait a minute . . .

Lacke had blood type B. He now recalled that he and Virginia had talked about that one time, that Virginia also had the blood group B and that therefore he could . . . yes. That was exactly right. That they could give blood to each other because they had the same blood type. And Lacke had B; he was completely sure of that.

He got up, walked out into the corridor.

Surely they don't make these kinds of mistakes?

He got hold of a nurse.

"Excuse me, but . . ."

She glanced at his worn clothes, put on an aloof air, said: "Yes?"

"I was just wondering. Virginia . . . Virginia Lind who you . . . admitted a while ago . . ."

The nurse nodded, looked positively dismissive now. Had perhaps been present when they . . .

"Well, I was just wondering . . . her blood type."

"What about it?"

"Well, I saw there's a big A on the bag that . . . but she doesn't have that."

"I'm afraid I'm not following this."

"You see . . . uh . . . do you have a moment?"

The nurse looked around down the corridor. Perhaps to check if there was help to be had if this deteriorated into something, perhaps to underscore that she had more important things to do, but she did agree to accompany Lacke into the room where Virginia lay with closed eyes, the blood slowly dropping down the tube. Lacke pointed to the bag of blood.

"Here. This A, it means that . . ."

"That it contains type A blood, yes. There is such a shortage of blood donors these days. If people knew how—"

"Excuse me, yes. But she has blood type B. Isn't it dangerous to . . ."

"Of course it is."

The nurse was not unfriendly, exactly, but her body language suggested that Lacke's right to question the competence of hospital staff was minimal. She shrugged lightly, said: "If one has blood type B. But this patient does not. She has AB."

"But . . . the bag says A . . ."

The nurse nodded, as if she was explaining to a child that there were no people on the moon: "People with the blood type AB can receive blood from all blood groups."

"But . . . I see. Then she has changed her blood type."

The nurse raised an eyebrow. The child had just claimed that it had been to the moon and seen people up there. With a hand gesture, as if she were slicing a ribbon, she said: "That's just not possible."

"Is that a fact. Well, she must have been wrong, then."

"She must have been. If you'll excuse me I have other things to attend to."

The nurse checked the catheter in Virginia's arm, adjusted the IV stand slightly, and with a last look at Lacke that said that these were important things and god save him if he so much as looked at them, she left the room with energetic steps.

What happens if you get the wrong kind of blood? The blood . . . coagulates.

No. It must have been Virginia who couldn't remember correctly.

He walked to a corner of the room, where there was an armchair, a small table with a plastic flower. Sat down, looked around the room. Bare walls, shining floor. Fluorescent lights in the ceiling. Virginia's bed of metal tubing, over her a pale yellow blanket printed with COUNTY ADMINISTRATION.

This is how things end up.

In Dostoevsky, illness and death were almost always dirty, impoverished affairs. Crushed beneath wagon wheels, mud, typhus, bloodstained handkerchiefs. And so on. But damned if that weren't preferable to this. Slow disintegration in a polished machine.

Lacke leaned back into the armchair, closed his eyes. The chair back was too short, his head slumped back. He straightened up, put his elbow on the armrest, and leaned his head in his hand. Looked at the plastic flower. It was as if they had put it there simply to emphasize the fact that no life was allowed here; here order reigned.

The image of the flower stayed on his retina when he shut his eyes again. It transformed into a real flower that grew, became a garden. A garden attached to the house they were going to buy. Lacke stood in the garden, looked at a rosebush with shining red flowers. From the house came the long shadow of a person. The sun set hastily and the shadow grew, became longer, stretched out over the garden . . .

†

He jumped and was suddenly awake. His palm was wet with saliva that had run out of the corner of his mouth as he was sleeping. He rubbed his mouth, smacked his lips together, and tried to straighten his head. Couldn't. His neck had seized up somehow. He forced it to straighten out with a crackling of the ligaments, stopped.

Wide open eyes staring right at him.

"Hi! Are you . . ."

His mouth closed. Virginia was lying on her back, restrained by the straps, with her face turned toward him. But her face was much too still. Not a flicker of recognition, joy . . . nothing. Her eyes didn't blink.

Dead! She is . . .

Lacke flew up out of the armchair and something cracked in his neck. He threw himself on his knees next to the bed, grabbed the metal tubing, and moved his face close to hers as if to will her soul back into her face, from her depths, by the sheer force of his presence.

"Ginja! Can you hear me?"

Nothing. And yet he could have sworn that her eyes in some way looked back into his, that they were not dead. He looked for her, all the way through them, casting hooks from deep within himself, into the holes that were her pupils, in order to reach through the darkness for . . .

Her pupils. Is that what you look like when you . . .

Her pupils were not round. They were stretched lengthwise, to little points. He made a face when a cold stream of pain washed over his neck, put his hand on it, rubbed.

Virginia blinked. Opened her eyes again. And was there.

Lacke gaped idiotically, still rubbing his neck mechanically. A wooden click as Virginia opened her mouth, asked: "Are you in pain?"

Lacke removed his hand from his neck, as if he had been caught doing something he shouldn't be.

"No, I just . . . I thought you were . . ."

"I'm tied down."

"Yes, you . . . put up a bit of a fight before. Wait a second and I'll . . ." Lacke put his hand in between two of the bars on the bed frame and started loosening one of the straps.

"No."

"What?"

"Don't do it."

Lacke hesitated, the strap in his fingers.

"Are you planning to do some more fighting?"

Virginia half-closed her eyes.

"Don't do it."

Lacke dropped the strap, didn't know what to do with his hands now they had been robbed of their task. Without getting up he turned on his knees, pulled over the little armchair to the bed—with a new burst of pain in his neck as a result—and clumsily crawled up into it.

Virginia nodded almost imperceptibly. "Have you called Lena?"

"No. I can—"

"Good."

"Do you want me to? . . ."

"No."

A silence fell between them. The kind of silence that is particular to hospitals and that stems from the fact that the very situation—one person in the bed, sick or injured, and a healthy person at her side—says it all. Words become small, superfluous. Only the most important can be said. They looked at each other for a long time. Said what could be said, without words. Then Virginia turned her head in line with her body, stared at the ceiling.

"You have to help me."

"I'll do anything."

Virginia licked her lips, breathed in, and let out the air with a sigh so deep and long that it seemed to draw on hidden reserves of air in her body. Then she let her gaze slide up Lacke's body. Searching, as if she were taking a last good-bye of the body of a loved one and wanted to imprint his image in her mind. She rubbed her lips against each other and finally got out the words.

"I am a vampire."

The corners of Lacke's mouth wanted to pull up into a silly grin, his mouth say something soothing, perhaps funny. But the corners of his mouth didn't move and the comment took a wrong turn somewhere, never got anywhere near his lips. Instead all he got out was a: "No!"

He massaged his neck in order to change the atmosphere, to break the stillness that made all words the truth. Virginia spoke in a low voice, controlled.

"I went to Gösta. To kill him. If it hadn't happened. What happened. I would have killed him. And then . . . drunk his blood. I would have done that. It was my intention. With it all. Do you understand?"

Lacke's gaze wandered over the walls of the room as if it were searching for the mosquito, the source of the insufferable, buzzing sound that in the silence was tickling his brain, making it impossible to think. Finally stopped at one of the overhead lights.

"That damned sound."

Virginia looked up at the light, said: "I can't stand light. I can't eat. I have horrible thoughts. I'm going to hurt people. You. I don't want to live."

Finally something more concrete, something he could respond to.

"You can't say things like that," Lacke said. "Ginja, you are not allowed to talk like that, you hear? Do you?"

"You don't understand."

"No, I probably don't. But you are not going to die, damn it. Here you are, you're talking, you are . . . it's OK."

Lacke got up out of the chair, took a few aimless steps over the floor, held his arm out.

"You're not allowed to . . . you're not allowed to say those things."

"Lacke. Lacke?"

"Yes!"

"You know. That it's true. Don't you?"

"What?"

"What I'm talking about."

Lacke snorted, shook his head while his hands patted his chest, his pockets. "Need a smoke. That . . ."

He found the crumpled cigarette packet, the lighter. Managed to get out the last cigarette, put it into his mouth. Then he remembered where he was. Took the cigarette out.

"Damn, they'll have me out on my behind if I . . ."

"Open the window."

"Now you're telling me to jump, too?"

Virginia smiled. Lacke walked over to the window, opened it all the way, and leaned out as far as he could.

The nurse he had talked to could probably catch the whiff of a cigarette a mile away. He lit the cigarette and inhaled deeply, making an effort to exhale the smoke so it didn't blow back in the window. Looked up at the stars. Behind him, Virginia started to talk again.

"It was that child. I've been infected. And then . . . it has grown. I know where it's centered. In my heart. The whole heart. Like cancer. I can't control it."

Lacke blew out a column of smoke. His voice echoed between the tall buildings around them.

"Nonsense. You seem . . . normal."

"I'm making an effort. And they've given me blood. But if I let go. At any moment I could let go. And then it would take over. I know it. I feel it." Virginia took a few deep breaths, continued, "You are standing there. I'm looking at you. And I want to . . . eat you."

Lacke didn't know if it was the kink in his neck or something else that sent a shiver down his spine. He suddenly felt vulnerable. He quickly stubbed out the cigarette against the wall, flicked the butt away in an arc. Turned back into the room.

"This is complete utter insanity."

"Yes, but that's how it is."

Lacke crossed his arms over his chest. With a forced laugh he asked: "What do you want me to do?"

"I want you to . . . destroy my heart."

"What? How?"

"However you want."

Lacke rolled his eyes.

"Can you hear yourself? How this sounds? It's crazy. Like I should . . . drive a stake into you or something."

"Yes."

"No, no, no. You can forget about it in that case. Have to think of something better." Lacke laughed, shaking his head. Virginia looked at him as he walked to and fro across the room, with his arms still folded across his chest. Then she nodded gently.

"OK."

He walked over to her, took her hand. It felt unnatural that it was . . . restrained. He didn't even have enough room to put both his hands around it. But her hand was the warm one, squeezed his. With his free hand he stroked her cheek.

"Are you sure I shouldn't undo these things?"

"No. It can . . . come back."

"You're going to get well. It'll work out. I only have you. Do you want to know a secret?"

Without letting go of her hand he sat down in the armchair and started to tell her. Told her everything. About the stamps, the lion, Norway, the money. The little cottage they were going to buy. Red Falu paint. Spun out a long fantasy about what the garden was going to look like, what flowers they would have, and how you could put out a small table, make a little shady patio where you could sit. . . .

Somewhere in all of this the tears started to flow from Virginia's eyes. Quiet, translucent pearls that found their way down her cheeks, wet her pillowcase. No sobs, just tears that streamed down, jewels of sadness . . . or joy?

Lacke grew silent. Virginia squeezed his hand, hard.

Then Lacke walked out into the corridor and managed to half-convince, half-plead his way to an extra cot. Lacke positioned it so it was exactly next to Virginia's. Turned out the light, took off his clothes, and crawled down into the stiff sheets, fumbled for and found her hand.

They lay like that for a long time. Then came the words. "Lacke. I love you."

And Lacke did not reply. Simply let the words hang in the air. Become encapsulated and grow until they were a large red blanket that floated around the room, that lowered itself onto him and kept him warm all night.

4:23, MONDAY MORNING, ICELAND SQUARE:

A number of people in the vicinity of Björnsonsgatan are awakened by loud screams. One person who calls into the police believes it is an infant crying. When the police arrive on the scene ten minutes later the screams have stopped. They search the area and find a number of dead cats. On some the extremities have become separated from the body. The police find contact information on the cats with collars and make a note of names and telephone numbers with the intention of notifying the owners. Street services are contacted for clean up.

✝

Half an hour until sunrise.

Eli is reclining in the armchair in the living room. He has been here all night, morning. Packed up what there is to pack.

Tomorrow evening, as soon as it gets dark, Eli will go to a telephone booth and ring a taxi. He doesn't know which number to call, but it's probably something that everybody knows. Just have to ask. When the taxi comes he'll load his three boxes into the trunk and ask the taxi driver to take him . . .

Where?

Eli shuts his eyes, tries to imagine a place he would like to be.

As usual, the first image he sees is of the cottage where he lived with his parents, his older siblings. But it is gone. Outside Norrköping where it once stood there is now a roundabout. The stream where his mother rinsed their clothes has dried up, become overgrown, a depression next to the intersection.

Eli has a lot of money. Would be able to ask the taxi driver to take him anywhere, as far as the darkness allows. North. South. Could sit in the back seat and ask the driver to drive north for two thousand kronor. Then get out. Start over. Find someone who . . .

Eli throws his head back, screams up at the ceiling:

"I don't want to!"

The dusty cobwebs sway slightly in his exhalation. The sound dies in this sealed room. Eli puts his hands up on his face, presses his fingers against his eyelids. Feels it in his body, the approaching sunrise, like a worry. He whispers:

"God. God? Why can't I have anything? Why can't I . . ."

It has been brought up many times before, this question.

Why can't I be allowed to live?

Because you should be dead.

Only once after he had been infected did Eli meet another infected person. A grown woman. Just as cynical and hollow as the man with the wig. But Eli received an answer to another question that had been nagging him.

"Are there many of us?"

The woman shook her head and had said with theatrical sadness: .

"No. We are so few. So few."

"Why?"

"Why? Because most of us kill ourselves, that's why. You must understand that. Such a heavy burden, oh my." Her hands fluttered; she said in a shrill voice: "Ooooh, I cannot bear to have dead people on my conscience."

"*Can* we die?"

"Of course we can. All you have to do is set fire to yourself. Or let other people do it; they are only too happy to oblige, have done so through the ages. Or . . ." She held out her index finger and pressed it hard into Eli's chest, above the heart. "There. That's where it is, isn't it? But now my friend, I have a wonderful idea . . ."

And Eli had fled from that wonderful idea. As before. As later.

Eli put his hand on his heart, felt the slow beats. Maybe it was because he was a child. Maybe that was why he hadn't put an end to it. The pangs of conscience were weaker than his will to live.

Eli got up out of the armchair. Håkan would not turn up tonight. But before Eli went to rest he had to check on Tommy. That he had recovered. He had not become infected. For Oskar's sake he wanted to make sure that Tommy was fine.

Eli turned off all the lights and left the apartment.

Down in Tommy's stairwell all he had to do was pull the cellar door open; a long time ago when he was down here with Oskar, he had tucked a piece of paper into the lock so it would stay unlatched when the door closed. He stepped into the cellar corridor and let the door fall shut behind him with a muted thud.

He stopped, listened. Nothing.

No sound of a sleeping person's breathing; only the cloying smell of paint thinners, glue. He walked quickly along the corridor to the storage area, pulled open the door.

Empty.

Twenty minutes until sunrise.

✝

During the night, Tommy had glided in and out of a daze of sleep, half-wakefulness, nightmares. He didn't know how much time had gone by when he started to wake up properly. The naked bulb in the cellar was always the same. Maybe it was dawn, morning, day. Maybe school had already started. He didn't care.

His mouth tasted of glue. He looked around bleary-eyed. There were two bank notes on his chest. Thousand kronor notes. He bent his arm to pick them up, felt a tugging on his skin. A large Band-Aid was pasted over the inside of his elbow, a small blood stain in the middle of the patch.

But there was . . . something more.

He turned in the couch, searching along the inside of the cushions, and found the roll he had dropped during the night. Three thousand more. He unfolded the bills, put them together with the bills from his chest, felt the whole lot, made them crinkle. Five thousand. Anything he wanted to do.

He looked at the Band-Aid, chuckled. Not bad for just lying back and closing your eyes.

Not bad for just lying back and closing your eyes.

What was that? Someone had said it, someone . . .

That was it. Tobbe's sister, what was her name . . . Ingela? Turning tricks, Tobbe had told him. And she got five hundred for it, and Tobbe's comment was:

"Not bad for . . ."

Just lying back and closing your eyes.

Tommy squeezed the bills in his hand, scrunched them up into a ball. She had paid for and drunk of his blood. An illness, she had said. But what kind of fucking illness was that? He had never heard of anything like it. And if you had something like that, you went to the hospital, then they gave you . . . You didn't fucking go down into some basement with five thousand and . . .

Swish.

No?

Tommy sat up in the couch, pulled off the blanket.

They didn't exist. No. Not vampires. That girl, the one in the yellow dress, she must somehow believe that she is . . . but wait, wait. It was that Ritual Killer that . . . the one they were searching for . . .

Tommy leaned his head in his hands; the bills crinkled against his ear. He couldn't figure it out. But in any case he was damn scared of that girl now.

Just as he was thinking about going back up to the apartment after all, even if it was still night, come what may, he heard the door to his stairwell open. His heart fluttered like a frightened bird and he looked around.

Weapon.

The only thing he could see was the broom. Tommy's mouth was pulled up into a smile that lasted for a second.

The broom—a good weapon against vampires.

Then he remembered, got up and walked to the safety room while he stuffed the money into his pocket. Cleared the corridor in one step and slid into the safety room as the cellar door opened. Didn't dare lock the door since he was afraid she would hear it.

He sank into a crouch in the dark, tried to breathe as silently as possible.

†

The razor blade glimmered on the floor. One corner was stained with brown, like rust. Eli tore off a corner of the cover of a motorcycle magazine, wrapped the paper around the razor blade, put it into his back pocket.

Tommy was gone; that meant he was alive. He had left on his own, gone home to sleep, and even if he put two and two together he didn't know where Eli lived, so . . .

Everything is as it should be. Everything is . . . great.

There was a wooden broom with a long handle leaned up against the wall.

Eli picked it up, broke it over his knee, almost as far down as the head of the broom. The surface of the break was rough, sharp. A thin stake, about an arm's length. He put the point against his chest, between two ribs. Exactly the place that the woman had put her finger.

He took a deep breath, squeezed the shaft, and tried on the thought.

In! In!

Breathed out, loosened his grip. Squeezed again. Pressed.

For two minutes he stood with the point one centimeter from his heart, the shaft held firmly in his hand, when the handle of the cellar door was slammed down and the door glided open.

He removed the wooden stake from his chest, listened. Heard slow, tentative steps in the corridor like from a child who had just learned to walk. A very large child who had just learned to walk.

†

Tommy heard the steps and thought: *Who?*

Not Staffan, not Lasse, not Robban. Someone who was sick in some way, who was carrying something very heavy . . . Santa Claus! His hand went up to his mouth to smother a giggle as he imagined Santa Claus, the Disney version—

Hohoho! Say "Mama!"

—come staggering through the corridor with his enormous bag on his back.

His lips trembled under his hand and he clenched his teeth to stop them from chattering. Still in a crouch, he shuffled back from the door, one step at a time. Felt the corner of the room at his back at the same time as the spear of light from the door was darkened.

Santa Claus had stopped between the light and the shelter. Tommy put his other hand over the first to stop himself from screaming, waited for the door to open.

†

Nowhere to run to.

Through cracks in the door he could see a fragmented outline of Håkan's body. Eli stretched the stake out as far as it went, nudged the door. It swung out about ten centimeters, then the body outside stopped it.

One hand grabbed hold of the edge of the door, threw it open so it banged into the wall, tearing off one of the hinges. The door sagged, swung back leaning on its only remaining hinge, hitting against the shoulder of the body that now filled the door opening.

What do you want from me?

There were still patches of blue on the shirt that covered the body to the knees. The rest was a dirty map of earth, mud, stains of something Eli's nose identified as animal blood, human blood. The shirt was torn in several places revealing white skin etched with scratches that would never heal.

His face had not changed. It was still a clumsily fashioned mass of naked flesh with one single red eye thrown in as if for fun, a ripe cherry to top a rotten cake. But his mouth was open now.

A black hole in the lower half of the face. No lips that could cover the teeth that were therefore revealed; an uneven semicircle of white that made the oral cavity seem even darker. The hole increased and decreased in size with a chewing motion and out of it came:

"Eeeiiiij."

You couldn't hear if the sound was supposed to mean "Hi," "Hey" or "Eli" since the "L" had to be formed without the help of lips or tongue. Eli pointed the stake at Håkan's heart, said, "Hi."

What do you want?

The undead. Eli knew nothing about them. Didn't know if the creature in front of him was limited by the same restrictions as he was. If it even helped to destroy the heart. That Håkan was standing still in the doorway seemed to imply one thing: that he needed an invitation.

Håkan's gaze ran up and then down over Eli's body, which felt unprotected in the thin, yellow dress. He wished there were more to the fabric, more protection between his body and Håkan. Tentatively Eli held the stake closer to Håkan's chest.

Can he feel anything? Can he even feel . . . fear now?

Eli experienced a feeling that he had almost forgotten: fear of pain. Everything healed of course, but there was such an overpowering sense of threat emanating from Håkan that . . .

"What do you want?"

A hollow, rasping sound as the creature pressed out air and a drop of yellowish, viscous liquid ran out of the double hole where the nose had been. A sigh? Then a damaged whisper: "Aaaaaaijjjj . . ." and one arm flinched quickly, cramplike,

baby movements

clumsily grabbed the shirt down at the hem, pulled it up.

Håkan's penis stood out from his body to one side, craving attention, and Eli looked at its stiff swolleness crisscrossed with veins and—

How can he . . . he must have had it the whole time.

"Aaeejjlll . . ."

Håkan's hand pulled the foreskin aggressively up and back, up and back, and the head of his penis appeared and disappeared, appeared and disappeared like a jack-in-the-box while he uttered a sound of pleasure or suffering.

"Aaaee . . ."

And Eli laughed with relief.

All this. To be able to jack off.

He could stand there, rooted to the spot until . . . until . . .

Can he even get it off? He's going to have to stand there . . . forever.

Eli imagined one of those obscene dolls that you wound up with a key; a monk whose cape went up and he started masturbating as long as the mechanism allowed.

clickety-click, clickety-click . . .

Eli laughed, was so occupied with the crazy image that he didn't notice when Håkan stepped into the room, uninvited. Didn't notice anything until the fist that had just been sealed around an impossible pleasure was raised above his head.

With a flashing spasm the arm came down and the fist landed over Eli's ear with a force that could have killed a horse. The blow came sideways and Eli's ear was folded in with such force that the skin split and half the ear was separated from his head, which was thrown abruptly down, meeting the cement floor with a muffled crack.

†

When Tommy realized that the thing that was out in the corridor was not on its way to the shelter, he dared to take his hand from his mouth. He sat pressed into the corner and listened, trying to understand.

The girl's voice.

Hi. What do you want.

Then her laugh. And then that other voice. Didn't even sound like it came from a human being. Then muffled thuds, the sounds of bodies moving.

Now there was some kind of . . . rearranging going on out there. Something was dragged across the floor and Tommy was not planning to find out what it was. But the sounds disguised those he would make as he stood up and felt his way along the wall to the stacked boxes.

His heart was pattering like a toy drum and his hands shook. He didn't dare light his lighter, so in order to concentrate better he shut his eyes and searched with his hand over the top of the boxes.

His fingers clenched around what they found. Staffan's shooting trophy. He carefully lifted it from its place, tested it in his hand. If he held the figure's chest the stone base made a kind of club. He opened his eyes, found that he could vaguely make out the outline of the little silver pistol shooter.

Friend. My little friend.

With the trophy pressed against his chest he sank down into the corner against the wall and waited for all this to finally be over.

†

Eli was being handled, like an object.

While he was swimming to the surface of the darkness he had sunk into he felt how his body, at a distance, in another part of the sea . . . was being handled.

Intense pressure against his back, legs that were forced up, back, and iron rings pulled tight around his ankles. Now the ankles with their iron rings were on either side of his head and his spine was tight, so stretched it felt like it was about to snap.

I'm going to break.

His head felt like a container of gleaming pain, as his body was doubled over by force, folded up like a bolt of fabric and Eli thought he was still having an hallucination because when his eyes started to see again, they only saw yellow. And behind the yellow a massive, billowing shadow.

Then came the cold. Something was rubbing a ball of ice across the thin skin between his buttocks. Something tried, first poking, then thrusting, to force its way into him. Eli gasped; the fabric of the dress that had been spread over his face was blown aside, and he saw.

Håkan was lying over him. His only eye was staring fixedly at Eli's spread buttocks. His hands were locked around Eli's ankles. His legs had been brutally bent back so that his knees were pressed to the ground on either side of Eli's shoulders and when Håkan pressed harder Eli heard how the tendons in the back of his thighs broke like tightly pulled strings.

"Noooo!"

Eli screamed into Håkan's shapeless face where no feelings at all could be discerned. A strand of drool came out of Håkan's mouth, stretched and broke, falling onto Eli's lips, and the taste of corpse filled his mouth. Eli's arms fell out from his body as limp as a rag doll's.

Something under his fingers. Round, hard.

He tried to think, forced himself to create a sphere of light inside the black, whirling insanity. And envisioned himself in the pool of light, holding the stick in his hand.

Yes.

Eli squeezed the handle of the broom, locking his fingers around the delicate savior while Håkan kept pushing, poking, trying to enter.

The point. The point has to be on the right side.

He turned his head to the stick and saw it was lying the right way.

A chance.

Everything went quiet inside Eli's head as he visualized what he had to do. Then he did it. In one movement he raised the stick from its prone position and thrust it up toward Håkan's face with all his might.

His underarm brushed against the side of his thigh and the stick formed a straight line that . . . stopped a few centimeters from Håkan's face when Eli, because of his position, could not manage to bring his arm further.

He had failed.

For one second Eli had time to think that maybe he possessed the ability to will his body to die. If he turned off all . . .

Then Håkan thrust himself forward and at the same time dropped his head down. With the soft sound of a wooden spoon pushed down into thick porridge, the sharp end of the stick went into his eye.

Håkan did not scream. Perhaps he did not even feel it. Maybe it was simply surprise over not being able to see that made him loosen his grip around Eli's ankles. Without feeling anything from his damaged legs, Eli wriggled his feet free and kicked straight out at Håkan's chest.

The soles of his feet met skin with a moist smacking sound and Håkan fell back. Eli pulled his legs under him and with a wave of cold pain from his back he got to his knees. Håkan had not fallen, only been folded up, and like an electric doll in a ghost house he now straightened up again.

They faced each other, on their knees.

The stick in Håkan's eye was pulled downward in stages, inching down with the regularity of a second hand and then fell out, drummed out a few beats on the floor and then it lay still. A translucent fluid started to seep out of the hole where it had been, a teary flood.

Neither of them moved.

The fluid from Håkan's eye trickled down onto his naked thighs.

Eli concentrated all of his strength into his right arm, made a fist. When Håkan's shoulder jerked to life and his body made an effort to stretch out to Eli, to pick up where it had left off, Eli hit his right hand straight into the left side of Håkan's chest.

The ribs cracked and the skin was stretched to its limit for a moment, then gave way, broke.

Håkan's head bent down to see what it couldn't see as Eli fumbled inside his chest cavity and found his heart. A cold, soft lump. Unmoving.

It's not alive. But it has to . . .

Eli squeezed the heart until it went to pieces. It gave way too easily, allowed itself to be broken like a dead jellyfish.

Håkan only reacted as if a particularly persistent fly had settled on his skin. He moved his arm up to remove the irritating element and before he had time to grip Eli's wrist Eli pulled his hand out with remnants of the heart quivering in the clenched fist.

Have to get away from here.

Eli wanted to get up but his legs would not obey him. Håkan was groping blindly with his arms in front of him, trying to find him. Eli rolled over on his stomach and started to crawl out of the room, his knees whispering on the concrete. Håkan turned his head in the direction of the noise, put his arms out, and got a hold of the dress, managed to tear off one sleeve before Eli reached the door, got up on his knees again.

Håkan stood up.

Eli had a few seconds of reprieve before Håkan found his way to the door. He tried to order his broken joints to heal enough to enable him to stand, but when Håkan reached the door his legs were only strong enough to allow Eli to stand braced against the wall.

Splinters from the rough planks punctured the tops of his fingers as he scratched with his hand along them in order not to fall. And he knew now. That without a heart, blind, Håkan would pursue him until . . . until . . .

Must . . . destroy . . . must . . . destroy him.

A black line.

A vertical, black line in front of his eyes. It had not been there before. Eli knew what to do.

"Aaaaa . . ."

Håkan's hand around one edge of the door frame and then the body that came staggering out of the storage unit, his hands groping the air in front of him. Eli pressed his back into the wall, waiting for the right moment.

Håkan came out, a few tentative steps, then stopped exactly in front of Eli. Listened, sniffed.

Eli leaned forward so that his hands were the same height as Håkan's shoulder. Then he braced himself against the wall, rushed forward, and put everything into throwing Håkan off balance.

He succeeded.

Håkan took a mincing step to the side and fell against the door to the shelter. The crack in the door that Eli had seen as a black line widened as the door opened inwards and Håkan tumbled into the darkness, his arms waving for help, while Eli started to fall headlong into the corridor, managed to stop himself before the floor met his face, then crawled to the door, and grabbed the lower of the two locking wheels.

Håkan lay still on the floor inside as Eli pulled the door shut and turned the wheel, locked it. Then he crawled out to the cellar office, got the stick, and threaded it in between the locking wheels so that it could not be unlocked from the inside.

Eli continued to concentrate his energy on healing his body and started to crawl out of the basement. A rivulet of blood snaked out of his ear. At the door out of the cellar he was healed enough to be able to stand up. He pushed the door open and managed to go up the stairs on wobbly legs.

rest rest rest

He pushed open the door at the top of the stairs and stepped out into the hall lamp. He was beaten, humiliated, and the sunrise threatened just under the horizon.

rest rest rest

But he had to . . . exterminate. And there was only one way he knew to do that. Fire. Staggering, he made his way across the yard, heading to the only place he knew where he could find it.

7:34, MONDAY MORNING, BLACKEBERG:

The burglar alarm at the ICA grocery store on Arvid Mörne's Way is set off. The police arrive at the scene eleven minutes later and find the store window broken. The store owner, who lives next door, is there. He says that from his window he saw a very young dark-haired person leave the place running. But upon searching the store nothing is found to be stolen.

7:36, SUNRISE.

The hospital blinds were much better, darker, than her own. There was only one place, where the blinds were damaged, where they let in a thin ray of morning light that made a dust-gray slash in the dark ceiling.

Virginia lay outstretched, stiff, in her bed, staring at the gray slice of light that trembled when a gust of wind made the window vibrate. Reflected, weak light. No more than a mild irritation, a grain of sleep in her eye.

Lacke snuffled and wheezed in the bed next to her. They had stayed awake for a long time, talking. Memories, mostly. Close to four in the morning Lacke had finally fallen asleep, with his hand still in hers.

She had had to disentangle her hand from his an hour later when a nurse had come in to check her blood pressure, found it satisfactory, and left them with a glance, actually a tender look at Lacke. Virginia had heard how Lacke pleaded to stay, the reasons he had given. Thus the tender glance, she supposed.

Now Virginia lay with her hands strapped at her sides, fighting her body's desire to . . . turn off. *Fall asleep* was not an adequate expression for it. As soon as she did not consciously concentrate on her breathing, it stopped. But she needed to stay awake.

She hoped a nurse would come back in before Lacke woke up. Yes. The very best thing would be if he could sleep until it was over.

But that was probably too much to hope for.

✝

The sun caught up with Eli in the courtyard, a glowing tong that pinched his mauled ear. Instinctively, he backed up into the shade of the vaulted entrance to the yard, squeezed the three plastic bottles of denatured alcohol to his chest, as if to shield them from the sun as well.

Ten steps away was his front door. Twenty steps to Oskar's. And thirty steps to Tommy's.

I can't do it.

No, if he had been healthy, strong, he would perhaps have tried to make it to Oskar's entrance through the flood of light that grew in intensity for every second he waited. But not to Tommy's. And not now.

Ten steps. Then up the stairs. The big window in the stairwell. If I trip. If the sun . . .

Eli ran.

The sun threw itself over him like a hungry lion, biting itself into his back. Eli almost lost his balance as he was thrown forward by the sun's physical, howling force. Nature vomited its disgust at his transgression: to show himself in sunlight for even one second.

It sizzled, bubbled, like someone pouring boiling oil on Eli's back when he reached the front door, threw it open. The pain almost made him faint and he moved toward the steps as if drugged, blinded; didn't dare open his eyes for fear that they would melt.

He dropped one of the bottles, heard it roll away across the floor. Couldn't be helped. With head bent, one arm wrapped around the remaining bottles, the other on the banister, he limped up the stairs, reached the landing. One flight left.

Through the window the sun delivered a last swipe at his neck, snapped at him, then bit him in the thighs, calves, heels while he moved up the stairs. He was burning. The only thing missing was flames. He got the door open, fell into the wonderful, cool darkness inside. Slammed the door shut behind him. But it was not dark.

The kitchen door was open and in the kitchen there were no blinds in front of the window. The light was weaker, grayer than what he had just experienced and, without hesitation, Eli dropped the bottles onto the floor, continued on. While the light clawed relatively tenderly at his back as he crawled down the corridor to the bathroom the smell of burnt flesh wafted into his nose.

I will never be whole again.

He stretched his arm out, opened the bathroom door, and crawled into the compact darkness. He pushed a couple of plastic jugs out of the way, closed the door, and locked it.

Before he slid into the bathtub he had time to think:

I didn't lock the front door.

But it was too late. Rest turned him off at the same moment as he sank down into the wet darkness. He wouldn't have had the energy anyway.

†

Tommy sat still, pressed into the corner. He held his breath until his ears started to ring and he saw shooting stars in front of his eyes. When he heard the cellar door slam shut he dared to let his breath out in a long panting exhalation that rolled along the cement walls, died out.

It was completely quiet. The darkness was so complete that it had mass, weight.

He held one hand in front of his face. Nothing. No difference. He touched his face as if to convince himself that he existed at all. Yes. His fingertips touched his nose, his lips. Unreal. They flickered to life under his fingers, disappeared.

The little figurine in his other hand felt more alive, more real than he did. He squeezed it, held it close.

†

Tommy had been sitting with his head bent down between his knees, his eyes tightly shut, his hands held against his ears in order not to have to know, not to hear what was going on outside in the storage unit. It sounded like that little girl was being murdered. He would not have been able to do anything, not dared do anything, and therefore he had tried to deny the whole situation by disappearing.

He had been with his dad. On the soccer field, in the forest, at the Canaan baths. Finally he had paused at the memory of that time on the Råcksta field when he and his dad had tried a remote-control airplane that his dad had borrowed from someone at work.

Mom had come along for a while, but in the end she thought it was boring to look at the airplane making circles in the sky, had gone home. He and his dad had kept going until it got dark and the airplane was a silhouette against the pink evening sky. Then they had walked home, hand in hand, through the forest.

Tommy had been in that day, far from the screams, the insanity going on a few meters away. The only thing he was aware of was the furious buzz of the airplane, the warmth of his father's large hand on his back while he nervously maneuvered the plane in wide circles over the field, the graveyard.

Back then Tommy had never been in the graveyard; had imagined people walking aimlessly around the graves, crying large shiny comic book tears that splashed against the headstones. That was then. Then Dad had died and Tommy had learned that graveyards rarely—all too rarely— look like that.

His hands tightly pressed against his ears, killing away those thoughts. Think about walking through the forest, think about the smell of the airplane's special gas in the little bottle, think about . . .

Only when he—halfway through his soundproofing—heard a lock being turned, had he taken his hands down and looked. To no avail, since the safety room was even blacker than the darkness behind his eyelids. Started to hold his breath when the second wheel thundered into place, kept holding it in case whatever-it-was was still in the basement.

Then that distant bang from the door to the stairwell, a vibration in the walls, and here he was. Still alive.

†

It didn't get me.

Exactly what "it" was, he didn't know, but whatever it was it had not discovered him. Tommy got up from his crouched position. A tingling trail of ants ran through his numb leg muscles as he groped along the wall, toward the door. His hands were sweaty with fear and the pressure against his ears; the statuette almost slid out of his hand.

His free hand found the wheel of the closing mechanism and started to turn it.

It went about ten centimeters, then it stopped.

What is this . . .

He pressed harder, but the wheel wouldn't budge. He dropped the statuette in order to be able to grab the wheel with both hands, and it fell to the floor with a

thud.

He froze.

That sounded funny. As if it landed on something . . . soft.

He crouched down next to the door, tried to turn the lower wheel. Same thing. Ten centimeters, then stop. He sat down on the floor. Tried to think practically.

Damn, am I going to be stuck here.

Like that, sort of.

But it still came creeping . . . this terror he had had a few months after his dad died. He had not felt it for a long time, but now, locked in, in the pitch blackness, it was starting to make itself known again. Love for his dad that through death had been transformed into a fear of him. Of his body.

A lump started to grow in his throat, his fingers stiffened.

Think now! Think!

There were candles on a shelf in the storage room on the other side. The problem was making his way over there in the dark.

Idiot!

He slapped his forehead, laughed out loud. He had a lighter! And anyway: what was the use of looking for those candles if there wasn't anything to light them with?

Like that guy with thousands of cans and no can opener. Starved to death surrounded by food.

While he dug around in his pocket for his lighter he reflected that his situation wasn't *so* hopeless. Sooner or later someone would come down into the basement, his mom—if no one else—and if he could just get some light in here, that would be something.

He got the lighter out of his pocket, lit it.

His eyes that had adjusted to the dark were momentarily blinded by the light, but then when they adjusted again he saw that he was not alone.

Outstretched on the floor, right next to his feet, was . . .

. . . Dad . . .

The fact that his father had been cremated did not register with him as, in the fluttering flame of the lighter, he saw the face of the corpse and it met his expectations of how one would look after having been in the earth for many years.

. . . Dad . . .

He screamed straight into the lighter so the flame went out, but the split second before the light went out he had time to see his dad's head jerk and . . .

. . . it's alive . . .

The contents of his bowels spilled into his pants in a wet explosion that splattered warmth over his rear end. Then his legs crumpled up, his skeleton dissolved, and he fell into a heap, dropped the lighter so it bounced away across the floor. His hand landed straight on the corpse's cold toes. Sharp nails scratched the palm of his hand and while he continued to shriek—

But Dad! Haven't you trimmed your toenails?

—he started to pat, to stroke the cold foot as if it were a frozen puppy that needed comforting. Kept petting up the shinbone, the thigh, felt the muscles tense under the skin, move while he screamed in fits and starts, like an animal.

The tips of his fingers felt metal. The statuette. It lay nestled between the thighs of the corpse. He grabbed the figurine by the chest, stopped screaming, and returned for a moment to the practical.

A club.

In the silence after his scream he heard a dripping, sticky sound when the corpse raised its upper body. And when a cold limb nudged the back of his hand he pulled it back, squeezing the statuette.

It is not Dad.

No. Tommy drew back, away from the corpse, with excrement clinging to his buttocks, and thought for a moment that he could *see in the dark* as his sound impressions transformed into vision and he *saw* the corpse rise up in the darkness, a yellowish shape, a constellation.

With his feet tap-dancing over the floor, he shuffled backward to the wall; the corpse on the other side uttered a short exhalation:

"...aa..."

And Tommy saw...

A little elephant, an animated elephant, and here comes (toooot) the BIG elephant and then... trunks up!... and toot "A" and then Magnus, Brasse, and Eva enter and sing "There! Is Here! Where you are not...."

No, how did it go...

The corpse must have bumped into the stack of boxes because he could hear thuds, the rattle of stereo equipment that fell to the floor, as Tommy slid up against the wall, hitting the back of his head and seeing a kind of static. Through the roar he could hear the smack of stiff, bare feet walking across the floor, searching.

Here. Is There. Where you are not. No. Yes.

Just like that. He wasn't here. He couldn't see himself, couldn't see the thing that was making the noise. So it was only *sound*. It was just something he was listening to as he stared into the black mesh of the speaker. This was something that didn't even exist.

Here. Is There. Where you are not.

He almost started to sing out loud, but a sensible remnant of his consciousness told him not to. The white buzz started to die down, leaving an empty surface where he started to stack new thoughts, with effort.

The face. The face.

He didn't want to think about its face, did *not* want to think about...

Something about the face that had been momentarily illuminated by the lighter.

It was getting closer. Not only did the footsteps sound closer, now hissing across the floor, no, he could feel its presence like a shadow more impenetrable than the darkness.

He bit down on his lower lip until he tasted blood, shut his eyes. Saw his own two eyes disappear out of the picture like two . . .

Eyes.

It doesn't have eyes.

A faint breeze on his face as a hand went through the air.

Blind. It is blind.

He wasn't sure, but the lump on the creature's shoulders had not had any eyes.

When the hand went through the air again Tommy felt the caress of air on his cheek one tenth of a second before it reached him, had time to turn his face so the hand only brushed against his hair. He finished the movement and threw himself flat on the floor, started to snake along the floor with his hands circling in front of him, swimming.

The lighter, the lighter . . .

Something poked into his cheek. A wave of nausea when he realized it was the thing's toenail, but he quickly rolled over so he wouldn't be in the same place when the hands came groping for him.

Here. Is There. Where I am not.

An involuntary chuckle issued from his mouth. He tried to stop it, but couldn't. Saliva sprayed out of his mouth and out of his hoarse-from-screaming throat came hiccoughs of laughter or crying, while his hands, two radar beams, continued searching the floor for the only advantage he maybe, maybe had over the darkness that wanted to devour him.

God, help me. Let the light of thy face . . . God . . . sorry about that thing in church, sorry about . . . everything. God. I will always believe in you, however you want, if you just . . . let me find the lighter . . . be my friend, please God.

Something happened.

At the same moment that Tommy felt the thing's hand flailing across his foot the room was illuminated for a split second with blue-white light, like from a flash, and during that split second Tommy really did see the boxes that had tumbled to the floor, the uneven surface of the walls, the passageway into the storage rooms.

And he saw the lighter. ·

It was only one meter from his right hand, and when the darkness engulfed him again the location of the lighter was burned onto the inside of his eyelid. He yanked his foot from the thing's grip, flung his arm out and managed to grab the lighter, held it firmly in his hand, jumped up onto his feet.

Without thinking about whether it was too much to ask, he started to chant a new prayer inside his head.

Let the thing be blind, God. Let it be blind. God. Let it be blind. . . .

He flicked the lighter. A flash, like the one he just experienced, then a yellow flame with a blue center.

The thing stood still, turned its head toward the sound. Started to walk in that direction. The flame flickered when Tommy slid two steps to the side and arrived at the door. The thing stopped where Tommy had been three seconds earlier.

If he had been able to feel joy, he would have. But in the weak light from the lighter everything suddenly became mercilessly *real*. It was no longer possible to escape into some fantasy that he was really not here at all, that this wasn't happening to him.

He was locked into a soundproofed room with the thing he was most afraid of. Something turned in his stomach but there was nothing more to be emptied. All that came was a little fart and the thing turned its head again, toward him.

Tommy pulled at the wheel of the locking mechanism with his free hand so that the hand holding the lighter trembled, and the flame went out. The wheel didn't budge, but out of the corner of his eye Tommy had had time to see how the thing was coming toward him and he threw himself away from the door, in the direction of the wall where he had been sitting before.

He sobbed, snuffled.

Let this *end*. God, let it end.

Again the big elephant who raised his hat and with his nasal voice said:

This is the eeeend! Blow the trumpet, trunk, toooot! This is the end! I'm going crazy, I . . . it . . .

He shook his head, flicked the lighter on again. There on the floor in front of him was the trophy. He bent over, picked it up, and jumped a few steps to the side, kept going toward the other wall. Looked at the thing groping the space where he had just been.

Blind man's bluff.

The lighter in one hand, the trophy in the other. He opened his mouth to say something but only managed a hoarse whisper.

"Come on, then. . . ."

The thing appeared alert, turned around, came toward him.

He raised Staffan's trophy like a club and when the creature was half a meter away he swung it at its face.

And like in a perfect penalty kick in soccer, when at the same moment as your foot meets the ball you feel that this one . . . this one has hit the spot exactly, Tommy felt the same thing already halfway into his swing, that—

Yes!

—and when the sharp stone corner met the thing's temple with a force that continued in an arc along Tommy's arm, he was already feeling triumph. It was only a confirmation of this feeling when the skull crumpled and with a crack of splitting ice, cold liquid splashed onto Tommy's face and the thing crashed to the ground.

Tommy remained in place, panting. Looked at the body that was laid out on the ground.

He has an erection.

Yes. The thing's penis was sticking out like a minimal, half overturned gravestone and Tommy stood there staring, waiting for it to wilt. It didn't. Tommy wanted to laugh, but his throat hurt too much.

A throbbing pain in his thumb. Tommy looked down. The lighter had started to burn the skin on his thumb that was holding the gas tab down. Instinctively he let go. But his thumb didn't obey him. It was locked in a cramp over the tab.

He turned the lighter the other direction. Didn't want to turn it off anyway. Didn't want to be left in the dark with this . . .

A movement.

And Tommy felt how something important, something he needed in order to be Tommy, left him when the creature lifted its head again, and started to get up.

An elephant balancing on the little, little thread of a spiderweb!

The thread broke. The elephant fell through.

And Tommy hit again. And again.

After a while he started to think it was fun.

Monday

9 NOVEMBER

Morgan walked through the controls, waved the monthly pass that had expired six months ago, while Larry dutifully stopped and pulled out a wrinkled coupon strip and said "Ängbyplan."

The ticket collector looked up from the book he was reading, stamped two coupon spaces. Morgan laughed when Larry came over to him and they started to walk down the stairs.

"What the hell do you bother to do that for?"

"What? Get my ticket stamped?"

"Yeah. It's not like you're some model citizen."

"It's not that."

"What is it?"

"I'm not like you, OK?"

"But come on . . . the guy was just . . . you could have shown him a picture of the king for all he cared."

"Yes, fine. Quit talking so loud."

"Think he's going to come after us or something?"

Before they opened the doors down to the platform Morgan cupped his hands into a makeshift megaphone and shouted back up to the station hall: "Alert! Alert! Illegal riders!"

Larry slunk away, taking a few steps toward the platform. When Morgan reached him he said:

"You're pretty childish, you know that?"

"Absolutely. Now, run the whole thing by me again. From the top."

Larry had called Morgan already that night and given a summary of what Gösta had told him ten minutes earlier on the telephone. They had agreed to meet at the subway station early in the morning in order to go to the hospital.

Now Larry went over it all again. Virginia, Lacke, Gösta, the cats. The ambulance that Lacke had climbed into with her. Added a few extra details of his own, and before he was done the subway train to the city arrived. They got on and claimed a four-seater for themselves, and Larry finished his story with:

". . . and then it drove off with sirens going full blast."

Morgan nodded, chewing on a thumbnail, looking out of the window while the train climbed out of the tunnel, stopped at Iceland Square.

"What the hell made them go off like that?"

"You mean the cats? I don't know. Something made them all crazy."

"But all of them? And at the same time?"

"You have a better suggestion?"

"No. Damn cats. Lacke must be completely crushed and all."

"Mm. Wasn't doing so great before either."

"No," Morgan sighed. "I feel damned sorry for the guy, actually. We should . . . I don't know. Do something."

"What about Virginia?"

"Yeah, yeah, yeah. But you know, being injured. Sick. What can you do. You have to lie there. The hard part is sitting next to the bed and . . . no, I don't know, but he was right . . . last time, when he . . . what the hell did he ramble on about? Werewolves?"

"Vampires."

"Yeah. That's not a sign that you're doing so damned great, is it?"

The train pulled into the Ängbyplan station. When the doors closed Morgan said:

"There. Now we're in the same boat."

"I think they're more lenient if you have at least two stamped sections."

"That's what you *think*. But you don't know."

"Did you see the results of the poll? For the Swedish Communist Party?"

"Yes, yes. It'll straighten itself out after the election. There're a lot of people, who are leftist at heart, that when they stand there with the ballot still vote according to their conscience."

"That's what you think."

"No. I know. The day the Communists are pushed out of parliament is the day I start believing in vampires. But of course: there's always the conservatives. Bohman and his lot, you know. Talk about bloodsuckers . . ."

Morgan launched into one of his monologues. Larry stopped listening somewhere near Åkeshov. There was a lone police officer outside the greenhouses, looking up at the subway. Larry felt a brief pang of conscience when he thought about his understamped ticket, but immediately suppressed the thought when he remembered why the police were there.

But this police officer looked simply bored. Larry relaxed; the occasional word in Morgan's rambling made its way into his consciousness while they thundered on toward Sabbatsberg.

†

A quarter to eight, and no nurse had yet appeared.

The dirt-gray strip of light on the ceiling had turned light gray, and the blinds let in enough light to make Virginia feel like she was on a tanning bed. Her body was hot, throbbed, but that was all. It wouldn't get any worse.

Lacke lay in the bed next to her, snarling, chewing in his sleep. She was ready. If she had been able to press a button to summon a nurse, she would have done so. But her hands were bound and she couldn't.

So she waited. The heat in her skin was painful, not excruciating. What was worse was the constant effort to try to stay awake. One moment's forgetfulness and her breathing stopped, lights started to go off in her head with increasing speed, and she had to open her eyes wide and shake her head in order to get them to turn on again.

At the same time, this necessary wakefulness was a blessing; it stopped her from having to think. All her mental energy went to keeping herself awake. There was no room for hesitation, regret, an alternative.

The nurse came in at exactly eight o'clock.

When she opened her mouth to say "Good morning, how are we today!" or whatever it was that nurses said in the morning, Virginia hissed: "Shhhhhh!"

The nurse closed her mouth with a surprised click, and she frowned when she walked through the dim room to Virginia's bed, leaned over her and said, "and how—"

"Shhh!" Virginia whispered. "Sorry, but I don't want to wake him up." She made a gesture with her head in Lacke's direction.

The nurse nodded, said in a lower voice, "No, of course not. But I need to take your temperature and a little blood."

"Sure, whatever. But could you . . . take him out first?"

"Take him . . . do you want me to wake him up?"

"No. But if you could . . . roll him out while he's still sleeping."

The nurse looked at Lacke as if to determine if it was even physically possible, then smiled, shook her head and said: "I think this will be alright. We'll take your temperature orally, so you don't have to feel . . ."

"It's not that. Couldn't you just . . . do what I'm asking?"

The nurse cast a glance at her watch.

"You'll have to excuse me, but I have other patients and I—"

Virginia snapped, as loud as she dared:

"Please!"

The nurse took half a step back. She had clearly been informed of Virginia's actions during the night. Her eyes quickly went to the bindings holding Virginia's arms. She appeared to be reassured by what she saw, went back up to the bed. Now she talked to Virginia as if she was weak in the head.

"You see . . . I need . . . we need, in order to be able to help you get better again, just a little . . ."

Virginia closed her eyes, sighed, gave up. Then she said: "Would you be so kind as to open the blinds?"

The nurse nodded and walked over to the window. Virginia took the opportunity to kick off the blanket, exposing her body. Held her breath. Kept her eyes tightly shut.

It was over. Now she wanted to turn off. The same function she had been resisting all morning she now consciously tried to let forth. But she couldn't. Instead she experienced that thing that you heard about: seeing your life pass before you like a strip of film in fast forward.

The bird I had in the cardboard box . . . the smell of freshly mangled sheets in the laundry room . . . my mother leaning over the cinnamon bun crumbs . . . my father . . . the smoke from his pipe . . . Per . . . the cottage . . . Len and I, the big mushroom we found that summer . . . Ted with mashed blueberries on his cheek . . . Lacke, his back . . . Lacke . . .

A clattering noise as the blinds were raised, and she was sucked down into a sea of fire.

†

Oskar's mom had woken him up at ten past seven, the usual. He had climbed out of bed and had breakfast, as usual. He had put his clothes on and then hugged his mom good-bye at half past seven, as usual.

He felt like normal.

Filled with anxiety, dread, sure. But even that wasn't unusual when he was heading back to school after the weekend.

He packed his geography book, the atlas, and the photocopy he had not finished. Was ready at twenty-five minutes to eight. Didn't need to leave for fifteen minutes. Should he sit down and do that worksheet anyway? No. Didn't have the energy.

He sat down at his desk, stared at the wall.

This must mean he wasn't infected? Or was there an incubation period? No. That old man . . . that had only taken a few hours.

I'm not infected.

He should be happy, relieved. But he wasn't. The phone rang.

Eli! Something has happened to . . .

He shot up from the table, out into the hall, yanked up the telephone receiver.

"HithisisOskar!"

"Oh . . . hello there."

Dad. It was only Dad.

"Hi."

"Well, so . . . you're at home."

"About to leave for school."

"Right, in that case I won't . . . Is your mother home?"

"No, she's left for work."

"I see, I thought as much."

Oskar got it. That was why he was calling at this strange time: because he knew Mom wasn't home. His dad cleared his throat.

"So I was thinking . . . about what happened Saturday night. It was a bit . . . unfortunate."

"Yes."

"Yes. Did you tell your mother about . . . what happened?"

"What do *you* think?"

There was silence on the other end. The static crackle from one hundred kilometers of telephone lines. Crows sitting on them, shivering, while people's conversations darted past under their feet. His dad cleared his throat again.

"You know, I asked about those ice skates and it worked out. You can have them."

"I have to go now."

"Yes, of course. Hope you . . . have a good day at school."

"OK. Bye."

Oskar put the receiver down, picked up his bag and left for school. He felt nothing.

†

Five minutes left until the lesson started and quite a few members of the class were standing in the corridor outside the classroom. Oskar hesitated for a moment, then tossed his bag onto his shoulder and walked toward the door. All eyes turned toward him.

Running the gauntlet. Gang attack.

Yes, he had feared the worst. Everyone knew what had happened to Jonny on Thursday, of course, and even though he couldn't pick Jonny's face out of the crowd it was Micke's version they had heard on Friday. And Micke was there, with his idiot grin pasted on his face, like usual.

Instead of slowing down, preparing to escape in some way, he *lengthened* his stride, walking quickly toward the classroom. He was empty inside. He didn't care what happened anymore. It wasn't important.

And sure enough: a miracle occurred. The sea parted.

The group assembled outside the door broke up, created room for Oskar to get to the door. He had not expected anything else actually. If it was because of some strength emanating or because he was a stinking pariah who had to be avoided; it didn't matter.

He was different now. They sensed it, and slunk back.

Oskar walked into the classroom without looking to either side, sat down at his desk. He heard murmuring from the corridor and after a few minutes they streamed back in. Johan gave him the thumbs up when he walked past. Oskar shrugged.

Then the teacher came in and five minutes after the lesson started, Jonny arrived. Oskar had expected him to have some kind of bandage over his ear, but there wasn't anything. The ear was, however, dark red, swollen, and didn't look like it belonged to his body.

Jonny took his seat. He didn't look at Oskar, didn't look at anyone.

He is ashamed.

Yes, that must be it. Oskar turned his head to look at Jonny, who pulled a photo album out of his backpack and slipped it into his desk. And he saw that Jonny's cheeks had turned bright red, matching his ear. Oskar thought about poking his tongue out at him, but decided against it.

Too childish.

†

Tommy started school at quarter to nine on Mondays so at eight o'clock Staffan got up and had a quick cup of coffee before he went down to have his man-to-man talk with the boy.

Yvonne had already left for work; Staffan himself was supposed to report for duty at nine in Judarn in order to continue a search of the forest, an undertaking he sensed would be fruitless.

Well, it would feel good to be outside and it looked like the weather was going to be decent. He rinsed the coffee cup out under the tap, deliberated for a moment, then went and put on his uniform. Had considered going down to see Tommy in his normal clothes, talk to him like a normal person, so to speak. But, strictly speaking, this was a police matter, vandalism, and anyway, the uniform imbued him with a shell of authority that he, although he didn't think he lacked in his everyday person, nonetheless . . . well.

And anyway it was practical to be ready for work since he was heading off to work after this. So Staffan pulled on his work clothes, the winter jacket, checked in the mirror to see the impression he made and found it pleasing. Then he took the cellar key that Yvonne had put out for him on the kitchen table, walked out, closed the door, checked the lock (work habit) and walked down the stairs, unlocked the door to the cellar.

And speaking of work . . .

There was something wrong with this door. No resistance when he turned the key, the door could simply be opened. He crouched down and checked the mechanism.

Aha. A wad of paper.

A classic trick of burglars: make up some excuse to visit a place you wanted to rob, tamper with the lock, and then hope the owner wouldn't notice it when they left.

Staffan unfolded the blade of his pocketknife, picked out the piece of paper.

Tommy, of course.

It didn't occur to Staffan to wonder *why* Tommy needed to rig the lock of a door that he had a key to. Tommy was a thief who hung out here and this was a thief's trick. Therefore: Tommy.

Yvonne had described the location of Tommy's unit for him, and while Staffan walked in that direction he prepared in his head the lecture he was going to hold. He had *considered* taking the pal route, taking it easy, but this thing with the lock had made him angry again.

He would explain to Tommy—explain, not threaten—about juvenile detention facilities, social services, the age at which you could be legally tried as an adult, and so on. Just so he understood what kind of path he was about to head down.

The door to the storage unit was open. Staffan looked in. Well, what do you know. The bird has flown the coop. Then he saw the stains. He squatted and pulled his finger over one of them.

Blood.

Tommy's blanket lay on the couch and even that had the occasional bloodstain on it. And the floor was—he now saw when he was looking for it—covered in blood.

Alarmed, he backed up out of the unit.

In front of his eyes he now saw . . . a crime scene. Instead of the lecture he was supposed to have delivered, his mind now started to flip through the rulebook for the handling of a crime scene. He knew it by heart, but as he was proceeding through the paragraphs—

immediate recovery of such material as may otherwise be lost . . . note the exact time . . . avoid contamination of locations where traces of fibers may potentially be recovered . . .

—he heard a faint murmur behind him. A mumbling punctuated with muffled thuds.

A stick was threaded through the wheels of the locking mechanism of the safety room. He walked over to the door, listened. Yes. The mumbling, the thuds, were coming from in there. It almost sounded like a . . . mass. A recited litany that he could not make out the words to.

Devil worshippers . . .

A silly thought, but when he looked closer at the stick in the door it actually frightened him, because of what he saw at the very tip. Dark red, lumpy streaks that reached about ten centimeters up the stick itself. Thus, and exactly thus, is what knives looked like when they had been used for violent altercations and had partly dried.

The muttering on the other side of the door continued.

Call for reinforcements?

No. There was perhaps something criminal going on behind that door that would be completed while he was upstairs making the call. Had to manage this on his own.

He undid the fastening on his holster in order to make easy access to his gun, unhooked the baton. With his other hand he picked out a handkerchief from his pocket and carefully wrapped it around the end of the stick and started to pull it out of the wheels while he listened closely to see if the scraping sound from the stick altered the noises from inside the room in any way.

No. The litany and the thuds continued.

The stick was out. He propped it up against the wall in order not to destroy any hand or fingerprints.

He knew that the handkerchief was no guarantee that prints would not be erased, so instead of grabbing the wheels he used two stiff fingers on one of the spokes and forced it to turn.

The wheel pistons gave way. He licked his lips. His throat felt dry. The other wheel was turned back all the way and the door slid open one centimeter.

Now he heard the words. It was a song. The voice was a high-pitched, broken whisper:

> *Two hundred and seventy-four elephants*
> *On a teensy spider weeeee—*
> (Thud.)
> *—eb!*
> *They thought it was*
> *Such jolly good fun*
> *That they went and got a friend!*
>
> *Two hundred and seventy-five elephants*
> *On a teensy spider weee—*
> (Thud.)
> *—eb!*
> *They thought it was . . .*

Staffan angled the baton away from his body, pushed the door open with it.

And then he saw.

The lump that Tommy was kneeling behind would have been hard to identify as human had it not been for the arm that stuck out of it, half separated from the body. The chest, stomach, face were only a heap of flesh, guts, crushed bone.

Tommy was holding a square stone with both hands that, at a certain point in his song, he thrust down into the butchered remains, which did not provide more resistance than that the stone went all the way through and hit against the floor with a thud, before he lifted it up again and yet another elephant was added to the spiderweb.

Staffan could not tell for sure that it was Tommy. The person holding the stone was covered in so much blood and tissue scraps that it was difficult to . . . Staffan became intensely nauseated. He restrained a wave of nausea that threatened to overwhelm him, looked down in order not to have to see, and his eyes stopped at a tin soldier lying by the threshold. No. It was the figure of pistol shooter. He recognized it. The figure was lying in such a way so the pistol was aimed straight up.

Where is the base?

Then he realized.

His head spun and, oblivious to fingerprints and crime scene protocol, he leaned his hand against the door post in order not to fall while the song continued repetitively:

> *Two hundred and seventy-seven elephants*
> *On . . .*

He must be pretty shaken up because he was hallucinating. He thought he saw . . . yes . . . saw clearly how the human remains on the floor, between each blow . . . moved.

As if trying to get up.

†

Morgan was a chain smoker; he was already putting out his butt in a flower bed outside the hospital entrance when Larry still had half of his left. Morgan pushed his hands down into his pockets, walked to and fro in the parking lot, swore when water from a puddle seeped in through the hole in his shoe and made his sock wet.

"Got any money, Larry?"

"As you know I'm on disability and—"

"Yeah, yeah. But do you have any money?"

"Why? I'm not going to lend you any if that's—"

"No, no, no. But I was thinking: Lacke. What if we were to treat him to a real . . . you know."

Larry coughed, looked accusingly at the cigarette.

"What . . . to cheer him up, you mean?"

"Yes."

"No . . . I don't know."

"What? Because you don't think it'll make him feel better or because you don't have any money or because you're too cheap to put out?"

Larry sighed, took another puff, coughing, then made a face and put the cigarette out with his foot. Then picked up the butt and put it in a sand-filled receptacle, looked at his clock.

"Morgan . . . it's half past eight in the morning."

"Yes, I know. But in a couple of hours. When stuff opens."

"No, I have to think about it."

"So you have money?"

"Should we go in, or what?"

They walked in through the revolving door. Morgan pulled his hands through his hair and walked up to the woman at the reception desk to find out where Virginia was, while Larry went and looked at some fish that were swimming sleepily through a large bubbling cylindrical tank.

After a minute Morgan came back, rubbed his hands over his leather vest to wipe off something that had stuck to him, said: "Damn bitch. Didn't want to tell."

"Oh well. Must be in intensive care."

"Can you get in there?"

"Sometimes."

"You seem like you know what you're doing."

"I do."

They moved in the direction of the Intensive Care Unit. Larry knew the way.

Many of Larry's "acquaintances" were in or had been in the hospital. At the moment there were two here at Sabb, excluding Virginia. Morgan suspected that people that Larry had only met briefly became acquaintances or even friends only at that moment that they landed in the hospital. Then he sought them out, went for visits.

Why he did this, Morgan had just been about to ask when they reached the swinging doors of the ICU, pushed them open, and caught sight of Lacke at the far end of the corridor. He was sitting in an armchair, in only his underpants. His hands were clutching the arms of the chair while he stared into a room in front of him that people were hurrying in and out of.

Morgan sniffed: "What the hell, are they cremating someone or what?" He laughed. "Damn conservatives. Budget cuts, you know. Let the hospitals take over the . . ."

He stopped talking when they reached Lacke, whose face was ashen, his eyes red and unseeing. Morgan sensed what must have happened, let Larry take the lead. Wasn't good at this kind of thing.

Larry walked over to Lacke, put a hand on his arm.

"Hey there, Lacke. How's it going?"

Chaos in the room closest to them. The windows visible from the door were wide open but despite this the sour smell of ash drifted out into the corridor. A thick cloud of dust was floating through the air, people were standing in its midst talking loudly, gesturing. Morgan caught the words "hospital's responsibility" and "we have to try . . ."

What they had to try he didn't hear because Lacke turned to them, staring at them like they were two strangers, said: ". . . should have realized . . ."

Larry leaned over him.

"Should have realized what?"

"That it would happen."

"What's happened?"

Lacke's eyes cleared and he looked toward the foggy, dreamlike room, said simply: "She burned."

"Virginia?"

"Yes. She went up in flames."

Morgan took a couple of steps toward the room, peeked in. An older man with an air of authority came over to him.

"Excuse me, this is not a public exhibition."

"No, no. I was just . . ."

Morgan was about to say something witty about looking for his boa constrictor, but dropped it. At least he had had time to see. Two beds. One with wrinkled sheets and a blanket thrown to one side as if someone had gotten out of it in a hurry.

The other was covered with a thick gray blanket that stretched from the foot end to the pillow. The wood of the headrest was covered with soot. Under the blanket he could see the outline of an unbeliev-ably thin person. Head, chest, pelvis were the only details he could make out. The rest could just as well be folds, irregularities in the blanket cloth.

Morgan rubbed his eyes so hard that his eyeballs were pressed a centimeter or so into his head. It's true. It's fucking true.

He looked around the corridor, looking for someone to work through his confusion on. Caught sight of an older man leaning against a walker, an IV stand next to him, trying to get a glimpse into the room.

"What are you looking at, you old fool? Want me to kick your walker out from under you too?"

The man started to retreat, in tiny intervals. Morgan balled his hands into fists, tried to control himself. Remembered something he had seen in the room, turned abruptly and went back.

The man who had spoken to him was on his way out.

"*Excuse* me, but what . . ."

"Yes, yes, yes . . ." Morgan shoved him out of the way, ". . . just getting my friend's clothes for him, if that's alright. Or do you think he should keep sitting out there in the buff?"

The man crossed his arms over his chest, let Morgan pass.

He grabbed Lacke's clothes from the chair next to the unmade bed, threw another glance at the other bed. A charred hand with outstretched fingers poked out from under the sheet. The hand was unrecognizable; the ring that sat on the middle finger was not. Gold, with a blue stone, Virginia's ring. Before Morgan turned away he also noted that a leather strap was fastened across the wrist.

The man was still standing in the door, his arms crossed.

"Happy now?"

"No. But why the hell was she restrained like that?"

The man shook his head.

"You can let your friend know the police will be here shortly and they will no doubt want to talk to him."

"What for?"

"How should I know? I'm not the police."

"No, of course not. Easy to make that mistake, though, isn't it."

Out in the corridor, they helped Lacke get into his clothes, and had just finished when two police officers arrived. Lacke was completely spaced out, but the nurse who had pulled the blinds up had enough presence of mind to be able to vouch for the fact that he had had nothing to do with it. That he had still been sleeping when the whole thing . . . began.

She was comforted by one of her colleagues. Larry and Morgan led Lacke out of the hospital.

When they had gone through the revolving front door Morgan drew a deep breath of the cold air and said: "Sorry, have to barf," leaned over the flower beds and deposited the remains of yesterday's dinner mixed with green slime over the bare bushes.

When he was done he wiped his mouth with his hand and dried his hand on his pant leg. Then held up the hand as if it were exhibit A and said to Larry:

"Now look here, you're fucking going to have to cough up."

†

They made their way back to Blackeberg and Morgan was given one hundred and fifty to spend at the alcohol shop while Larry took Lacke back to his place.

Lacke allowed himself to be led. He had not said a single word the whole time they were on the subway.

In the elevator up to Larry's apartment on the sixth floor he started to cry. Not quietly, no, he wailed like a kid, but worse, more. When Larry opened the elevator door and pushed him out onto the landing the cry deepened, started to reverberate against the concrete walls. Lacke's scream of primal, bottomless sorrow filled the stairwell from top to bottom, streamed through the mail slots, keyholes, transformed the high-rise into one big tomb erected in the memory of love, hope. Larry shivered; he had never heard anything like it before. You don't cry like this. You're not allowed to cry like this. You die if you cry like this.

The neighbors. They're going to think I'm killing him.

Larry fumbled with his keys while thousands of years of human suffering, of helplessness and disappointments, that for the moment had found an outlet in Lacke's frail body continued to pour out of him.

The key finally made it into the lock and, with a strength he had not believed he possessed, Larry basically *carried* Lacke into the apartment and closed the door. Lacke continued to scream; the air never seemed to give out. Sweat was starting to form on Larry's brow.

What the hell should I . . . should I . . .

In his panic he did what he had seen in the movies. With an open hand he slapped Lacke's cheek, was startled by the sharp slapping sound and regretted it in the same moment that he did it. But it worked.

Lacke stopped screaming, stared at Larry with wild eyes, and Larry thought he was going to get hit back. Then something softened in Lacke's eyes, he opened and closed his mouth like he was trying to get some air, said: "Larry, I . . ."

Larry put his arms around him. Lacke leaned his cheek against his shoulder and cried so hard he was shaking. After a while Larry's legs started to feel weak. He tried to untangle himself from the embrace so he could sit down on the hall chair, but Lacke hung onto him and followed him down. Larry landed on the chair and Lacke's legs buckled under him, his head sank down onto Larry's lap.

Larry stroked his hair, didn't know what to say. Just whispered:

"There, there . . . there, there . . ."

Larry's legs had fallen asleep when a change occurred. The crying had died down, and given way to a soft whimpering, when he felt Lacke's jaws tense up against his thigh. Lacke lifted his head, wiped away the snot with his sleeve and said:

"I'm going to kill it."

"What?"

Lacke lowered his gaze, stared right through Larry's chest and nodded.

"I'm going to kill it. I'm not going to let it live."

†

During the long recess at half past nine both Staffe and Johan came over to Oskar and said "great job" and "fucking awesome." Staffe offered him chewy candy cars and Johan asked if Oskar wanted to come with them and collect empty bottles one day.

No one shoved him or held his nose when he walked past. Even Micke Siskov smiled, nodding encouragingly as if Oskar had told him a funny story when they met in the corridor outside the cafeteria.

As if everyone had been waiting for him to do exactly what he did, and now that it was done he was one of them.

The problem was that he couldn't enjoy it. He noted it, but it didn't affect him. Great not to be picked on anymore, yes. If someone tried to hit him, he would hit back. But he didn't belong here anymore.

During math class he raised his head and looked at the classmates he had been with for six years. They sat with their heads bent over their work, chewing on pens, sending notes to each other, giggling. And he thought: *But they're just . . . kids.*

And he was also a kid, but . . .

He doodled a cross in his book, changed it to a kind of gallows with a noose.

I am *a child, but . . .*

He drew a train. A car. A boat.

A house. With an open door.

His anxiety grew. At the end of math class he couldn't sit still, his feet banged on the floor, his hands drummed against his desk. The teacher asked him, with a surprised turn of her head, to be quiet. He tried, but soon the restlessness was there again, pulling in the marionette threads and his legs started to move on their own.

When it was time for the last class of the day, gym class, he couldn't stand it any longer. In the corridor he said to Johan: "Tell Ávila I'm sick, OK?"

"Are you taking off, or what?"

"Don't have my gym clothes."

This was actually true; he had forgotten to pack his gym clothes this morning, but that was not why he had to cut class. On the way to the subway he saw the class line up in straight rows. Tomas shouted "buuuuu!" at him.

Would probably tell on him. Didn't matter. Not in the least.

†

The pigeons fluttered up in gray flocks as he hurried across Vällingby square. A woman with a stroller wrinkled up her nose in judgement at him; someone who doesn't care about animals. But he was in a hurry, and all the things that lay between him and his goal were mere objects, were simply in the way.

He stopped outside the toy store. Smurfs were arranged in a sugary cute landscape. Too old for stuff like that. In a box at home he had a couple of Big Jim dolls that he had played with quite a bit when he was younger.

About a year or so ago.

An electronic doorbell sounded as he opened the door. He walked through a narrow aisle where plastic dolls, krixa-men, and boxes of building models filled the shelves. Closest to the register were the packages with molds for tin soldiers. You had to ask for the blocks of tin at the counter.

What he was looking for was stacked on the counter itself.

Yes, the *imitations* were stacked under the plastic dolls, but the originals, with the Rubik's logo on the packaging, they were more careful with. They cost *ninety-eight kronor* apiece.

A short pudgy man stood behind the counter with a smile that Oskar would have described as "ingratiating" if he had known the word.

"Hello . . . are you looking for anything special today?"

Oskar had known the Cubes would be stacked on the counter, had his plan figured out.

"Yes. I was wondering . . . about the paints. For tin."

"Yes?"

The man gestured to the tiny pots of enamel paint arranged behind him. Oskar leaned over, putting the fingers of one hand on the counter just in front of the Rubik's Cubes while the other hand held his bag, hanging open underneath. He pretended to search among the colors.

"Gold. Do you have that?"

"Gold. Of course."

When the man turned around Oskar took one of the Cubes, popped it into his bag, and had just managed to return his hand to the same place when the man came back with two pots of paint and placed them on the counter. Oskar's heart was beating heat up into his cheeks, across his ears.

"Matte, or metallic?"

The man looked at Oskar, who felt how his whole face was a warning sign on which it was written, "Here is a thief." In order not to draw attention to his red cheeks he bent over the tins, said: "Metallic . . . that one looks fine."

He had twenty kronor. The paint cost nineteen. He got it in a little bag that he scrunched into his coat pocket in order not to have to open his school bag.

The kick came as usual when he was outside the store, but it was bigger than normal. He trotted away from the store like a newly freed slave, just released from his chains. Could not help but run to the parking lot and, with two cars shielding him, carefully open the packaging, take out the Cube.

It was much heavier than the imitation he owned. The sections slid smoothly, as if on ball bearings. Perhaps they were ball bearings? Well, he wasn't planning to take it apart and examine it, risk destroying it.

The box was an ugly thing made of transparent plastic, now that the Cube was no longer in it, and on the way from the parking lot he threw it into a trash can. The Cube looked better without it. He put it in his coat pocket in order to be able to caress it, feel its weight in his hand. It was a good present, a great . . . good-bye present.

In the entrance to the subway station he stopped.

If Eli thinks . . . that I . . .

Yes. That he, by giving Eli a present, somehow accepted the fact that Eli was leaving. Give a good-bye present, over and done with. Good-bye, good-bye. But that wasn't how it was. He absolutely didn't want . . .

His gaze swept across the station, stopped at the kiosk. At the rack of newspapers. The *Expressen* paper. The whole first page was covered in a picture of the old guy who had lived with Eli.

Oskar walked over and flipped through the paper. Five pages were devoted to the search in Judarn forest . . . the Ritual Killer . . . background and then: yet another page where the photo was printed. Håkan Bengtsson . . . Karlstad . . . unknown whereabouts for eight months . . . police turning to the public . . . if anyone has observed . . .

Anxiety dug its claws into Oskar.

Someone else who might have seen him, known where he lived . . .

The kiosk lady leaned out through the kiosk window.

"Are you buying it or not?"

Oskar shook his head, tossed the paper back into its place. Then he ran. It was only once he was down on the platform that he remembered he hadn't shown his ticket to the ticket collector. He stomped his feet on the ground, sucked on his knuckles, his eyes teared up.

Come on, please, subway train, come on . . .

✝

Lacke half-lay on the sofa, squinting at the balcony where Morgan was trying to coax over a bird who was sitting on the railing—without result. The setting sun was exactly behind Morgan's head, spread a halo of light around his hair.

"Come on . . . come, come. I won't bite."

Larry was sitting in an armchair, half-watching a public education course in Spanish. Stiff people in obviously rehearsed situations walked across the screen, said:

"Yo tengo un bolso."

"Qué hay en el bolso?"

Morgan bent his head, so Lacke got the sun in his eyes and closed them, while he heard Larry mutter:

"Ke haj en el bålså."

The apartment reeked of stale cigarette smoke and dust. The seventy-five was empty, lying on the coffee table next to an overfull ashtray. Lacke stared at a couple of burn marks on the table left by carelessly extinguished cigarettes; they slid around before his eyes like meek beetles.

"Ona kamisa y pantalånes."

Larry chuckled to himself.

". . . pantalånes."

✝

They had not believed him. Or rather, yes, they had believed him but refused to interpret the events in the way that he did. "Spontaneous combustion," Larry had said, and Morgan had asked him to spell it.

Except for the fact that the case for spontaneous combustion is just about as well-documented and scientifically proven as vampires. That is to say, not at all.

But of two equally implausible scenarios you probably choose to believe the one that demands the least amount of action on your part. They were not going to help him. Morgan had listened seriously to Lacke's account of what happened at the hospital, but when he got to the part about destroying the cause of all this, he had said:

"So, like, you mean we should become . . . vampire killers. You and me and Larry. With stakes and crosses and . . . No, sorry, Lacke, but I'm having a little trouble seeing it, is all."

Lacke's immediate thought when he saw their disbelieving, dismissive faces had been:

Virginia would have believed me.

And the pain had sunk its claws into him again. He was the one who had not believed in Virginia and that was why . . . he would rather have spent a couple of years in jail for mercy killing than have to live with the image he had seared on his retina.

Her body writhing in the bed as her skin blackens, starts to smoke. The hospital gown that rides up over her stomach, revealing her genitals. The rattle of the metal bed frame as her hips move, heaving up and down in infernal copulation with an invisible being as flames appear on her thighs, she screams, she screams and the stench of singed hair fills the room, her terrified eyes on mine and one second later they whiten, start to boil . . . burst . . .

Lacke had drunk more than half the contents of the bottle. Morgan and Larry had let him.

". . . pantalånes."

Lacke tried to get up out of the couch. The back of his head weighed as much as the rest of his body. He steadied himself against the table, heaved himself up. Larry stood up in order to give him a hand.

"Lacke, damn it . . . sleep a while."

"No, I have to get home."

"What do you have to do there?"

"I just have to . . . do something."

"But it's nothing to do with . . . the stuff we were talking about, is it?"

"No, no."

Morgan came in from the balcony while Lacke was teetering out toward the hall.

"Hey you! Where do you think you're going?"

"Home."

"Then I'll walk you there."

Lacke turned around, making an effort to shore himself up, appear as sober as possible. Morgan walked over to him, his hands out in case Lacke fell. Lacke shook his head, patted Morgan on the shoulder.

"I want to be alone, OK. I want to be alone. That's all."

"Are you sure you can make it?"

"I'll manage."

Lacke nodded a few more times, got hung up on this movement, and had to consciously put an end to it so he wouldn't be stuck standing there, then turned and walked out into the hall, pulling on his coat and shoes.

He knew he was very drunk, but he had experienced this state so many times that he knew how to unhook his movements from his brain, perform them mechanically. He would have been able to play pick-up-sticks without his hands trembling, at least for a short while.

He heard the others' voices from inside the apartment.

"Shouldn't we? . . ."

"No. If that's what he wants we should respect it."

But they came out into the hall to see him off. Hugged him clumsily. Morgan took him by the arms and bent down to look him in the eyes, said:

"You're not going to do anything stupid now are you? You have us, you know that."

"Yes, I know. Of course I won't."

✝

Once he was outside the high-rise apartment building he came to a standstill, looked up at the sun resting in the top of a pine tree.

Will never again be able to . . . the sun . . .

Virginia's death, the way she had died, hung like a lead weight in his heart, in the place his heart had been, made him walk doubled over, compressed. The afternoon light in the streets was a mockery. The few people moving around in it . . . a mockery. Voices. Speaking about everyday things as if . . . all over, at any moment . . .

It can happen to you, too.

Outside the kiosk a person had leaned up against the window, was talking to the kiosk owner. Lacke saw a black lump fall from the sky, attach itself to the person's back and . . .

What the hell . . .

He stopped in front of the rows of headlines, blinked, tried to focus properly on the photo that nearly filled the available space. The Ritual Killer. Lacke snorted. He knew better. What this was actually about. But . . .

He recognized that face. It was . . .

At the Chinese restaurant. The man who . . . bought him the whisky. Could it . . .

He took a step forward, looked more closely at the picture. Yes. It was. The same closely-set eyes, the same . . . Lacke put his hand to his mouth, pressed his fingers to his lips. The images whirled around, attempted connections.

He had let him buy him drinks, the one who killed Jocke. Jocke's killer had lived in the same building complex as him, only a few doors down. He had greeted him a couple of times, he had . . .

But he wasn't the one who did it. That must have been . . .

A voice. Said something.

"Hi Lacke. Someone you know, or what?"

The owner of the kiosk and the man outside were both looking at him. He said:

". . . Yes . . ." and started to walk again, toward his apartment. The world disappeared. In his mind's eye he saw the doorway the man came out of. The covered windows of the apartment. He was going to get to the bottom of this. He was.

His pace quickened and his spine straightened out; the lead weight was a pendulum now that beat against his chest, making him tremble, his resolve thundering through his body.

Here I come. By Jove . . . here I come.

†

The subway train stopped at Råcksta and Oskar chewed his lips, impatiently, with a touch of panic, thought the doors stayed open too long. When there was a click on the speaker system he thought the driver was about to announce a delay but—

"Step away from the doors. The doors are closing."

—and the train pulled away from the station.

He had no plan beyond warning Eli; that anyone, at any time could call the police and say they had seen the old guy. In Blackeberg. In that building. In that stairwell. In that apartment.

What happens if the police . . . if they break down the door . . . the bath-room.

The train rattled across the bridge and Oskar looked out the window. Two men were standing down at the Lover's newsstand and, half-covered by one of the men, Oskar could still discern the row of hateful front-page headlines blown up and printed on yellow fliers. The other man walked quickly away from the kiosk.

Anyone. Anyone can recognize him. He could know.

Oskar was already up and standing by the doors when the train started to slow down. He pushed his fingers through the rubber lips between the doors as if that would make them open faster, and leaned his forehead against the glass, cool against his hot skin. The brakes started to squeal and the driver must have been distracted because only now did he announce:

"Next stop. Blackeberg."

Jonny was standing on the platform. And Tomas.

No. Nonono. Not them.

When the train, rocking, pulled to a halt, Oskar's eyes met Jonny's. They widened, and at the same time as the doors slid open with a hiss, Oskar saw Jonny say something to Tomas.

Oskar tensed, threw himself out through the doors, and started to run.

Tomas' long leg flicked out, hooked his, and he fell headlong onto the platform, scraping the palms of his hands when he tried to break his fall. Jonny sat on his back. "In a hurry to get somewhere?"

"Let me go! Let me go!"

"Why should we?"

Oskar shut his eyes, balled his hands into fists. Took a couple of deep breaths, as deep as he could with Jonny's weight on his chest, and said into the concrete:

"Do whatever you want. Then let me go."

"Okie-dokie."

They grabbed him by his arms and pulled him to his feet. Oskar caught a glimpse of the station clock. Ten past two. The second hand hacked its way around the face. He tensed the muscles in his face, in his stomach, tried to make himself like a rock, impervious to blows.

Just let it be over fast.

It was only when he saw what they were planning to do that he started to struggle. But as if by silent agreement both of them had twisted his arms around so that every movement made it feel as if his arms were going to break. They forced him toward the edge of the platform.

They wouldn't dare. They can't . . .

But Tomas was crazy and Jonny . . .

He tried to brace himself with his feet. They danced across the platform while Tomas and Jonny led him up to the white line that marked the start of the drop down toward the tracks.

Some hair on his left temple was tickling his forehead, fluttering from the gust of wind coming out of the tunnel as the train from the city approached. The tracks started to hum and Jonny whispered:

"You're going to die now, you understand."

Tomas giggled, gripped him even harder by the arm. Oskar's head went dark: *they're really going to do it.* They forced him out so his upper body was hanging out over the tracks.

The lights on the approaching train projected an arrow of cold light over the tracks. Oskar jerked his head to the left and saw the train come hurtling out of the tunnel.

BAAAAAAAAAAH!

The train's signal sounded and Oskar's heart leaped in its deaththrows at the same time as he wet his pants and his last thought was—

Eli!

—before he was pulled back, his field of vision filled with green when the train rushed past, a few centimeters in front of his eyes.

†

He lay on his back on the platform, his breath coming in puffs of smoke from his mouth. The wetness in his groin grew colder. Jonny squatted next to him.

"Just so you get it. How things are going to be around here. Understand?"

Oskar nodded, instinctively. Put an end to it. The old impulses. Jonny gingerly touched his injured ear, smiled. Then he put his hand across Oskar's mouth, pushed his cheeks together.

"Squeal like a pig if you get it."

Oskar squealed. Like a pig. They laughed. Tomas said: "He was better at it before."

Jonny nodded. "We'll have to start training him again."

The train on the other side arrived. They left him.

Oskar lay where he was for a while, empty. Then a face came floating through the air in front of him. Some lady. She was holding her hand out to him.

"You poor dear. I saw the whole thing. You have to report them to the police, that was . . ."

The police.

". . . attempted murder. Come, I'll help . . ."

Oskar ignored her hand and jumped to his feet. While he was limping toward the doors, up the stairs, he could still hear the lady's voice:

"Are you sure you're alright?"

†

The cops.

Lacke winced when he walked into the courtyard and saw the patrol car parked in the corner. Two police officers were standing outside the car; one was writing something on a pad. He assumed they were after the same thing as him, but that their information source was not as good. The officers had not noticed his hesitation, so he kept going to the first entrance in the row of buildings, walked in.

None of the names on the wall told him anything, but he knew which one it was anyway. Ground floor, to the right. Next to the basement door there was a bottle of T-Röd. He stopped, looked at it as if it could give him a clue as to what he should do next.

T-Röd is flammable. Virginia went up in flames.

But the thought stopped at that point and he only felt that dry, screaming rage again, continued up the stairs. A shift had occurred.

Now his mind was clear and his body clumsy. His feet slipped on the steps and he had to steady himself with the railing in order to maneuver himself up the stairs, while his brain clearly resonated:

I go in. I find it. I drive something through its heart. Then I wait for the cops.

In front of the door with no name plate he remained standing.

And how the hell am I going to get in.

As a kind of joke he tossed out one arm and felt the door handle. And the door opened, revealing an empty apartment. No furniture, rugs, paintings. No clothes. He licked his lips.

It's gone. There's nothing for me here. . . .

There were two more bottles of T-Rö on the floor in the hall. He tried to decide what that meant. That this creature drank . . . no. That . . .

Only means that someone has been here recently. Otherwise that bottle back there would be gone.

Yes.

He stepped in, stopped in the hall and listened. Heard nothing. Did a quick round of the apartment, saw there were blankets hanging in the windows in several rooms, understood why. Knew he was in the right place.

Finally he ended up standing in front of the bathroom door. Pushed the door handle down. Locked. But this lock was no problem; all he needed was a screwdriver or something like that.

Again he concentrated entirely on his movements. To perform the movements. He shouldn't think beyond that. No need to. If he started thinking he would hesitate and he wasn't going to hesitate. Therefore: movements.

He pulled out the kitchen drawers, found a kitchen knife. Walked to the bathroom. Inserted the blade into the handle and turned it, clockwise. The lock gave way; he opened the door. It was pitch black in there. He groped around for a light switch, found one. Turned it on.

God help us. Damned if it isn't . . .

The knife fell out of Lacke's hand. The bathtub in front of his feet was half-filled with blood. On the bathroom floor were several large plastic jugs whose translucent plastic surfaces were smeared with red. The knife clattered against the tile floor like a little bell. ·

His tongue stuck to the roof of his mouth as he leaned forward to . . . to what? To . . . investigate it . . . or something else, something more primal; the fascination of such quantities of blood . . . to dip his hand into it, to—bathe his hands in blood.

He lowered his fingers against the still, dark surface and . . . plunged in. His fingers appeared to be severed, disappeared, and with a gaping mouth he lowered his hand until it felt—

He screamed, pulled back.

He quickly drew his hand out of the bathtub and drops of blood flew in an arc around him, landing on the ceiling, walls. In a reflex motion he put his hand over his mouth. Only realized what he had done when his tongue, lips registered the sweet stickiness. He spit, dried his hands on his pants. Put the other, clean hand over his mouth.

Someone's lying . . . down there.

Yes. What he had felt under his fingertips had been a belly. That had yielded under the pressure of his hand, before he pulled it out. In order to stave off the feeling of revulsion, he scanned the floor, found the knife, picked it up and squeezed the shaft.

What the hell am I . . .

If he had been sober he would perhaps have left at this point. Left this dark pool that could be concealing just about anything under its once more still, polished mirror surface. A butchered body, for example.

The stomach is maybe . . . it maybe is just a stomach.

But the intoxication made him merciless even to his own fear so when he saw the thin chain that led from the edge of the bathtub down into the dark liquid he stretched out his hand and pulled on it.

The plug was pulled out down there, there was a filtering, clucking sound from the pipes and a faint whirl formed on the surface. He kneeled in front of the bathtub, licked his lips. Felt the harsh taste on his tongue, spit on the floor.

The surface became gradually lower. A sharply delineated dark red edge became visible along its highest level.

It must have been here a long time.

After a minute the contours of a nose appeared at one end. At the other a set of toes that, as he watched, became two half feet. The vortex on the surface became narrower, stronger, positioned exactly between the feet.

He crept with his gaze along the child's body that was gradually being revealed on the bottom of the bath. A couple of hands, folded across the chest. Knee caps. A face. A muffled slurp as the last of the blood drained out.

The body in front of his eyes was dark red, blotchy and slimy like a newborn. It had a navel, but no genitals. A boy or a girl? It didn't matter. When he looked closely at the face with its closed eyes he recognized it only too well.

†

When Oskar tried to run, his legs froze up. Refused.

During five desperate seconds he had really believed that he was going to die. That they were prepared to push him. Now his muscles were having a hard time getting past the idea.

They gave out in the passageway between the school and the gymnasium.

He wanted to lie down. Tip back into those bushes, for example. The jacket and his lined pants would protect him from sharp twigs; the branches would provide gentle support. But he was in a hurry. The second hand; its staccato progress along the clock face.

The school.

The red-brown sharp-edged brick façade of stone laid against stone. In his thoughts he swooped like a bird along the corridors, into the classrooms. Jonny was there. Tomas. Sat at their desks and smiled mockingly at him. He bent his head, checked his boots.

The shoelaces were dirty, one about to become untied. A metal hook toward the top had been bent open. He walked slightly pigeon-toed; the leather imitation on both shoes was slightly stretched at the heels, worn to a shine. Even so he was going to be wearing these boots all winter, most likely.

Cold in his wet pants. He lifted his head.

I won't let them win. I. Won't. Let. Them. Win.

Warmth streamed into his legs. The straight masonry lines of the brick façade dropped away, were rubbed out, disappeared as he started to run. His legs stretched out, the dirt squelched and sprayed up around his feet. The ground flowed out from under him and now it felt as if the Earth was turning too fast, he couldn't keep up.

His legs took him stumbling past the high-rises, the old Konsum store, the coconut factory, and with his speed in combination with old habits he rushed into the courtyard, past Eli's door, and straight to his own building.

He almost ran into a police officer who was heading the same way. The officer opened his arms, received him.

"Hey there! You're in quite a hurry."

His tongue stiffened. The officer let go of him, looked at him . . . with suspicion?

"Do you live here?"

Oskar nodded. He had never seen this police officer before. Admittedly he looked quite nice. No. He had a face that Oskar would *normally* think looked nice. The officer pinched his nose and said:

"You see . . . something's happened here. In the building next door. So now I'm going door to door around here asking if anyone's heard anything. Or seen anything."

"Which . . . which building?"

The officer nodded his head toward Tommy's building and the immediate panic left Oskar.

"That one. Well, not in the building per se . . . more like, the basement. You wouldn't have happened to hear or see anything unusual around there? The past few days?"

Oskar shook his head, his thoughts spinning so chaotically that he technically wasn't thinking anything at all, but he suspected his anxiety was shining from his eyes, fully visible to the officer. And the officer really did incline his head, scrutinizing him.

"How are you doing?"

". . . fine."

"There's nothing to be afraid of. It's all . . . over now. So there's nothing you need to be worried about or anything. Are your parents home?"

"No. My mom. No."

"OK. Well, I'm going to be walking around here for a while, so . . . you can always think a little about what you may have seen."

The police officer held the door open for him. "After you."

"No, I was going to . . ."

Oskar turned and did his best to walk naturally down the hill. Halfway down he turned and saw the police officer go into his building.

They've taken Eli.

His jaws started to chatter, his teeth clicking an unclear Morse code message through his bones while he pulled open the door to Eli's building, continued on up the stairs. Would they have put that kind of tape on the door, sealed it off?

Say that I can come in.

The door was ajar.

If the police have been here, why did they leave the door open? That wasn't something they did, was it? He put his fingers on the handle, pulled the door open gently, crept into the hallway. It was dark in the apartment. One of his feet bumped into something. A plastic bottle. At first he thought there was blood in the bottle, then he looked and saw it was lighter fluid.

Breathing.

Someone was breathing.

Moving.

The sound came from the corridor in the direction of the bathroom. Oskar walked toward it, one step at a time, folded his lips inward to stop his teeth from chattering and the shivering moved down toward his chin, his neck, the suggestion of an Adam's apple on his neck. He turned the corner, looked into the bathroom.

That's not a policeman.

A man in shabby clothes was kneeling next to the bathtub, his upper body leaning over the edge, outside Oskar's field of vision. He only saw a pair of dirty gray pants, ripped up shoes with the tips pointed down toward the tiled floor. The hem of a coat.

The old guy!

But he's . . . breathing.

Yes. Hissing inhalations and exhalations, almost like sighs, came from the bathroom and Oskar crept closer without consciously thinking about it. Little by little he saw more of the bathroom, and when he was almost level with the bathtub itself he saw what was happening.

†

Lacke couldn't do it.

The body at the bottom of the tub looked completely defenseless. It wasn't breathing. He had put his hand on its chest and registered the fact that its heart was beating but only with a few beats a minute.

He had been expecting something . . . terrifying. Something in proportion to the horror he had experienced at the hospital. But this little bloody rag of a person didn't look as if it could ever get up again, much less hurt anyone. It was only a child. A wounded child.

Like seeing someone you love wasting away with cancer, and then being shown a cancer cell through a microscope. Nothing. *That? That did this? That little thing?*

Destroy my heart.

He let out a sob, his head falling forward until it hit the edge of the bathtub with a dull, echoing thud. He could. Not. Kill a child. A sleeping child. He simply couldn't. Even though . . .

That's how it has managed to survive.

It. It. Not a child. It.

It had attacked Virginia and . . . it had killed Jocke. It. The creature lying in front of him. This creature who would do it again, to other people. This creature that was not a person. It wasn't even breathing, and even so its heart was beating . . . like an animal in hibernation.

Think about the others.

A poisonous snake living among people. You think you shouldn't kill it, simply because for the moment it appears defenseless?

But in the end that wasn't what helped him make up his mind. It was when he looked at the face again; the face covered in a thin film of blood, and he thought it looked like it was . . . smiling.

Smiling at all the evil it had done.

Enough.

He raised the kitchen knife above the creature, moved his legs back a little so he could put all his weight behind the thrust and—

"AAAAHHH!"

†

Oskar screamed.

The old guy didn't flinch; he simply froze, turned his head toward Oskar and said slowly: "I have to do it. Do you understand?"

Oskar recognized him. He was one of the drunks who lived in the apartment complex and said hello to him from time to time.

Why is he doing this?

But that was neither here nor there. The important thing was that the guy had a knife in his hands, a knife that was pointing directly at Eli's chest as he lay there in the bathtub naked, exposed.

"Don't do it."

The guy's head moved to the right, to the left, more as if he was look- ing for something on the floor than signaling refusal.

"No . . ."

He turned back to the tub, to the knife. Oskar wanted to explain. That the thing in the bathtub was his friend, that it was his . . . that he had a present for the thing in there, that . . . *that it was Eli.*

"Wait."

The point of the knife lay against Eli's chest, pressed in so hard it al- most punctured Eli's skin. Oskar didn't know exactly what he was doing when he shoved his hand into the pocket of his jacket and took out the Cube, showed it to the guy.

"Look!"

Lacke only saw it in the corner of his eye as a sudden burst of color in the midst of all the black, gray that surrounded him. Despite the bubble of determination that enveloped him he couldn't help turning his head toward it, to see what it was.

One of those Cubes in the boy's hand. Bright colors.

Looked completely sick in the current context. A parrot among crows. For a second he was hypnotized by the toy's vividness. Then he turned his gaze back to the bathtub, to the knife that was on its way down between the ribs.

All I need to do is . . . press . . .

A change.

The creature's eyes were open.

He tensed in order to drive the knife in all the way, and then his temple exploded.

†

The Cube creaked when one of the corners smashed into the guy's head and it was wrenched from Oskar's hand. The guy fell to one side, landing on a plastic jug that gave way, hitting the side of the tub with a thundering noise like a bass drum.

Eli sat up.

From the bathroom doorway Oskar could only see the back of his body. The hair was plastered against the back of his head and his back was one big open wound.

The guy tried to get back on his feet but Eli didn't so much jump as fall out of the bathtub, landed in his lap: a child seeking comfort from his father. Eli wrapped his arms around the guy's neck and pulled his head to him to whisper tender words.

Oskar backed away from the bathroom as Eli bit the guy's neck. Eli hadn't seen him. But the guy saw him. His gaze locked with Oskar's, held him fast as Oskar moved backward toward the hall.

"Sorry."

Oskar didn't manage to get any sound out, but his lips formed the word before he turned the corner and the eye contact was broken.

He stood with his hand on the door handle as the guy screamed. Then the sound stopped abruptly as if a hand had been clamped over his mouth.

Oskar hesitated. Then he closed the door. And locked it.

Without looking to the right he walked down the hall to the living room. Sat down in the armchair.

Started to hum in order to drown out the noise from the bathroom.

Part Five

LET THE RIGHT ONE SLIP IN

These days this is
my only chance to say my piece . . .
　　　　　—bob hund, "Struggling Against the Current"

Let the right one in
Let the old dreams die
Let the wrong ones go
They cannot do
What you want them to do
　　　　　—Morrissey, "Let the Right One Slip In"

From *The Daily Update* 16:45, Monday, 9 November, 1981

The so-called Ritual Killer was apprehended by police on Monday morning. He was tracked down in a basement office in Blackeberg, in west Stockholm.

Police spokesman Bengt Lärn:

"A person has been apprehended. That is correct."

"Are you sure that it is the same man you have been looking for?"

"Quite sure. Certain factors, however, complicate a positive identification at this time."

"What kind of factors?"

"Unfortunately I can't go into further details at the moment."

After the man was apprehended he was transported to the hospital. His state was described as critical.

Together with the suspect, the police also found a sixteen-year-old boy. The boy was physically unharmed but is said to be in a state of severe shock and has been taken to the hospital for further monitoring.

The police are searching the area in order to gather further information regarding the chain of events.

His Royal Highness Carl Gustaf today opened the new bridge over the Almö sound in Bohuslän. During the opening speech . . .

From diagnostic notes made by the surgeon Professor T. Hallberg, copied for police files

... preliminary investigation complicated by ... spasmodic muscle action ... unlocalized stimulation of central nervous system ... heart function suspended ...

Muscle movement stops at 14:25 ... autopsy yields hitherto unobserved ... severely deformed inner organs ...

Like the eel that dead and butchered jumps in the frying pan ... never before observed in human tissue ... ask to retain the cadaver ... sincerely ...

From the newspaper *Western Suburbs*, week 46

WHO KILLED OUR CATS?

"The only thing I have left is her collar," says Svea Nordström, pointing to the slushy field where her pet and eight others belonging to neighboring homeowners were found ...

From the television news program *Current Events*, Monday, 9 November, 21:00

Earlier this evening police entered the apartment believed to belong to the so-called Ritual Killer, who was apprehended this morning.

A call from a member of the public helped police to finally locate the apartment in Blackeberg, some fifty meters from the place where the man was apprehended.

We have our reporter Folke Ahlmarker at the scene:

"Emergency technicians are right now carrying out the body of a man found in the apartment. The man's identity is not known at this time. It appears the apartment is unoccupied, although there are certain indications that people have been in the apartment recently."

"What are the police doing right now?"

"They have been going door to door all day but if they have gained any further information in the process they have made no announcement to that effect."

"Thank you, Folke."

The Tjörn bridge, which was finished six weeks before the estimated completion date, was opened today by His Royal Highness, Carl Gustaf ...

𝕸𝖔𝖓𝖉𝖆𝖞

9 NOVEMBER

Pulses of blue light across the bedroom ceiling.

Oskar is lying in bed with his hands behind his head.

Under his bed there are two cardboard boxes. There is money in one, masses of bills, and two bottles of T-Röd; the other is filled with puzzles. The box of clothes was left behind.

In order to conceal the boxes Oskar has placed his hockey game at an angle in front of them. Tomorrow he'll carry them down into the basement, if he has the energy. His mom is watching TV, shouting out something about how their building is on the screen. But he only has to get up and go to the window to see the same thing, from another angle.

✝

He threw the boxes from Eli's balcony over to his own while it was still light, while Eli was washing himself. When he came out of the bathroom the wounds on his back had healed and he was slightly intoxicated from the alcohol in the blood.

They lay in bed together, held each other. Oskar told him what had happened in the subway. Eli said:

"I'm sorry. About starting this."

"No, it's alright."

Silence. For a long time. Then Eli asked, hesitantly:

"Would you want to . . . become like me?"

". . . no. I would like to be with you, but . . ."

"No, of course you don't. I understand."

In the evening they finally stood up, put their clothes on. They were standing with their arms around each other in the living room when they heard the saw. The lock was being removed.

They ran to the balcony, jumped over the railing, landing fairly softly in the bushes below.

From inside the apartment they heard someone say:

"What in the world . . ."

They curled up under the balcony. There was no time.

Eli turned his face to Oskar's, said:

"I . . ."

Closed his mouth. Then pressed a kiss on Oskar's lips.

For a few seconds Oskar saw through Eli's eyes. And what he saw was . . . himself. Only much better, more handsome, stronger than what he thought of himself. Seen with love.

For a few seconds.

†

Voices in the apartment next door.

The last thing Eli had done before they got up was remove the piece of paper with the Morse code. Now strange feet are clomping around in the room where Eli once lay and tapped on the wall to him.

Oskar holds his hand up against the wall.

"Eli . . ."

Tuesday

10 NOVEMBER

Oskar did not go to school on Tuesday. He lay in his bed and listened to the sounds through the wall, wondered if they would find anything that would lead them to him. In the afternoon it grew quiet and they had still not come by.

At that point he got up, put his clothes on, and walked over to Eli's building. The door to the apartment was sealed. No one was allowed in. While he stood there looking a police officer walked by on the stairs. But Oskar was only a curious boy from the neighborhood.

When the sun went down he carried the boxes into the basement and put an old rug over them. Would decide later what he would do with them. If some thief decided to break into their storage unit he would hit the jackpot.

He sat in the darkness of the basement for a long time, thought about Eli, Tommy, the old guy. Eli had told him everything; that he hadn't meant for things to turn out the way they did.

But Tommy was alive and would be fine. That's what his mom had told Oskar's mom. He was going to be coming home tomorrow.

Tomorrow.

Tomorrow Oskar would go back to school.

To Jonny, Tomas, to . . .

We'll have to start training him again.

Jonny's cold hard fingers across his cheeks. Pressing the soft flesh against his jaws until the corners of his mouth were unwillingly forced up.

Squeal like a pig.

Oskar interlaced his fingers, leaned his face against them, looked at the little hill that the rug over the boxes made. He got up, pulled the rug away and opened the box of money.

One thousand kronor notes, one hundred kronor notes, all mixed up, a few bundles of bank notes. He dug around with his hand among the bank notes until he found one of the plastic bottles. Then he went up to the apartment and got some matches.

A lone spotlight cast a cold, white glow onto the schoolyard. Outside its circle of light you could see the outlines of playground structures. The Ping-Pong tables that were so cracked you couldn't play on them with anything other than a tennis ball, were covered in slush.

A few rows of school windows were illuminated. Evening classes. For this reason one of the side doors was unlocked.

He made his way through the darkened corridors to his homeroom. Stood for a while looking at the desks. The classroom looked unreal at night like this, as if ghosts silently whispering were using it for their school, whatever that would look like.

He walked over to Jonny's desk, opened the lid, and sprayed a few quarts of T-Röd onto it. Tomas' desk, same thing. He stood without moving for a second in front of Micke's desk. Decided not to. Then he went and sat at his own desk. Letting it soak in, like you do with charcoal.

I'm a ghost. Booo . . . booo . . .

He opened the lid and took out his copy of *Firestarter*, smiled at the title and slipped it into his bag. The exercise book where he had written a story he liked. His favorite pen. They all went into the bag. Then he stood up, made a final round of the classroom and enjoyed simply being there. In peace.

Jonny's desk gave off a chemical smell when he raised the lid again, took out the matches.

No, wait . . .

He went and got two rough-hewn wooden rulers from a shelf at the back of the classroom. Rigged up Jonny's desk with one so it would stay open, Tomas' with the other. Otherwise they would stop burning the moment he let the lids drop.

Two hungry prehistoric animals gaping for food. Dragons.

He lit one match, held it in his hand until the flame was large and clear. Then dropped it. It fell from his hand, a yellow drop, and—

WHOOSH

Damn . . .

His eyes stung when a purple comet's tail shot up out of the desk, licked his face. He sprung back; had expected it to burn like . . . charcoal, but the desk was fully lit, one big bonfire reaching up to the ceiling.

It was burning too much.

The fire danced, flickered across the classroom walls, and a garland of large letters made of paper, hanging over Jonny's desk, broke off and fell to the floor, the P and Q burning. The other half of the garland swung in a large arc and fell onto Tomas' desk which immediately burst into flames with the same

WHOOSH

a searing explosion while Oskar ran from the classroom with his schoolbag bouncing on his hip.

What if the whole school . . .

When he reached the end of the corridor the bells started to ring. A metallic clatter that filled the building and it was only when he was a good ways down the stairs that he realized it was the fire alarm.

Out in the schoolyard the large bell rang fiercely to assemble students who were not there, gathered up the school's ghosts, and followed Oskar halfway home.

Only when he reached the old Konsum grocery store and he no longer heard the bell did he relax. He walked calmly the rest of the way.

In the bathroom mirror he saw that the tops of his eyelashes were rolled up, singed. When he touched them with his finger they broke off.

𝔚𝔢𝔡𝔫𝔢𝔰𝔡𝔞𝔶

11 NOVEMBER

Home from school. Headache. The phone rang around nine. He didn't answer. In the middle of the day he saw Tommy and his mom walk past outside the window. Tommy walked bent over, slowly. Like an old person. Oskar ducked down under the windowsill as they went by.

The phone rang every hour. Finally, at twelve o'clock, he picked it up. "This is Oskar."

"Hi. My name is Bertil Svanberg and I am, as you may know, the principal of the school that you . . ."

He hung up. The phone rang again. Oskar stood there for a while, looking at the ringing phone, imagining the principal sitting in his checkered sport coat, fingers drumming on the desk, making faces. Then he put his clothes on and went down into the basement. Picked at the puzzles, poked at the little white wooden box where the thousand pieces of the gold egg glittered. Eli had only taken a couple of thousand and the Cube. He closed the lid of the puzzle box, opened the other, mixed up the rustling bank notes with his hand. Took a fistful of them, threw them on the ground. Pushed them down into his pockets. Took them out one by one, played "The Boy with the Gold Pants" until he grew tired of it. Twelve wrinkled thousand kronor and seven hundred kronor bills lay at his feet.

He gathered up the thousand kronor notes into a pile and folded them up. Put the hundred kronor notes back, closed the box. Walked up into the apartment, found an envelope that he stuffed the money into. Sat with the envelope in his hand and wondered what he should do. Didn't want to write, someone could recognize his handwriting.

The phone rang.

Stop it. Understand that I don't exist anymore.

Someone wanted to have a long talk with him. Someone wanted to ask him if he realized the gravity of what he had done, which he did. As did Jonny and Tomas probably. Quite well, in fact. Nothing more to talk about.

He walked over to his desk and took out his rubber letters and ink set. In the middle of the envelope he stamped a 'T' and an 'O.' The first 'M' went askew, but the second one was straight, like the 'Y.'

When he opened the door to Tommy's building with the envelope in his coat pocket he was more nervous than he had been at his school the night before. His heart thumping, he gingerly eased the envelope through the mail slot in Tommy's door so no one would come to the door or catch sight of him through the window.

But no one came and when Oskar was back in his apartment he felt a little better. For a while. Then it sneaked up on him again.

I won't . . . be here.

At three o'clock his mom came home, several hours earlier than usual. At that point Oskar was sitting in the living room with the Vikings' album. She walked into the room, lifted the needle, and turned off the record player. By her face he sensed that she knew.

"How are things with you?"

"Not so good."

"No . . ."

She sighed, sat down on the couch.

"The principal called me. At work. He told me that . . . there was a fire there last night. At your school."

"Really. Did it burn to the ground?"

"No, but . . ."

She closed her mouth, her gaze getting stuck in the hooked rug for a few seconds. Then she lifted her eyes and met his.

"Oskar. Was it you?"

He looked straight back at her and said:

"No."

Pause.

"No. It's just that it seems that although much of the classroom was destroyed, that . . . that Jonny's and Tomas' desks . . . that it was there it had started."

"Oh."

"And they were apparently quite sure that . . . that it was you."

"But it wasn't."

His mom sat on the couch, breathing through her nose. They sat a meter apart, an endless distance.

"They want to . . . talk to you."

"I don't want to talk to them."

It was going to be a long evening. There was nothing good on TV.

✝

That night Oskar couldn't sleep. He got up out of bed, tiptoed to the window. He thought he saw something in the jungle gym down on the playground. But it was just his imagination, of course. Nonetheless he continued to stare at the shadow down there until his eyelids grew heavy.

When he got back into bed he still couldn't sleep. He gently tapped on the wall. No answer. Just the dry sound of his own fingertips, knuckles against the concrete, knocking on a door that was closed forever.

Thursday

Oskar threw up in the morning and was allowed to stay home another day. Despite the fact that he had only slept a few hours the night before he was unable to rest. There was a gnawing anxiety in his body that forced him around the apartment. He picked things up, looked at them, put them back.

It was as if there was something he had to do. Something absolutely necessary, but he simply couldn't think of what it was.

At the time he had thought he was doing *it* while he set fire to Jonny's and Tomas' desks. Then he had thought *it* was giving the money to Tommy. But that wasn't *it*. It was something else.

A great theater performance that was now over. He paced back and forth on the emptied, darkened stage and swept up that which had been left behind. When it was something else. . . .

But what?

When the mail arrived at eleven there was only a single letter. His heart made a somersault in his chest as he picked it up, turned it over.

It was addressed to his mom. "South Ängby School District" was printed in the upper right-hand corner. Without opening it he ripped it into pieces and flushed them down the toilet. Regretted it. Too late. He didn't care what was written in it, but there would be even more trouble if he started messing around with this, than if he just let it be.

But it didn't matter.

He undressed, put on his bathrobe. Stood in front of the mirror in the hall, studied himself. Pretended he was someone else. Leaned over to kiss the glass. At the same time that his lips met the cold surface the phone rang. Without thinking he lifted the receiver. "Hi. It's me."

"Oskar?"

"Yes."

"Hi. Fernando here."

"What?"

"Ávila. Mr. Ávila."

"Oh. Yeah. Hi."

"I just wanted to ask . . . are you coming to the training tonight?"

"I'm . . . a bit sick."

Silence on the other end. Oskar could hear Mr. Ávila's breaths. One. Two. Then "Oskar. If you did. Or did not. I do not care about this. If you want to talk; we talk. If you do not want to talk; we don't. But I want you to come to the training."

"Why?"

"Because Oskar, you cannot sit like *caracol*, how do you say . . . the snail. In the shell. If you aren't sick, you will get sick. Are you sick?"

". . . Yes."

"Then you need physical fitness training. You will come tonight."

"What about the others?"

"The others? What are the others? If they are stupid I will say boo, they stop. But they are not stupid. This is training."

Oskar didn't reply.

"OK? You'll come?"

"Yes . . ."

"Good. See you later."

Oskar put the phone down and everything was quiet around him again. He didn't want to go to the workout session. But he wanted to see Mr. Ávila. Maybe he could go there a little earlier, see if he was there. Then go home again when the session started.

Not that Mr. Ávila would accept that, but . . .

He completed another round of the apartment. Packed his workout things, mainly to have something to do. Lucky he hadn't started the fire in Micke's desk, since Micke would be going to the gym. Although maybe it got destroyed anyway because it was right next to Jonny's. How much had actually been destroyed?

Something to ask . . .

The phone rang again around three o'clock. Oskar hesitated before picking it up, but after the flicker of hope he had felt after seeing the lone envelope he couldn't resist answering it.

"Hello, this is Oskar."

"Hi. It's Johan."

"Hi."

"What's up?"

"Nothing much."

"Want to do something tonight?"

"When . . . what?"

"Oh . . . about seven, or something."

"No, I'm going to . . . the gym."

"Oh. OK. Too bad. Catch you later."

"Johan?"

"Yeah?"

"I . . . heard there was a fire. In our classroom. Did . . . a lot get destroyed?"

"Naw. Just a couple of desks."

"Nothing else?"

"Naw . . . some . . . papers and that."

"Oh."

"Your desk is fine."

"Oh. Good."

"OK. Bye."

"Bye."

Oskar hung up with a strange feeling in his stomach. He had thought that *everyone knew* it was him. But that's not how Johan had sounded. And his mom had said that *a lot* had been destroyed. But she could have been exaggerating, of course.

Oskar chose to believe Johan. He had *seen* it, after all.

†

Oh, for christ's sake . . ."

Johan hung up, and looked around, hesitantly. Jimmy shook his head, blew smoke out of Jonny's bedroom window.

"That was the worst I've heard."

In a meek voice Johan said: "It's not so easy."

Jimmy turned to face Jonny, who was sitting on the bed rubbing a tassle from the bedspread between his fingers.

"What happened? Half the classroom burned down?"

Jonny nodded. "Everyone in the class hates him."

"And you . . ." Jimmy turned toward him again, "you say that . . . what was it you said? 'Some paper.' Do you think he'll go for that?"

Johan lowered his head, embarrassed.

"I didn't know what to say. I thought he would . . . get suspicious if I said that . . ."

"Yes, yes. Done is done. Now we just have to hope he turns up."

Johan's gaze flew back and forth between Jonny and Jimmy. Their eyes were empty, lost in images of the coming evening.

"What are you guys going to do?"

Jimmy leaned forward in his seat, brushing away a little ash that had fallen on his sweater, and said slowly:

"He burned it. Everything we had from our dad. So what we're going to do is something that . . . that doesn't concern you. Understand?"

†

His mom came home at half past five. The lies, the distrust from the night before still hung like a cold cloud between them, and his mom went straight to the kitchen, started making an unnecessary amount of noise with the dishes. Oskar shut his door. Laid on his bed and stared up at the ceiling.

He could go somewhere. Out into the yard. Down into the basement. To the square. Take the subway. But there still wasn't any place . . . no place where he . . . nothing.

He heard his mom walk to the phone and dial a lot of numbers. His dad's probably.

Oskar shivered a little.

He pulled the blankets over him, sat up with his head against the wall, listening to the sound of his mom and dad's conversation. If he could talk to dad. But he couldn't. It never happened.

Oskar pulled the blanket around himself, pretending to be an Indian chieftain, indifferent to everything as his mom's voice rose. After a while she started to yell and the Indian chieftain fell down on the bed, pressed the blanket, his hands over his ears.

It's so quiet inside your head. It is . . . like outer space.

Oskar made the lines, colors, dots in front of his eyes into planets, distant solar systems that he traveled through. Landed on comets, flew for a while, jumped off and hovered freely in weightlessness until something pulled on his blanket and he opened his eyes.

Mom was standing there. Her lips twisted. Her voice abrupt and sharp as she talked:

"So. Now your father has told me . . . that he . . . on Saturday . . . that you . . . where were you? Tell me. Where were you? Can you tell me that?"

His mom pulled on the blanket up by his face. Her throat tensed to a hard, thick sinew.

"You're never going there again. Never. You hear me? Why didn't you say anything? I mean . . . that bastard. People like him shouldn't have children. He is not going to see you anymore. And then he can sit there and drink as much as he likes. You hear me? We don't need him. I am so . . ."

His mom twirled abruptly away from the bed, slammed the door so hard the walls shook. Oskar heard her rapidly dial the long number again, swearing when she missed a digit, had to start over. A few seconds after she finished dialing she started to yell.

Oskar crept out from under his blanket, grabbed his workout bag, and walked into the hall where his mom was so preoccupied with yelling at his dad that she didn't notice the fact that he had slipped on his shoes and walked up to the front door without tying them.

It was only when he was standing in the stairwell that she saw him.

"Wait a second! Where do you think you're going?"

Oskar banged the door shut and ran down the stairs, kept running, the soles of his shoes pattering, on his way to the pool.

†

Roger, Prebbe . . ."

With his plastic fork, Jimmy jabbed in the direction of the two guys emerging from the subway station. The bite that Jonny had just taken from his shrimp sandwich lodged halfway down his throat and he was forced to swallow again in order to get it down. He looked quizzically at his brother but Jimmy's attention was directed at the guys on their way over to the hot dog stand, greeted them.

Roger was thin and had long, straggly hair, a leather jacket. The skin in his face was punctured by hundreds of small craters and appeared shrunk since the cheekbones stood out sharply and his eyes seemed unnaturally large.

Prebbe had a denim jacket with the arms cut off and a T-shirt under that, and nothing else, even though it was only a couple of degrees above zero. He was a big guy. Spilling out over the edges, cropped hair. An out-of-shape paratrooper.

Jimmy said something to them, pointed, and they took off in the direction of the transformer-station above the subway tracks. Jonny whispered:

"Why . . . are they coming?"

"To help out, of course."

"Do we need it?"

Jimmy sniffed and shook his head as if Jonny didn't know the first thing about how these things worked.

"How were you planning to get around the teach?"

"Ávila?"

"Yeah, you think he would just let us walk on in and . . . you know?"

Jonny had no answer for this, so he just followed his brother in behind the little brick house. Roger and Prebbe were standing in the shadows with their hands in their pockets, stamping their feet. Jimmy took out a metallic cigarette case, flicked it open, and held it out to the other two.

Roger studied the six hand-rolled cigarettes inside, said: "My, my, pre-rolled and everything, why thank you," and used two thin fingers to nab the thickest one.

Prebbe made a face so he looked like one of the old balcony guys on *The Muppet Show.* "They lose their freshness if they sit around."

Jimmy wiggled the case in an inviting way, said:

"Quit your whining, you old woman. I rolled them an hour ago. And this isn't any of that Moroccan shit you run around with. This is the real thing."

Prebbe sucked in his breath and helped himself to one of the cigarettes. Roger helped him light it.

Jonny looked at his brother. Jimmy's face was sharply silhouetted against the light from the subway station platform. Jonny admired him. Wondered if he would ever be someone who dared to say "you old woman" to someone like Prebbe.

Jimmy also took one of the cigarettes and lit it. The rolled-up paper at the tip burned for a moment before it simply glowed. He inhaled deeply and Jonny was enveloped by the sweet smell that always clung to Jimmy's clothing.

They smoked in silence for a while. Then Roger held out his joint to Jonny.

"You want a drag, or what?"

Jonny was about to hold his hand out for it, but Jimmy hit Roger on the shoulder.

"Idiot. Want him to turn out like you?"

"That so bad?"

"OK for you, maybe. Not for him."

Roger shrugged, took back his offer.

It was half-past six when everyone was done smoking, and when Jimmy spoke it was with an exaggerated articulation, every word a complicated sculpture he had to get out of his mouth.

"OK. This . . . is Jonny. My brother."

Roger and Prebbe nodded knowingly. Jimmy took hold of Jonny's chin with a slightly clumsy movement, turned his head so the other two saw it in profile.

"Check out his ear. That's what this squirt did. That's what we're going to . . . take care of."

Roger took a step forward, squinted at Jonny's ear, smacked.

"Shit. It looks bad."

"I'm not asking for an . . . expert . . . opinion. You just listen. Then this will be . . ."

✝

The steel gates in the corridor between the brick walls were unlocked. The echo from Oskar's footsteps went *ka-ploff ka-ploff* as he walked over to the door of the swimming pool, pulled it open. A damp warmth wafted over his face and a cloud of vapor billowed out into the cold corridor. He hurried in and shut the door.

He kicked his shoes off and kept going into the locker room. Empty. He heard the sound of running water from the shower room, a deep voice singing:

> *Bésame, bésame mucho*
> *Como si fuera esta noche la última vez . . .*

Mr. Ávila. Without taking off his jacket, Oskar sat down on one of the benches, waited. After a while both the splashing and the singing stopped and the teacher came out of the shower area with a towel around his hips. His chest looked completely covered in black, curly hair with splashes of gray. Oskar thought he looked like something from another planet. Mr. Ávila saw him, smiled broadly.

"Oskar! So you crawl out of your shell after all."

Oskar nodded.

"It got a bit . . . stuffy."

Mr. Ávila laughed, scratched his chest; the tips of his fingers disappeared in the fuzz.

"You are early."

"Yes, I was thinking . . ."

Oskar shrugged. Mr. Ávila stopped scratching himself.

"You were thinking?"

"I don't know."

"To talk?"

"No, I just . . ."

"Let me take a look at you."

Mr. Ávila took a couple of rapid strides up to Oskar, studied his face, nodded. "Aha. OK."

"What?"

"It was you." Mr. Ávila pointed to his eyes. "I see. You have burned your eyebrows. No, what is it called? Underneath. Eye . . ."

"Lashes?"

"Eyelashes. Yes. A little in the hair as well. Hm. If you don't want anyone to know for sure you have to cut your hair a little. Eye . . . lashes grow fast. Monday it is gone. Gasoline?"

"T-Röd."

Mr. Ávila expelled air through his lips, shook his head.

"Very dangerous. Probably . . ." Mr. Ávila touched Oskar's temple ". . . you a little crazy. Not a lot. But a little. Why T-Röd?"

"I . . . found it."

"Found? Where?"

Oskar looked up at Mr. Ávila's face: a damp, kindly stone. And he wanted to tell him, wanted to tell him all of it. He just didn't know where to start. Mr. Ávila waited. Then he said:

"To play with fire is very dangerous. Can become a habit. Is no good method. Much better physical exercise."

Oskar nodded, and the feeling disappeared. Mr. Ávila was great but he would never understand.

"Now you get changed and I show you a little technique with bench press. OK?"

Mr. Ávila turned to go back to his office. Stopped outside the door.

"And Oskar. You don't worry. I say nothing to nobody if you don't want. Sound good? We can talk more after the training session."

Oskar changed his clothes. When he was finished Patrik and Hasse came in, two guys from 6A. They said hi to Oskar, but he thought they looked at him a little too long, and when he walked into the gym he heard them start whispering to each other.

A sense of despondency settled in the pit of his stomach. He regretted having come here. But shortly thereafter Mr. Ávila came in, now in a T-shirt and shorts, and showed him how you could get a better grip on the bench press bar by allowing it to rest against the tips of your fingers, and Oskar managed twenty-eight kilos, two kilos more than last time. Mr. Ávila noted the new record in his notebook.

More guys came in, among them Micke. He smiled his usual, cryptic smile that could mean everything from that he was about to give you a nice present, to he was about to do something terrible to you.

†

It was the latter that was the case, even if Micke himself did not understand the full extent of it.

On the way to the training session Jonny had come running up to him and asked him to do something, since he was planning to set Oskar up. Micke thought that sounded cool. He liked pranks. And anyway Micke's complete collection of hockey cards had burned up Tuesday night, so paying Oskar back was something he was more than happy to participate in.

But for now he smiled.

†

The session went on. Oskar thought the others were looking at him strangely, but as soon as he tried to meet their eyes they looked away. Most of all he would have liked to go home.

. . . no . . . go . . .

Just go.

But Mr. Ávila was watching over him, bolstering him with peppy comments, and there was kind of no possibility of leaving. And anyway: to be here was at least better than being at home.

When Oskar was done with the strength training he was so exhausted he didn't even have the energy to feel bad. He walked off to the showers, lagging a little behind the others, showering with his back facing the room. Not that it mattered. You still showered naked.

He stood for a while by the glass divide between the shower room and the pool, used his hand to make a small peephole in the condensation covering the glass, looked at the others jumping around in the pool, chasing each other, throwing balls. And it came over him again. Not a thought formulated in words, but as a virulent feeling:

I am alone. I am . . . completely alone.

Then Mr. Ávila caught sight of him, waved for him to enter, to jump in. Oskar shuffled down the short staircase, walked over to the edge of the pool, and looked down into the chemically blue water. He had no spring left in his body, so he climbed in from the ladder, one step at a time and let himself be enveloped by the rather cold water.

Micke sat down on the edge of the pool, smiled, and nodded at him. Oskar took a few strokes in the other direction, toward Mr. Ávila.

"Orre!"

He saw the ball come flying in the corner of his eye, a moment too late. It landed in the water exactly in front of him and splashed chlorinated water into his eyes. They stung as if from tears. He rubbed his eyes and when he looked up he happened to see Mr. Ávila looking at him with a . . . pitying? . . . look on his face.

Or disdainful.

Perhaps it was only his imagination, but he hit away the ball floating in front of his face and sank. Let his head glide down under the surface of the water, his hair billowing out and tickling around his ears. He stretched his arms out from his body and floated with his face under the surface, bobbing with the water. Pretended he was dead.

That he could float here forever.

That he would never have to get up and meet the gazes of those who in the final analysis only wanted to hurt him. Or that when he finally lifted up his head the world would be gone. Just him and all this blue.

But even with his ears under the water he could hear the distant sounds, banging sounds from the world above, and when he pulled his face out of the water it was there: echoing, noisy.

Micke had left his place at the edge of the pool and the others were engaged in some kind of volleyball. The white ball flew into the air, clearly defined against the darkness of the frosted windows. Oskar paddled into a corner of the deep end of the pool, stood there with only his nose above the water and watched.

Micke came walking rapidly from the shower room at the other end of the hall, shouted, "Teacher! The phone in your office is ringing!"

Mr. Ávila muttered something and stomped away along the edge of the pool. He nodded to Micke and disappeared up into the shower rooms. The last Oskar saw of him was a blurry contour behind the fogged-up glass.

Then he was gone.

†

As soon as Micke had left the changing rooms they had taken up their positions.

Jonny and Jimmy slipped into the exercise gym; Roger and Prebbe pressed up against the wall next to the door post. They heard Micke call out from inside the swim hall, prepared for action.

Soft barefooted footsteps that approached, passed through the gym, and a few seconds later Mr. Ávila walked in through the doors to the changing rooms and over to his office. Prebbe had already wound the double tube socks filled with small change one time around his hand in order to get a better grip. As soon as the teacher reached the door and stood with his back to him, Prebbe stepped out and swung the weight at the back of his head.

Prebbe was not particularly coordinated and Mr. Ávila must have heard something. Halfway into the swing he turned his head to the side and the blow caught him right above the ear. The effect was nonetheless the desired one. The teacher was thrown forward and to one side, hit his head on the doorpost, and fell to the floor.

Prebbe sat on his chest and tucked the heavy ball of coins into his palm so that he would be able to deliver a more controlled blow if needed. Didn't seem like it. The teacher's arms were trembling slightly, but he didn't put up the slightest resistance. Prebbe didn't think he was dead. Didn't look like it, was all.

Roger came over, leaned over the prone body as if he had never seen anything like it.

"Is he Turkish or what?"

"Damned if I know. Get the keys."

While Roger was fumbling for the keys in the teacher's shorts he saw how Jonny and Jimmy walked out of the gym and toward the pool hall. He got out the keys, tried one after another in the office door, shot a look at the teacher.

"As hairy as an ape. He's got to be a Turk."

"Oh, come on."

Roger sighed, kept trying the keys.

"I'm only saying it for your sake. Probably feels a little better if . . ."

"Fuck it. And come on."

Roger found the right key and unlocked the door. Before he walked in he pointed to the teacher and said:

"You probably shouldn't be sitting like that. Probably can't breathe if you do."

Prebbe slid off his chest, sat down next to the body with his weight at the ready in case Ávila tried something.

Roger searched through the pocket of the coat he found inside the office, pulled out a wallet with three hundred kronor. In a desk drawer that, after a short search, he found the key in, there were also ten unstamped subway cards. He took them as well.

Not much in the way of bounty. But that wasn't what this was about. Pure payback.

†

Oskar was still in the corner of the pool blowing bubbles in the water when Jonny and Jimmy walked in. His first reaction wasn't fear, but annoyance.

They were wearing their outdoor clothes.

They hadn't even taken their shoes off, and Mr. Ávila who was so concerned about . . .

When Jimmy stopped at the edge of the pool and started looking out over the pool, the fear came. He had met Jimmy a few times, briefly, and thought he seemed horrible even then. Now there was also something about his eyes . . . the way he was moving his head . . .

Like Tommy and those guys when they have . . . .

Jimmy's gaze found Oskar's and he realized with a shiver that he was . . . naked. Jimmy had clothes on, armor. Oskar was in the cold water and every centimeter of his body was exposed. Jimmy nodded to Jonny, made a semicircular movement with his hand and, one on either side of the pool, they started to walk toward Oskar. While he walked Jimmy screamed to the others:

"Get out of here! Everyone! Out of the water!"

The others were standing still or treading water, indecisive. Jimmy placed himself at the edge of the pool, took a stiletto out of his jacket pocket, unfolded it, and held it like an arrow directed at a group of boys. Thrust it in the direction of the other end of the pool.

Oskar was pressed up into the corner, watching shivering while the other boys quickly swam or waded their way to the other end and left him alone in the pool.

Mr. Ávila . . . where is Mr. Ávila . . .

A hand gripped him by the hair, fingers taking hold so firmly that his scalp stung and his head was forced back all the way into the corner. Above him he heard Jonny's voice.

"That's my brother, you fucker."

Oskar's head was banged backward a couple of times against the tile ledge and water splashed up into his ears while Jimmy walked over to the corner of the pool and crouched down with the stiletto in his hand.

"Hi there Oskar."

Oskar took in a mouthful of water and started to cough. Every shaking motion of his head that the cough induced made his scalp, which Jonny had grasped even more firmly, burn more. When his coughing spell was over Jimmy clinked the blade against the tiled edge.

"You know what? I was thinking like this. That we should have a little competition. Now don't move . . ."

The stiletto passed right above Oskar's forehead as Jimmy handed it over to Jonny, taking over the grip on Oskar's head. Oskar didn't dare do anything. He had looked into Jimmy's eyes for a few seconds and they looked completely crazed. So filled with hate he couldn't look at them.

Oskar's head was pressed into the corner of the pool. His arms were helplessly fumbling in the water. Nothing to grip. He looked for the other boys. They were standing at the shallow end of the pool. Micke was in front, still smiling, in anticipation. The others looked mostly scared.

No one was going to help him.

"So here's the deal . . . it's pretty easy, see. Easy rules. You stay under the water for . . . five minutes. If you can do that we'll just put a little scratch in your cheek or something. A keepsake. If you can't do it . . . well, then when you come up I'll take out one of your eyes. OK? Understand the rules?"

Oskar got his mouth above the surface. Water was spurting out of his mouth as he said, shivering:

". . . can't do it . . ."

Jimmy shook his head.

"That's your problem. You see that clock. We'll start in twenty seconds. Five minutes. Or your eye. Better take a breath now. Ten . . . nine . . . eight . . . seven . . ."

Oskar tried to push away with his legs, but he had to stand on tiptoe to even get his whole head above the water and Jimmy's hand was holding him by his hair, making all movement impossible.

If I pull my hair away . . . five minutes . . .

When he had tried it on his own he had managed three at most. Almost.

"Six . . . five . . . four . . . three . . ."

Mr. Ávila. Mr. Ávila will come back before . . .

"Two . . . one . . . zero!"

Oskar only managed to take half a breath before his head was pushed down under the water. He lost his foothold and the lower half of his body slowly floated up until he lay with his head bent toward his chest a few decimeters under the surface, his scalp burning like fire as the chlorinated water came into contact with the rips and tears in the skin.

No more than a minute could have gone by before the panic came.

He opened his eyes wide and only saw light blue . . . veils of pink that swirled from his head past his eyes when he tried to take hold with his body, although it was impossible, since there was nothing to hold onto. His legs were kicking up at the surface rippling the pale blue in front of his eyes, refracted in light waves.

Bubbles rose from his mouth and he threw his arms out, floating on his back, and his eyes were pulled to the white, to the swaying halogen tubes' glow in the ceiling. His heart was throbbing like a hand against a glass pane, and when he happened to draw water in through his nose a kind of calm started to spread in his body. But his heart was beating harder, more persistently, wanted to live, and again he thrashed desperately, tried to get a grip where there was no grip to be had.

And his head was pushed down further. And strangely enough he thought:

Better this. Than an eye.

†

After two minutes Micke started to feel really uncomfortable.

It seemed like . . . like they really wanted to . . . He looked around at the other boys, but no one seemed prepared to do anything, and he himself only said a half-muffled:

"Jonny . . . what the hell . . ."

But Jonny didn't seem to hear him. He was absolutely still on his knees next to the pool with the tip of the stiletto directed into the water, at the refracted white shape moving down there.

Micke looked up at the shower rooms. Why the hell wasn't the teacher back yet? Patrik had run up to get him; why wasn't he coming? Micke pulled further up into the corner, next to the dark glass door that looked out onto the night, folded his arms across his chest.

In the corner of his eye he thought he saw something fall down from the roof outside. Something banged on the glass door so hard it rattled in its frame.

He stood on tiptoe, peeked out of the window of regular glass at the very top, and saw a little girl. She lifted her face up to his.

"Say 'Come in!' "

"W . . . what?"

Micke looked back at what was happening in the pool. Oskar's body had stopped moving but Jimmy was still leaned over the edge, holding his head down. Micke's throat hurt when he swallowed.

Whatever happens. Just make it stop.

A banging on the glass door, harder this time. He looked out into the darkness. When the girl opened her mouth and shouted at him he could see . . . that her teeth . . . that there was something hanging from her arms.

"Say that I can come in!"

Whatever happens.

Micke nodded, said almost inaudibly:

"You can come in."

The girl pulled back from the door, disappeared into the darkness. The stuff that was hanging from her arms shimmered for a moment, and then she was gone. Micke turned back to the pool. Jimmy had pulled Oskar's head out of the water and taken the stiletto back from Jonny, moving it down to Oskar's face, aiming.

A speck of light was visible in the dark middle window and a split second later it shattered.

The reinforced glass didn't shatter like regular glass. It exploded into thousands of tiny rounded fragments that landed with a rustle at the edge of the pool, after flying out into the hall, over the water, glittering like myriad white stars.

Epilogue

Friday the thirteenth . . .

Gunnar Holmberg was sitting in the empty principal's office, trying to get his notes in order.

He had spent the whole day at the Blackeberg school, studying the scene of the crime, talking with students. Two technicians from downtown and a bloodstain analyst from the National Laboratory of Forensic Science were still securing evidence down by the pool.

Two youths had been killed there last night. A third . . . had disappeared.

He had even talked to Marie-Louise, the class teacher. Had realized that the missing boy, Oskar Eriksson, was the same one who had raised his hand and answered his question about heroin three weeks ago. Holmberg remembered him.

I've read a lot and stuff.

Also recalled that he had thought the boy would be the first to come out to the police car. He would have taken him for a spin in it, maybe. If possible, bolstered his self-confidence a little. But the boy had not shown up.

And now he was gone.

Gunnar scanned his notes from his conversations with the boys who had been at the pool last night. Their accounts basically matched up, and one word had turned up frequently: angel.

Oskar Eriksson had been rescued by an angel.

The same angel who, according to the witnesses, had ripped Jonny and Jimmy Forsberg's heads off and left them in the bottom of the pool.

When Gunnar told the crime scene photographer, who had used his underwater camera to eternalize the image of the two heads in the place where they had been found, about this angel he had said: "Hardly one from heaven, in that case."

No . . .

He looked out the window, tried to think of a reasonable explanation. In the schoolyard the flag was at half-mast.

Two psychologists had been present for the boys' questioning, since several of them were showing worrying signs of talking too lightheartedly about what they had witnessed, as if it were a film, something that had not happened in reality. And that was what one would most like to believe.

The problem was that the bloodstain technician to a certain extent corroborated what the boys had said.

The blood had run out in such a course, left traces in such places (ceiling, beams), that the immediate impression was that it had been made by someone who was . . . flying. It was this he was now trying to explain. Explain away.

And would probably succeed in doing.

The boys' gym teacher was in intensive care with a serious concussion and would not be available for questioning until tomorrow at the earliest. He would probably not give them anything new.

Gunnar pressed his hands against his temples so that his eyes narrowed, glanced down at his notes.

". . . angel . . . wings . . . the head exploded . . . the stiletto . . . trying to drown Oskar . . . Oskar was completely blue . . . the kind of teeth like a lion . . . picked Oskar up . . ."

And the only thing he managed to think was:

I should go away for a while.

✝

Is that yours?"

Stefan Larsson, the conductor on the Stockholm-Karlstad line, pointed to the bag on the luggage rack. You didn't see many of those these days. A real old-fashioned . . . trunk.

The boy in the compartment nodded and held out his ticket. Stefan punched it.

"Is someone meeting you at the other end?"

The boy shook his head.

"It's not as heavy as it looks."

"No, of course. What have you got in there, if you don't mind my asking?"

"A little bit of everything."

Stefan checked his watch, punched the air.

"It will be evening when we arrive, you know."

"Mmm."

"The boxes. Are they also yours?"

"Yes."

"Look, I don't mean to . . . but how are you going to manage?"

"I'll get help. Later."

"I see. Right. Have a good trip, then."

"Thanks."

Stefan pulled the door to the compartment shut and walked over to the next one. The boy seemed like he knew what he was doing. If Stefan had been sitting there with that much luggage he would hardly have looked so *happy*.

But then, it's probably different when you're young.